Barrett's Promise

While this story is written with purpose, it is a work of fiction; names, characters, places and incidents are solely of the author's imagination. Any resemblance to an actual person, living or dead, events or town similarities are entirely coincidental. Some existing towns have been used as a backdrop to provide a general location.

Bible references are taken out of the Authorized King James Version with the exception of occasional author paraphrase's which are noted.

Credits:
Cover Picture by [Sergii Pavlov] @123rf.com
Cover Design: B.A. Shields
Formatting assistance: Robert C. Ray
Helpful assistance: Caitlin Warren

ISBN-13 978-1463571818
ISBN- 10 146357181X

Printing revision, November 2016

Editing assistance: Barbara J. Layow & Lisa Revall

Special Thanks

TO MY LOVING HUSBAND
Jim, who constantly provides
unconditional love and support.
I love you.

MY CHILDREN
Who have encouraged me in their unique
ways to finish the book,
Ginger Warren, Robert C. Ray,
Angel Milligan, James Warner

ENCOURAGEMENT OF FRIENDS
For the unique support each one gave me
on this journey: Linda Woodie,
Cheryl Terry & B.A. Shields
And for my lifelong friend: Barbara J. Layow
for standing by me through every process.
Lisa Revall who jumped in with
teaching skills to help edit the final pages.

MY ETERNAL FRIENDS
Sherry Coykendal Shirey, Linda Hall
& Carolyn Dickerson,
for their consistent encouragement,
who are now residing with Jesus.

MANY FRIENDS
Who have been waiting patiently with prayers;
Thank you.

I dedicate this book to

My Aunt Irene

Irene Fahner,
94 years of age,
before going her Eternal Home
would continually encouraged
me to finish the book;
she is forever beautiful
& I love her.
Until we meet again!

Aunt Irene went home with Jesus.
July 12, 2011

Letter from the Author

Dear Reader,

If you are looking for a literary masterpiece, this may not be for you. However, if you want to know the story God shared with me and discover hidden truths within the greater parable as the story unfolds, please read on.

If you decide to journey with me through these pages, I pray you will benefit as much as I have, by writing it down.

I confess none of this story came from my own experiences or anyone else's that I know, but every time I sat at the computer and prayed I began a new adventure and wrote as I was inspired. I was the first to read His story.

God has been very patient with me putting it to paper. I have only to obey and tell the story He gave me.

Forgive my mistakes.
Enjoy His Story.
And be blessed.

In Christ's Love,
Mary Autumn Grace

Visit me on facebook

Barrett's Promise

By Mary Autumn Grace

I acknowledge that I can do nothing without Jesus Christ; Without Him there would be no parables to tell.

Chapter 1

His coal brown eyes were fixed upon her, as they attached themselves profoundly to hers, a solitary gaze held her breathless. Even though their skin never embraced, it was undeniable, their souls touched.

He infiltrated her existence deeper than anyone ever had, yet without violation. With distinct purity, this man was able to reach in one private glance places within her reserved for the man she would wed. Feeling embarrassed, she blushed slightly and glanced away wondering, could this be the one? Perhaps the one she would marry… *Lord who is this man?* Feeling timid and in fear of rejection, she kept moving. She has waited for so long for the right man…saving herself for God's perfect choice. Although moments of hopelessness emerged more often this past year, she still waited, but the fact remains, Raine Jordan would soon turn 42 and still was veiled in innocence.

Being 45 and never having the opportunity to marry, Price Barrett spent his life occupied with the functions of his deaf parent's ranch, since they were without vocal speech he took care of the business side and all negotiations. He never viewed being there for them as a hardship; rather felt it was a blessing to work at their side. His Aunt Arnett was the one who taught him to speak and read; his lessons were compiled daily of Scriptures taken from the Holy Bible, the only book in the house. Out of those early lessons, Price developed a sincere unwavering devotion to God. When Aunt Arnett passed away several years ago, Price became the sole support for his parents, while caretaking the ranch to meet all their needs. Just recently, he lost both to influenza, dying within a day of each other. For the duration of their illness he tended to them daily, never leaving their side. God's favor was on him during all of this, for he escaped the disease and never suffered a day of poor health. Being the solitary survivor in his family, Price was now alone for the first time, yet not totally, there was God and his dog. Even through all that had happened he still held onto the belief that he would marry one day. It saddened him, realizing his parents would not be around to partake in his joy.

Throughout the years, the Scriptures wove a manual for life, providing him with strength and purpose. Price spent endless hours of wandering the desert, praying and walking as he read pages from the Good Book. It was there, in those captivating moments, God met with Price, immersing him with a powerful influence that dictates his life to this day. He found it hard to understand why he experienced great comfort in his personal relationship with the Lord, while it appeared to be uncommon for men to have this closeness to God. Price observed with fervor how other men ordered their lives; he paid attention to the encounters he had with some of the men he met at Coles Trading Post and on his occasional trips into New Crossing. In his many observations, he thought it odd that he never met one man who demonstrated a harmony of soul. Out of his frequent visits with Father God, he felt blessed because he had developed a harmonious relationship in his own life. It surprised Price; this was not something men sought after. Nevertheless, Price Barrett was a friend of God. He conversed daily with his dearest companion about everything, including a bride.

Price was loading his wagon at the General Store

when she passed by. The sight of her startled him, piercing his heart with a profound awareness, knowing he has just set eyes upon the woman Father God told him about endless times; *Now Lord?* Price questioned. Succumbing to an unexplainable calm mind and gathering his focus to the task at hand, he saw no reason to introduce himself today. Trusting the Lord would keep her close and protected and until His divine time. At this hour Price was on a different undertaking; he had come into town to buy lumber to build two burial boxes for his loving parents. In spite of this fact, Price understood distinctly, this was the woman, the one saved for him alone and one day before long he would come back for her.

On the walk back to the schoolhouse, Raine was bedazzled by the incident of the stranger in town. Coming upon the schoolyard where the children were playing, she decided to set the episode aside and focus on the present. This was the last year she would be teaching these students. As a going away present she had planned to buy sweet sticks for her class a week ago, but her procrastinating had ordered her steps to the General Store today during lunch break. This year's summer school closing was tough on her; she was emotionally attached to these students. Raine had taught most of them several consecutive years in a row and she regretted there would not be another year to enjoy them. Nevertheless, she had to make a choice, other people's children or a life to obtain her own. Her plans were set in motion to leave town and go back East this summer. Yes, the timing was right to leave, determine to be settled in a town where the population was bustling with eligible men by summer's end.

Raine was no longer settling for a small one horse town, some last stop location before entering into the barrens of the desert, or before venturing further west to find their dream town on the coast, or going north for gold. Which describes New Crossing, only a small amount of people have settled here in the middle of nowhere, generally out of desperate needs…her family was one of them. The area just recently became a part of the United States and was called the Arizona Territory. Raine did not dislike New Crossing, in fact, it was not really an undesirable place to live; she held wonderful memories of growing up this town. The people were friendly enough; yet the reality of it was that the area simply did not hold much promise for a woman who wanted matrimony in her future.

For the past ten years Raine was looked on a spinster who dwelt alone. The only company she regularly entertained was her books and an occasional visit from one of her students. Her three dearest friends, whom she grew up with, were married years ago and held their own personal family interests. No one deliberately set Raine aside, it just happened; she was unattached and the others married. It was only the force of nature that their common interests matured differently. The girlish dreams did not progress as anticipated, least not for Raine Jordan. At an early age she came to the conclusion it was definitely too scary to leave important choices to chance, so one night after witnessing her mother's friend crying over her husband's infidelity, she prayed earnestly for God's will for her life. She gave Him the ultimate permission to choose His choice of a husband for her. After that initial commitment Raine continued to have many conversations with the Lord about her singleness; always believing one day the perfect man would come along. However, as time went on the pickin's got slimmer, until there were no longer any decent single men in town. Raine was hesitant about leaving a town where she knew everyone, a place where her family lived and died, yet her perception of how to meet Mr. Right had changed. In order to meet God's perfect man, she would have to move to a larger town.

Before entering the classroom Raine took the liberty of letting her thoughts drift, recalling the stranger outside the store. *I wonder where did this man come from,* she pondered. *I am acquainted with everyone in town and most of the surrounding homesteads as well, yet I never once set eyes on this particular man before…I would have remembered!* Her heart fluttered at the thought of him.

Price felt no urgency to get back to the ranch considering the finality of what he had to do. As he rode he mulled over the purchase made several times, *sure glad I met that outsider at Cole's Trading Post; he was certainly right about where to find juniper lumber. Adam's General Store had plenty; I believe I got enough for the boxes and maybe a little extra for a couple of chores I've been putting off…The burial boxes…*Price felt sorrowful. There was something final about putting his parents in the ground, yet he wanted to comply with his father's wishes, to be buried in a juniper coffin. Remembering how his father raved about the superior quality of the wood, not to mention how his Pa cringed at the idea of an old pine box. He could hear his father's words, as he recalled the story given to him many times, *"Crazy men indicated in their many snide remarks, how they were going to put me in a pine box."* Price could still see his father ranting with his hands about it. A lump formed in his throat, he swallowed, then cried out, "Pa it is juniper!" With a whisper he said it again, "It's juniper". Miserable and heartbroken, there was a touch of satisfaction in locating the wood to fulfill his Pa's wishes.

Price did not venture into town much after Aunt Arnett died; he stayed close to the homestead, with them being deaf he was not comfortable traveling too far away. Just the thought of leaving them alone was heart wrenching...what if they should need him? So many things could go wrong; an accident or strangers could come by and frighten them. It was not worth the risk or the worry. The times he did endeavor to go far away, he was anxious to return and grateful to find his parents safe.

A cool breeze brushed his face; it felt good. Price clearly saw one door of his life slam shut and there was nothing he could do to open it again, yet in the midst of grief, another door was cracking opening...*could this be God's divine providence, so I would not be alone*? The idea mulled over in his head several times brought a form of healing, one of hope for a future, when this morning he had no hope at all.

Price closed his eyes for a split second and the vision of her beauty surfaced. Surprised, that her beautiful eyes were already embedded in his memory; brown hazel, with flakes of gold dancing through them. She had a natural uncomplicated beauty. Not painted like some he'd seen, but beautiful in an effortless way. The way she held herself portrayed a confident yet gentle spirit. *She is not a very tall woman,* he recalled, quite a contrast with him being six foot three. His mother often referred to him with hand signs, saying *I was her very own gentle giant*. The thought made him smile; he loved Mama, and would miss her deeply.

Focusing back on his future, Price was satisfied with

the Lord's choice; this attractive creature was more delicate and lovely than he could have hoped for. *Why should it surprise me that the Lord even created her with my favorite hair color, black as a raven's feather?* Even though she wore it tied up, the twisted braid hid elegant long hair; he anticipated seeing it flow down on her back.

On the way into New Crossing this morning, Price could barely lift his head, sickened with his loss and nothing to look forward to, but a burial, sorrow and immense loneliness. Now he had hope and visions of a future with a beautiful wife. The woman occupied his thoughts as he rode. He could not quit rendering a multitude of thanks to the Lord for revealing her to him today. Price appreciatively knew God had given him a wonderful expectation of a life still yet to live.

♥

Chapter 2

As Price approached the barn, his eager sidekick was there to greet him. Trader was a stray dog he found three years back hanging around the trading post. Cole the proprietor had no use for another dog and even though he showed lack of interest, the dog would not leave. When Price saw the dog he took a liking to him right off; he was medium in size, black with a few freckles of white. Tracker Joe was there at the time and said the dog looked to be an elkhound that probably got lost from a wagon train. If he ran off, the trainmaster's schedule would not wait for some dog's wandering curiosity. Price never owned a dog and any information was appreciated. Joe said the breed was known for loyalty and for fighting off dangerous animals like bears; it was not uncommon for voyagers to acquire a dog of this breed for protection along the trip. After a few close calls, Price was convinced Tracker Joe knew what he was talking about; this old dog was not afraid of anything! Trader took on snakes, a mountain lion, javelina, and anything looking harmful to Price. All in all, Joe was right about the breed's fearlessness and Trader proved to be a useful companion; Price never regretted bringing the dog home.

"Hi boy," Price ruffled the dog's head, giving Trader assurance of his pleasure to see him. The ol' dog stretched upward with his whole body arching, welcoming the touch.

"Told him you not be long, he just watch road…for you to come." The voice was of his friend Caleb, formerly known as Crooked Eye, an Indian Price befriended in the desert over fifteen years ago. Caleb's eye was slightly wandering, so his father gave him the name Crooked Eye. However the eye did not restrict his aim with a shotgun or bow, nor did it hinder any of his abilities, it was simply noticeable. After Price was acquainted with Crooked Eye six months, he gave him a new name. Not a name to draw attention to his friends weakness, but one to speak of his character; Price called him Caleb from this time on. He chose the name Caleb because this Indian was a positive thinking man. Price shared his faith with Caleb and it was not long after the new name he adopted the faith in Jesus Christ.

Looking up from the dog, his friend was a welcome sight after the long trip. "Hello Caleb, I was afraid he would do that, but it was necessary for me to be alone and accept my loss. Thanks for watching Trader and the ranch; it was really a hard thing to leave him behind. Believe me, it was not any easy choice and I worried about him all the way to New Crossing. You know we have never been separated since the day I got him." Price ruffled Traders head affectionately and the forgiving ol' dog was soaking it all up.

"He good dog and good friend, he stay where you left him…no move, no eat…Must be hungry as bear…see jerky," he pointed, "There…not gone." Caleb reached down, picked up the jerky and offered it to Trader. The starving dog did not have any trouble demonstrating his contentment by eating it without hesitation. Caleb shook his head at this action.

"I finished stitching bags and added Old Woman's spices, to help with odor. I still not understand why you do not set them on fire."

"We talked about this Caleb." Being travel weary he did not feel like explaining it again. However he did have to chuckle remembering the conversation they had before he left. "Thanks for sewing the bags for me; it was a difficult job I was not looking forward to." Price lay his hand upon the pile of juniper lumber, "After we unload the wood I will begin turning these planks into burial beds...Come, and help me unburden the wagon."

Price and Caleb proceeded to unload the lumber into the barn, stacking it near the place where Price would be assembling the burial boxes. When the task was done Caleb took his leave. "I will come back first light to do your custom of burial," he announced in a matter of fact tone.

Once the last piece of wood was down on the stack, Price straightened his back, rubbing the lower part with both hands to ease the pain. Then turning to face Caleb, he wiped the sweat off his brow as he spoke, "Thank you my friend, it gives great honor to my parents for you to be here. For many years you have been such a welcome guest at our table. I too will be honored to have you at my side tomorrow."

Caleb mounted his horse and rode out before darkness set in. Inside, the barn was already darkening; Price lit lamps to bring light in his work area. He would be working throughout the night to have things ready for the burial service. He took a stick of jerky from a sack on the wagon floor. While chewing on a piece he began to calculate a sketch in his head of what he needed to do. After giving another stick of jerky to Trader, he began the process of building two boxes; tailor fashioned to embrace the precious bodies of his parents.

Price thought as he worked about where he would dig the graves. It was an area already established by his family. They selected the spot when Sharla, his sister died; she was seven. At that time a particular piece of land was set aside for the family grounds. *Pa and I built a small fence around it,* he thought; *it was already known as the burial garden when we buried Aunt Arnett.* The location was in a peaceful section of the property, perfectly situated in the direction of the mesa and viewable distance from the porch.

Price recalled the year his mother carefully dug up some wild ocotillo's and planted them on the outside of the fence, *now they overtook the area behind the site; yet when they produce flaming reddish-orange tubular flowers, it gave Mama pleasure. It does provide a beautiful array of color.* He thought of her collecting flowers to make hibiscus tea after the crop increased. *As she sipped from her cup Mama always referred to having tea with little Sharla and later she added her sister Arnett to the tea party.* He managed a faint smile in the midst of these welcomed thoughts, pleasant ones and sad ones. *All the times I observed Mama's heart breaking as she walked around the grave site feeling melancholy.* His mother increased her visits to the burial garden after the loss of her sister; Aunt Arnett was always his mother's safeguard, looking after and protecting her since they were very young. *Now you girls are having a tea party in Heaven,* he perceived.

Price labored most of the night fashioning the burial boxes with precise calculations the way his father taught him. When he accomplished the constructing of the coffins, he went into the house and retrieved the bodies. Price carried his parents in the sewn bags, one at a time, into the barn and placed them into their new resting beds. With the weather temperatures still dropping at night and the spices Caleb sewn into the bags, the odor was not noticeable. He was appreciative; considering his mother had left three days ago and rigor mortis was set in on both bodies. He felt so unprepared for an experience such as this and wished he could handle it better. He was second guessing himself, *how can anyone possibly be prepared.* Price skillfully positioned the top on each burial box, sealed them shut with nails and carved inscriptions on both lids.

Martha Nadine Haden Barrett, wife of Theodore, Born February 18, 1847; United with the Lord April 3, 1912. Then for his father he inscribed, Theodore Bernard Barrett, Born April 26, 1842; United with the Lord April 4, 1912 because he could not bear life without his beloved.

Price could not get away from adding the last aspect on top of his father's box, recalling the silent conversation they had shortly after his mother left her body. It would remain permanently etched in his mind forever. How could he disregard this moment when even now it wrenched at his heart? After informing his father about his mother's passing, in his father's fragile and sickly condition he managed to gain the strength to present the sign for "love" followed by the sign for "broken." Price watched his father laying there in the bed, tears running down the side of the old man's face, his burly hands folded upon his chest, Price perceived his father was in prayer. When his father finally opened his eyes, he immediately gave the signs, "God's answer good," followed by "Take care of yourself, my son. You are a good son. I love you." Price knew at that moment he would also be losing his father. His father did not fight to live any longer, but followed his mother into glory.

Price constructed two crosses and put the same inscriptions on them as he did on the burial lids, only this time he added "beloved of children, Sharla and Price". He made the crosses three feet high above ground with boards wide enough to write out their tribute. He could have inscribed endless words telling of their unselfish love and devotion to each other and towards him. He could have told of their love for God and His land, among many other countless noble feats he had personally witnessed in their lives, but Price would have to cherish all these in his heart. A tear ran down his cheek as he stood there looking over the finished boxes in the back of the wagon.

Price put out the lamps and propped himself up on a stack of hay in a corner of the barn; he could not bear to leave his parents out here unattended tonight. Beside him laid his faithful companion, Trader. While smoothing the fur on the old dog's back and feeling exhausted, Price drifted off to sleep.

♥

Chapter 3

The shrilling pitch of a rooster's crow startled Price awake; still groggy he staggered to his feet. He stretched a full arm-body stretch and glanced upward only to see his friend Caleb watching over him from the upper loft. The large frame Indian sat with his feet dangling over the edge, his hands folded on his lap in a casual position and chuckling, appearing to be quite amused.

"What are you doing up there...and what in tarnation is so humorous?" Price asked in an unbelievable tone.

"You snore louder than Trader and you jump like a girl."

Price shook his head not believing his ears; it was way too early for all this comedy. Yet with an ever so slight grin he tried not to divulge, he replied, "I'll give you 'a girl'! With only two hours sleep, I am entitled to be somewhat spooked." Price yawned, "Oh...enough justification...why are you up in the loft, Caleb?" Price reached over and affectionately petted Trader, ruffling his ears and with a loud whisper so Caleb could hear him, "Why did you not wake me when this scoundrel came in?"

"I come when sun is on mesa and you friend, are sleeping good. I know we have much light to finish white man's traditions...burying the Old Ones. I am in no hurry...I climbed up here to wait...it is good place to look at your work." The Indian cocked his head from one side to the other peering down at the burial boxes, "I studied words while you sleep, I wonder what words mean...you are not awake...I ask the Great One to explain to me."

"Did He?"

Never taking his eyes off the burial lids Caleb answered thoughtfully, "Yes my friend, He did…they are memory symbols of your parents. I think words speak of who they are deep in heart; did I hear right?"

Price smiled briefly as he rubbed the back of his neck; for his neck was beginning to ache with his head tilted up in this stretched position, "I believe you heard accurately…come down and I will read it to you."

Caleb complied, although he did not use the ladder, but spontaneously jumped down and landed on his feet, springing into a standing position with one continuous flow of movement.

"I want to learn how to do that!" Price confessed.

"You too old to learn now, it is for boy."

"I am not old, my life is just beginning." Price said with joyful expectancy, smacking his hand on Caleb's shoulder in a friendly manner. "In fact, just yesterday, I set eyes on the woman I have been promised."

"The woman God promised you?"

"Oh yes Caleb, I believe she is the one," Price's lips curved to a full smile, enjoying a few moments of pleasure by letting the memory of her encompass his thoughts. He wanted to indulge in daydreaming a little longer, but the reality of the day prompted him to the present. "I will tell you of this meeting later." Walking up to the crafted burial boxes, he put his hands upon them affectionately with reverence, "Let me read to you what I have carved on these burial boxes."

Caleb moved closer as he listened to what a good son would inscribe on the boxes and crosses loved ones; he wanted to understand this unfamiliar custom of the white man. Price was a blood brother in the faith and a devoted friend in the traditions of his way of life, which was enough for Caleb to walk respectfully beside Price while he finished this journey.

Since Price did not take time to secure the coffins for travel the night before the two men rearranged the boxes in the wagon and set the crosses securely beside them. Caleb tied his horse near the barn so he could ride in the wagon with Price and Trader to the sacred burial ground. There were several minutes of silence before the wagon pulled up at the revered site. Price was pleased when he noticed a few of the ocotillos already in bloom, *a miracle,* he thought. Caleb and Price would be digging most of the day preparing the resting spots.

The men worked several hours digging but the soil was not cooperating to have a clear hole; the sand was loose and caving in. Nevertheless, after a lot of perseverance and physical exertion the gravesites were finished, awaiting burial. Price realized how filthy he had gotten digging, grime clung to his sweaty body and he smelled like an animal. Taking a quick assessment of Caleb's appearance, he scratched his head in amazement. *He worked beside me all morning digging these holes, how in tarnation has he managed to avoid looking soiled?* Price took another glance at his grimy arms; *I must look dreadful, like I have war paint on with all the sweat streaks.* While sizing up his dirt-ridden situation, he remembered his mother's firm instructions at the time of Aunt Arnett's burial service, *"it is a matter of reverence to the one departed for us to come to their funeral cleaned up", she would say...boy did she stress that point to me.* Looking at his arms again, he certainly knew he was not in any condition to give a respectable burial to his parents. How could he continue after remembering his mother's words? It was inconceivable to even think of lowering their burial boxes into the ground being this dirty and improperly dressed. Now humbly recognizing the need, Price had no choice, but to return to the house and clean up before the burial.

Price explained to Caleb that he needed to go back to the house before having the burial service, but before leaving the site he needed him to help situated both burial boxes on top of the graves. They made them ready to be lowered into the grave with ropes, using stakes to hold them up securely. The crosses were placed in position at the head of both sites. They had everything in order for burial when they returned.

Price and Caleb got into the wagon, giving a quick whistle for Trader, who promptly jumped into the back. The three headed back to the homestead so he could clean up and dress for the service; his faithful friend did not understand, but complied with this tradition.

At the house, Price offered Caleb a dipper of water to quench his thirst, then took a drink himself. Caleb sat down at the end of the table to wait. Price tossed a piece of jerky to him, then a stale piece of bread, "good catch!" he said as Caleb caught the bread in midair. Caleb just shook his head slowly and smiled, but said nothing. Price also gave him a cup of herbal tea to wash the bread down; after the Indian took one bite of the hard bread, he was immensely grateful for the tea. Price also provided fresh water for Trader; it was a hot morning and he had not thought about taking any water with them to the burial grounds. It could have helped with the digging if he had the notion earlier to carry a couple of water buckets.

While gnawing on a piece of jerky he proceeded to look for some respectful clothing. Finding suitable attire he set them out on his bed. Checking the water for the wash bowl and found it warm enough, he set up his wash station and proceeds with the cleansing act as

Caleb would say.

Caleb sat quietly drinking his tea while his friend scrubbed his mud-sweat body with a wet rag. The Indian noticed it took several jugs of water to clear the sludge from his face, not to mention the unusual matting of his hair. He wondered why Price did not choose to go down to the river; it was a lot more efficient. It may have been cooler this time of the year, but certainly tolerable, Caleb and his family began using the river water many moons back.

Caleb pondered, as Price put on fresh clothing, if he were appropriately dressed for white man's custom and wondered if he too needed a burial costume. So he asked Price, who informed him courteously that his present garments were suitable. Then he explained that the Old Ones would expect this of their son out of respect for them. However no regulations were imposed on guests. The answer satisfied Caleb, it was not unusual for the customs to be very different between the white man and the Indian. In fact, in his clan the one who was crossing over received the customary bathing.

Price was now standing before him dirt free with clean brushed hair, unsoiled clothes and apparently ready to go back out. Caleb noticed Price had the Holy Bible clutched tightly in his hands, which made Caleb particularly interested in what Price would teach him regarding the participation of the Great God in a white man's burial. The two men and the dog left for the burial garden to finish laying Price's parents to rest.

After the students completed their end of the year exams, Miss Raine Jordan opened her desk and retrieved the sweet sticks she had bought the day before. As she started to pass them out she announced to her class as delicately as she could that New Crossing would be employing a new schoolteacher for next year because she would not be teaching. This news was not embraced by her students, resulting in a loud uproar of disgruntled children; it took Raine several minutes to gain control of the class and quiet them down. They were getting angry with the school board and various parents they thought were firing her. It touched her heart seeing how much the students didn't want her to leave. Nonetheless she bravely and gracefully informed them, the town did not release her from teaching, rather it was her choice because she was moving back East in midsummer. Raine Jordan observed a disappointed look on several students faces. It grieved her having to tell the children about her leaving; she felt affection for all of them. The students she had for several years were like her own, so leaving them was extremely difficult. Looking out at her class wishing there were another way.

Following her announcement, several of the children approached wanting to be near her. She received a flood of hugs and some cried, which only brought tears to her eyes. She noticed Billy Sprats in the back of the classroom, scrunching his face, trying to express clearly that he could care less. As indignant as he could, he stood up tall and expressed he was glad there would be a new teacher for him to train next year. He did however, enlighten Raine, how he thought she was a good challenge and finished by saying "Miss Jordan you can hold your own quite well," with that remark he left the room hastily. Raine was not sure how she felt about this rowdy whippersnapper of twelve letting her know she had spunk, but she could tell under his pigheaded demeanor, he too was saddened by her leaving even if he could not bear to show it.

Letting out a sigh, she drew the class together and concluded school was now officially over for the year. Miss Jordan encouraged the children to have a good vacation break and to help their parents on their small farms, ranches and places of town labor. The children reluctantly left, scurrying for home or to a buggy with their awaiting parents. Raine stood at the door of the old schoolhouse and watched each one disappear out of sight, knowing she would miss each one, including Billy Sprats. As she waved to the last one, she could not help feeling somewhat melancholy while at the same time relieved, the day was finally over.

Raine finished clearing the classroom of her personal belongings. With a little cleaning, she made the room tidy for a new teacher. Once all of her possessions were loaded into her buggy, she met the prudent Mrs. Grayson at the schoolhouse door, arriving to lock it up for the season. Raine was hoping not to see anyone from the board; however in this awkward moment she was cordial. She told Mrs. Grayson that she would pray God would bring the right teacher next year, with this remark Raine departed the school leaving a portion of her heart locked behind those doors. She rode off trying to hold back the tears, but a few escaped and trickled down her cheek. Raine took a deep sigh and quoted from the Scriptures, "this too shall pass." With a quick swipe of the hand she brushed the tears away, held her head up and began anticipating a brighter future.

♥

Chapter 4

Raine would have to keep focused, she only had ten weeks to sell the family belongings and pack or she would not be ready to depart come July. Mrs. Adams, from the General Store was graciously providing the transportation. She & her brother were going to visit their aging grandmother in Albuquerque for the summer and had invited Raine to ride along.

In Albuquerque, Raine could obtain passage to Chicago, where she had relatives. However, Raine was beginning to have some other ideas scrambling through her head and soon a decision would have to be made on just how far east she really wanted to go. Mrs. Adams informed her how Albuquerque was a booming town with an increasing population. The inspiration of staying there for a while began to entwine in her plans; maybe she would not go directly to Chicago after all. Maybe stay through the winter in Albuquerque, if the life there did not suit her or held no promises for her future, she could always move to Chicago next spring. This notion sounded better to her each day and the more she entertained the idea the more firmly planted it became. Yet she still waivered at times because the idea of having family close by in Chicago was just as exciting. She needed to make a decision and stick to it. After mulling over a few pros and cons her assessment was over, settling on what she thought was a reasonable conclusion. *Simple enough, I will stay in Albuquerque until spring before venturing back to family*. Raine already knew Mrs. Adams would be there for the summer and when she returned to New Crossing, Raine would be settled in at the boarding house for the winter. *Who knows, I may even stay longer if God's perfect choice is in that city*. The decided change of plans began to fill her with fresh optimism and enthusiasm.

Later when Raine was cooking dinner, she began to consider the family belongings, what she could take and what needed to go. *Obviously, this is not going to be easy. Just thinking about it is exhausting, so many decisions to make, from Grandma's lace tablecloth to Mama's fine quilts.*

Raine began stirring the simmering pot of soup on the stove; it was warm enough to eat. *I made too much again! I should stick to doing one thing at a time…cooking or packing. Oh my…this is far too much for one person*! With a sigh, Raine already knew what to do; *guess I'll share with the Bartley's again.* In the past her mistakes blessed the family of ten, especially with the two older boys who were always ready to eat.

Raine prepared the dinner table for two; it had become a practice for her to set an additional setting at suppertime. It was her way of showing the Lord she still believed in His promise of a perfect mate. Raine was quite aware of how much the Lord kept a watchful eye on her, so she was delighted to show Him every chance, her faith on the issue of marriage. Her timing on "when" would have been years ago, but she yielded to the belief that the Lord's timing was always perfect. One day the man will reveal himself, she was certain of it! Raine bowed her head, prayed for the meal and for His promise. In a flicker before she opened her eyes, she saw clearly a man's face, recognizing immediately it was the man she saw yesterday loading his wagon at the General Store. Reflecting a moment, she recalled the man's coal brown eyes infiltrating every fragment of her being with such dignity and honor; she flushed even now at the thought of him, although alone, she felt somewhat embarrassed because of the intimacy this stirred within her, as if she had known him all her life. Raine lifted her hand and rapidly fanned her face, hoping to cool her rosy cheeks.

Raine tried to quit thinking about this stranger, but it was unsuccessful; *he looks like a man of great strength, a giant in his form, yet by his mannerism, I perceive he is gentle natured. I find his appearance pleasing; wavy amber hair with such dark eyes, almost ebony.* She took pleasure in recalling all his features, his full lips and straight teeth, a broad smile ready to burst out in a hardy laugh at any moment...she found the memory delightful, at the same time she detected a backdrop of sadness on him and wondered why? It surprised her how she was able to take in all this information just passing by him to enter the General Store. Although once inside, she did take the liberty to observe him a little closer through the store window as he continued loading lumber into his wagon. She carefully stayed back so he did not see her watching him. Then he was gone.

She took a deep sigh; *maybe You have a man like him for me in Albuquerque, Lord, that would be real nice!* She thought it, but knew the Lord did not take her requests seriously; she had shared with Him quite a few silly requests about men over the years, without any avail. Yet this time there was something exhilarating about pondering over this mysterious man, recalling again how he intimately looked at her and wondered if she would ever see him again; she privately hoped so.

Raine took another deep breath, then finished eating her soup and relinquished daydreaming for the time being; it was time to focus on checking the exam papers. As a teacher, this was the last official thing left to do. According to the rules the school board set, she was expected to post the results of the final exams on the schoolhouse door, informing which students would be passing into the next grade. However, she chose not to comply with the board's ruling about posting the test grades, but rather sent private notes to the parents. She had done it this way for fifteen years, from the time she had taken over the teaching job and even though this was the last time, she was not about to do it any other way, even if it meant more work.

Raine Jordan could not bear to hurt any student, it bothered her to make a spectacle of the any child who barely made it, not to mention the humiliation it would be for the student who did not pass. She protected the information so no one would tease a child about their accomplishment. Raine believed each child responded to learning in individual ways and each uniquely grew at his or her own pace. They all were a success story to Raine. She wondered if the new teacher would keep this practice or give in to the bullies on the board.

Passing by the pictures of her parents assembled neatly on the mantle only reminded Raine of how deeply she missed them. Recalling the day they received the news about her father; the telegram arrived in the afternoon, stated: "WITH REGRET WE WISH TO INFORM THAT CLAY JORDON WILL NOT RETURN TO NEW CROSSING DUE TO HIS UNFORTUNATE DEATH. HE WAS BURIED RESPECTFULLY ALONG THE PATH OF THE RAILROAD ON AUGUST 21, AS IS THE NORMAL PROCEDURE WHEN SOME ONE EXPIRES ON THE JOB. THE CREW REPORTED HE WAS GRABBING HIS CHEST WHEN HE FELL. THE PAY DUE HIM WILL FOLLOW BY MAIL CARRIER." "It was heart failure, it happens sometimes," Doc informed while consoling her mother, who at the time was wailing over the loss of her husband. Doc Walker was a trusted family friend and knew her father personally. He traveled with her family on the wagon train when they first settled in New Crossing. Preacher Matthew came to her home that day also, to aid in comforting her mother. *Everyone was so compassionate, yet Mama was never the same.* The days following her father's death were stressful for Raine, watching her mother's pain and feeling her own grief, she found herself wishing often her father would not have taken the railroad job as if it were the railroad's fault. Now after some years, she knew differently, God gives life then takes it back at will, we must care for each of our days and not live them frivolously.

Raine recalled the next eight years; she took work anywhere she could to help her mother make ends meet. It was her enjoyment of children which led her to help out at the school a few hours a week, until tragedy took Mrs. Evans, which secured the position for Raine to take over as the primary teacher.

Raine's mother took a job helping Doc Walker for the next several years, then in 1902, her mother died of hypertension. *Doc being well aware of her condition tried to persuade her not to push herself so hard, however no one could make Mama slow down, not even Doc.*

Feeling a little melancholy, Raine began to amble about the old home; pausing briefly at many unique items which brought back special memories. At times feeling overwhelmed about leaving it all, selling her memories was a hard thing to do. *This is the right time to go and with the Lord's help, I will accomplish this task as painless as possible.* She kept in mind that her future was still ahead and one day soon she would live and breathe the Promised life God purposed for her and this sadness will fade. Hanging on to this positive thought, Raine turned in for the night, deciding tomorrow would be soon enough to start sorting and packing.

♥

Chapter 5

After the school season would come to an end, Raine would sleep in late for a week straight. She felt completely justified indulging in some lazy days after a long year where she was required to be punctual and diligent. There was not anyone who could substitute in the class to relieve her. Also her home hours would be busy with lesson plans and checking papers, often late in the night. However, this morning instead of sleeping in, Raine arose in the early hours of daylight, just like she had done all year long. Since she was leaving in July, she wanted to get the student's promotion letters in the mail along with a note about her resigning. It would be better if the parents received them earlier, so they could evaluate their students' progress and if they had any questions or concerns, she would be available. Invariably one of the families would wait until just before school resumed before making contact with her. Actually, Raine felt there was no rational reason to leave them waiting until the end of May; Mrs. Evans, the previous teacher, set up this method and it became standard procedure. She wondered why she never changed it before now. *Maybe I needed to take it slower myself when school let out.*

Looking over the results of the examinations she felt delighted, the outcome was the evidence of a successful school year. Each one of her students was promoted to another grade level, except for Billy, who continued to stagnate once again, as he had for the past two years. *Maybe Mr. Sprats would finally give up and let his son stay home this year,* she thought, convinced this was Billy's ultimate plan. *With the resistance he gives daily, it would indubitably be a blessing for a new teacher to start the class without his hassles.*

Raine was still idling on who the school board would find to teach next year, with the local population being few in number there weren't many to choose from. Frustrated with her concerns, she decided to not to waste time pondering on it any longer. Whether the school board obtained another teacher or if the officials were still searching, was really no concern of hers. Besides, she gave the board six months' notice and certainly, they could have already secured someone to take the job. *More people are coming West at a rapid pace and some Back-East-Teacher has undoubtedly relished this challenging adventure already.*

The pleasant walk to the store was helping Raine in put her thoughts in order. She realized she was taking on the whole responsibility of uninterrupted education for the town, when it really was not her problem to solve. She wished it was not so difficult to shake the guilt feeling; as if she were abandoning her children. *Lord, ease my mind and bring the right teacher.* Putting it in the Lord's hands was just what she needed to do.

Now at Adams General Store, Raine handed the letters containing the student evaluations to Mrs. Adams, who was busy sorting the morning mail. She felt confident these notices would be in the hands of the parents before the week was out. After spending a few minutes being cordial with Mrs. Adams, Raine noticed Mr. Adams stocking shelves across the room.

In appearance, Mr. Adams was much older than his wife, who was closer to Raines's age if she guessed right; making the man about twenty-five years her senior. Raine did not judge the arrangement as being a bad choice, even though many said from the time Myra Harper came back to town, "she was out to get married and it did not matter to whom". Raine understood the woman position; there certainly were not a large number of middle-aged men for Myra to select from in New Crossing. Nor had she seen an assortment of gracefully aging unattached women for lonely Mr. Adams to choose. Over the past five years since their wedding, Raine curiously observed the two of them making marriage work. Mr. Adams showed his new wife polite affection and was accustom to pampering the frail middle-aged woman; Myra on the other hand showed a deep respect for her husband.

While browsing through the store, Raine kept one eye on Mr. Adams as he concentrated heavily on stocking rolls of new fabric on high shelves and she feared he would fall off the stepladder; he looked unsteady. She wanted to speak to him, but did not want to take him off guard and create an accident, so she waited.

As Mr. Adams continued to wedge the roll of cloth into the slot on the shelf, his latter teetered slightly and Raine silently prayed. She wondered if she could get up the nerve to talk with him on the subject. Raine had frequently rehearsed her opening question before she left the house, but after becoming preoccupied with thoughts of the children during her walk, she forgotten her opening lines. Mr. Adams eased himself safely to the floor and Raine was greatly relieved. Her relief sparked an unintentionally loud, "Mr. Adams." The words moved spontaneously out of her lips at the very sight of him being safe.

Carefully steadying himself and regaining his manly confidence, he turned towards her, "Yes Miss Jordan, what can I help you with today?"

"I was wondering if you would allow me to bring some of my belongings in here to sell; I would give you a fair profit. Besides, to tell you the truth, I really do not know how much to ask for most of it and I was hoping you would help with pricing." She sidestepped her real question, hoping to muster up enough courage during the conversation before she left.

Scratching his head for a minute he thoughtfully replied, "Well frankly, I have helped folks in the past and you being a woman alone, without a man, most certainly I can help. Tell you what, bring in a number of items every day and we will see if we can get them sold. Make a list of items you are planning to part with and post it on the Trade Wall. This will let people know what you have; update it as you include more things." He paused and was silent for a moment while scratching his balding head again. He appeared to be deep in thought and then added, "The timing could be perfect. A number of new homesteaders are settling around the area and we are also beginning to get a flow of wagon trains coming through town, there seems to be a few more every month. After getting this far west, many of the trekkers are realizing what they gave up and might find your items a helpful replacement to what they left behind."

"Thank you kindly Mr. Adams, you have encouraged me. I am convinced with your assistance everything I have will sell right on schedule. It is exceptionally gracious of your wife, Mrs. Adams, to offer me a ride to Albuquerque when she leaves with her brother." Raine gave a fleeting look at Mrs. Adams who was behind the mail counter consumed with mail packages, yet, when she heard Raine's remark she glanced up, keeping her silence and offered a genuine smile. "Without the two of you being so helpful I don't know how I could ever accomplished this enormous task of moving.

Raine moved around the store as she was talking, stalling for time by picking up some food items. She needed additional minutes to muster up the courage to casually inquire without being obvious. "I trust you will not find me presumptuous or too bold in my asking." She moved closer to where Mr. Adams was working, "There was a man in the store the other day who bought some lumber." She paused, searching for the words to attach to this most blunderbuss beginning.

Mr. Adams quickly responded before Raine was finished, as this was his only lumber sale this week. "Yes, I remember him, Mr. Barrett, nice fellow. What about him do you want to know?"

"He looked familiar to me, but I cannot place him... does he live close by?" There was a connection when their eyes met so she did not feel like this was an untruth about the familiarity.

"I am pretty sure you do not know this man Miss Jordan, he comes from the other side of the river. I believe he owns land out towards the Painted Sands. He rarely comes to town; I think the last time he was in the store must have been in 1897. I remember it well because Mrs. Evans and her son died from the home fire tragedy and I was about to close up to attend the funeral walk when he arrived." Mr. Adams was always connecting people with situations to help identify them. "Actually, come to think of it, I have seen him a couple of times since then, but certainly not many." He tapped his finger on the wooden fabric counter as if it gave him a memory boost before adding, "He came in more often when he was younger. Often with a woman he called his aunt. She would look over the periodicals and made several orders, along with selecting a few supplies in the store. Come to think of it, I have not seen her for several years...she probably moved back East because she was always interested in the most up to date conveniences."

Mr. Adams was good at collecting particulars about people; simply a good business practice. The General

Store became the local-news-informer on what was going on around town; people would post all their announcements on the stores Trade Wall. The town acquired a small newspaper two years ago and even now, the journalist came into the store frequently to collect any information he missed for his weekly paper.

Raine appeared satisfied with the answer, but inside she wondered how she could reside so close to such a magnificent man without meeting him, *he must not be the one,* she concluded. "Well thank you Mr. Adams, I will not be troubling my mind about it any longer. I have never been anywhere near the Painted Sands, for that matter, I haven't been on the other side of the river. I must have been mistaken." She got her small sack of flour along with four potatoes she purchased and headed for the door.

"Miss Jordan, before you leave New Crossing, I think you may want to consider a pleasure trip to visit the Paints. They are spectacular and with you living so close all these years, it would give you a grand story to tell your family back East. Since there are no deserts in Chicago, it would be something their imaginations will get to experience through your eye-witness-tale."

Pausing at the entrance, Raine turned back to finish the conversation. "I appreciate your suggestion, yet I sincerely doubt I will be efficient enough with my time to view them before I leave...with all the toil I have in front of me these next few months... it is a fine thought, just the same." Turning towards the door and lifting her hand to wave, she rendered, "Good day to you, Mr. and Mrs. Adams," then with polite confidence she moved out the door.

"Oh wait Miss Jordan!" Mrs. Adams bellowed in haste. "I almost forgot with all the sociable conversation, a letter for you arrived this morning." She retrieved it from the counter top and briskly brought the letter to Raine, placing the envelope directly into her hand, as if it held great importance.

Raine viewed the envelope, "A letter from Aunt Margaret back in Chicago." She was not exceptionally thrilled, because now she had to inform her aunt of her decision not to return to her birth town until spring, if at all. She tucked it into her pocket.

"I imagine she is looking forward to your arrival," Mrs. Adams encouraged, wondering if she had observed a twinge of unsettledness in Miss Jordan's expression.

"I imagine she is," Raine was short and finished. She did not feel confident enough to reveal her decision to stay on in Albuquerque yet, so she bit her lip and bid her good bye a second time.

On the walk home Raine had much to think about. *It would be a frivolous excursion for me to consider,* she laughed, *going across the river to look at the Paints.* She mulled, *who would even offer to take me on this venture, as I certainly could not go alone. Even then, how would I ever find a man or his land over there in unfamiliar territory?*

She knew the Paints stretched a great many miles, so to navigate an unknown area with silly hopes of running into him would be very implausible. Besides if this Mr. Barrett owned land, he probably had a wife and children also. The idea was entirely inconceivable; nevertheless Raine recited his name in her head several times, *Mr. Barrett.*

♥

Chapter 6

Raine felt good about her meeting with Mr. Adams and was ready to get busy selecting particular items to deliver at the General Store tomorrow. Her thoughts were to transport ten things a day, not all of them big items, but a good variety. New Crossing was a travel crossroads town with routes going in all directions. She never thought to consider the variety of people who frequented Adams General Store every week. This may work out better than she had hoped and maybe people would take pleasure in her priceless treasures. She could never have done this without Mr. Adams help. *Thank You, God, for giving Mr. Adams a charitable heart to assistance me in my time of need. I can see why Myra Adams has grown to appreciate him.*

Raine gathered several items and had them loaded into the buggy before she recalled the unread letter from Aunt Margaret. Taking it out of her pocket she paused for a moment, reflecting on her latest idea to stay in Albuquerque over the winter; she wished she could take back her previous letter informing Aunt Margaret of her intentions to return to Chicago. Raine hoped her change in plans would not be a great disappointment. She felt torn and a bit remorseful about letting her relatives think they could be expecting her arrival. Looking at the letter in her hand and realized it was not getting read this way. It is a good time for a break I have been diligent all afternoon. She pouring a cup of hot coffee and sat down to read Aunt Margaret's letter.

My Dearest Raine, What a pleasant surprise, it has been years since we have heard anything from you, not since Deloris' passing. You cannot imagine how delighted we were to receive this wonderful letter of your plans to return to Chicago the home of your birth, and take residence once again among us, your family. What fabulous news! We do hope these are still your intentions, as it has been several months since we have gotten your loving correspondence. Dear, a lot has happened which prevented me from answering promptly as I will share later in this letter.

First I want to say your intention to travel now is astuteness. After all, you are not getting any younger and to begin such a long journey at an older age would become extremely difficult. Just like it would be for me to be able to visit you now, I am presently seventy-three, and Deloris would have been seventy-five this year; my how time flies.

Raine allowed the letter to rest on her lap while she sipped her coffee and reflected on what Aunt Margaret reminded her, *mother's birthday is only two days away; it is hard to believe mother would have been turning seventy-five.* She released a deep lonely sigh accompanied by a single tear trickled which down her cheek; *I miss you Mother.* Wiping her cheek, Raine picked up the letter and proceeded to read.

I realize from your letter that you are still hoping for matrimony, for you expressed this irrational notion of the Lord saving someone for you. Seriously dear, if He had marriage in mind for you, don't you think He would have already provided the gentleman? You must know this to be true because soon you will be too old to have children. Starting a family at your age now is precarious, not to mention you do not have a specific man in mind yet. I hope you do not mind my speaking frank about this, as I know Deloris would have wanted me to instruct you as she would have done. She certainly would not want her daughter to be caught up in some fantasy that would bring her heart pain. However, you are a bright woman and I would not want you to be in the least bit disheartened Dear, your life has great purpose. Look at all the children you have taught who are benefiting from your instructions. Even now, God may have a different destiny in store for you, one you have not thought of. You will not be alone anymore, so a man will not be the only solution to your loneliness, because by coming here, you will have a home with us for as long as you want. We are family.

It took all of Raine's strength not to toss the letter on the floor before finishing the conclusion. Inside she was fuming; she had not felt such fury in a long time. Holding the letter rigidly in her hand, eyes glaring at the paper, her lips parched and with a defiant attitude, she proceeded to read further.

I am sorry to divulge now the reason for our delay in answering your pleasant letter. Uncle Bentley met with some illness a couple of months ago and he is stiff on one side of his body, he is in a chair with wheels and needs help with everything from eating to dressing. The work is strenuous for me to endure, but I have a renewed optimism again, after your correspondence. I see your returning as a divine providence and a ray of hope to me, because together we can care for him. The Children and I did not want to put him into a convalescent center because this has always been his home; we are proud people and we must provide for our own. Our children help when they can, but they have lives of their own and families to care for. However, now with the blessing of you coming you will be providing another hand to help us with Uncle Bentley. We have a beautiful guest room to accommodate you, no need of looking for a place to live; there will be no expenses to live with us. Also you do not have to concern yourself with another teaching job when you arrive; we have plenty of money and have carefully thought of everything to make it easy on you and on us. It will be a great relief to have you here.

Uncle Bentley needs some lunch so I should close and tend to him. We are all looking forward to your coming.

Waiting your reply as to when we might expect your arrival.

Love, Aunt Margaret

Raine hastily flung the correspondence letter of Aunt Margaret's onto the floor; she could barely comprehend all she read. She was shocked and felt disturbed over Uncle Bentley's illness, perceiving it probably was a tremendous struggle for Aunt Margaret to care for him, especially with her being so aged. As much as Raine wanted to cling to the feelings of sympathy, she could not erase the taunting words that were expressed about her personal life, regarding her promise from the Lord. She sat fuming without uttering any known syllables for several minutes, her foot tapping rapidly on the floorboards as she released indescribable sounds into the room. After a short while of gibberish, her words began to form, "Whooo…who does she think she is, saying I am too old to marry and God would have already provided a husband for me…IF He wanted me wed? How dare she have the nerve to write me relaying that I will be without children…what does she understand about the plans of God in my life? I should have never exposed my hearts intent to such a faithless woman. How could I possible know that her faith was so shallow! Lord, how could she be so manipulatively self-absorbed? Just because she needs a house nurse for my dear uncle, why does her need allow her the right to tear down the Promise You have given me since I was seventeen."

Raine was in tears of anger. She herself had feared the very things her aunt had mentioned, but never allowed her mind to give into the temptation. Now they were hanging in mid-air like dynamite waiting to explode. She paced the floor displaying a stormy temperament, letting out a few groans and releasing every bit of her frustration while at the same time trying to find a way to get a grip on her emotions. *It is a good thing I received this letter, because my plans from here out will never include my returning to Chicago,* "NEVER!" she shouted.

In the midst of her anger, Raine had a moment when she seriously contemplated for several minutes if God really wanted her to go assist Aunt Margaret with Uncle Bentley, and asked Him if caring for them was this truly her destiny. In a flicker she remembered of all the things Father God conveyed to her over the years and decided to hang on every promise. "No! No!" she exclaimed, "You would not have told me to wait. You would have prepared me so I would not include matrimony in my plans. You are not a God who plays tricks on the hearts of those who trust You." She unrelentingly continued to pace the room, taking deep breaths and wiping her cheeks from the continual flow of angry tears.

Trying to recapture the faith she held only minutes ago, Raine began to utter aloud her affirmations to the Lord. "I trust You Lord, it is not Your way to cause confusion...Your word to me is truth and I am holding tightly to the Sacred Promise. Forgive my weakness, Lord, I do not believe You are cruel, playing a game with my emotions. You are trustworthy and faithful. I believe I will marry young enough to have a child. You certainly have given me examples in the Bible, for Sarah and Elizabeth were older than I am, when they had a child. I am choosing to trust you Lord." Raine decided she would, without reservation, ignore her aunt's opinion of Chicago being her destiny. *No, I am not destined to be a spinster nursemaid,* she concluded, *I am going to be a wife and a mother as You have told me.*

Swiftly she scooped up the letter from the floor, "Oh, the gall of this woman! She is so faithless and in her need, manipulative." Raine tore the letter into tiny shreds and tossed it into the fireplace before she was tempted to re-read it and be tempted to consider everything all over again.

After wearing out the floorboards, Raine sat down in her mother's rocker and began to rock gently getting her emotions under control. As calmness replaced her fury, Raine's faith was being restored and solidifying inside her heart again. She lifted her voice to the Lord, but this time without any trace of anger; her fiery temperament had burnt itself out. Raine picked up the Holy Bible and with her arms crossing over it, she embraced the Book close to her heart and vocally prayed with remorse and trusted hope.

"Lord, please forgive me for letting my aunt's letter invoke such anger in me. I cannot count on my fingers how many people in this world actually believe as my Aunt Margaret, however, I know Your Promise is a truth for me to believe and hold on to. You alone have kept me pure from any man's desires and allowed me to observe a wholesome life. With Your help I have resisted the temptations to follow after my worldly desires, because I have always believed Your Sacred Promise to me." Raine lifted one hand to the sky and offered praise, "Thank You Lord for this refreshing." She stared upward towards heaven, with endearment and anticipation rising in her spirit. "I know You will bring Your perfect choice to me soon. I feel Your Promise nearer today than when You first conveyed the arrangement for me as a young woman. I will not compromise nor will I quit believing in Your faithfulness. Thank you my Lord for being close to me and loving me. I will stand on the Sacred Promise just as firmly as I believe the Scriptures to be true. In Jesus Name, Amen."

Raine began to contemplate situations in her life that were meant to derail her stand. Well-meaning friends who even went as far to suggest she go to the saloon hall to dance with the strangers passing through town, thinking maybe she would snag one for keeps. However, Raine refused to do anything to entice a man. The elderly widowers in town were even suggested. Once a person recommended Mr. Adams as a choice; although he was a nice older man, Raine never once believed he was the Lord's selection. Obviously, Mr. Adams did not either, as he never approached her in an unfitting manner. Yet all these years Raine held strong to her convictions and waited just as the Lord asked her to do; she was grateful for the strength he gave her to endure. This trial is no different.

Reminded of the past, she felt even more convicted of what the Lord had spoken to her years ago. If Abraham and his wife Sarah had to wait for their Son of Promise, how arrogant she was to think she would not have to wait for God's Promise as well; certainly waiting was a special part of God's plan.

Raine returned to her work assembling selections to take to the General Store. With renewed faith she sang out boldly an old hymn her mother taught her. "Come thou fount of every blessing, tune my heart to sing Thy grace. Streams of mercy never ceasing, call for songs of the loudest praise. Teach me some melodious sonnet, sung of flaming tongues above. Praise Thy mount I'm fixed upon it, mount of Gods unchanging love." When she quit singing the words, she hummed it more loudly and it penetrated her spirit abundantly with TRUST.

♥

Chapter 7

Raine proceeded to pack her belongings into a couple of sturdy trunks, feeling confident they were constructed to handle the long treacherous journey. She was grateful Myra Adams and her brother had prearranged to save an adequate amount of space in the covered wagon to accommodate them. She walked carefully throughout the home looking to see if she had missed anything. The only things left were a bed, table, two straight chairs, a few dishes and cooking pots, just enough to sustain her for the next few days. It was strange to hear footsteps echo in the vacant rooms and words ricochet off the walls when she spoke out loud, all confirming the emptiness that surrounded her.

Mr. Adams had done a sufficient job of unloading her belongings. She requested for him to get the remainder of her furnishings after she was gone, she could not bear to see the place entirely lifeless. With his help, she acquired more than a sufficient amount to cover the cost of the journey; Myra was adamant about not needing anything for the trip since they were already going there. Raine on the other hand, felt she should give them some money for taking her. Even with setting aside what she considered a fair amount of money to bless them, she was still in good financial shape. Certainly she would have no trouble securing a room to rent in Albuquerque; in fact she had enough to sustain her for a couple of months while she sought employment. As she finished packing her last trunk, she praised the Lord in song for meeting all her needs.

Raine's respect for Mr. Adams had grown over the past two months, after working closely with him on selling her items. She also gained a fresh appreciation of his marriage relationship to Myra, she found him to be gentle natured and kind to her. Raine formed a positive opinion of the man that she once felt neutral about. Now she knew him to be a fair and honest man with incorruptible character; he certainly did her right. With her being a woman alone he could have taken advantage of the situation, but that was not in George Adams. She was convinced God smiled on him.

Raine talked with Mr. Harrisburg, who was not only the proprietor of the Land Settlement Office, but also her father's dearest friend and made a verbal agreement concerning the family home. Mr. Harrisburg promised to look after the sales transaction and should someone be looking for property in town, he assured her that he would show them the Jordan homestead. He gave his solemn guarantee that he would work diligently to get a fair offer and he would do this at absolutely no cost to her. This was his personal tribute to the memory of his friend, Clay, Claiborne Jordan. Mr. Harrisburg agreed to direct any exchange of deeds and settlements to the New Crossing Post Office; knowing the Adams would be notified of her new forwarding address. Everything was falling into place and Raine was completely comfortable with all the arrangements.

Moving also gave Raine opportunity to spread some unrecognizable charity to several needy families by giving them the overflow articles that she would not be selling. Many of the folks were extremely proud people and did not take kindly to any charity. Understanding this, Raine convinced them they would be doing her a great favor. She explained the item could not be sold and it would not be right to leave behind a houseful of objects and this approach seemed to satisfy them.

Among the distribution, a few items were actually set aside for specific folks she had purposed in her heart to bless. There were a few quilts and some cookware she knew would be very useful to the Bartley's. Raine took pleasure in giving Billy Sprat's mama her mother's favorite rocker; the woman needed a place she could relax for a few stolen moments with her rowdy crew.

Raine's packing was finished and everything was in order for her journey. While waiting for her departure on Saturday she planned a few days of relaxation along with reading her Bible. Raine would be leaving New Crossing in four long days, with no plans to ever return. Her passage into a new life would begin and somehow she was feeling a little melancholy about it.

After all she had a wonderful childhood growing up in this town, a life which Delores and Clay Jordan gave her. Raine began to store her treasured memories, one at a time, in a safe place inside her heart; a place where she would not feel loss, but a place she would be able to cherish them forever. Sitting on the edge of the bed and thumbing through the Family Bible, reading for the second time the lists of births, marriages and death registries of the family tree; it was all recorded, she had a great heritage and understood moving would not change anything. Raine was going to carry a precious legacy wherever she ventured.

Raine was peaceful; her heart, outlook, and belongings were all in proper order. Yet a stirring in her began and she started to speculate if she missed something. She went through everything from clearing the house, putting it up for sale, her last details as a teacher, her family treasures...then she remembered, *Oh My, I almost forgot!* Without hesitation, Raine went to the kitchen to obtain a sack of flower bulbs she had set aside days ago and abruptly left the house. Feeling quite foolish, *how could I forget something this important!*

Approaching the church graveyard she went directly

to the Jordan family gravesite. Sitting down on the ground as a child would come before their parent waiting to talk, *Mama, I miss you so...You also Papa...* With tear-filled eyes Raine looked towards the memorial cross. She had it carved as an honor to both father and mother, since her father was buried in an unknown spot without a marker; thanks to the railroad crew. Her hands went right to work as she spoke, and the flower bulbs found their home being planted near the cross; *I hope you are proud of how I have handled the estate and our possessions. It is not going to be easy leaving this area behind, but I know you would understand Mama, no matter what Aunt Margret said. God has a husband out there for me somewhere and I must follow His lead to meet him.* Since this would be the last time tending on her parent's gravesite she found it difficult. Over the years when she felt emotional struggles Raine would come visit the site, she needed someone to talk to. *I am well aware you both are no longer here, however, I did enjoy a few mother and daughter talks, especially since I got to do all the talking!* She gave a faint smile. Putting in the last bulb, the peaceful feeling she previously felt in the bedroom returned; only now it was complete, as if she received her parent's approval to leave. Standing up, fully satisfied she felt free to embark on her new life. *Sleep well, my loves, until we meet again.* With that thought Raine gave a deep sigh and left the cemetery.

However, not everything was finished, for it was on the walk home when Raine realized she still had not answered Aunt Margaret's letter, in fact, she purposely put off writing it. Even now, sitting on the porch steps, there was a struggle taking place inside of her over the idea. Reluctantly, she conceded, only because it was the right thing to do. *I might as well do it now, so Aunt Margaret will not be expecting my arrival,* sighs...

It was not because Raine was still upset with the old woman that warranted her procrastination; she felt a sincere compassion for Aunt Margaret, considering the load her aunt was carrying now with Uncle Bentley being ill. It was simply the fact Aunt Margaret assumed Raine would be coming as a caretaker for her uncle, without even getting her consent to this arrangement that troubled her. Not to mention her aunt's faithless response to Raine's promised husband. Just the same, Raine Jordan did not relish the fact that her news would certainly bring disappointment. She went inside, gathered a piece of writing paper, envelope, ink and feather pen. Sitting down at the table, wishing she still had the abominable letter as a guideline for her to write. She began:

Dear Aunt Margaret, I am writing to thank you for your kind and generous offer, but I am sorry to inform you that I will not be coming to Chicago this year. I have decided to stay in Albuquerque for the winter and regretfully I will not be there to assist with Uncle Bentley. I do hope you are finding some relief and getting the help you need. Do Anne and Melvin come over to help with their dad? They live close enough, so I am sure they have taken turns giving you some time for needed rest. Maybe you would consider hiring a live-in-housekeeper, and then you could just work with uncle yourself and not have to do both jobs. A woman who does house cleaning is a lot cheaper than a nurse caretaker. I realize you are getting up there in years and the added help around the house would be a benefit. Nevertheless, I am praying for your needs and Uncle Bentley's return to health. I am sorry for the delay in my writing to you, as I did not have my plans solid enough to share them until this month.

May God bless you,
Your Niece, Raine Jordan.

Raine intentionally did not respond to her aunt about her difference in opinion of waiting on God's perfect man, as when the time comes, Aunt Margaret will receive the blessed announcement of her marriage. She folded the paper and slid it into an envelope and addressed the outside, than concluded, *it's done…that wasn't so bad.*

As Raine held the letter, a respectful awe overcame her which left her speechless, sitting motionless with her mind completely blank for several minutes. It was an extremely peaceful feeling being void of a single opinion. As Raine adapted to this sensation, words began to form and she responded in a heartfelt prayer about Uncle Bentley's health and the issues concerning his care. She asked for strength and the needed help for Aunt Margaret. She was engulfed in a deep conversation with Father God concerning her two elderly relatives when she was interrupted by an abrupt, hasty loud knock at the door.

Raine approached the entrance cautiously, still in the manner of prayer, and quite surprised to see Myra Adams standing on the porch with a bewildered look on her face. "What a pleasant surprise, Mrs. Adams, please come in." Opening the door enough for her guest to walk through, "What can I do for you? I did not expect to see you at my door today." Raine anticipated the visit was about their departure schedule and wondering if they would be leaving sooner.

Myra Adams entered the home without the appearance of someone bringing good news, but rather looking perplexed, which made Raine concerned to what prompted the visit. Myra sat down and straightened her skirt, "Raine, honestly I came to tell you as soon I knew…forgive me, but I will not be able to depart for Albuquerque this year. I am expecting a baby and George forbid me to travel, as I have lost two children before. Doc Walker agrees with him and has instructed me to rest in bed, in hopes that taking these precautions with a little pampering will help me to carry this baby full term."

At first Raine was flooded with a mirage of mixed emotions, not knowing what to say, feeling let down. She glanced around her empty homestead, *all my memories sold and now…nowhere to go, not to mention I am no longer an employed teacher at the schoolhouse. Certainly my position has been filled by now. What am I going to do?* Raine's mind raced simultaneously in many directions, some positive and some devastating. Thankful for her unwavering faith in a sovereign God which penetrated her spirit before a word was spoken; now being filled with the right determination, it was apparent she would have to find another way. "What a surprise blessing…I am very happy for you and Mr. Adams. I will be praying fervently for your baby…I agree, we certainly want to protect this one. Don't fret and be distraught about not being able to go to Albuquerque as planned, it seems God had a different one. Your health and the health of the baby is far more important so I will simply have to locate another way. I am sure the Lord will provide something for He has never let me down."

Mrs. Adams could not believe how gentle Raine handled this unexpected news and appreciated the kindness this woman displayed to her; Myra definitely would miss Raine. "You're such a gracious woman and I cannot believe that you are so resilient when having your plans changed so abruptly. Yet I must confess, it actually saddens me to think of you leaving New Crossing. Through our attempted travel venture, we have gotten to know each other better and I feel like we have developed a friendship…I wish we would have gotten more acquainted before this…probably my fault, being so occupied with my life. I do have a simple request that I have wanted to ask of you for some time…could you please call me Myra? I realize it is polite and cordial to call someone by their last name with a title. Yet, I feel so distant and older when you call me Mrs. Adams. I think I am close to your age."

"I believe we are the same age and I would love to call you Myra; it was not entirely your fault. I was busy with school and kept occupied myself. Nonetheless, the fact that we never got to know each other personally all these years is a great loss to me too…a loss I will not quickly forget. I guess my being unmarried has not given me a lot of common ground to socialize with many…maybe I need to change this isolation strategy when I get settled." Raine and Myra laughed at the way Raine described her solitude lifestyle.

"Yes, most certainly you need to trust us old married folks!" Myra smiled. "It is my loss too. We do seem to get along well and it has amazed me from the start on how much we have in common…simple things we both are fond of."

Both were quiet for a few minutes, then Myra broke the silence, "Would you mind writing and staying in touch with me, once you are settled back East? I would dearly love to hear from you and know how you are getting on…we could be pen pals."

Raine smiled at the thought of making a friend, even if it were to be a long distance one. "I would love that Myra, besides I will want all the details about your little one. You can let me know what it feels like to actually be a mother. I have grown attached my students, but I still hope to have children myself one day after I marry."

Myra Adams hoped for Raine to get her wish. She deserves to be married to a fine man and have children, especially after waiting for so long. Which brought up the age factor in her mind and knew time for miracles would soon run out. Myra was only too grateful to meet George when she came home for a visit five years ago.

Myra looked at this extraordinary woman; she admired her character. She had hesitated about coming here today with the news so close to the time of leaving. What an eminence relief she felt knowing Raine was not upset with her over the change of plans. In fact, she felt closer to Raine and was sincere about cultivating a friendship, even if it had to be developed by letters. *What can I do to help this gracious woman find a ride to Albuquerque? There must be some way to get her there…she has sold everything.* Myra observed the empty home and knew she was totally responsible for Raine's unfortunate dilemma.

"Would you like to have some tea? I have a pot already made," Raine offered, still wondering how it was all going to work out for her to leave.

"Actually, I hope you do not think me rude, I really should get back to the store…George will be worried if I am gone too long. He dotes over me so much, but more so since we got the news of the baby yesterday." Myra Adams stood up to leave, but then quickly sat back down with a hopeful look in her eye. "It just might work," she said to herself. The remark made Raine curious to what was on Myra's mind.

Without holding back, the frail mom-to-be initiated her hopeful idea, "Well, all may not be lost, I know my brother is still planning to go to Albuquerque and see Gram's. Since he no longer has to wait on me, Max has decided to leave tomorrow morning. I do not see why you could not ride with him, I am sure he would love the company… it's such a long trip."

"Wait just a minute Myra, what about Max's wife

Elizabeth? Think about it, how would she feel about us journeying together for days alone, without being chaperoned? I am sorry Myra, I know you want to help and I appreciate the offer, but I do not perceive this to be such a good idea." Even though she was polite about the proposal, inside Raine shuddered at the memory of how Max would examined her with unclean eyes when they would pass in town and how on several occasions he spoke suggestively to her when picking up his son, Daniel, from school. *That man makes me feel eerie and frightened. I have purposely avoided being caught alone with him for years; this is not an option, I will not consider traveling with just him alone!* This was not at all a comfortable arrangement for Raine.

"Maybe you are right," she relented, "I truly am sorry Raine, I know I have created a problem for you, if I think of anything to help you get to Albuquerque, I will let you know...possibly a family going back East, or maybe someone traveling all the way to Chicago will come into the store... you just be ready, something will turn up." Myra stood up and went to the door then turning back looked at Raine with still another idea. "Maybe Elizabeth will decide to go now that I cannot travel."

"If Elizabeth were to accompany Max, I would have no problem accepting a ride with the Harper's," Raine confessed, joining Myra at the door.

"Alright, I will ask her," she softly touched Raine's arm empathetically, "it is the least I can do."

"Thank you Myra, I appreciate your checking for me...I will come to the store later to verify what Elizabeth plans are."

Raine closed the door. Feeling despair she slumped aimlessly into a chair; her dreams were vanishing before her eyes. When she glanced around the empty room;

there was none of the familiar things sitting on the mantle. The home was virtually void of all the cozy belongings her mother acquired, which made the home feel comfortable and safe. The two wardrobe trunks sat in middle of the floor with a few unseen treasures packed away. On top was a carry satchel holding a few clothes to change into along her trip. What was she going to do now there was no alternative plan? Could she possibly go with Myra's brother? Would it be safe for her, even with Elizabeth? *Oh Lord, help me to know what to do. I feel so displaced right now.*

♥

Chapter 8

After Raine's few moments of self-indulged-pity, she turned to the Lord and bared her heart in prayer; persevering for several hours until she felt peace again. She began to feel slightly optimistic about the situation and knew everything would work out, although she had absolutely no idea how.

It had been several hours since Myra left, plenty of time to have met with Elizabeth and inquire if she considered traveling with Max to Albuquerque. So Raine took a stroll to the General Store with a sense of buoyancy. She was surprised to see Elizabeth and her son Daniel at the counter speaking with Myra and Mr. Adams when she entered the door.

Elizabeth was a stately woman, tall with broad shoulders, although not in the least bit heavy, solid. Her auburn hair was smartly pulled back to elegantly cascade flowing down her back. She was the kind of woman who would turn a man's eye when she walked through town, but with Max as her husband, those eyes were quick to readjust elsewhere. Daniel looked like his mother, tall for his age with the same reddish color hair.

Elizabeth looked up, greeting her kindly, "Good afternoon Raine." Being straight forward in nature, she immediately got to the issue, "You are such a precious woman. I genuinely understand your hesitation to travel with Max alone to Albuquerque. Matter of fact, I would feel identical, if I were departing on a journey across country with a married man who was not my husband." She took hold of Raine's hand, holding it firmly, yet gentle, speaking earnestly to her as one would speak to a friend. "My dear Raine Jordon, I assure you, if it was any other woman in this town, I would be concerned over the arrangement, but certainly not you." Elizabeth let go of Raine's hand to adjust her hair and then continued maintaining direct eye contact, "Throughout the years I have witnessed the sincerity of your faith and I have the deepest respect for you. I trust you completely, I do not have a single concern about you being anything but decent." After this remark, Myra verbalized agreement of Raine having a reputation of one who follows her faith and was not in the least bit considered a woman of moral decay. Mr. Adams also added his accord that everyone in New Crossing knew Raine was a decent woman without question.

Raine felt her face flush slightly; she was flattered with all the high respects they gave her. However, she was not concerned about her responses to Max, knowing she would be more than proper, but rather she was extremely disturbed about how his dealings would be towards her. "Thank you for the complements," turning her remarks to Elizabeth, "from this I assume you will not be journeying with Mr. Harper to Albuquerque?" Desperately hoping she was wrong.

Elizabeth spoke up, "Raine we have known each other a long time and there is no need to be so formal with me, I am still the Elizabeth you went to school with." She paused a moment to check on Daniel, making sure he was not touching anything in the store. "As it turns out, Max and I will not be traveling collectively to Albuquerque as much as I would have appreciated the time away. My responsibility now is to be of assistance to Myra; she will be bedridden and will need a great deal of help to not lose the baby." At this remark, Mr. Adams lowered his head and found something to busy himself. Raine noticed the anxiety enveloping his expression and she felt compassion for him.

Raine's disappointment tried to surface, but she

masked her true feelings, knowing her sensitivity was bred in selfishness, "I can definitely see the wisdom in your staying here, Elizabeth." She glanced at Myra who still was feeling the impact of it being her fault for the complications. "It is obvious you will certainly need someone to help, please forgive me, Myra, for not considering your great need. It is a good idea for Elizabeth to stay with you." Raine felt trapped, how could she possibly leave with Max in the morning. Her knees trembled underneath her skirt. She did all she could to keep her lip from quivering publicly.

"I have a suggestion," Elizabeth spoke confidently. "I could send Daniel with his dad and then you would not have to travel alone."

Raine could not hold back her snicker and spontaneously blurted out her feelings verbally without thinking, "Daniel is 9; that really makes me feel ok about it." She was being sarcastic; however, the women did not receive it that way.

"Great, this is the perfect plan! I will be able to focus on Myra without having Daniel to care for and he can spend time with his great grandparents. Would you like that Daniel?" The boy became excited over the fantastic idea and began asking countless questions, "Not now Daniel, we'll cover everything at home with your father," Elizabeth instructed. She then gave her attention back to Raine and continued, "This will give Max someone to return with; it will work out perfect for them to have time together." In the excitement, Elizabeth's voice resounded off the store walls, "This is simply ideal for all of us." Glancing over at Myra, the two of them began to giggle and agree in a cheerful manner. The assembly of the three, Myra, George and Elizabeth, were increasing their enthusiasm in favor of the perfect arrangement while young Daniel bounced around the store hootin-an-hollarin'!

Raine was certainly not as joyful as the four of them, in fact, she felt trapped. She stood in the midst of them going on about what a wonderful plan, working out for everyone's best interest. While trying to accept this arrangement she considered, *Maybe it will not be so bad with Daniel there, and I could keep Daniel close by for protection, certainly Max would have to mind himself with his son there.* "Alright, I would feel better to not be totally alone with your husband, even though you trust me," she managed to say. "I heard Max was leaving in the morning, what time?" Raine spoke affirmatively, but inside extremely reluctant.

Myra spontaneously spoke up, "We were leaving at first light on Saturday so I 'spect they will leave at first light tomorrow, don't ya think Elizabeth?"

Elizabeth agreed.

"Then I will arrive outside the store with my wardrobe trunks at the morning's light. Which reminds me, I must get back as the Bartley twins have offered to load my two trunks in the buggy for me and I will need to inform them that I will require their help tonight...I really must return to the house." Edging towards the door feeling extremely anxious, Raine felt like dashing out of the store in a full run, but she restrained her feet to walk calmly. Raine could not wait to get alone with her private thoughts. Half way to the entrance, she slid her hand into her pocket, *Aunt Margaret,* "Oh...I almost forgot Mrs. Adams...Myra. I have a letter to mail out!" She came back and laid it down quickly on the counter and left. She could hear the two women chattering; they were cheerfully satisfied with the solution, but Raine held much apprehension.

♥

Three months swiftly passed and Price had not ventured back to New Crossing to collect his promised bride. Looking down at the homemade calendar his mother constructed, he wondered how July arrived so quickly. Since the day of the funeral, he had not allowed himself any time to be melancholy, grieving the loss of his parents. Although he did have a variety of moments when he felt as if they should still be here. Instead of dwelling on what could have been and making his life sad, Price set his sights on the future. He occupied his days with thoughts of having a wife. A single moment did not pass, where he did not cling to the memory of the beautiful woman in New Crossing. His heart anticipated her arrival. In fact, each daily activity revolved around her coming to Barrett Ranch. He labored endlessly fixing up the homestead, making those needed repairs he had put off. His intentions were to spiffy up the ranch so it would appear welcoming to his bride.

Price finished the last thing on his mental list this morning. The completion presented him with a surge of eagerness, realizing it was time to take a trip to New Crossing. Price had a lot of time to think about how he would approach things when the day arrived. He would search for her at the very spot they exchanged the wedding glance, the Adams General Store. However, if this did not disclose her whereabouts, he predetermined to stay in town until he located her. He had every intention of proposing matrimony to the woman the Lord saved for him.

His dog situated at his side was pleading for a gentle head rubbing, so Price obliged. "Well Trader, what do you think? Will she like the home we have prepared for her?"

Price looked around the home. His family had already made an exquisite house, so there was nothing to change in this respect. He knew the repairs should have been tackled long before this. The house has so much to offer, he should not had let it go unattended for so long. Nevertheless it is now done.

Today he put the finishing touches on the homes. It was his first attempt at decorating anything and the reason for his folly made him smile. He put a clean tablecloth on the table, the one his Aunt Arnett always used for special dinners. In addition, he placed his mother's favorite vase in the middle of the table; she cherished it because it came from Grandmother Hayden, back in Ohio. Inside it held Desert Holly and Fluff Grass he carefully selected the way he watched his mother do plenty of times. He arranged the best coverlets on the two beds in the back room, but decides to close the door and pick up the things laying around later. He saved the quilt his mother finished last winter for the front room bed, the one he would be sharing with his new wife. *Mama referred to it as a wedding quilt,* informing him it was made for his time of matrimony. Price remembered questioning her why she felt he was getting married, and with anticipation waited her insight. They had a good conversation that day about how she felt strongly he would soon be meeting the woman of his dreams and would marry her. *Mama was always such a great encourager…wish she were here to see her premonition for me come true.* After this she took ill.

The front room looked good to him, almost like one of those pictures in the periodicals Aunt Arnett browsed through at the General Store. He was proud of his work. Price learned from observing his mother and aunt that these little things were minor touches women seemed to notice. It actually did not make a lot of sense to him, but it felt like they had been instructing him every step of the way. *They made sure I knew*! He laughed out loud as the memories flashed before him.

Price realized the many repairs he completed on the ranch would probably escape his bride's view. He would be the only one to reflect on the mending of the broken fence, the hole in the corner of the roof and the repairs to the barn. However, if they had stayed in their worn out condition he was certain she would notice the run down appearance and that would not be good. Price was satisfied with all the repairs behind him. Now he would be pleased if she simply liked the place. Tonight it felt good to take the liberty of relaxing with no list on his mind. His focus was solely on his soon-to-be-bride void of drifting off to sleep in the chair from exhaustion like he had been doing for many nights.

"Well boy, what do you think, should we go to New Crossing and locate my bride tomorrow?" Trader would agree and be content with anything Price had to say especially if it accompanying a nice rub to the head. The ol' dog leaned in as Price scratched behind his ears. Price contemplated the idea, "Yep, I am thinking its time. We are leaving at first light, so go curl up on your rug and get some sleep." Price stood up, selected a stick that was lying in the corner and swiftly swooped up several cobwebs he had noticed. Meanwhile Trader moseyed over to his favorite spot and got comfortable.

Price retrieved the washtub and placed it in front of the cook fireplace. He took his standing bath, lathering down from hair to feet and rinsing off. The goal was to look as appealing as he possibly could when he met his bride. He certainly would not want to have her meet him with a reeking body. He may be a man, but he still had a nose!

After Price dried off and was carrying the washtub to

the door so he could dump the water outside, he looked over at Trader laying contently. "Hey old friend, how about you, do you want to spruce up a bit before you meet the lady?" Trader did not budge or pay him any mind. The dog was definitely not interested. Price chuckled. Recalling the past times when he had tackled the job, he could guarantee the old boy would not be an easy wash. Price chose not to attempt it tonight and took the water out.

Price put away the bathing apparatus, wiped up the water on the floor and wondered, *How am I going to approach her, what will I say?* Father God quickly reminded him of a conversation they had this morning…*Forgive me Lord, I know You told me You already spoke to her*. His anxiousness was overcome by peace by remembering, *"She will understand your approach comes on the wings of My love and will accept your proposal without reservation"*. Price anticipated this fulfillment, never thinking it could be so simple. He reconciled not to give into doubt, but believe. Simply because Father God said it would be so.

Peacefully Price proceeded to prepare the house for nighttime. Taking a last look over the ranch yard and out towards the barn…everything was quiet. He checked the cook fireplace to be sure the fire was contained. Now he needed to get his rest, tomorrow would be coming soon enough.

♥

Chapter 9

It was a restless night, Price tossed and turned desperately trying to get to get some sleep, but it was useless, every momentary struggle defeated. "What is the use?" he mumbled, stroking his hair away from of his face with his fingertips. *Apparently, this is not working, no slumber tonight.*

The excitement of the day was finally here for him to meet his chosen bride and it was more than Price could handle. He got out of bed, pulling up his trousers, slipping the suspenders over his shoulders, and walked over to the door. Opening it, a surge of fresh air revitalized him while he gazed over the ranch's moonlit landscape. "This sure is a beautiful night Lord. What an enormous moon! Of course you know...You placed it there." The brightness of the moon made everything on the horizon visible. On a night like this your vision was almost as clear as daylight. Noticing Trader comfortably stretched out on the new woven rug from Ruth, Caleb's wife, he concluded, *Ol' boy is not having a sleepless night.*

He moved onto the front porch and sat down on the bench, *it feels warmer tonight.* Price was having difficulty toning down his excitement with his mind racing, thinking about his God-chosen-bride. After fifteen minutes, he was not any closer going back to bed. He was wide awake. *Why not...I should leave tonight*! He took his Pa's timepiece out from his pocket to check the time, *Hum, almost 3:00 a.m. Yes, I could leave now and get into New Crossing around 7:00 in the morning. An early start would certainly be better than sitting on this porch until daybreak*. It was decided.

Price went inside and began to gather a few travel items. "Trader," he called waking the dog from his rest.

"Come on boy, let's go find the beautiful gem of New Crossing." Since Trader was slow to move he tossed in a convincing word, as if the dog could be conned, "I promise she'll spoil you." The old faithful dog was ready to comply, standing up stretching his back legs. He moved slowly away from his cozy spot to follow his master out the door.

On the way to the barn Price stopped by the chicken coop and tossed out extra feed for the flock. Once inside the barn he fed the goats. While he was laying out hay for the horses he remembered how his mother and Aunt Arnett insisted on riding in the buggy-wagon. They claimed it was more comfortable with the springs in the seat, so he hitched the team to it instead of his faithful work wagon and set out for New Crossing.

Anxiety plagued him again with doubt and fickleness before he ever reached the trail leading to town. *Won't this woman think I am a lunatic if I approach her with a proposal of matrimony at our first meeting?* The Lord understood the pressure he felt and was patient with Price. As quick as the insecurity hit him, the Lord responded, "You worry too much my son. I have told you before, I have prepared her heart. She is waiting for you." Although the words were the same encouraging reminder as before, yet this time the Lord included another instruction which ricocheted deep into Price's heart, "Hurry my son…do not hesitate." This instruction had an urgent boldness attached to it which made Price shudder. He questioned, why he was to hurry, but quickly dismissed it being reminded of the stories of men in the Holy Book. They taught him it was not a good idea to question God's instructions, but do them exactly as He speaks them. At this, Price prodded his team of horses to increase speed. *I can cut a half hour of travel time off the trip if I stay diligent. Trader rather enjoys a fast ride anyhow*. The dog sat in the seat next to Price with the refreshing wind tousling his fur...nothing could be better!

♥

Before Raine went to bed the Bartley twins put her two trunks into the back of the buggy. So this morning all she had to do was transport them to the General Store where she was to meet Max with the covered wagon. She would be leaving the horse-and-buggy there and someone in the Bartley family would retrieve it later in the day. They were very gracious to her and agreed to pay the low-price she quoted them. With their assistance over the last month helping load and unload all of her goods to sell...it was the least she could do to repay them for their selflessness.

Raine was apparently early. The covered wagon had not yet arrived at the store. She positioned the buggy in front of the store so it would be there for the Bartley's. Looking at her father's chronometer, she seen it was already 5:30 a.m. The sun's light was not even outlining the horizon yet. *Certainly, I am not late for it is still partially dark*. Raine retrieved the lap blanket from beneath the seat and covered her legs. *It feels a bit nippy this early in the morning*. She tried to relax while waiting for Max & Daniel to arrive, however she felt extremely uncomfortable. She still had uncertainties about journeying for several days with Max. The only protection from this sinister father was his nine-year-old boy.

Waiting only gave Raine time to fret about how wearisome the trip was going to be. She would have to be perpetually on guard with Max Harper. There really was no other choice, if she wanted to get herself to

Albuquerque. Taking a deep sigh, resigned to this fact she would endure. Once in the big city she could put this trip behind her and lighten her spirit once again. Only after she is safe will she have the pleasure to approach her new life with optimism. As she considered everything, she decided the favorable goal was worth the risk. After all she had the Lord's Promise to keep her focused. *I will speak about the Lord with Max and Daniel along the trip and with the Lord's words being discussed, he might keep his distance.* She sincerely hoped Max had a healthy fear of God's power and might. Because Max was no wee man, with his large frame he could easily overpower her without much effort. Nevertheless she took extra precautions and was ready for any advances he might make. *If he even tries to get familiar with me, I have a surprise for him*! In her satchel was her mother's Colt pocket revolver ready for a quick retrieval, hoping she would never come close to using it. If he gave her any indication of becoming crude she would transfer it to her pocket. In fact, she chose to wear her skirt with the large pockets just for this reason.

Raine glanced down the walkway and spotted Mr. Adams coming towards her. It was time to open the General Store. As he came closer he gave a quick wave and loudly informed her a pot of coffee would be brewing on the wood stove. He offered for her to come inside and wait where it was warm, but Raine declined. She preferred her solitude in the buggy, praying and trying to convince herself it was going to be all right. Actually, she was wavering on her worth-the-risk decision and was trying to muster up the nerve to leave. Knowing the new conditions surrounding her trip had the ambiance for disaster.

Raine noticed the time, *6:20 a.m.* She was extremely nervous, wondering why the covered wagon hadn't shown up yet. *I should abandon this venture and start over again in New Crossing*. Yet the major question remained, where would she meet the man God has promised her? While she was deep in thought Mr. Adams startled her. "Raine, this will help keep you warm. I do not know where Max is, I thought he and Daniel would be here by now." He was standing by the buggy with a cup of coffee he graciously brought out for her.

"I am sure they will be along soon," she replied trying to act confident and at ease. "Congratulations on the coming birth of your child," she spoke as he was walking back to the store.

Mr. Adams paused a moment before her turned to look at her. At first he revealed a big smile which faded quickly, replaced by his request, "Thank you. Pray for my Myra and the child, Raine." He then continued his pace towards the store.

"I will," she was able to assure him before he disappeared inside. The worrisome expression on Mr. Adams face moved her with deep compassion. Immediately she rendered a prayer for the Adams family and their new unborn child. When she opened her eyes she noticed the covered wagon heading her way. She became quickly aware that Daniel was not up front with his father. *Where is he? Maybe he is sleeping in the back.*

Max purposely angled the covered wagon in front of the buggy, making it difficult for her to pull away. His burly frame shot out of the covered wagon vigorously and in haste.

"Where is Daniel?" She nervously requested to know.

"Oh, Daniel won't be coming, he caught a bad case of summer sniffles and I thought it best he not travel in a weakened condition...are those your trunks in the back?"

Raine felt the blood drain out of her face, leaving her pale white. *How did this happen? What can I do now? I cannot go with this man…I do have my mama's package,* thinking of the revolver. "Yes," she barely got it out.

Max being strong as an ox, abruptly whipped the two travel trunks, depositing them onto the back of the covered wagon as effortless as cloth garments, before she could speak another word or catch her breath.

Slowly with reservations, Raine climbed timidly out of the buggy while clutching her satchel tightly. Hesitating, she stared extensively at the huge covered wagon, feeling overwhelmed with fear and apprehension.

"Guess it is just us Missy, let me help you up." Max grabbed Raine around her waist and when his hands touched her body he slid them places that were unnecessary. Acting like it was accidental as he boosted her up in the front of the wagon. Now she already felt violated and they had not yet pulled away from the General Store. She took a seat, still being petrified, retrieved her revolver and placed it into her pocket while Max went to the back of the wagon to tighten the latches. *Oh Lord, I wish I were not here.*

Max climbed in the seat beside of her and prepared to move out. He had just picked up the reins, when Mr. Adams shouted for him to wait, causing Max to grumble under his breath. Mr. Adams went back inside the store and returned with a package from Myra to her grandmother. Max instructed him to put it in the back, to which Mr. Adams complied and then waved good-bye.

Max snapped the reins and placed his wide strong hand on Raine's knee. "I have been waiting a long time for a chance like this, Missy."

She abruptly moved his hand and shot daggers at him with her eyes. Max was not easily intimidated and gave out a hardy diabolical laugh. Raine slid her hand in her pocket, grasped the revolver and prayed fervently for the Lord to rescue her from Satan's snare.

♥

Chapter 10

A covered wagon was approaching when Price arrived in town. As it drew closer he noticed his future bride riding in the front seat. There was no spiritually bonding glance which occurred the first time he saw her, nor did her eyes touch his with the same intensity that penetrated his heart. This time she scarcely looked in his direction. However, the look on her face communicated something desolate. *Her eyes are so empty Lord, what shall I do...is this man her husband...have I been wrong in my assumptions?* Immediately his mind was flooded with all the things the Lord spoken to him. He remembered the Lord's last instruction, *'Hurry and do not hesitate!'*

Price knew his Heavenly Father would not instruct him wrongly. This reminder was all that was needed to inspire him to act boldly. He quickly turned the wagon around and set out to prevent the covered wagon from leaving town. The earliness of the morning left the streets of New Crossing empty, making it trouble-free to catch up to them. He positioned the buggy-wagon in stride alongside the large covered wagon so he could communicate with the woman and driver. He motioned for them to bring their wagon to a halt.

Max had no intentions of complying. In fact he was extremely irritated about the attempt to delay him. Jabbing Raine's side with his elbow, he crudely asked if she knew the man.

Raine was preoccupied with her own predicament and oblivious to what was taking place at the time Max inquired. Slowly turning her head, she apathetically looked over at the buggy-wagon traveling with them in perfect step. Recognizing the driver, her heart leaped. *It's him!* Astonish, she could not turn her eyes away.

Meanwhile Max was becoming more demanding inquiring irrationally to the driver's identity. She quick wittedly replied, "Max, I think you should stop the wagon, this man has traveled a long way."

"So you do know this irritant." He grumbled and snarled while reluctantly pulling up on the reins bringing the covered wagon to a standstill. Then retorted, "Whatever his business is, be quick about it. I want to get on the trail."

Price pulled his wagon to a halt and climbed down and proceeded boldly to where Raine was sitting. "Hello Mam," he said taking off his hat. Holding it politely in front of his chest as he spoke with confidence. "I think you are going the wrong way." With these words, he looked directly into her eyes and the tender bonding of their souls were stirred once again.

With the morning sun reflecting off his amber hair amplifying his good looks, leaving Raine captivated. She noticed every gesture, how he stroked back his hair and tucking the shoulder length strands behind his ears. Never breaking the lock of their eyes. He waited patiently for her response as she processed everything. It occurred to her this man was her answered prayer of rescue...*a way off this wagon and out of the control of the devil himself.* She spoke affirmatively in a voice that made Price's heart race. "Yes, I believe you are correct, I am going the wrong way. Will you help me down?"

Max abruptly grabbed a hold of Raine's arm in an attempt to stop her. With a quick jerk she was able to pull out of his grasp...amazed how it released so easily.

Placing his hat on his head, Price reached up to take hold of Raine's hand. Noticing her touch was delicate and frail made it difficult for him to concentrate. Helping her to descend by taking her waist and lifting her to the ground, *she is light as a feather*. He did not let go until he was sure her footing was stable.

"Hey!" Max bellowed gruffly, "What in blazes are you doing?" He was utterly enraged over the situation and mulling silently over his private intentions, *I almost had the wench alone and out of earshot of a living soul*. His anger soared, *this no-account is foiling my plans…who is he*? "Raine," he shouted firmly, "climb back in the wagon, we need to move out…this joker ought to have placed his farewells yesterday!" Hovering over the side glaring at them from the wagon, Max could not hide his enrage. He was sporting a beet-red-face revealing an ill-tempered disposition was brewing underneath, which only solidified with each angry remark.

Feeling extremely relieved, Raine peered up from her safe position knowing she had wreaked havoc on his filthy intentions and instructed smugly. "I will need my wardrobe trunks out of the back of the wagon please. I will not be departing for Albuquerque today."

Albuquerque, Price instantly realized why the Lord called him to make haste on his trip. How close he had come to having her vanished from his life! *Lord the timing was extremely crucial,* he rendered thanks privately.

Max got down and continued to display his conniption-fit with profanity and name calling rolling off his lips, "Strumpet." He abruptly snatched the wardrobe trunks out of the wagon compartment, slamming them roughly in the dirt street. He was not about to put them into the other wagon. In fact, Max would not have complied with any of this if he had not been so close to his own homestead and feared Elizabeth might be watching. *If I were further down the road I would have outrun this mudsill and not even stopped,* Then his diabolical mind rethought…*better yet shoot this intruder and claim it was a holdup.* He mulled furiously as he stomped to the front of the covered wagon and climb in.

Price lifted the first trunk from of the dusty ground. Raine tried to give assistance because she knew how heavily she packed them. However, Price was not a weakling, rather a man with great physical strength and insistently refused her help. He slid the trunk into the back of the wagon, and then as he was taking hold of the second trunk, he displayed a broad grin. It was his way of assuring her he was perfectly capable of handling the load.

Raine stood there being impressed with his gentle manner and well-built vigor. Watching closely as he pushed the trunk into a secure place. Her attention on Mr. Barrett was interrupted by a child's voice calling out. She turned to see who it was.

Nine-year-old Daniel was running towards the covered wagon, "Paw, Paw, you came back. I knew you were just joshing me." Both Price and Raine stood motionless as they observed the young lad climbing into the front of the covered wagon. Max snapped the reins harshly and pulled away leaving a spray of dust.

Price and Raine were still standing in the middle of the road when Max left abruptly. Spontaneously they both turned away from the dust flailing all around them. After hearing Daniel's remark to his father, Raine silently rendered thankfulness to the Lord for saving her. She glanced back at the wagon as it vanished within the dust. God had delicately rescued her from an evil scheme.

Promptly redirecting her attention to Mr. Barrett. The sight of him made her lightheaded. She was dumfounded and could not comprehend all that had just taken place. *I do not understand...how is it that you of all people came to my rescue…I am so glad you did*! Yet unbelievable as it was…God sent her a hero and nonetheless the handsome Mr. Barrett. Just the man she wanted to meet. Raine was completely mesmerized in his company. How could she even begin to speak to him and what would she say? *'Mr. Barrett I am so glad it is you who come to rescue little ol' me'…Oh my, I have to stop thinking like a schoolgirl and get myself together before he finds me completely foolish.*

Raine was not the only one who was having a hard time making something of this situation as they each stood awkwardly in the road. Price felt almost hypnotized having her so close. He still could not get over the fact that she was about to leave for Albuquerque. Although he realized his timing was critical, he was still unaware of all the dangers that awaited his promised bride had he not arrived on time. *What were the odds she would actually step off the covered wagon and change her direction at my request? But she did! God told me. He prepared her to meet me. Wonder what He told her about me*?

Feeling a bit uncomfortable just standing there, he broke the awkward silence with a slight stammer, "Mm…Mm...Mam, allow me to help you up in the buggy-wagon." He guided her to the side of the wagon, while instructing his faithful sidekick Trader to get in the back. The obedient dog responded, jumping into the wagon without hesitation. Price gently lent a hand assisting Raine in the front seat. He then went around to the other side and climbed into the seat alongside of her.

Not knowing what to do next, he asked, "Do you have a particular place in mind you would like to go?" He was finding it difficult to be debonair being so captivated by her. Inside he was stumbling all over himself trying not to not let her notice how much he was admiring her. *More lovely than I remember!*

Raine was insecure over the quick change of plans and did not know quite how to answer Mr. Barrett. "No...well maybe...actually I don't rightly know. I just closed up my home this morning under the presumption that I was leaving for Albuquerque. I dropped a Property-Release letter into the door-box at the Land Settlement Office this morning so they could begin to find a buyer for my house. It looks like I will need to get it back. Only the Settlement Office will not be open to do business for several hours. I suppose you could take me back to my house...I could sit on the porch." She realized the explanation was pathetic, as she stumbled through her answer, but it was accurate.

Considering the obvious dilemma, Price offered a solution in his charming, yet humorous way. "Mam, rest easy I have no intention of kicking you out of the wagon. It would be a ruthless thing to leave you stranded with two trunks in the middle of New Crossing after asking you to not go on your journey. I have a lot of time and I do not have to be anywhere. You are welcome to sit in the wagon with me until the Settlement Office opens up. Actually I would welcome your company. That is if you do not mind...we could wait together for it to open up," *I would welcome your company for life,* were his silent thoughts.

Raine smiled when he invited her, she did not want to leave him so soon. She nervously replied, "Yes, I would like that. I think you would be fine company." *Did I actually say that?* Surprisingly she was flirting. She did find him amusing, and was fascinated by his how a cheerful mannerism flowed out of him. Deep inside she had a hunch he was interested in her too.

Price looked intently at her, studying her, reflecting over the situation privately in his mind. He wanted to tell her why he was here. Yet questioned if he could possibly risk it so soon? He certainly did not want to frighten her away. Nevertheless the compulsion to speak was stronger than he could endure. His heart was pounding so fast, but Price could not restrain himself and blurted out the whole idea. "This may sound presumptuous to you, especially with you not knowing me and yet I am compelled to offer a different suggestion, in hopes it might be compatible with you."

Raine chuckled nervously, "I believe I am open for suggestions. Look at me, I just got off a wagon at the request of a man I never met, and at the same time it felt like the natural thing to do." *Am I still flirting... oh stop it Raine!*

Price proudly took the bait and moved forward with assurance. "It seems apparent to me that it was your preference to leave New Crossing this morning. With your homestead registered with the Land Settlement Office and since your belongings are packed and in the back of my wagon, maybe there is no need for you to stay in this town? I have a godly idea which you might find is a suitable proposition." Price pulled the buggy-wagon over to the side of the road, enabling him to talk more freely.

While Raine waited for him to finish his suggestion, her puzzled mind questioned what Mr. Barrett was trying to suggest. Maybe he needed a housekeeper or a child caretaker. If a married man, he could have come into town to find a person he could employ to assist his wife. *Oh I wish I knew...this could be disappointing.* Fear of his being attached to someone else tried to invade her hopes. She felt a twinge of panic inside, she did not want him to be married. Children were not a problem, *maybe he is a widower?*

Nonetheless, if Mr. Barrett was not going to finish his

suggestion without knowing her possible interest she would have to take the risk to find out. There were no other options. *He did say a 'godly idea'.* "Well Sir, you are accurate, I do not really have any reason to stay in New Crossing at present, so I am open to hear your godly idea."

Price took a deep breath, mustering courage. he boldly reached over and gently took hold of her hand placing her delicate fingers reverently in the palm of his own. Raine surprised and completely mesmerized by this action. She allowed him to hold her hand although she did have a moment of reservation thinking, *maybe I should pull my hand away, incases there is a Mrs. Barrett.* However liking the action, she did not have the strength to do it. She was trembling with an overwhelming desire inside to welcome his tender touch. Raine permitted the dashing Mr. Barrett to hold her hand as she waited, longing to know what he had in mind.

Price focused his attention on her beautiful hazel eyes. He was searching for an approval. Her eyes danced and flickered and Price took this as consent to continue holding her hand and proceeded to reveal his proposal. "I have prayed daily for a wife all of my manhood years without fail. Not for just any woman, but one of God's choosing. I have waited a long time following His instructions with endurance and hope. I am now 45 years old and I believe with all my heart the Lord God has brought me here today to ask you to be my wife." There, it was out and surprisingly he was not worrisome over it, but with anticipation awaited her reply.

Raine's heart fluttered when she realized Mr. Barrett was not already given in matrimony to anyone, rather he was asking her to fill that position. She began to tremble considering carefully the offer he presented. *Could this be true? A man who had asked the very thing she has asked of the Lord. Why not? The Lord asked me to wait and it would only be His divine way if He had a man to do the same.* Overflowing with hope, she held back her tears of joy. Amid quivering lips Raine fought off the urge to instantly reply yes. She hesitated but only for a moment, "But Sir, you do not even know my name or anything about me."

"It was not your name the Lord gave me insight to, but your character. I do not need to know your name to know you are the woman that the Lord in His loving mercy saved for me."

Raine melted instantly at his simple explanation because she knew it to be true...she felt the same about him. If it were not for Mr. Adams she would not have a name to attach to him and her feelings would be unchanged. With a soft and trembling voice, she replied, "I have also waited for the Lord's Promise. A man who He saved for me to marry," she modestly confessed. "The Lord advised me at the age of 17, not to be flirtatious in the ways women are to seduce men to take notice, because He had someone created especially for me. At the time, I was advised to be patient, and sir, I have been patient a long time."

When Raine explained her side, a powerful surge of faith and appreciation entered the core of Price's heart. Lifting his eyes upward, he felt deeply embraced by a loving God. Marveling over the construction of this magnificent plan. Price looked at her delicate hand cupped in his own bulky overworked one and gently caressed it with his fingers. Giving her hand an affirming squeeze he spoke, "I am aware you have waited as I have...the Lord God informed me of this detail. Yet I must tell you, I never dreamed He would have chosen such an attractive woman to delight my eyes as a part of His plan...you are beautiful...accept my offer and marry me."

Raine flushed at the compliment and glad she pleased his eyes as he also pleased hers. She noticed her personal effects sitting in the back of the wagon, knowing they were without explanation placed in the buggy-wagon by divine intervention. There was no doubt that this was the Lord's arranging. The timing was perfect with the moving plans, the selling of her home and belongings, letting go of her job, everything was orchestrated for this moment. *Yes, Lord, I see You were at work all a long and are fulfilling Your Sacred Promise to me.*

An emotional lump in her throat prevented her from speaking for several moments, while Price waited patiently with confidence. Once she caught her breath, the words began to form on her lips and she answered, "Yes...I will marry you."

Did he hear her correctly? Yes, she said yes! Price felt ecstatic and a broad smile crossed his face showing a straight set of white teeth. "My name is Price Barrett and yours?"

"Raine Jordan."

"Beautiful, what a unique name, I do not believe I have ever met or heard of anyone being named Raine; I like it...Raine," he spoke it again, "Beautiful name for a beautiful woman."

It was a rare occurrence for Raine to receive any compliments, let alone two back to back. *How could this attractive man with just a solitary glance infiltrate my very soul, and pay me such extravagant compliments*? She was modestly embarrassed. Feeling her face flush, she lowered her head and wondered. *Could I love him already, is there such a thing as love at first glance?*

Price could not hold back his enthusiasm. He let go of Raine's hand momentarily and burst out in a hardy laugh, throwing his arms spontaneously up in the air rendering bold lip service to Father God. "Praise be to You Lord God of the whole universe. This is the day I have waited for." He corrected, "We have waited for. Thank You for Your tremendous faithfulness and Your overwhelming love to us." He realized his zeal was exuberant, but he could not restrain. Knowing no one could receiving a promise of 25 years. Have it placed in their grasp and not offer unrestrained thanksgiving to the One who brought it all about! Looking again at his beautiful woman invoked a smile that would not ease up, "Golly Moses! Is there a Gospel Sharp in town, Raine?"

Raine blushed and chuckled by the way Price showed so much happiness openly. She liked how he did not attempt to hide his feelings, or pretend to be aloof. This display of appreciation to God only made her admire him even more. He was unashamed and spoke loud enough for anyone to hear. Two men passed by on horses did hear and looked strangely at them, but they did not care if the world knew.

Raine answered shyly, "There is a little chapel on the east side of town. Preacher Matthew lives next door."

Price reconsidered his words, he did not want to take advantage of the situation. Just because she got off the wagon did not signify she felt at peace with the arrangement so quickly as to marry him today. He offered, "Do you really desire to take this leap of faith to marry me today, a stranger? I certainly do not want to force you. We can take our time if you are not totally comfortable with the speed of our engagement." Price was hoping she would be brave, but was willing to wait.

Raine felt comforted, hearing the compassion and the consideration he expressed for her. "I do want to marry you…I do not consider you a stranger. I have waited for you all my life and I recognize you are the one God sent.

Yet I still have many questions because I am still mystified about how we got to this place. I feel like I am in a whirlwind. Help me to understand better, Price, what brought you here on this morning at the precise moment when I was leaving town. I know you reside on the other side of the river, towards the Paints, so how did it happen for you to be in New Crossing at this time?"

Price was flattered she knew his location without ever telling her. Another confirmation the Lord prepared her for this moment. "I respect your question even though neither of us may not fully understand the hand of God. I was planning on coming here today to search for you to ask you to marry me. However, I was restless and I could not sleep last night so I decided to leave. I could see clearly to travel with the brightness of the moon. Once I was in route to New Crossing the Lord spoke to me and instructed for me to hurry and not to hesitate. With that encouragement I picked up the speed allowing me to arrive just in time of your departure. In a brief moment of discouragement after passing you in the covered wagon I almost abandoned my quest until the Lord reminded He said, 'Hurry and not to hesitate'. That was all I needed to act boldly on what I believed or to go home without you in my life."

"I did not notice you passing me. I am glad that you turned around," she said in a positive tone.

"When I saw you riding away in the covered wagon, I wondered if I had misunderstood the Lord. He did not let me wallow too long in self-pity before turning me around to catch up with you."

"You recognized me and remembered me from the General Store three months back?" Raine asked.

"You remembered me from three months back." Price grinned.

Raine blush, "I did."

"I believe the divine connection the Lord instilled in us that day at the General Store sealed our lives. When you follow God's ways and obey His principles He will not disappoint you. " Price spoke confidently.

At that moment, Raine began to admire Price for his character. She could hardly wait to have their unique personalities and the history of their lives unveiled one layer at a time. *It will be wonderful getting to know more of him. I am so impressed already with this little bit...I even like his name, Price.*

For a brief moment their faces were close enough to feel each other's breath. Price did not take advantage for the marriage vows were not affirmed to have permission for a kiss. Instead he spoke the question on his heart. "And what might I ask, caused you to be departing New Crossing in a covered wagon, with a foul-mouthed man heading to Albuquerque?"

Raine felt rightfully humiliated after he put the facts so bluntly, but the question deserved an explanation. "Good question, I have been feeling for a year I was supposed to move away from New Crossing. After giving my job notice, I sold all my family belongings to afford the trip. I acquired a ride with Mrs. Adams, who is the General Store proprietor's wife. Mrs. Adams and her brother were going to see their aged grandmother in Albuquerque. Yesterday, she came by the house to inform me she was with child and too weak to travel. I tried to get out of the trip with her brother, but his wife and the Adams insisted it would be fine, considering Daniel, his son, would be journeying with us. I figured it had to be safe with the boy along, but as you observed, he tricked his son to leave without him." Raine turned pale at the remembrance of how close she came to being out of earshot of anyone. "I was in a very dangerous position when you arrived and I believe you were the answer to my prayer of rescue."

Price heard the tremendous fear in her voice as she spoke of her situation on the covered wagon and he did not ever want her frightened like this again. "We must praise the Lord. He was well informed of your situation Raine. You are safe now and I promise you I will never let the likes of that man near you again." Price picked up the reins and promptly began to lead the horses east of town where Raine had instructed he would find the New Crossing Chapel.

Raine felt incredibly safe knowing both God and this man was capable of protecting her. This peace enabled her to set aside her fearful thoughts and look toward her future…after all it was her wedding day!

♥

Chapter 11

Preacher Matthew began his day in the usual way. Awakened long before dawn, he was encased in stillness on his knees, humbly presenting himself before God. While in prayer, Matthew received a vision, a pair of white doves, and he knew instinctively they were lifetime mates. He inquired of the Lord about the meaning, but even now as light broke on the horizon, there was no understanding. The fence was in need of repairs, so he decided to work on it while Bonita, his wife, prepared breakfast.

Matthew's thoughts were preoccupied with the vision while mending the parsonage fence. He was interrupted occasionally with stomach growling stirring his appetite, yet his mind was perplexed by the vision. It had been a long time since the Lord brought something so vivid to his mind's eye. He knew it had to be important for the Lord to draw his attention in this way, but he did not have any revelation other than the lifelong partnership.

On the other hand Bonita had wanted the fence mended for quite some time. So he had to concentrate on this project. He wanted to have it done before joining her in the kitchen.

While steadying the board for nailing, he observed a wagon stopping in front of the Mission Chapel. Rarely were there unexpected visitors at the small community church, let alone this early in the morning. Matthew wondered if there was a death. *There have been rumors around town about an outbreak of influenza among the settlers, perhaps someone has died. The deathly illness was said to have already claimed two lives from a nearby ranch.* Not everyone calls out the preacher so he had not personally buried anyone. He hammered the nail to set the board in place while watching the people walking his way. *Looks like Raine Jordan.*

Raine saw Preacher Matthew at his fence, pointing him out to Price as they walked over to where he was working. Matthew set down his tools and stood to greet them. Even though Raine knew Preacher Matthew most of her life by faithful attending Sunday Meetings, it was Price who began speaking assertively. "Hello, my name is Price Barrett," he held out his hand for a friendly hand shake.

Matthew cordially responded, "Matthew here, what can I do for you, Mr. Barrett?" He glanced over at Raine, noticing an unusual glow on her face before turning his attention to Price.

"I have a simple problem Matthew. I need to return to my ranch today, which is four hour west of here and I was hoping to take this beautiful woman home with me. However, we are not married. So I am asking if you would do the honor of joining Raine Jordan and I in matrimony." Price glanced at Raine to see if she wanted to add anything, but she stayed silent, with an I-told-you-so-smirk for Matthew.

On the spot, Matthew was refreshed with all he knew about Raine. She was a young lady when he met her. Even then, she had already acquired an eccentric reputation. It was common knowledge around the community about Raine's strong convictions. She believed the Lord promised to provide a husband of His choosing, if she would wait. The townspeople thought of her as a spinster with strange flights of imagination, but Matthew was not easily convinced. He met personally with Raine a few times and found her to be credible and convincing in her convictions. The way she put it: *'God set standards and if I follow His ways, He will not let me down and one day He will fulfill His Sacred Promise'.* Knowing the Scriptures in the Holy Bible, Matthew could not disagree with her. He truly admired her for staying true to what she believed. He wished more demonstrated the same kind of faith. *Now here she stands today in front of me alongside of a man who obviously adores her. I only wished her mother and father was still alive to see their daughter have her Sacred Promise fulfilled.*

Before Matthew could speak the still small voice of God whispered, "My children are connected by My love". *The doves!* He instantly understood the vision was to prepare him about this couple. He was confident Raine chose a way that pleased the Lord. A huge smile broke forth on Matthew's lips, "It would be an honor Mr. Barrett...Raine." Preacher Matthew called to his wife, who was inside the house. "Bonita, hold off on breakfast and come join us the Chapel."

Raine wore a high collared blouse, trimmed in yellow lace. Her skirt was a dark tan. Her hair was tucked neatly in a delicate pale yellow bonnet. Price could not help thinking, *without her knowing, how fitting she looked to be a bride today*. He did however fancy the idea of what her beautiful hair would look like unrestrained, flowing gently on her back. After staring so intently, mesmerized once again, he gave an open smile showing all his teeth, with pleasure he squeezed her hand.

Turning his attention to Matthew he replied, "Thank you, it would mean a great deal to us." Meanwhile Raine gave Matthew a look expressing her full agreeance. Noticing the glow & smile on her face that preacher Matthew never saw prior to this moment, gave him a deep satisfaction. Miss Raine Jordan was not disappointed in the Lord selection. Moreover, God was faithful in His promises.

After securing the last fence board Matthew gathered his tools, set them on the porch, glancing in the door to see if Bonita heard him, which she had. Then walked with the couple over to the Chapel.

Once inside the Chapel, Matthew proceeded to get the formalities out of the way, while waiting for Bonita to arrive. He asked the required questions for registering the official papers. Informational facts. What were their full names and if they had a middle name? Price was eager to comply, "Price Theodore Barrett." Raine followed with hers, "Raine Leigh Jordan."

Matthew wrote the names down carefully with help on the correct spelling, and then asked for their birth dates.

Price gave his, "September 3rd, 1867."

"July 20th, 1870" Raine offered and Price took special note to remember it.

Bonita, after hearing the conversation at the fence from inside the house, cheerfully entered the front door of Missions Chapel carrying a bouquet of fresh picked flowers from her garden.

"Bonita, we have a wedding this morning." Matthew spoke and then looked at her suspiciously. He was taken off guard by her obvious knowing. Meanwhile Bonita was thrilled to place the small fresh bouquet graciously into Raine's hand. The women exchanged a smile and Bonita hugged her, she always liked Raine. After the women were finished exchanging polite gestures, Matthew instructed Price and Raine to come before the altar. "Please join hands."

The ceremony was about to get started when the door opened and Gustavo entered, surprised to see a wedding taking place. Gus was the oldest man in town and respected by everyone. He was a quiet gentle man and often went for long walks around town, politely speaking with townsfolk along the way. It was his scheduled routine every morning to go to the Chapel and sit quietly in prayer before starting out. No one ever noticed him coming here before, not even Preacher Matthew. He was looking forward to this quiet time today because it was a special morning; it was Gretchen and his anniversary. They would have been married sixty-eight years if she had not departed six years previously, and now ironically a wedding was taking place. It instantly brought back fond memories.

Preacher Matthew looked up and motioned for him to come forward and join them. "Welcome Gus, as you see, we are having a wedding this morning, please join us." Gustavo noticing the one getting married was his dear sweet friend Raine Jordan, who always took time to speak with him when their paths crossed. He quietly took pleasure in joining the wedding ceremony, giving her an affirming smile. He placed himself next to Price, steadying himself with his walking stick. Bonita stood on the other side next to Raine.

Raine was delighted to see Gus. He was like a father figure to her in many ways, although she never told him how she felt.

Matthew began the ceremony by repeating, "Please join hands."

Price took a hold of Raine's hand. When their hands embraced, she immediately felt weak at the knees and had to refocus her attention on Matthew. She rendered a quick silent prayer for strength to remain standing as opposed to fainting.

Matthew proceeded to give a serious matrimonial challenge informing them in no uncertain terms they would be entering into this union for better or worse. Not to make this solemn commitment before God lightheartedly, but with conviction. He then picked up the Holy Bible and read from the pages, "Charity beareth all things, believeth all things, hopeth all things, endureth all things. Charity never faileth." He lowered the Bible, "What God has joined together no man can separate. This morning in a vision I saw a pair of doves who were lifetime mates. You two, standing before me, are the two doves in my vision." God spoke to me after you walked up saying, "My children are connected by My love." Matthew words were more surprising to him than to Price and Raine, as they seemed to accept the truth of it with pure simplicity. "Therefore, since God has ordained this union" he continued, "Do you Price Theodore Barrett take Raine Leigh Jordan to be your wife before God in His Holiness as long as you both shall live?"

"I do," Price spoke proudly the resonant affirmation.

Matthew looked at Raine "Do you Raine Leigh Jordan take Price Theodore Barrett to be your lawful husband before God in His Holiness as long as you both shall live?

"I do," Raine replied soft and clear.

Matthew directed his words to Price, "If you have a ring place it on her finger." Price looked down forlorn, it never occurred to him to have a ring. He was about to speak when he was interrupted by Gus.

Witnessing the disappointed look on Price's face, Gustavo, without thinking slipped his hand into his pocket and grasped a ring he had carried for six years. *Now it is going to find a home,* he professed silently to Gretchen.

Simultaneously, Raine squeezed Price's hand and whispered, "I do not need a ring." While Gus was placing a ring into Price's free hand, "This belonged to my Gretchen and I would love for Raine to wear it as a symbol of your marriage, please accept it."

When Raine realized that Gus had come to the rescue of their awkward moment it melted her heart. It was a beautiful and unselfish sentiment from her old friend. Price accepted the ring and slid it onto her finger, but found the ring too large. Matthew suggested he try placing it on the pointer finger, as was a Jewish custom. So Price slid the ring onto Raine's pointer finger and it fit perfectly.

Raine admired the beautiful gold band with carved olive leaves circling it. *This is a symbol of both of my loves; my husband and my God, plus the memory of Gus and Gretchen.* She would treasure this ring for all the sentiments it held.

Gustavo was pleased the ring had found Raine's finger to reside. He and Gretchen were never blessed with children nor did they have any family to leave a love token. He was honored and felt Gretchen was standing beside the Lord Jesus smiling, she also adored Raine. He could hear her words, *"If I had a daughter I would want her to be like Deloris Jordan's daughter, Raine".* The old man smiled proudly, it was the first time in six years he felt like he and Gretchen were together in this decision.

Matthew proceeded, "I now, under the authority of Almighty God and the Christian Faith in the Arizona Territory, pronounce you man and wife, Mr. and Mrs. Price Barrett. You may now kiss your bride."

Price gently lifted Raine's chin and leaned down to kiss her lips. It was the first kiss that either of them had ever experienced, and the magnitude of power that transpired in a single moment was beyond earthly knowledge or understanding.

Price opened his eyes first and viewed the gift of beauty before him, *what a precious gift*. Gaining back his senses Price asked Matthew, "Is it alright with you if I say a prayer before the ceremony is officially over?" Raine added her desire to pray also. Matthew nodded in agreement.

Raine knelt down at the altar beside her husband, who simultaneously took the humble position. Matthew followed their lead and knelt beside Price with Gus on one knee at his side and Bonita took a place beside Raine. All on their knees in humble respect, bowing before God asking for His favor.

Price did not hesitate to open the prayer, "Father God, I come before You with a thankful heart, for giving me such a generous gift, Raine, my wife. I vow before these three witnesses to love and protect her, to treat her always with kindness. I will always put You and Raine before myself. Grant our love to grow as You have ordained. This is a special sacred bond of matrimony, and I will be mindful of the importance of our union. Thank you for fulfilling Your promise. Your timing is exceptional. May our lives together bring honor to Your Name and may You find pleasure in our children." He gave way to silence while solemnly considering the seriousness of the moment. He could feel the Lords presence and knew it was good.

In the silent pause, Raine also was mindful of the significance of the vow she made before the Lord and began to pray, "Thank You Lord God, for the fulfillment of the Sacred Promise. I do not regret waiting, seeing this man of great character beside me. Thank You for my husband, Price Barrett, he is far more amazing than I ever hoped. May we never forget Your merciful love. Thank You Lord, I am humbled this day at Your goodness and I promise to be a Proverbs thirty-one wife." She was silent for a moment, and then added "Thank You for bringing Gus to our wedding and for his precious wedding gift to us."

Price added a last word to close the prayer. "Lord as we go forth from this day as man and wife, we ask You to join us in this marriage. Make this a marriage of three instead of two, because my wife and I cannot bear having a life without You being a part of it. You were with us in the beginning preparing us for this day and we want you to be in in the middle of our everyday together. Stay close to us and offer Your direction in all our upcoming decisions, Thank You. In the name of Your Son Christ Jesus I pray, Amen."

Raine followed with an "Amen". Matthew and his wife also added an "Amen." Gustavo wiped a tear from his eye and humbly said in a low respectful voice, "Amen", touching the heart of each one present. They all stood and hugged one another and rejoiced over this blessed union. Each one experienced the presence of God in the sanctuary this morning.

Raine took Gus aside and gave him a hug. She told him how much she appreciated the sacrifice of the ring, knowing it meant so much to him. Gus reaffirmed how glad he was to give it. "Today was Gretchen's and my anniversary. It is a fitting thing to do on our day. I may be 92, but I can still see the level of love Gretchen and I held living on in the two of you. This pleasures me."

His story touched Raine's heart and she expressed to Gus how she always looked forward to their paths crossing. Also how she appreciated the kindness he had shown her all these years. Raine then made her heart transparent and revealed her secret about the way she viewed him as a father, since her natural father died. How grateful she was for all his encouragement. Gus was honored and he shared how Gretchen felt about Raine being the daughter she would have wanted. This made Raine tearful for she never knew Gretchen thought so much of her. It was a tender moment between them.

After Matthew signed the official paper, and Gustavo and Bonita signed as witnesses, he gave the marriage certificate to Price, who then handed it to Raine, "Put this in your satchel so it does not get lost."

The Barrett's thanked Matthew and Bonita, giving Gus another hug and handshake before leaving Mission Chapel. After they left, Gus went to the back row of the sanctuary where he usually sat each morning and continued his normal prayer meeting with the Lord.

Up at the pulpit, Matthew placed his arm around Bonita, starring down the aisle at the entrance door where the couple vanished. "My dear Bonita, we have just witnessed a marriage that God has truly ordained, and wasn't it beautiful." She agreed. He asked, "We have become the Arizona Territory now, haven't we?"

"I think so, Matt dear."

"I will have to be certain before the next wedding I perform," he chuckled. "Now how about that breakfast Bonita, I'm starved." He then looked over at Gustavo, "Join us at the house Gus when you are finished, Bonita is cooking a tasty breakfast this morning." Gus conferred he would be glad to join them in a little while, but first he wanted to talk with the Lord to express his gratitude for this morning.

Outside Mission Chapel Price greeted Trader by ruffling his fur. He was a good loyal dog, patiently waiting in the buggy with Raine's belongings.

Once they were settled into the wagon's buggy seat, Price looked over at his new bride, "I am flattered to have you as my wife Raine Barrett. Are you happy?"

"Raine Barrett, I like how that sounds, and I am pleased to be your wife… Yes…Yes, I am happy."

"Well, my beautiful wife, I am planning on you carrying the Barrett name for eternity, so I am glad you like it. Just so you know I am ecstatic, never have I been so happy over anything."

Price proceeded to pick up the reins, but before he headed out, he took pleasure in another kiss making it difficult to concentrate on his journey back home to Barrett Ranch. The kiss left Raine flushed and lightheaded. She put her arm through his and rested her head on his shoulder, she felt heavenly. Trader also seemed content to snuggle-up on the floorboard under Raine's feet where she suggested he ride for the long journey.

The weather for the journey home was beautiful with the sun shining on everything making it look brilliant. To Mr. and Mrs. Barrett the whole world looked extraordinary today.

During the beginning of the ride, they experienced a welcomed silence as each adjusted to their new roles. There was no need to rush into conversation, realizing a four-hour trip would give ample time to become acquainted. Raine hummed gently a peaceful tune, while admiring the ring Gus so graciously provided. Price enjoyed the music and wondered how he managed to ride anywhere without the accompaniment of a sweet melody.

♥

✞ Father God sanctioned the marriage covenant between Price and Raine Barrett. He delighted in His children because faithfully with endurance they obeyed His standards. Now He would show His favor on them and bless their lives as He promised.

No evil will come near them, no plague will come on their ranch. Angels were dispersed to guard them with divine protection. Whenever they call on the Name of the Lord, He will hear their appeals and come to their rescue in the storms of life. As they trust Him, His hand alone will guide them into a safe harbor.

Concept inspired by
Ps. 91:10, 11, & 15; Matt.19:4-6

♥

Chapter 12

Raine was amazingly peaceful about being married to Price Barrett. In reality they were strangers, yet spiritually they were connected. After traveling the first hour along the river, Price approached a location where he knew it was not dangerous to take the wagon across. The whole idea of crossing the river made Raine apprehensive and rigid, as she was unfamiliar with the technique of river crossing. Noticing her inflexible demeanor, Price assured her, "The Lord certainly did not bring us this far in His plan to allow us to be swept away in the current…we are going to be fine." Hearing her husband's faith-motivated-logic, Raine took a deep breath focusing her attention on the Lord in silent prayer, knowing only He could lighten her tension. God showed His faithfulness and her fearfulness began to ease. In a moment of sensible reasoning, she became conscious of a simple fact; if she were ever to travel to New Crossing for supplies in the future, she would have to get use to crossing the waterway. This made her face up to her skittishness and embrace courage.

Once safely on the other side Raine felt her fear was conquerable. Her husband was skilled at this maneuver and she would have to learn from him. In all the years living in New Crossing Raine never once considered crossing the river before. With all the dreadful stories she heard in town over the years from travelers she felt it was just fine on her side of the river. Although when she heard Mr. Barrett lived on the other side maybe the thought did cross her mind momentarily.

Now traveling with the view of the waterway to her left, Raine was relieved to be on dry ground. She looked at the energy of the water, *How magnificent the water looks rambling in motion towards town. Price sure looks confident, I wonder if...* She wanted to pursue more about the man she'd be with the rest of her life. *Maybe I could ask a simple question, let's see...ahhh,* "How did it come for your parents to name you Price? Is it a family name?"

Price busted out laughing when he heard the question and Raine wonder why her asking was so funny. Actually Price's memory flashed to his parents, *they loved to tell this story in sign language about how I got my name and then hearing Aunt Arnett confirm it was the absolute truth, all the while the three of them laughing hysterically...* sigh, *priceless memories!* "Actually it was a mistake; I was named by the doctor who delivered me." Remembering how much the family had fun with the account made Price chuckled; it never occurred to him that he would be explaining the events to anyone.

Pursuing the issue, Raine echoed, "A mistake?" while observing Price's whole body shaking in amusement, *His laughter is contagious;* she began to chuckle also, his humor beckoned her to join him.

Since both of them were laughing silly, it only made it harder for them to get their emotions under control. Price put forth a great effort to gain his composure, while Raine simply looked away to help settle her laugher down. When Price felt that he could continue without laughing, he began to explain, "Yes, truthfully it really was a mistake. You see, my parents were speechless, they spoke with their hands. So, when Pa was trying to ask the doctor what was the price he owed for the delivery, the doctor thought it was the name of the baby he was trying to convey. Since the doctor found it difficult to communicate with either of them, he wrote my father's name down for the middle name on his own initiative. Thus, on the birth registration I became Price Theodore Barrett. My parents laughed so much about this over the years; they actually came to love my name, for it made them happy." Price chuckled lightly and added, "It makes me happy too, because they were going to name me after my great grandfather Hector. Somehow, I do not feel like a Hector, my aunt use to tell me the name Hector meant bully and that's not a legacy I want to be attached to. Therefore, I believe Price was God's name for me; it reminds me of the price Jesus paid at Calvary for my salvation."

Raine could not help herself; she let out a gentle laugh periodically while he was revealing the account. When Price was finished, she added, "You are right the name Hector does not suit you. I noticed how mannerly you handled yourself with Max and how you spoke to Preacher Matthew…No, you are definitely not a Hector, beside, I know in my heart, God would not have promised me a bully for a husband." she smiled confidently. "It's a good thing God intervened on your name, because in the Bible names always mean something important for the individual, like Judah means praise and Isaac meant laughter. To me, Price sounds like something of value." Price liked her meaning.

After spending a few moments in silence watching the landscape, the lighthearted atmosphere mellowed and Raine inquired more about his parents' speechlessness. "Was the problem with your parents not being able to speak because of their vocal area or was it their hearing?"

"My parents were deaf, and could not perceive sounds to be able to form the syllables into any words, although, my mama had a voice, she screamed so loud at the sight of a spider or snake, I could hear her all the way out to the barn," he smiled, "and both gave a hardy laugh. Words were much harder".

Raine listened carefully and treasured every tiny piece of information Price shared with her; she found it interesting how his parents communicated with their hands and not with a voice of words. She was looking forward to meeting them, which did present a small problem, but knew she would work it out; *I wondered how quickly I can learn to speak to them using my hands.* "I love your name, even if I must admit it is a funny story on how you acquired it. Were you born here in the Territory?" She fidgeted in the seat trying to get comfortable; the ride was longer than any she had remembered, least not since the wagon trip out West when she was young and resilient. *Wonder how I would have ever made it to Albuquerque?*

"No, I was actually born in Ohio and my parents took the adventurous trek out West in 1880. Enough about me for now, what about you Raine Barrett, how did you acquire your beautiful name?"

"It was not an accident," she chuckled, "My mother gave birth on a rainy day and decided rain had to be something special. For that reason, she called me Raine and Leigh…well…that was her middle name. As for Barrett, I have to confess this I acquired by divine providence," she proudly revealed.

Price smiled at her analogy of now possessing the Barrett name. "Your mother must be an intelligent and wise woman, as it appears she knew Raine Leigh Barrett would turn out to be an exceptionally special woman and I am inclined to agree with her assumption."

Accepting the compliment she replied, "Thank you, Mr. Barrett it is polite of you to say so." She reached down to run her fingers across the top of Trader's head; she enjoyed being with Price and his dog, it was comfortable. Somehow it felt normal for her to be riding with them, like she had done this many times before. *Oh*

Lord, You continue to amaze me after waiting so long...only You could have orchestrated all of this and brought everything together so naturally. How else could I feel this much at ease in Price's company so quickly?

Listening to Raine express her ideas and opinions, Price found her fascinating and was grateful the Lord had created her to be so interesting. Nothing passed his attention, he took everything into account and he even observed how she would crinkle her nose when she was deep in thought. Price loved how Raine seemed to be comfortable with beginning their life together. She showed no signs of being timid about it; rather she gave the appearance of a confident woman. Yes indeed, he liked this quality very much.

They rode a while in silence. There was no need to rush anything they had their whole lives ahead of them. Raine observed terrain she never viewed before, noting, *it is extremely beautiful here*. However, she detected the heat difference; it felt much warmer with the noon hour approaching. In fact it was a lot warmer than it was in New Crossing, yet she found it tolerable, as long as the breeze kept blowing.

Price was quiet, deep in thought. He wondered about many things, for one, how Raine would like the ranch. She was obviously a woman who was used to living in town and having more neighborly conveniences. His mind wandered, remembering how hard he worked with his father to make life more comfortable for his mother after Aunt Arnett died in 1892. Price's aunt had been a valuable helper to his mother and also the family. Recalling the explanation Aunt Arnett told him. *"It was my idea to come looking for land in this new uncultivated western territory... I wanted a place where my sister and her husband did not have to put up with all the ignorant people that dwelt in the city."* Price understood precisely what she meant. It was difficult for his parents to live around people with little understanding about their lack of hearing and speech. However, he was grateful his parents had the opportunity to meet at a school for the deaf. Recollecting Arnett's story further, *"this move out West opened avenues of hope for them to have a normal life. When they lived back East, simply being married and having children did not alter the way people viewed them...nor did it shelter you kids from the cruelty of your classmates." It took much coaxing from Aunt Arnett to persuade my parents, but after the last confrontation Pa had with rude neighbors, Pa began to believe the move out West was the only solution to raising children without the evils of discrimination.* Price had not given much thought about this in many years. Yet after the memory jog, he felt open to share more details of his life and family with Raine.

"Raine, my parents moved onto this land with the help of my Aunt Arnett and Uncle Cuate'. They facilitated the cultivating of our ranch, the layout of the buildings, barns and need sheds. My uncle was originally from Mexico, so he was quite knowledgeable in the art of constructing adobe homes; he also knew how to survive in the desert. Both my aunt and uncle were very good to my parents and taught them how to sustain in this barren area." He had Raine's full attention, she seem to hang on his every word. "Now let me tell you, the house Uncle Cuate' had us construct is not a small structure by any means. You will see it's quite stately...a far cry from the small quarters where we resided back in Ohio. But this grand adobe would have to meet all our needs and this place Uncle Cuate' designed did just that...the six of us lived graciously under one roof." Pausing slightly then added, "I had a sister, who passed away our first year."

Raine felt compassion for Price losing his sister, even if it were years ago, she realized Price never had a sibling growing up, since his sister passed he was like an only child. "I am sorry for the loss of your sister…did she get injured on the ranch, was it sickness, or did she have poor health?"

"Sharla Jane was only seven when she became very ill, burning up with a fever Mama could not break. Her death was especially hard on Mama, although she remained a strong woman and managed to adjust to her loss for my sake and Pa's."

"I am certain it must have been a dark time of the soul for her." Raine perceived her husband was being contemplative about the unspoken details; she wanted to comfort him, make the sad memories go away, she slid her hand under his arm connecting their arms together and leaned into him in a tender way. "How old were you, Price, when you journeyed out here?"

He welcomed her closeness, "I was almost thirteen, old enough to be of some valuable help. It was a pretty difficult time, the ranch was not green as it is today; everything was dry and really barren. We all worked extremely hard, many times I felt I would drop, yet surprisingly our labor paid off. We pretty much had the major things running for our survival, like an outhouse, a windmill, the well dug and all within the first couple of months while we were living out of the wagons. My uncle was an unbelievable help to my father. I also learned an enormous amount of important stuff about building and running the ranch from Uncle Cuate'; he used to refer to me as his first-rate-apprentice after we built the main house; a Spanish style adobe manor." Price let out a short chuckle welcoming the memories of the good ol' days. "Everything had come together and things were running quite well on the ranch. We had a garden, some livestock, and the forging shed to help us. Mama and Pa were happy and feeling free to enjoy life on the ranch, moving around without fear or restrictions. My aunt and uncle had achieved their goal. They also seemed to relax and take pleasure in the ranch as well; everyone looked pretty happy to me."

Price took a deep breath and then proceeded with a more solemn tone to his voice. "Then Uncle Cuate' received a letter from his youngest brother telling him news regarding his two older brothers. They had been disabled in the war and died within a year of each other. This letter arrived about our fifth year on the ranch. Uncle Cuate' felt guilty for leaving his family, thinking he should have stayed there to help everyone; he even said he should have gone to war with them. The guilt penetrated deep in his heart, tormenting him night and day, he had to appease his conscience and return home. There was no shaking the pull these tragedies had on him, drawing him like a giant magnet. He cultivated an idea in his mind; it was a plan to bring his mother and younger brother's family back here to the ranch the following spring. At the time I wanted to go with him, I was eighteen and struggled severely with the notion. Uncle Cuate' was not only my uncle, but working together he had become my friend. Nevertheless, the truthful facts prevailed, my parents would need me even more with Uncle Cuate' gone, so I abandoned the idea and stayed.

"With all the treacherous miles between here and Ohio there had to be a measure of uncertainties for his safety. This must have been extremely difficult on your Aunt Arnett." Raine offered sympathetically.

"Aunt Arnett was extremely torn. She wanted to go with him, but succumbed to her reality that she was still needed here with my mother. I think she found it hard to let go of helping Mama, so to her it was better to stay behind and make things ready for the rest when they came. Uncle Cuate' assured her he would be fine and promised he'd be back with the others in the spring before planting season was over. Aunt Arnett could not accept the separation; she never let the memory of him die out as she waited his return. Then the months turned into years. She never received a single letter from him or anyone in his family. The letters she wrote to his mother's address were never answered and by the following autumn Aunt Arnett was losing hope of his returning. Yes, I guess it was very difficult on her. I think she grieved and worried herself into an early grave. It may have been easier if she had heard something regarding him, then her life might have been different, but she never even knew if he made it back to Ohio or not. Five years after my uncle left, she died. I am not sure what the actual cause of her death was from, but Mama said 'she died of a broken heart'."

Raine eyes were misty, *such a sad story,* "I am sorry you lost both your aunt and uncle too," she manage to say without her voice cracking. Perceiving the memories were hurtful, she decided to bring up some present day ideas hoping to change the outlook, "Well, I am glad I will be there to help your Mama, I know you must be concerned about your parents being alone on the ranch? How much farther is it?"

Price was startled at her remark, realizing he had not conveyed the fact his parents were also with the Lord and thoughtfully chose his words to explain. "Raine, forgive me for not explaining sooner, but you will not get to meet my parents, and I am extremely sorry they will not get to meet you."

Raine wondered why she would not be meeting these two wonderful people; feeling disappointed and puzzled, she waited for him to clarify.

"Remember the morning at Adams General Store when we first saw each other while I was loading

Juniper lumber into my wagon? I had bought the wood to build burial boxes for my parents. They had become severely ill with a deadly case of influenza; losing their appetite, because nothing stayed down. It got so bad they lost the desire to even take a drink, I figured they suffered dehydration. They were both very weak and too sick to have a desire to live. Within two days of each other my father and mother went to be with the Lord. That is the reason I did not prolong my stay in town to come talk with you that morning, as much as I would have liked to. I had to return home speedily to care for their burial." Price had dealt with the loss, but explaining it to his new wife was not as easy as he thought it would be, he still missed them both.

Large tears ran down Raines cheeks, "Oh my, forgive me, I am speechless, I do not know what to say. My heart is breaking for your loss. This has to be overwhelmingly devastating for you…to lose everyone in your family; you have only barely begun to endure without them." She felt deep compassion for him, knowing firsthand how it was to be alone in a world that once was your comfort. She embraced his arm with both of hers and laid her head on his shoulder, wiping away her tears with her hand. "I too am alone."

It was ironic, both of them were destined to begin a family; they were the only living link to their parent's legacy. By their joining in marriage, they were given an opportunity to preserve their heritage.

Price welcomed her closeness and appreciated her expressing concern. It was *peculiar* though, *both without family*. "Raine, I did not come into New Crossing to seek a woman because I was alone. I was not looking for a wife when God pointed you out. But from the moment I saw you I knew you were my promised bride. I admit, I thought at the time it was an untimely moment, yet I have come to recognize it is simply our Father's decisive planning. I have had over two months to think about it and believe me I thought a great deal about you. I have come to accept what the Lord God sets before me; learning to rely on His wisdom has been a valuable lesson for me. Although He revealed you to me when it appeared to be untimely, according to His reality it is perfect timing. I know this even more now because He chose the time before you left town." Price looked over at Raine several times trying to convey his thoughts, "I am looking forward to our life together with such great expectations. I definitely miss my folks, but I have peace knowing they are singing out loud in heaven and I would not take that splendor away from them to return home to me."

"That is a beautiful perception," she commented. Raine straightened herself in the seat as her back was feeling the stress of the trip, "And for you to perceive the ways of the Lord in such a manner, even in your trials...well, I have never heard it expressed with so much assurance and faith. I am happy to be a part of that by becoming the woman God picked for you." She felt blessed, and pondered a moment before adding her personal history. "I lost my parents a few years back. I have no siblings; my mother was unable to carry a baby over a couple months, so she believed that I was her miracle. Now you and I are no longer without family...the Lord has given us each other; we can build a family legacy through our children that will carry on the Barrett name." She spoke confidently.

"I do believe that," Price agreed completely. "God joined our lives together so we would be fruitful and have our children to pass on a legacy of faith."

Price and Raine set aside the detailed discussion of their lives, placing their focus on the simplicity of the ride. Both pondered the personal history the other has shared and their attachments to grief. Now that those issues were covered, they could begin to look forward to happier times, facing new beginnings. Price would occasionally point out interesting landmarks to Raine; he found enjoyment showing her the magnificent sights of the desert.

It slowly dawned on Price about bringing Raine into a home where disease had claimed lives. How this might be a concern for her and thought he needed to offer some assurance. "In case you are slightly uneasy about the house being full of influenza contaminations, I want to assure you that I did have the house disinfected before I left for New Crossing to find you, I had the home filled with smoke to cleanse out all influenza germs."

"Smoke?" She questioned.

"Yes, smoke," he grinned, "I have a native Indian friend who teaches me interesting ways of his culture. By living in the desert far back in his ancestry they have come to be knowledgeable of many things; he says burning certain herbs will clean the air of disease. He brought me the ones the old woman in his pueblo picked out for me to use and I did exactly what he said to do."

"I am really not worried; however, I find this Indian technique very interesting. I would love to learn this ancestral desert knowledge, if you will teach me."

Price smiled and gently laughed, "Raine Barrett, you are most fascinating woman. Instead of turning up your nose and telling me the idea is completely hogwash, you simply say you want to learn about them. You really amaze me." Price just shook his head in wonderment of this outstanding woman that God chose for him. "Possibly my friend Caleb's wife, Ruth, will teach you the customs regarding desert plants."

"I definitely would welcome her knowledge and her

friendship, especially if our husbands are good friends; I think we already have something in common. How did they come by their names? Caleb and Ruth are not native names!"

Price smiled realizing how much he needed to explain, things she could not possibly know, "I gave those names to them when they joined our faith in Jesus; actually their given names are Crooked-eye and Sure-fire."

"Good questions," he grinned, "but they are fine with the Bible names. Jesus changed Peter and Paul's names, so these new titles are their Christian names. I have to admit, my first reason for changing Crooked-eye's name was different, I felt his name drew attention to his weakness, a wandering eye from birth. Being a man born with a positive character like Caleb in the Bible, this name suited him far better. By my changing his name, I was hoping to emphasize his good character, not his weakness. After Caleb told his wife Sure-fire the news about Jesus, she said if this was his faith she wanted it too, like Ruth told Naomi 'where you go I will go and your God will be my God.' Because her husband was given a Christian name when he joined the faith, she wanted one too, and Ruth was a perfect choice."

"What a beautiful account of these two lives…you witnessed to this man and then his household has come to know the Lord. I find your witnessing is not only appealing, but you are an incredibly God inspired man, Price Barrett." She adjusted herself again in the seat trying to get comfortable.

Noticing her fidgeting, Price asked, "You must be travel weary, would you like to stop for a while?" Without waiting for an answer, he pulled on the reins; bring the wagon to a pace where he could find a place to rest. "Forgive me for not stopping before this; you probably have not ridden very far in a long time."

"Not since we first settled there and everything is fairly close in New Crossing, so I guess my wagon trips have been ten minutes at the most."

"Are you hungry? We have not eaten anything?" Price proceeded to get a sack from under the seat and took out a few pieces of jerky. He shared them with her and gave a small piece to Trader. "I regret I haven't more to share with you, I guess I did not plan very well for a trip with a new bride." He thought again and confessed, "Actually I have been surviving off jerky for some time now."

She smiled, understanding most men could survive off most anything to avoid cooking; however she knew they also enjoyed a good cooked meal. "Well then, I will have to cook you a meal once we get to the ranch, I am sure your mother has some prepared food stored up. As for the jerky, it is truly sufficient; I am too excited to eat much right now anyway." Desiring to get her aching body out of the buggy so she could stretch some and yet not wanting to be too anxious about it, she gently asked, "Will it be ok to walk down by the river for a little while?"

"Of course, it's a great idea to stretch our legs by the riverbank, and Trader will benefit from walking around too." As soon as Price found a suitable place to stop, the dog jumped out of the wagon with little urging. Price climbed out and assisted his wife down. Raine slid her feet to the ground securing her footing, and then looked upward into her husband's ebony eyes; she realized he had not moved away as he did before. She wanted him to kiss her. Price noticed her eyes beckoning a response. He still had his hands resting on her waist, sliding them up her back tenderly he willingly obliged.

♥

Chapter 13

The river's cool breeze gently brushes Raine's face, refreshing her with tranquility. How could she feel so wonderful, she wanted to pinch herself to see if she would wake up? Yet she did not want to disturb this dream. There he stood more handsome than any man she ever seen before, continually captivating her. *He is very handsome for 45, I never thought at my age I would have such a good looking man*. Yet she knew there was more to this man than mere appearances. He was polite speaking, confident and his profundity in God absolutely intrigued her. She felt lighthearted and slightly giddy, like she was soaring far above the earth; a feeling she had only experienced during her quiet moments with God. Now Price Barrett was stirring these same lifted feelings inside of her. There was something else…something she had not experienced before. *Yes…a stimulating freedom;* like she could let down her protective barriers…*it feels splendid,* unworried and open.

Raine relaxed by the edge of the water, enjoying the fresh air, completely at peace and wondered if it was alright to feel such pleasure. The water moved along entrancing her in her own thoughts. She was really married! Thinking back how young she was when she made a pledge to the Lord, *oh…so long ago*. Raine was just barely becoming the appropriate age for a serious courtship, one that would lead to matrimony. Yet after committing herself to what she felt the Lord was asking, she never allowed herself to be attentive to any suitors until she knew for certain he was the one the Lord had in mind. Reviewing the selections that cropped up throughout the years, confirmed why it was easy to keep this commitment, *there was hardly a whopping number of good male prospects residing in New Crossing*. She had to laugh inside, shaking her head slightly trying to shake the thought of the assortment, when another old memory got her attention.

It was a flicker of courtship, if you could call it one; nevertheless it was the only one she ever experienced. It was the week after her 16th birthday, before her talk with the Lord. She was at a respectable age to begin to consider marriage and a particular suitor started paying attention to her, Randall O'Malley. *Ho-hum, I haven't thought of him in years, twenty-five to be exact!* However, the would-be romance was short lived; barely two weeks in its entirety. At the time of this budding courtship, Randall's parents decided to pack their old covered wagon and continue to follow their dream westward, to the new booming town of Sacramento. Apparently, Randall's father had greater expectations for the family than New Crossing had to offer. At the time, Raine thought it was peculiar that after all these years his parents decided to finish the trip to California since no one else ever felt the need to finish the expedition.

Raine's parents were heading for California when they decided to settle down in New Crossing. One third of the people from their wagon train did not venture on further, but also settled in the area and became their neighbors; the O'Malley's were among them.

Randall suggested she come with them to Sacramento, but Raine was not ready to move so far away from her family on a mere two-week flirtation, so she broke his heart, as he proclaimed. Randall O'Malley left with his family on schedule without her. It was almost a year after this when she heard the still small voice of God asking her to wait and not look for a relationship. He had chosen a husband for her, and IF she followed His standards and waited He would bring them together.

At first, after Randall left, Raine wasted a lot of time wondering what her life would have been like if her parents did not reconcile to make their home in the wayside settlement, named for its location, New Crossing. She understood when they explained it to her about not having sufficient funds to sustain them going the distance and start a homestead. However, the practical choice to stay and start a new life in the settlement decided their fate. How different would it have been if they continued? At the time when her parents made the decision Raine really didn't mind giving up daily tiresome travel. Besides, she knew their home would be full of love no matter where they settled, not to mention a lot of her friends from the caravan were staying also.

It took several months before Raine was at peace about not leaving with Randall. When she no longer looked for greener grass, life in New Crossing became good again and her relationship with God began to grow immensely, making life meaningful…Thoughts of Randall fell by the wayside.

Raine contemplated the entire picture of her life as it unraveled quickly, everything which led up to this wonderful warm summer's day in July. Only two days after her 42nd birthday; clearly it was God's providence. *He holds the reigns of our life, we are the ones who choose to let Him lead or to pull away,* and she realized by obeying her vow, she had chosen the right way.

The day was warming up, even with the breeze off the lake. She noticed Price, who was a few yards away squatting near the river's edge affectionately petting his dog. Raine reached into the river and retrieved water to splash on her face. The coolness of it felt good, patting it onto her forehead and cheeks and gathered a second handful to dab on her neck. Feeling repentance, she offered a brief silent prayer, *Lord Thank You for helping me endure my waiting. I am sorry for complaining this past year and trying to rush You, I was afraid I would give up and disappoint us both. Now, I see your plan and he is worth the time...he is perfect. Help me be a good wife. Bless our marriage. Amen.*

Raine decided not to interrupt Price, he appeared peaceful and in deep thought, *maybe he is praying too.* Raine walked the edge of the riverbank a few steps away not wanting to disturb him. Silently enjoying this beautiful resting spot, It has so many things for eyes to behold...God's beauty was artistically painted all around her. No bride could be happier.

Price was in deep contemplation and did not want Raine to notice his dilemma; squatting down by his dog was a good smokescreen. He was wondering just how to court a woman in the married way. When Price turned eighteen his uncle took time to fill in a few details before leaving to go back East, yet inside, he was never comfortable with his uncle's explanation of the animalistic traits of man. Price understood about procreation, when man first began his plight on earth, *but now the world has people everywhere, Father God, You knew this would happen so there has to be more to the act than simply making babies. I know You do nothing without a purpose.* Price was certain of that much, yet now feeling awkward and foolish he had never thought to discuss the matter with Father God before this. *At 45 I am reduced to feel like a boy!*

Price recalled the times he observed how tender his father would treat his mother and seemed to court her, even though married. He figured, *if Pa treated Mama like an animal, I doubt she would have been be so flirtatious with him. For that matter, Uncle Cuate' & Aunt Arnett appeared to be very romantic...animals don't court.* Recalling only brought to mind more questions without explanation. Price held several uncertainties plaguing his mind, yet no peace about any of it. This was not going to be the end of the conversation. He was dedicated to pray silently while traveling the rest of the way, anticipating there would be some meaningful insight from the Lord on exactly how to approach his new bride tonight. Catching Raine's reflection in the river, *Lord, just the touch of her closeness stirs a passion I've never experienced before.* The thought only made him more anxious and actually a little frightened, which is a very unfamiliar feeling to Price Barrett. *How can I be so brave in the desert and with men, yet this woman has my gut in turmoil. I definitely do not want to do anything wrong and make her wish she did not marry me. Father I really need your counsel.* Trying to act nonchalant, he cupped his hand and took a drink of water. *Certainly, she cannot tell what I have been thinking about...Golly I've lived a sheltered life!*

Price looked up from his pretension with Trader, observing Raine; noticing how pretty she looked with the sun's reflection off the water adding a radiant glow to her skin. While admiring her beauty, he realized she seemed to be mesmerized with something down the river; another glance quickly revealed that she was captivated with the colorful scene of distant rocks, so he offered, "Our ranch is before those rock formations."

She looked his way, "They are lovely."

"They are. I never get tired of seeing them, especially from this location." There was silence as they enjoyed the view together, then he added, "The terrain gets a bit rugged close to the river at this point, so we will be moving into the desert clearing for the rest of our journey." He pointed up stream, "Can you see how the river curves beyond that big boulder? The ranch is located just a little past the curve. Our lands boundary line is the river."

Raine was attentive to Price's explanation about the location of his ranch, "Thanks for pointing it out, I admit I've been curious about where exactly the ranch is located…so it is near the river!" She gave a welcoming smile, "I am certain it is in a beautiful location and I am eager to see…my new home…our home." Raine looked towards the desert and wondered if the route through the barren region would lose the gentle breeze, which had aided in keeping her cool.

Price was glad she was interested, "I want to show you our home." Moving closer he noticed a strand of hair in her eye and he spontaneously brushed it away. It reminded him how much he anticipated seeing her hair down. "It's time to get back on the trail."

Leaving the breathtaking view of the rocks, Price and Raine walked peacefully back to the buggy wagon with Trader following closely, looking eager to finish the journey himself.

Before helping Raine into the wagon Price took another opportunity to kiss her. "I could really get use to this," he smiled and lifted her up to the wagon-step; she blushed. He turned away briefly to see Trader jumping into the back, settling near the travel trunks. Then he climbed in beside his bride, he was happy man yet his mind lingered on his ongoing one-sided discussion with God by the riverbanks. He could not help wondering if his bride was concerned about tonight as much. *Do women think about such things?*

Raine was dazed, amazed how kissing Price could leave her limp and weak with her head spinning; she loved the feeling. Noticing the adorable grin on Price's face, *he finds pleasure in me*, the mere thought made her blush again. She quickly turned her head away so he did not notice the fluttering she was feeling.

Price snapped the reins lightly and gave a clicking sound, guiding the horses onto the trail that lead away from the river. Raine straightened her skirt and situated herself for the least impact, *Oh my, how am I ever going to make it all the way, I hope he doesn't notice my discomfort.* Just then the wagon hit a bump, *Ouch!* She subdued in silence, *I am so grateful for this installed buggy seat. I cannot imagine how hard the traveling would be with a regular wagon seat that does not have a cushion and springs.*

The temperature was warming up, the further away from the river the hotter she felt; Raine wiped the dampness off her neck. She was glad Price took the extra time to water the geldings by the riverside. She now understood that it was not just a polite courtesy to the horses, but rather a necessary precaution measure to help them endure the hot desert.

The sky opened up far as the eye could see, enhancing the skyline with a small number of towering plateaus God strategically placed along the tranquil landscape. The vast portions of barren land had a spellbound effect on Raine, making her forget the heat. She remembered Mr. Adams telling her about the general location of Barrett Ranch. Thinking about it only perked her curiosity to inquire, "Do you actually live in the Paints?"

It tickled Price for her to know the direction in which he lived. *This is the second time she let this out; I think she has inquired of me.* Speaking before he flattered himself too much, "No...no Beautiful, a person could not live in the Painted Desert, it's a magnificent place to see, but not where anyone would want to settle." Having a second thought, "Then again, if you were an Indian you might...I believe they can dwell just about anywhere." Explaining a little more, "The main part of our ranch is not located on the riverbanks, although we own half of the waterway. In that area, there is a steep upgrade in the terrain from the river. However, we fashioned a stair-like path so we could make good use of the river. The land on the high ground was a more suitable to establish a ranch. It's really a perfect location because from the main house you can enjoy both desert and the river. If we were not close to water we would not be able to sustain out here, not to mention, the riverside's neighboring vegetation being a benefit to our survival. I'll be the first to admit our location makes survival more delicate. Merely living this close to the Paints creates an entirely different climate than you have in New Crossing. Having the river close by changes everything about the land…it supplies ample water to turn the watermill, which provides power for the bellows in the forging shed and for the small grinding mill. It also provides water for our irrigation ditches so we are able to grow our own food. There is a windmill up on the high ground which draws water to the well which is located near the barn. I always wanted to put a well closer to the house, but that is saved for a future project. The land north of us is massive with deep gorges, God created its spender, it's magnificent. Between us and the gorge is Cole's Trading Post, a good place to pick up supplies. Covering his mouth with his hand and pausing briefly, "I am rambling on; you must be getting tired hearing me explain our ranch in detail when you will be seeing it soon enough."

Without hesitation Raine spoke up, "Not at all, please keep talking, I find each detail interesting. It appears your family thought of everything needed to establish a ranch here in this barren land."

"They definitely did," confirming her remark, "Are you certain I am not boring you!"

"I do not find you or the topic boring…really go on."

Price continued bragging about the ranch, he was rather proud of it. "My family considered many options and details to what was needed in this area for survival. Uncle Cuate' knew precisely what to look for; being raised half of his life in the Mexican desert." He paused to adjust his hat. Then with pride added, "The ranch is like an oasis with beautiful views of the mesa to the west and when sitting on the veranda you can also watch the river rambling by to the east…there are exhilarating sunrises and sunsets and with the location and openness we can easily see both. You will be surprised, it is not just an efficient piece of land, it is quite scenic. I am confident you are going to be captivated and will come to love every inch of the land, as much as I do…I seriously could not consider living anywhere else after residing here."

It moved Raine to see the passion Price felt for a piece of land. She was already captivated by him, why not the land. *I believe I would love anywhere you are Price Barrett.*

"One day we will take a journey to the Painted Desert. I will enjoy showing it to you; the beauty is mind-boggling on how something so desolate could be so spectacular. Also one day we'll go up the westward trail past Coles, then you can discover with your own eyes the splendor of the deep gorge, with the river at its bottom. Actually it is more feasible for us to visit those places than for us to go into New Crossing, they are closer"

Raine thought viewing the Paints and the gorge with Price as her guide was something she would look forward to. Nevertheless she was presently distracted with the soreness she felt and simply could not consider another journey any time soon. *I will have to make some travel pillows before the opportunity comes up; I certainly do not want to be known as a whiny wife with a frail backside.* Raine looked up at Price and smiled, "yes, I would love to see both places...it sounds exciting." Her bottom was in agony, at the same time her mind was excited. Raine was beginning to grasp small fragments of what the homestead was going to be like and she could hardly wait to see it...*the sooner the better.*

Raine was completely impressed with what Price's courageous family managed to establish in the middle of nowhere. *Not many people would consider carving out a place for themselves, this far from the major settlements.* The thought occurred to her how much other people may be missing by not taking the risk; she began studying the landscape with anticipation.

It was a tranquil moment in time; both feeling relaxed in each other company as they rode in silence; Raine wide-eyed, taking in everything with a growing expectancy of her new home. Meanwhile, Price was conversing quietly with the Lord about things he neglected to ask about a woman. Nothing could have been any better in their silence...then...Raine saw them first! Panic mixed with terror surged inside of her. "Look!" she exclaimed, pointing to three Indians charging on horseback whooping and howling.

Seeing them, Price vigorously snapped the reins and the brown geldings picked up speed, causing the dust to flail high behind them. Raine kept looking over her shoulder keeping track of the savage's location. The color to her cheeks grew pale and she wondered what would become of them. She clung tightly onto Price arm, bouncing slightly off the seat as the wagon moved rapidly down the trail. "They are getting closer!" she informed. The panic in her voice caused Price to become sympathetic, making it difficult for him to keep up the charade. Left with no choice he slowed the horses to an easy trot. With this action Raine became weak and was feeling faint, as the Indians overtook their wagon.

"What are you doing Price?" bellowed Caleb as he rode his pinto up alongside of the wagon, keeping in step.

At the sound of his friend's voice Price gently brought the wagon to a halt. He started chuckling profusely, with his whole body quaking...before bursting into wild laughter; afraid to look at Raine. He tried to speak, but found it difficult. Finally muttering, "What am I doing?" all the while trying to curb his laughter.

Caleb studied him in quiet amusement, when Price made another attempt, "What might I ask...were you doing...creating all that whooping clamors...it was loud enough to spook my horses!" He could not control his humor; burying his face into his hands allowing the laughter to roll out full heartedly.

Price peeked over his large hands which were concealing his glazed laughing eyes; sheepishly looking at Raine, who by now had recovered her fright and was feeling very foolish. Realizing she was a part of a practical joke, conducted by her ornery husband and his friends. Being a schoolteacher helped. she was familiar with children often playing pranks on her. Which over time this cultivated in her an acceptable take-it-in-stride attitude; even when she was the brunt of the humor. However, not wanting to let Price know this quality, she gave him the uncompromising wide-eye-look while holding her lips tight. Although, it was becoming hard not join in on the laughter. In fact, she almost lost control several times because Price's repetitive laughter was infiltrating everyone.

Caleb enjoying the humorous event interrupted his own laughter to speak, maintaining an enduring smile. "I come as welcome party. Happy greetings for marriage to you and woman...My friend, you pick up speed...I ride faster...catch up to you." He shook his head and laughed, "You loco."

Price's laughter was still unrestrained, "I'm sorry Raine...really," still laughing in his deep manly voice.

Price tried to get himself under control but it was just too funny. He gave a pitiful attempt at introducing everyone with a cracking voice, "This is...my dear friend...Caleb." Then he slid his arm around Raine's shoulders, "My beautiful wife Raine, who has suffered my ruthless folly."

Price was still trying to gain composure, looking down at the floorboard. Then Caleb started chuckling again along with his two laughing companions. Raine glanced back and forth at the two of them, "Ok you two, I mean four...I think you had a good laugh at my expense, but...it was not that funny!" As soon a she got the words out, her smugness began to fade giving into a mild giggle. "Well, maybe it was," bumping her elbow into Price's side then with a dumbfounded expression looked away. She knew they had gotten the best of her. Gathering her emotions she turned her attention to the Indians, "Hello Caleb, in spite of my husband's orneriness, I have heard only good things about you."

Caleb replied respectfully, "I have waited many moons to meet you; I welcome you to our land, Rainwater. I give you Indian name...does this please you?"

Raine was impressed and wanted to express her approval, "Thank you Caleb, yes I find it very pleasing, Rainwater is a very beautiful name. My parents did not know this name, so they called me Raine, but you may call me Rainwater...I will be honored."

"It is Christian custom to give new name to friend. You will be Rainwater...you coming to our land is good sign...I think the Great God of this ground will bless us with much water."

"I will pray for it." she responded.

After listening to the sincerity of conversation expressed between Caleb and Raine, Price was able to gained control of his laughter. He appreciated the way his new bride accepted the name so graciously. He looked to Caleb and nodded, showing his approval.

Caleb introduced the young men with him, "This brave is my son, Shinning-Light and his friend Black-Bird." He directed his gestures to indicate which one was the son and which the friend.

"A pleasure to meet you both," Raine replied. The two young braves nodded with huge smiles on their faces; they were still at the edge of laughter, but restrained.

Caleb spoke to Price, "We ride with you to fork in trail...I bring Ruth back in two moons to meet Rainwater."

"It will be good to see Ruth again, it has been several months since the folks passed and my mourning is over now." Price knew it was a respectful thing for Ruth to not come calling close after his parent's death, allowing him a time of grieving. Price recalled how his friend often looked over the ranch when he was away, so he inquired, "Caleb, have you been by the ranch today?"

"Yes, I come by at first light to see if you need anything. I saw mother Barrett's wagon gone from stall and chickens fed too much; I knew you went on long journey. Goats need milking; I took good milk to my pueblo...women pleased."

"Thank you, I am glad you took some milk home, those women spoil you and will have prepared a good meal for you when you return...How is your clan? Is everyone well?

"Strong," Caleb nodded his head towards one of the

riders, "My son has sought a bride from high ground…clan of my grandfather's brother. He has already left bundle at squaw's door and she accepted. He talk to squaw's parents they have agreed. The squaw ground the traditional cornmeal and brought it to Ruth and mother accepted. Now we move forward with wedding plans. Our tradition says Shining-light would move into their home. We have talked with parents and made a new plan. Shining-Light will stay 6 moons in their home and will work hard for them, then bring his bride home to our pueblo. Every year he must return to her father's home for 3 months and work hard for family needs. We make new dwelling in pueblo, get ready for his marriage and next young Christians." He smiled big, knowing his words about sharing the Christian faith would please Price.

"I am confident God will carry countless blessings your way my friend and make you a grandfather of many young braves and squaws." Price looked to Shinning-Light, "Good news, God will bless your wedding." The young man smiled and nodded with a mild gesture, relaying that he accepted Price's words.

Price waited for Caleb and the young braves to ride ahead on the trail before he apologized to Raine for scaring her as he did. "It was simply a reaction to the moment and if I had seriously thought about it I would have shown more consideration. Will you forgive me?"

Raine was not annoyed, her breathing was ordinary and her heart rate was back to normal, although it was certainly a good laugh on her. There was no cause for him to feel regretful about it, without hesitation she accepted his apology.

Raine and Price discussed the different traditions for marriage his friends had. Price shed light on why Caleb was insistent the squaw live with them. It was to raise children to know Christian life. Both thought he had great wisdom to work out this arrangement without offending the bride's family.

Raine began to notice something on the horizon that looked like buildings. It was hazy with portions fading and she wondered if it was real or her imagination. It held her attention captive, but she did not want to ask for fear of it being a mirage. She had never actually seen one before, but she read about them. As they rode closer it did not disappear, the illusion was becoming a reality. *It has to be the ranch*, she excitedly thought. Raine clung tight onto Price's arm as they followed Caleb and his sons up the trail.

With Caleb in full sight it was easy to think about him, so Price began sharing with Raine a little of Caleb and Ruth's history. "After they became Christians, my friends did not want to lose sight of their heritage and many of their traditions which were passed down by their ancestors, these were very important to them. At the same time, they wanted to incorporate this new faith into their lifestyle. One of these choices came with what to call the children without offending the old ones more than they already have by their acceptance of the Christian faith. Caleb is a very wise man and he began inquiring about certain scriptures I would mention and he chose what fit each child from those discussions. Caleb fathered six children, two girls, Morning-Dove and Healing-Waters. He has four sons and named them Shinning-Light, Faith-Walker, Good-Follower and Peacemaker. They already had three children by the time we met, Shinning-Light, Morning-Dove and Faith-Walker. The older children accepted their new names without question, just as Caleb and Ruth accepted theirs."

"That must have been extremely difficult for them all

to get used to, especially with their family knowing the children by their other names…didn't the family continued to call them their old names?"

"It was complicated for a while, but Caleb being a strong man insisted, the relatives complied and learnt the new names. Now it is normal for them all, no one ever brings up the fact that Caleb changed his children's names when they were 8, 6, and 5."

"Thank you for sharing their story, it makes me feel like I know them a little."

When they came to a fork in the trail, Caleb and the young braves waved, riding off to the right in a gallop. Price veered to the left and followed a trail that appeared a little less traveled. The silhouettes of the buildings were clear now and Raine knew what she had been watching on the horizon was not a mirage; it was the Barrett Ranch that Price loved so much. As they began their approach to the homestead, Raine was speechless. Her eyes took in every detail, realizing this place was far more than she could have ever imagined, even with Price's description. She held her breath and began silently to render thanks to the Lord who made it all possible. Sitting before her a new life, and the door of destiny open wide, timelessly waiting for her to walk through. She was overwhelmed by the promises of God, whose love surely rewards obedience.

♥

✞ Father God watched from His balcony as the Barrett's entered the ranch where they will begin sharing their lives together. He was delighted to have the opportunity to establish them in a way He rarely had the privilege. God stretched forth His heart towards the Barrett homestead and abundant blessings began flowing out of His immense love. Determined to stay close to Price and Raine with a watchful eye, for they give him much pleasure.

Father God's own reputation of being a loving Father is upheld, giving immeasurable satisfaction to call them as His own. He will not turn His back on His children.

Concept inspired by
1 Samuel 12:22

♥

Chapter 14

Traveling up the trail to the ranch, Price could not help noticing the sheer excitement dancing in Raine's eyes, she was taking in everything. The smile on her face was worth all the suspense of the trip to get here. He was pleasingly satisfied to be able to present Barrett Ranch to her. He could not be any prouder of the homestead his family toiled fervently to carve out of the barrens, than he was right now. It was going to be their home together, a place for them to entwine blended dreams for the land and to raise their children. He was excited about the life they were going to live; carrying on their own family traditions. It was going to be a good life, he just knew it.

Raine surveyed every detail. Looking over her right shoulder was the most beautiful mesa on the landscape. It was located beyond the ranch, yet she was convinced it would still be viewable on the property; *anything so beautiful would certainly be kept a focal point.* As they embarked closer she noticed the windmill blades turning in the late afternoon breeze. It was located near the barn which expanded her vision to notice even more. There was an attached corral to the barn, constructed for horses. *What a beautiful and inspiring sight on the landscape, a painter would embrace such a scene. Oh my…what an outstanding view beyond the barn, yes indeed, the backdrop of a Master Painter!*

Raine became aware of four adobe structures resting dignified on the land, one main adobe elegantly expanding both up and outward, looking like an extravagant artistic Spanish mansion. *I've only seen an elegant home like this in books.* Although the other three adobes were fairly smaller structures, they all were large enough for private dwellings.

Coming now into view were two small wood

buildings, *one could possibly be a henhouse*. Then she turned her head to look past Price towards the river and seen rooftops peeking up from what appeared to be a downgrade in the land. When she noticed the watermill turning she remembered Price telling her about it. Recalling details of the conversation, Raine figured those rooftops were the grinding mill and the forging shed. It amazed her how self-sufficient the ranch appeared. *It has everything one would need, maybe even better than in town...It's like a small town!*

Trying to take all of this in left Raine speechless, if that were possible. She never considered the dashing Mr. Barrett had a piece of paradise to offer her. It was so breathtaking she could hardly process everything.

Raine appreciated Price's sensitivity in his silence, he allowed her to explore the ranch without any interjections. As she observed all the buildings a possibility occurred to her that she never considered from their talks, *this really is a small community, even with the advantage of a few neighbors*. On the other hand, she did not see a single person moving.

After passing where the barn was situated the wagon moved into a circular clearing located in the middle of the adobes. She noted that two were on one side and the smallest of the three located on the other side near the wooded buildings. Straight ahead was the stately one. The total arrangement was comfortable, positioned in a u-shape of homes. Each home had adequate space and even though the Spanish mansion was elegant it did not distract or over take the rest of the adobes, but sort of brought them all together. At the end of this u-shape housing was the barn, now behind them.

Price gently brought the wagon to a halt facing the beautiful mansion. It had a veranda as long as the home itself and was designed with several a curved arches.

Raine noticed two chimneys, one on each side, foretelling two fireplaces were located inside. Raine could not hide her amazement seeing the splendor of what was obviously going to be her home.

Price lowered the reins, turning towards Raine hoping her expression would portray her opinion of the house, which it did. Her eyes were opened wide, her mouth softly parched open, and a smile slightly forming, evidence that his bride was pleased. "Well Mrs. Barrett, I want to welcome you to our home, on the Barrett Ranch."

When he spoke, Raine notice the brand insignia hanging in the middle of one arch on the veranda, recalling the same one was over the barn door, an encircled B and R mixed together, she thought it appropriately cleaver. "It's beautiful," she managed, "Price this ranch is simply beyond words. I never in my wildest dreams thought anyone could possibly create such a magnificent spread in this area. I must confess I am seriously in shock."

Trader who did not give one hoot about the thrill of the moment promptly jumped out of the wagon, happy to be on familiar ground; this was simply home.

Price stepped down off the wagon and extended his hand to assist Raine. She complied, but once on the ground she stood still not making any effort to move towards the door.

Price could not figure out why Raine did not move eagerly to go inside the home and explore, so he asked, "Would you like to go inside?" Hoping she would take his offer, but instead in her stillness he observed a tear trickle down her cheek "Is there something wrong?"

Raine looked up at this handsome man, observing his hair blowing carefree in the wind, his ebony eyes searching desiring to understand her tear. How she could be so fortunate to have such compassion in a husband. "If you would have brought me to a simple broken down shack, I would have been content to make it a home and be Mrs. Barrett, but here I am besieged with astonishment, I never expected to be living on such a grand estate. This dream is far beyond me, I am a simple teacher and I have only experienced exposure of such grand places to live through the reading of books. My only dream was you, my husband of Promise, a couple of children, and a home. I never ventured beyond these simplicities in my thoughts. Mr. Price Barrett you have provided a great deal more than I deserve. I do not know how to act or respond to this grandeur."

Price felt love for this woman already. He gazed at her for a few quiet moments not know how to answer her. With his finger he trailed the tears running down her cheeks, then gently kissed the trails of moisture. Stooping lower to bring his face to see her at eyelevel, he spoke, "Does not the Scriptures teach us our loving God will supply more abundantly than we ask? In the development of this ranch Father God had you, Raine Leigh Barrett, in mind to live here and He conceived us to bring Him glory from this place. My dear adorable wife, I believe where we live is barely the surface of His immense blessings on our lives." He hoped these words would bring peace to her to understand this was God's plan for her, for them.

Price straightened his posture and took a hold of her hand and proceeded to move towards the front porch. "Let's go inside, I want to show you the rest of your new home." However, he was brought to an abrupt halt in his step because Raine was immoveable with her footing planted firmly in place. It felt like tugging on a boulder. It didn't take Price long to figure out she was not moving away from the wagon. He wondered if she was concerned about consummating the marriage vows and maybe she was frightened. *Lord how should I handle this?*

Raine could see Price was befuddled over her hesitation. It was becoming clear to her that Price was probably not familiar with the wedding tradition. If she desired to have it done she was going to have to explain. "In some traditions when a man takes a woman to be his wife and then brings her to their home for the first time, he carries her over the threshold." She paused for an instant noticing his attentiveness. "I always imagined I would be carried across the threshold of my first home when I married."

Thank you Lord! Greatly relieved to hear Raine's explanation Price took a carefree approach, "You did, well Mrs. Barrett I can accommodate that," and with that remark barely out of his mouth he happily scooped her briskly up in his arms; noticing once again she was as light as a feather. "Like this?"

Being taken off guard by his fast reaction she giggled, "Yes, it is supposed to be for good tidings on our life together."

"Raine, we are blessed already! Nonetheless, to please my beautiful bride I am more than happy to oblige." He stepped onto the veranda with Raine in his arms. Unlatching the front door he instructed her, "Close your eyes."

Moving cautiously through the doorway as not to hurt her, he hesitated close to the door to allow her to view all of the room when she opened her eyes. Price felt very contented holding Raine with her eyes closed tightly and her head tucked into him. He enjoyed the closeness so much he put off setting her down to relish the situation a little longer. To extend this moment he repeating the instruction, "Keep your eyes closed and no peeking." Price took time to admire her beauty, how her nose turned slightly up on the end, and her complexion clear with a translucent rose color on her cheeks. *She is so beautiful,* he thought, *her skin is so soft*. He was truly smitten by this wonderful gift from Father God. Price forced himself to surrender to the reality of the moment; it was time to unveil their home. Enjoying the embrace he hesitated one second more, but then offered, "Ok...open up your eyes."

Raine also was feeling closely intimate in her husband's arms, not wanting the moment to pass. After a few fleeting moments she surrendered to her husband's request and slowly opened her eyes. At first she looked into Price's face not seeing anything but him. He kissed her and she was swept away with pleasure; *How can he do this to me,* she wondered again.

The kiss ended, but he held her close and she was in no hurry to move either. Then both realized they need to move on and she looked out into the room.

Price took pleasure in observing Raine's eyes darting in all directions, "Do I really have to put you down?"

Raine rendered a feminine sigh, letting him know she felt the same way, in fact, it took a moment before she could actually speak any words, feeling strangely lightheaded in his arms after the kiss. "I truly love being in your arms Mr. Barrett, and yet, I guess it is time to put me down."

Price lowered Raine's feet to the floor; however he was determined to keep her close. He turned her slightly so she could lean back into his chest with his hands clasped loosely in front of her. The delicate scent of her hair under his nose was tantalizing, the sweet fragrance was hypnotic, *I feel weak like Samson in the Holy Bible, when Delilah cut his hair*, he noted. The home, everything, was secondary to the presence of Raine's nearness, he felt completely under her influence.

Raine felt safe in the tender muscular embrace of Price Theodore Barrett; the closeness was too much to handle. It made viewing the home difficult, she felt as if she could be absorbed right inside of him. Raine tried to evaluate her new feelings, but found no words to accurately describe them; it did not matter if the words were not coming, she loved how she felt. One thing was for sure just being here in Price's arms was more exciting than anything in his wonderful house.

♥

Chapter 15

Moments passed, Price and Raine were held captive in time enjoying their embrace. Without any words between them, closeness was growing and a settling was taking place in their spirits about their future together. Up to now it had been a whirlwind day, but reality became a calming salve helping them process this new life journey they were embarking on. They would have a marriage partner in everything they decided or did from this day forward because neither was alone in this world anymore.

Price would have loved to hold her close in his arms forever, but he realized there was a lifetime of to explore all the emotions he was experiencing. So it probably was time to let Raine explore the house and get settled in. Reluctantly Price released his hold from around her waist. Raine accepted the timing and started to get acquainted with her new home.

As Price watched his new wife moving around the room examining different things an old memory surfaced. Hearing it freshly in his mind; *a woman and her home were a very intimate thing*. His mama and Aunt Arnett made sure he knew this information as a young lad whenever he wanted to interject something about moving a chair where he thought would look best. The two of them impressed strongly on him that he needed to be sensitive to the ways the house was run. Basically it was the woman's job and she governed the home. In time, as he grew older he yielded to their ways and decided not to even question this plan, just simply accept the fact that this was how things worked.

Watching Raine become familiar with things Price figured she would probably take pleasure in organizing everything in a personal fashion also. He did not mind, the Lord knows he has enough to take care of on the ranch. He laughed inside recalling again how repetitive that message was given to him.

Raine wandered around the room, her eyes flashing back and forth taking in everything with perfect accuracy. To her left was an elite cooking fireplace. She had never seen one designed so efficiently. There were ledges built in the opening, a variety of cubbyholes to use for baking and warming shelters, depending upon location. The most ingenious idea she had ever seen was located on the far end of the fireplace. It was a waist high ledge with an open space in which a large metal water reservoir was placed for a continuous supply of warm water during the time of cooking. It would be available for hot tea, or to obtain water for dishes, and for an evening bath. She notice a lower shelf to the side of it that held two buckets filled with water. *So the reservoir could be refilled as needed,* she presumed. Above hung three sizes of scooping ladles for retrieving the water from the basin. Looking back at the cooking area, she noticed several rods to support hanging pots, some directly over the hot part of the flames and some set off to the side for lower heat. *What a magnificent cooking fireplace!* Raine could hardly wait for the opportunity to make use of it, being confident her cooking skills were satisfactory. Mastering the flame might be a challenge, yet she was eager to conquer it with delightful determination.

In front of the fantastic cook-fireplace a good distance from the heat, yet close enough to utilize was a workstation. Next to it sat a long wooden table with eight chairs and in the center of the table was a beautiful bouquet of desert flowers, which added charm to the room. The unique spray of flowers revealed the man she married was not only pleasant to look at, he was thoughtful and tender hearted. Raine tilted her head and made eye contact with Price, a simple smile let him know she approved of his bouquet. He proudly received the message; *it was a good idea to add the flowers, if only to see her to smile.*

Running her hand along the huge table, Raine unexpectedly gave into thoughts that made her blush. *This table would feed a large family…I wonder how many children will sit around this table.* Quickly calculating it would take six children and the two of them to fill all eight seats. Her imagination ran wild, *Yes, Four boys to help dad with the muscular chores and two girls for me to teach womanly things. Oh my, for six children I would be in the motherly way until I am fifty and that means...*being embarrassed by her thoughts, she looked away from Price, incase her face revealed what she was thinking. She quickly found a few other things to look at to distract her mind.

Just pass the water station on the side of the fireplace there was a slanted door. Raine thought it looked like a door one would see on an underground pantry. However those pantries were most commonly entered from the outside of a home, but this is attainable from inside. Feeling confused she asked, "Is this a pantry?"

Price nodded his head in agreement while walking over and opening the doors for her to take a look. Sure enough the steps led down to a storeroom, *what a wonderful idea to have it inside so close to the kitchen.* Price lit a candle sitting on a small ledge just inside the doorframe and the two proceeded down the dimly lit stairs into the pantry. Arriving at the bottom of the stairs Price lit another candle and the room filled with light. Raine noticed another entrance leading to the outside, latched from the inside. Price explained the outer door was to help with harvest loads that did not require any further preparation. Raine gave this room a lot of attention, she would certainly be using the items stored here and wanted to make a mental check on what was available. The shelves were stocked with canning jars of all kinds, meats and vegetables and what looked to be fruit. There was garlic, peppers and dried plants hanging from the rafters. She saw unique baskets placed on low ledges that were not very high off the floor. Inside them was something that looked like potatoes and a variety of other food items in different baskets. "I still find it difficult to fully grasp how your parents thought of everything!" Raine remarked.

"Actually it was Aunt Arnett and Uncle Cuate' who thought of all these convenient ideas, they wanted to make life easier for my parents. My aunt confided in me one day how she felt guilty for having perfect hearing and her sister could not hear the slam of a door. However, I never found a hearing loss to hinder Mama. She was capable of doing most anything she set her mind to. Just the same, she certainly did not complain about not needing any of the convenience they created for her." Price chuckled slightly recalling his mother's strong will. "You probably have noticed the many inspirational heart-prints my aunt left throughout the home to make Mama's life easier."

"Yes, I have noticed. It is evident your Aunt Arnett was concerned for your mother and with your uncle's help they achieved a brilliant arrangement. Both of your parents were very lucky to have them. I have to admit, I am going to feel exceptionally spoiled living in this house."

"It will give me great pleasure to have you feeling spoiled because from what I can see already you have a lot in common with my mother. Martha Barrett was a remarkable woman, she loved living here. Since you are so very much like her, I am positive it would delight her to know you are making this your home."

Price mind wandered back to a few weeks before his mother took ill. "Before Mama took ill, she called me aside for one of those parent-to-kid talks," Price laughed because he was well in his forties. "She was extremely excited about what she had to tell me that day. Which was, I would be getting married very soon and she did not just tell me about it, you could tell she really believed it. I have to admit at the time I did give it a lot of attention to it...yet thinking back, sometimes Mama instinctively knew things."

"I think your mama was right." She said happily.

"I'm glad she was!" Price replied.

Raine looked around at the dim lit pantry, *so efficient;* she felt humbled moving into her mother-in-law's unique home and to be cooking with the food items Mrs. Barrett prepared. *It would have been nice to have known her.* Raine followed Price up the stairs to the main floor; he set the unlit-candle back on the ledge then latched the pantry doors behind them.

Raine looked around the room, once more finding pleasure in the kitchen with the magnificent cook-fireplace. Straight in front of her on the other side of the room was a stately large bed. As she approached she admired the craftsmanship, with her hands stroking the tall skillfully carved wood posts. A beautiful quilt lay on top of a thick feather mattress; she smoothed out the wrinkles admiring the quality. At the foot of the bed was a long trunk of the same expert workmanship. On one side of the double bed was an oval mirror hanging on the wall over a marvelously crafted dresser stand with pull out drawers. She could tell each piece was constructed by the same carpenter; they had the same carvings of trees in them. "Who made all this furniture?

I have never seen anything quite this beautiful," Raine motioned with her hands pointing out everything.

Price felt honored to answered, "My father gets the praise for being an excellent carpenter, as you have unmistakably observed; he fashioned all our furniture. Uncle Cuate' and I constructed an adobe building to serve as a workshop for him. My uncle worked at supplying Pa with enough wood to do his projects. He would bring in a load of all kinds of wood every time he went anywhere. By fashioning wood Pa felt a sense of importance, he was contributing to this venture in the desert. I guess Pa found his worth in the Good Book, his carpentry creations, and in Mama, she was his world."

Every time Price unveiled another story of his family, Raine became more impressed. She was feeling more and more like she knew them personally. Without further hesitation she came to her own conclusion, that to establish such a grand place carved out of the barrens like this ranch, it most certainly would have to be the Barrett's! She was proud of her husband's heritage and she realized their children would own a great legacy. One they could feel satisfaction in knowing it was in their blood to work hard and built this ranch out of nothing. *Thank You Lord, you have thought of everything, even the blessing on our children.*

In this large room, that already contained the kitchen and the bedroom, there was a large sitting arrangement next to the sleeping area. Positioned in a half circle in front of a formal fireplace sat four comfortable chairs and a deacon's bench. On all of them were crafted stuffed pillows big enough to sit on and relax your back. The materiel used for the pillows were colored in soft greens, cream, yellow and a tad of light brown. All contributing to make the room look bright and cheery. Two of the chairs were rockers and two were stationary.

The furniture was set in such a way to make you feel comfortable. To divide the deacon's bench from the one of the rocking chairs was a round crafted table and on the top sat a Bible. Noticing how the chairs were arranged Raine could picture Price's family relaxing for the evening in front of the beautiful stone hearth fireplace. Situated on the floor that seem to pull this area together was a beautiful Indian woven rug. The print carried the same colors as the pillows; however there were additional bolder colors in the rug as well. The whole environment looked warm, cozy and inviting. Which reminded Raine how famished she was from the trip, but did not allow herself to linger on the thought too long. *These chairs will have to wait.*

Price was sitting down at the dinner table quietly observing Raine acquainting herself with her new home. He smiled frequently watching her. The expressions on her face intrigued him. He would love to know what she was thinking. *One day I will know you well my wife.*

Raine stood in the sitting area and let her imagination run wild. She pictured children lying beside Trader on the rug as their dad reads to them out of the Family Bible. As for her, she would be rocking the youngest in a chair beside him; a smile crossed her face. She was captivated and lost in the whole idea. When Price asked from across the room, "What's the grin for, Beautiful?" It startled her, she felt like he had entered into her secret thoughts which made her blush, but she did not divulge her fantasy. Privately hoping one day her dream would come true. Price could see she was taken off guard so he let it go, *she will share when she is more comfortable with me.*

The last thing to check out in the huge room was the front corner. Just past the sitting area near the stucco wall which also encompassed the front door. On this side of the room there was a two-layer high glass-bottle window with shutters that slid closed for storms and privacy. A sitting bench was positioned under the window, although it was not set there to enjoy the view. The glass was too thick to clearly see out of, but the light certainly did illuminate in through them which made the bench a well-lit area. Raine examined how exquisitely the window was made. Each layer of bottles was in sets of six, framed with wood and placed elongated, one on top of the other. The two sets made the whole room brighter allowing in more daylight. Raine was used to having windows in town to let the sun in, so she liked this creative idea.

Raine glanced to one side of the window towards the corner, where a spinning wheel sat and next to it was a quilting rack; *I will have to learn these tasks.*

Turning to Price, "I love this home and it is arranged so comfortable, I see your family heritage everywhere I look…special people."

Price responded to the compliment, "Thank you, they were exceptional, I have a lot to live up to."

Raine observed two entries off the large central room, she hesitated to explore with the doors being closed. One door was on the back wall between the kitchen and where the bed sat, and the other was located on the other side of the front door before the kitchen area. Raine was curious and inquired, while pointing, "Price, what is behind those two closed doorways?"

Price got up from the table where he was seated and addressed her question. "The one at the back leads to a room I used for a bedroom. It is as long as the house and was originally created to be Mama's work room for sewing projects and such things. On the far end of the room is an unfinished stairway that leads to the second floor. There are two unfinished room we were going to use for bedrooms, Sharla's and mine. We shared the room downstairs for the first year with a quilt hung in the middle. The plan was to finish the upstairs in a couple of years when the ranch was stable. After Sharla died, no one wanted to finish it so the downstairs became my room. Following the loss, I wanted to be close to my folks and I think they liked it that way. After a while we just ignored the upstairs was even there." He pointed to the ceiling, "Those vents have been closed for so long they probably won't open; maybe we can change that after we have children. The house needs a few overhauls anyways." Raine was quiet, she could feel how the death of his sister affected the whole family in such a deep way they never recovered from, and a touch of sadness hovered in the air. *I am going to pray joy into every corner of this house*, she thought.

Price continued, "I will show the room and upstairs to you, but will you give me an extra day because it is not very orderly...I never made the back room presentable before I came for you. I promise after I tidy up a few things tomorrow I will let you see it." Price wished he had tended to the room before his departure, but it was too late to consider it now. He did have an excuse for leaving in such a rush and if he'd reminded her she might agree, but he kept it to himself. *Then again that was not the only reason, I was anxious, I was restless and I felt an urgency to go propose to you*...a *good thing too,* remembering how he almost missed her.

"I can help you tomorrow, I don't mind. "

Price was embarrassed, "No, no, I will do it..."

Switching the conversation, "The other room behind the kitchen was where my aunt and uncle slept. Mama sealed it shut subsequently to Arnett's passing away. Another thing I did not attempt before coming to get you." He gave a shy smile, "It is a comfortable room with a private fireplace."

"I imagine one day when the Lord blesses us with a quiver," he continued, "you and I may decide to use that room for our bedroom and open up the main part of the house for our growing family. We will need all the space in the sitting area for our children to move about on cold days. Possibly fix up a boy's room and a girl's upstairs. We can keep the babies close by in our room and the younger ones my old room." Price chuckled at his outburst of 'a quiver ', wondering how Raine felt about having a large family. He always wanted a lot of children after living as the only child.

"Well with lots of children you generally do make needful adjustments," she replied, "but for now everything is just perfect as it is. I like the closeness for us alone. In a day or two I'll help clean your room and open up your aunt's old room in case we need an extra room for a stranded guest. As for the back room, it may be perfect to make our room there with a baby room next to it, and still stay close to the other children upstairs" She reached out for Price and initiated a kiss, and he was more than pleased to respond without any hesitation. He would agree easily to anything she suggested, besides he knew already she would have her own ideas about the home…it was her job. He smiled.

After just one kiss Price was pliable, "I could give up all my duties on the ranch to linger right here in the house and kiss you all day long!" Giving her a hearty squeeze, "Do you realize that you are going to be a real temptation for me to get lazy, Mrs. Barrett?"

Raine was flattered how much her husband expressed his affections; she had no idea a man could be this way. *I never heard Father be so expressive to Mother; if he did, he was private about it.* Price embraced Raine tightly in his arms, hugging her. She was content being in his arms, but she wondered if this was all a big dream and she would wake up finding herself still in New Crossing waiting to leave.

Price interrupted her whirlwind thoughts by finding her lips and tenderly kissing them, after this he lifted her up off the floor and spun them both around with such enthusiasm. He declared, "This is a happy, happy day Mrs. Barrett." Taking her of guard with the spinning left her a bit unsteady when he placed her feet on the floor, and she held on to him. "Only you, my sweet wife, can imagine how long the wait has been for this day to come, and now we are going to have such a great life together."

"Come, let's just sit for a minute," he took Raine by the hand guiding her over to a stuffed rocker, first sitting down himself and coaxing her on his lap. "The many long prayerful years waiting for this day to arrive has made this day difficult for me to contain my excitement…and I hope you are as thrilled with me as I am with you."

"My dear Price, what is not to be thrilled about?" she replied. "Even though you have provided me with a wonderful home and it truly is beautiful, but the house is not what I find the most fascinating. I find you are the basis for my joy. I have noticed integrity and strength in the man God chose for me. Not to mention your gentle caring demeanor…I would be a fool not to be delighted." She laid her hand on Price's cheek, "I am happy to be married to you, Price Barrett; you are a wonderful fascinating man and I promise I will do my best to make you a good Proverbs thirty-one wife; by being a fervent helpmate on your ranch."

"Our ranch," he corrected her, "I had no doubt the Lord's choice for me would be a woman with exceptional qualities. I am looking forward to exploring every element of your character and discovering all your abilities. I want to know everything about you and from what I have viewed already I expect I am going to be impressed daily." He could not contain himself; the moment was tender and most entrapping, holding her close and kissing her repeatedly.

He was delirious, and the real world vanished in the pleasures of kissing. Price briefly glanced towards the door...it was ajar, and his consciousness returned, *Oh my, the horses are still hitched to the loaded wagon.* "Woman, you can make me forget what day it is, I am lost in your charm and I have forgotten to unload the wagon. Relax for a while and I will pull myself together and start by bring your trunks in the house. Then I should probably care for the horses...I will be as fast as I can." He brushed her hair out of her eyes, took off her bonnet and placed it in her hands. Then he instinctively pulled the large ornamental pin out of her back braid releasing it to hang down her back, *one little step at a time*, he thought.

They stood up and Raine allowed the braid to fall just below the middle of her back, wondering why Price took her pin out. *Maybe he wanted to see how long my hair was or maybe I look too stuffy for a ranch owner's wife.* Either case she accepted it, "I could help you," she offered.

"I will be fine," he said firmly walking towards the door, remembering how humiliated he felt when she wanted to help put the trunks into the wagon in New Crossing. He noticed her anxiousness, *she would not be settling into a rocker to take it easy.* "If you are not going to take my advice and relax maybe you could try to get some relief from the stiffness you incurred on the trip. Stretch your limbs a little more and move around the house. After all, this was an enduring jaunt for your back-side." Price laughed out loud and almost did not finish sharing his account, "You thought I did not notice, didn't you? How could I miss observing your discomfort? You have been pampering your back-side from the time we took our break along the river?" Price moved towards the door, chuckling all the while, knowing he embarrassed her in sharing his observation. "I really felt bad for you, honest," he chuckled, "but you did look cute adjusting yourself so frequently…shall I assist with a massage?"

"No!" she exclaimed turning as red as a beet. She wondered if she would ever get use to his spontaneous sense of humor. He always seemed to catch her off guard, although, she actually liked his absurdities. Her face felt hot, quickly turning away from him so he could not get the pleasure of her coloring. "All right Mr. Barrett," she managed to say, "You unload the trunks and I will find a workable spot to STAND! Then maybe I could stretch my LIMBS around the room to see what I can find to cook us a meal." All the while she was facing away from him so he could not see her smirking.

"Cook…holy Moses, would you be telling me, Mam, that you can actually cook too…" tilting his head up, "Lord I have hit pure gold…I struck it rich!" tossing his hat in the air exclaiming, "whoopee, I am going to eat again!" Feeling quite witty, catching his hat and placing it on his head Price proceeded out the door to leave Raine to mosey around the house. Meanwhile he'd tend to her belongings and put the horses up for the night. Price allowed his happy-go-lucky demeanor to bounce off of him as he proceeded doing his tasks. Indeed Price Barrett was a happy man.

Price left singing and Raine being lighthearted could not quit smiling. This was the most joy she felt in her adult lifetime although she was not completely sure how to process what she was experiencing because the feeling was simply marvelous.

♥

While Price tended to the luggage and wagon Raine went to the pantry to search for what would be available to cook a meal. By the light of a candle, she spotted a few items that would be useful. As she gathered her choices she heard Price singing boldly while he set down her travel trunks in the main room. Reality was beginning to sink in; *this is not a dream I will wake up from, this is my home now and I am living with a very funny man.* She smiled and continued selecting items in the storeroom. She noticed the stationary candle Price had lit earlier and knew it would be helpful on organizing days, but for a now the candle in her hand was sufficient. There was some light entering from the stairwell also to invade the dark room.

The pantry maintained an excellent supply of provisions. There were twelve shelves; three were fully packed with canned meats along with four shelves holding a generous amount of various vegetables. There were however five lower ledges that were bare awaiting this season's harvest with the exception of two baskets one storing some potato like bulbs and a few onions in another. There was plenty to hold them over until harvest time.

Raine marveled how they were able to have such a stockpile of food, when it occurred to her; *Price and I will be growing them.* Recalling the garden she saw situated behind the two adobes and wondered when Price found time to plant with his parents taking ill and dying. She wasn't acquainted with the techniques of farming, let alone doing it in the desert. *Oh my…I have much to learn, Lord Help me learn fast so I will be a good helper to my husband.* She did learn from her students, if done properly you could have several seasons of harvest, compared to what they got back East. *That must be why there is such abundance.*

Raine selected a jar marked 'rabbit', and then located another jar which looked similar to carrots. Tucking the jars in her arms she proceeded to the basket on the floor, where she gathered four of that potato looking bulbs. Returning upstairs with her arms loaded, she set the jars down on the table and went back to retrieve the two root bulbs from the stairway she had dropped on the way up. Still holding the candle thinking, *there has to be an easier way, maybe the downstairs candle would be better, I will just have to make two trips.* She put it out, set it on the ledge and closed the pantry door.

After placing the two root bulbs on the table, Raine went to the front door and stepped out to see if she could see Price, she did not. Yet in her amazement she found more than she anticipated. The view from the veranda was breathtaking. A magnificent observation of the mesa to her left and to the right side of the barn; there was an awesome distant view of the bend in the river. Raine noticed the smaller adobe building on the right, which was next to the main house. *That must be his father's workshop,* she reflected. Alongside of the workshop were the two wood buildings and she was now certain one was a chicken house, as she viewed the rooster and a few white hens scratching dirt in front of it. She looked across the circle clearing at the two-adobe buildings and her mind wandered back to her first look at the ranch. The adobe buildings appeared to be close together, but actually there was an abundance of land around each and she wondered who lived in them since his aunt and uncle occupied a room inside the main house. As she surveyed the area she still did not see anyone moving around the ranch, which felt strange as the adobes gave the impression as neighbors. Nor did she see Price anywhere and assumed he was inside the barn. Raine returned inside the home to prepare the meal on the wonderful cooking fireplace.

The braid hanging down on her back felt awkward because she was used to having it pinned up. Yet since Price wanted it down for a reason unknown to her, she let it swing as she worked.

There were scraps of wood stacked neatly in the cook fireplace ready to light, and wondered if Price prepared it when she was in the pantry. Finding matches conveniently placed in the middle of the table she figured he did. Sufficient cooking tools were easily located to prepare rabbit stew. His mother had things organize efficiently and everything was in a good reaching distance. She decided there was not enough time to make any biscuits and hoped that Price would not mind quick bread as a substitute. She set the fritter skillet on the workstation.

First she needed to cut up the bulbs so they could begin cooking in the water. After it was hung over the fire she opened the canned rabbit and added it to the pot knowing the longer the rabbit cooked the better flavor the broth would be. After mixing up a batter of quick bread, she greased the fritter skillet and got it hot on a lower shelf before adding the batter. While it was cooking in one of the hotter cavities of the fireplace, she added the carrot looking stuff to the pot of stew. She boldly tested a few unfamiliar herbs by rubbing them together in her hand, smelling and then putting a tiny bit on her tongue. *These will do*, and added them into the pot. In no time, the stew was taking shape and the aroma permeated the home. *I do like this elegant cook fireplace, almost better than my hard wood stove;* she was amazed how easy it was to regulate heat. *Simply a matter of where you place the pots!*

Raine transferred the lightly browned quick bread to

a warming slot and moved the pot of stew to a slower cooking area to keep warm. Although this was no doubt a new way of cooking, after one time working with the cooking fireplace it felt like she was easily adapting to its size and the new methods of cooking. Amazingly her timing also was working out. *It does remind me of conducting an orchestra, like the one I read about in the paper from back East.* While giggling at the thought of how she must look moving her arms and body like some conductor, she managed to set the table. Locating a couple of bowls and putting them in place with spoons made the appearance of dinner inviting, especially with the pretty candle holders she found.

Raine tucked of a few loose strands of hair behind her ears and wiped her face with a damp cloth to make her presentable to serve Price dinner. Since it was their first dinner together she did not want to look worn-out, especially on her wedding night.

Raine retrieved sleepwear for the night from one of her trunks near the door and placed it neatly folded on the long chest located at end of the bed. Feeling a bit chilly she also obtained a shawl from the trunk and tossed it over her shoulders. *How can it be so dreadfully hot on the trip here and have it cool down so quickly*?

The front door was slightly ajar from earlier, when she had looked out. Her first intentions were to close it tightly, but instead she moved out on the veranda. Her eyes widened and she took a deep breath, for there was the most beautiful purple and mauve sunset she had ever seen. In the foreground Price was coming from the barn with Trader striding beside him. She stood watching them and enjoying the colors the Lord had set as a backdrop for this moment.

Price made a stop at the chicken coop, he looked up and noticed her and gestured a wave before scooting the last few hens inside. Then Price went to the other wood building and came out with two buckets.

While admiring the sunset, watching Price and his dog from the veranda, Raine's hand inserted into the large pocket of her skirt; startled when her fingers fell upon Mama's revolver. *Oh my*! She had forgotten it was still on her.

While approaching the house it pleased Price to see Raine standing there waiting for him. *This is nice Lord,* he thought, "You look mighty rosy tonight in that sunset Mrs. Barrett."

At first she did not understand what he meant by rosy, then turning slightly she noticed the once sand colored home had a beautiful rose cast to it. "I guess I must," she replied smiling, "I hope you are hungry, I prepared some rabbit stew and griddle cakes for our dinner."

"I am hungry. Remember I have been surviving on a diet consisting mainly of jerky. Trader and I have eaten most of our supply over the past couple of months. I was thinking I need to restock the jerky bin…after all, it's a staple here," he chuckled. "But rabbit stew…well that is like sitting at the kings table. It will be a real feast for a ravenous man."

After stepping on the veranda Price set the pails by the door and joined Raine to absorb the splendor of the moment. "It sure is a magnificent sunset coloring the landscape tonight." He slid his arm to rest around her waist, "Sorry it took so long out at the barn, I really needed to give the horses a good brushing after such a long hard trip. My personal riding horse, Girl, needed some feed and attention too, she was missing me. We have goats and I tended to them also. Truth be told, I had an ulterior motive for being so long…you see, if I finished the chores while I was there. I would not have to go back out tonight and I could stay inside with you," he smiled.

"I am glad you took the time, besides, I hadn't finished dinner much before now. So your timing is perfect…what is in the buckets?"

"Heat," he said trying to break the news politely.

"Heat?" she questioned looking perplexed about his answer.

"Yes, it's a mixture of manure, desert bramble and wood chips from my father's work. It will heat the house up for the night. The desert can be bitter at nighttime."

Her lip curled and her nose crinkled, "Does it smell bad?"

"Gee, I never noticed," chuckling, and then realized he ought to explain better, "I do not think it stinks while burning. You have to understand towns-girl," picking on her a little, "out in the desert wood is a rare treasure not easily accessible. We do have some desert willows along the stream and a few Joshua trees, but animal dung is always plentiful. You just have to know where to look and with my friend Caleb's teaching, rest assured I have attained the skills to find an ample supply." With that he stepped back, tipped his hat comically and gave a bow. As if he had achieved a high score on a test before he added, "Our own livestock also helps to provide us with fuel." He was all smiles.

Raine was not offended by him calling her a towns-girl, mainly because it was truer than he really knew. She had never worked a farm or around livestock, and she had much to learn. Yet, not wanting to admit her lack of experience she thought to ask, "What did I use to cook the food over?" Worried she cooked it over dung; because the sticks were already in the fireplace and all she had to do was light it.

Knowing her concern Price could not help but grin,

"We use bramble bush, sagebrush, a variety of dried twigs, leaves and any plant waste material because Mama never liked the idea of cooking over dung either.

Raine scrunched her nose and gave an abrupt shake of her head, but with grateful words replied, "Your mama was a very smart woman!" then let out a laugh, feeling total relief.

The whole conversation tickled Price especially watching her squeamish response. In fact he thought it was rather cute and feminine. "Actually, the rocks are the real clandestine to these fires because rocks hold heat. Did you happen to notice our fireplace contains a good many of them?"

"It was a new thing for me to see rocks in the fire, but I figured out the reason they were there. However, I must confess I never thought to go examine the pail near the other fireplace...guess I know what is in it now." Raine still was indecisive about this type of fuel for heating her home and felt prudish about it. Observing her husband pick up the pails to go inside she resigned to keep an open mind.

Price knew that seeing is better than thinking about it, "Come on, I will build a fire."

Walking inside with Price, Raine considered her mother's revolver and wanted to put it in a safe place. "Is there a suitable place I could keep this?" She took her hand out of her pocket exposing the pistol.

"Whoa," taking a couple steps backwards to be funny almost dumping the pails. "Do I frighten you? Had I known my life was in danger I would not have been so insistent on kissing you and I certainly would have left these pails outside," he spoke jokingly. He did love to tease.

Not expecting this tomfoolery made Raine giggle, "You didn't frighten me silly!" She began to explain, "I took it out of my satchel and placed it in my pocket for safety. I forgot that it was in there until just a few minutes ago."

After Price heard the word 'safety' she had his full attention and quit joking.

"Max made an inappropriate advance while helping me into the wagon this morning so I thought I may needed it." She looked down at the pistol in her hand and continued. "After the second advance I began fervent prayer beseeching the Lord to be rescued. All the while I kept my hand in my pocket as a back-up plan. I desperately hoped I would not have to use this weapon…I never shot anyone before." Raine looked up with a smile on her face, "Praise the Lord you came along and rescued me. My prayer was answered."

Reflecting on the urgency God put in him to travel speedily; he understood it was more than losing her to Albuquerque. "God certainly has impeccable timing," he replied. Price felt a surge of anger. It was a feeling he did not entertain much, yet the thought of someone trying to hurt Raine had his emotions soaring. Taking stock of the situation he realized, nonetheless she was safe. He could not change what had already taken place so he let go of it…for now. On the other hand, he was uncertain how he would handle himself if he were to ever run into this man called Max in the future. It may be hard to let it go face to face, *Lord, You will have to help me…or You may need to help him!*

Raine was still waiting for an answer and Price needed to switch his thinking to the present situation. "Why don't you place it somewhere in the cooking area, so you will have it close by when I am out hunting? We have never had any trouble on the ranch, but I guess there is always a first time, so it is probably a good thing to be safe."

"I never considered the fact that you would be leaving the ranch. Being alone on the ranch could be a little intimidating, living in a secluded area for me and not being used to it. Yes...placing it close by is a good idea." She gave the area a quick look over, "I will put it on the high shelf in the flour bin." She placed the pistol safely there and not wanting Price to be overly concerned she added, "Don't worry. I am sure I will get use to the surroundings in no time..."then she changed the subject.

"Would you like some coffee? I mixed some roasted chicory I had packed in the trunk with some coffee grounds like my mama use to do. I was glad to locate your coffee can...have you ever drank coffee made this way before?"

Price completely let go of his fury and stepped fully into the moment at hand. "Actually no I have not, but I would love a cup." Considering that a brisk cup of coffee would be great to refresh his energy as he was beginning to feel a little drained from his lack of sleep. He took a sip as Raine watched waiting his reaction, "perfect" he said. Raine smiled and went on to put supper on the table

The newlyweds enjoyed their first night together in their home. Price could not stop raving about how great a cook she was. Raine figured, any man on a prolonged diet of jerky would think anything tasted good. The evening was filled with laughter as they sat comfortably in rockers absorbing the heat from the fire and sharing stories that ranged from childhood to present day lives. Raine was amazed she did not notice any offensive odors from the fire; it was as Price had said.

Price found it interesting to find out Raine was a teacher. This was an unexpected added blessing from God, who thought to give him an excellent educator for their children. Living so far away from town this really was something he had thought about.

Raine found interest in everything Price shared about his family. She especially enjoyed hearing how his parent's life improved after moving on the ranch. It was an inspirational story, kind of like how God brought them together. She could listen all night to stories with happy endings. Raine was also fascinated about how his parents talked with their hands and insisted that Price teach her some words. Without ado Price responded gladly teaching her a few words in silence, "God loves you" and "I love you." He started with the very two phrases he wanted to teach his children one day, in hopes they would use them often in their home.

Trader sprawled out on the Indian woven rug in front of the fireplace and stayed motionless the whole evening, not paying attention to either of them. He was simply grateful to be back in his own home with a full stomach. Price accused Raine playfully of spoiling him with too many scraps of rabbit stew.

Price read a passage from the Holy Scriptures, while Raine listened attentively and feeling grateful to be married to this man. The moment was something she had dreamed about in her many days of waiting. To share the Scripture with her promised husband was on the top of her list. When he was finished he laid the Family Bible on the table and put out a few candles. It was time to retire.

Price was no longer concerned about how to treat his wife; he delighted Raine with ample tenderness and love. In the warm, cozy, dim lit room the newlyweds willfully consummate their wedding vows naturally with God's blessing.

❤

✝ God was pleased with Mr. and Mrs. Barrett's obedience to wait and He wanted to give the couple a heavenly wedding gift. He decided to shower on them the wisdom of love. "The two will now become one in everything and their blossoming love for one another will bind them together like a strong rope, never seeking their own selfish good, but always putting the other first." God delighted in implanting His blessing into each heart and sealed it with His Will. With the secured seeds deep in place He would watch their love flourish into a Christ-like love.

Concept inspired by
Genesis 2:24, 25; Proverbs 18:22
Ephesians 5:22-33 1 Corinthians 13:4-7

♥

Chapter 16

The daylight cast shades of light around the room intertwined with shadows from the shutter. Raine lay still for several moments observing the graceful outlines portrayed on the ceiling and the wall. She felt peaceful, safe, something beautiful took place yesterday and her life would be forever transformed. *Thank you,* she whispered, her heart grateful for the blessing.

Raine began to stretch awake and became aware that Price was still embracing her. She quickly went motionless, *my husband.* Noticing her night clothes at the foot of the bed still laying neatly folded on the crafted chest, she laughed within herself, *How foolish I was to think I would be wearing them,* blushing at the thought.

Raine never experienced this much contentment before. Happiness and pleasure entwined with tranquility engulfed her like a braid of delight. This had to be love. *Only the favor of the Lord could bestow within me love so quickly.* Gently lifting Price's arm she rolled over to face him, then propping herself up on her side she leaned over and awakened him with a kiss, "Morning," she whispered.

His eyes twinkled at first light, followed by a smile, noticing Raine beside him. Without a hesitation he caresses her raven black hair, running the long strands between his fingers. He loved how it draped delicately across her body, "Your hair is so pretty…will you wear it down for me today?"

Her whole face lit up accepting his compliment, "I will." *Is it possible to stay humble with an abundance of flattering words? Certainly his compliments will fade after a while.* It felt so unnatural to hear pleasantries about her personal appearance. The way Price spoke to her made her feel special. She gazed into his eyes, loving him, "I'm going to find tremendous satisfaction in fulfilling your every request, Mr. Barrett," she added.

Price did not hesitate to respond, "Umm…is that right?" His lip curled even more, considering a request.

Raine nodded innocently as he gazed at her with his ebony eyes sparkling like the sun dancing off the river. She suddenly felt bashful, but there really was nothing she would hold back, she would do all she could to make him as happy as she felt.

"Well then, Mrs. Barrett, I believe I may have another simple request for you to fulfill." Without any hesitation, his lips spontaneously found hers with passion.

Price finished the morning chores and returned to the house. Upon entering he noticed Raine had kept her promise, her silky raven black hair swayed reaching within a fraction of her waist. When she moved her hair followed and continued until it swept over her shoulder. *Beautiful*, her hair was truly radiant…more elegant than he could have ever imagined.

Raine, who did not notice her husband's gawking announced, "Breakfast is almost finished," then went right to pouring his coffee and handed him the cup.

Price was not only awestruck at her appearance, but in his observation he noticed her movement around the home was calm and collected, as if she had lived here all her life. Although inwardly he was completely mesmerized, outwardly he maintained a manly status. The reality of having a wife was beginning to sink in. How quickly his life has changed from what he formerly thought was normal. Price watched his bride serving him with a joyful spirit, his eyes following her. He was finding it difficult to keep an aloof appearance no matter how hard he tried. She had this sweet, yet spunky character which fascinated him. Time held no barriers. Even though they were married only twenty-four hours ago Price had opinions forming already about their relationship. He believed their life together would not be boring, but vibrant. Similar to the connection he witnessed in his parents. He was overcome with thankfulness so he prayed silently, watching her. *"Thank You Father, I am fortunate You helped me endure the long years of waiting because this woman is certainly worth every moment I spent dreaming about her. I can hardly wait to see what the days ahead will bring. With You in our lives, I am certain it will be satisfying because it is in Your character to do things for our good. Amen"* Price continued to ponder on many things about his marital blessing while sitting at the table sipping coffee and waiting breakfast.

Raine finished the breakfast preparations and sat down to join Price, pausing momentarily to pass a few scraps into Traders dish.

"Shall we pray," Price suggested. Raine followed his lead. Closing her eyes and bowing her head in the normal fashion, she waited politely. Price became inspired to initiate something different, instead of a singular custom of folded hands he wanted to incorporate a more united one. Price reached across the table and took Raine's small delicate hand from its folded position, startling her momentarily, although she quickly adjusted. Holding it thoughtfully he began to pray. "Lord, I…err…my wife and I humbly render thanks for our union of marriage. May we never become neglectful or thoughtless of this miracle You have done in our lives. We ask for Your infinite wisdom and grace in all of our endeavors this day. May we bring honor to Your most Holy Name. Please bless our food that You have graciously provided. Thank You for Your abundance. In the Name of Christ Jesus, Amen."

Raine was pleased with how much her husband was attentive to God. His adoration and respect for the Lord was more than she had witnessed in any man including her dear father. She added her own quick silent prayer of thankfulness before vocally saying, "Amen".

During breakfast, Raine recalled the conversation she was having with the Lord before Price came in. Having an inquisitive nature only made her curiosity enhanced; she found it difficult to keep her thoughts to herself. "Price, I know you told me one of the adobes was built for your father's carpenter shop, but what did your family uses the other two for?"

Price expected many questions would be forth coming. "Since we owned 480 acres, my uncle had this grand idea about needing a lot of workers on the ranch to help maintain it. He wanted to make sure we had ample housing available when the time came; therefore, we built the two buildings to lodge the help. One was set up merely as a bunk house; it has several cots and bunks built into it. The other one is like a small home to accommodate a family, or possibly a foreman, someone to help oversee the work and the ranch-hands. However, both buildings have sat empty for years awaiting the workers. Apparently we never got big enough to require a superintendente." Noticing the strange expression on Raine's face…realizing he spoke as his uncle, "Sorry I was around Uncle Cuate' many years and picked up his jargon."

He took a bite of the biscuit in his hand that he was waving as he spoke, nodding his head in pleasure, "Good," referring to the biscuit.

Price ate silently for a few more bites, enjoying every one of them and then continued, "Yet our personal labor created only enough for our own survival, so we never had a real need for workers. We survived well and grew a sufficient amount of food; you saw the pantry shelves. We never found any reason to expand our gardens and livestock to justify hiring help. There was no need to work all of the acreage if we could manage with what we had. Besides as time went on my parents felt the provisions were satisfactory and were content not to expand the ranch. At the time I tended to agree with them, they were comfortable and happy with their life just the way it was. This was a successful move, considering the discriminated life they led back in Ohio. Why change it?"

Raine listened closely, she heard the tone in his voice and watched the expression on his face, all unveiling how important it was for Price's family to make the move into the desert. Here they were able to build a haven for their lives and their children. There was no need of having strangers around the land; some could be like the ones they left behind.

As Price continued to explain, Raine realized for many years everything in Price's life has circled around this one decision. It left a print on all he cared about. Living here in the barrens shaped his character. It was also clear he developed a protective nature for his parents and continually watched over them. She respected this in him and knew this quality of love would now be given to her. He may go hunting, but he would never be far; she felt safe.

Raine dunked her biscuit into her coffee, a habit she got from her father, and eagerly listened to the rest of the story.

Price noticed the unusual taste for coffee soaked biscuits, but did not mention it. Laying his fork down, he took a sip of coffee before continuing his explanation of the two vacant adobes. "Even though Aunt Arnett and Uncle Cuate' spoke often about how one day we will expand the ranch and hire ranch-hands. Pa and Mama had a secret idea, one they never felt the need to share with my uncle and aunt. The only people they ever hoped to live in those two adobes were Sharla and I," he paused.

"Then Sharla passed away. I recall the day Pa told me I had my choice of either adobe. It was an awakening moment for me for I realized Sharla would never be my neighbor and I would not watch her grow old. Nor would I see the man she would marry or watch her children grow and play in the yard with mine."

These expressed thoughts made Price's voice crack and Raine's heart broke for him. He continued, "After a few years Pa had an even bigger secret. He was hoping Aunt Arnett and Uncle Cuate' would decide to move into one of the adobes and out of the main house. However, they never did. My aunt was afraid to leave her sister in the house alone and she watched over my mama like a hawk. This use to bother Pa because he felt he was able to care for Mama. Yet there was one fact my aunt could not overlook; in slumber a silent ear cannot hear danger. So she stayed inside the main house to the very end."

Raine wanted to say something comforting, but found no words. To break the silence she just said whatever came to her mind. "Contrary to the plans people make things seem to take their own direction, we may think it will be one way and find out later it was meant to be another. Doesn't it say somewhere in the Scriptures that a man makes plans, but God orders his steps?"

"I think so, maybe in Proverbs."

"Then we can rest in His wisdom and trust Him, no

matter how hard we want it another way." This was a revelation to her as she spoke it.

Price delighted in the wisdom and knew there is no use fretting over what the Lord had willed.

Raine still had many questions about the adobes, but hesitated to ask. The timing did not feel right. They continued eating and talking on lighter topics. He asked how she liked the cook fireplace and what did she think of the ranch so far? Raine only had good things to say. She filled his plate for the second time noticing he was truly a hearty eater. They laughed and enjoyed the time together.

After Price had his fill of breakfast, they continued to stay seated and drink coffee; he was in no hurry to leave the house. Raine felt maybe this was the time to continue to ask her questions, the ones she had been pondering on with the Lord while she was cooking.

Setting down the filled coffee cups, Raine asked, "Are the two adobe houses still suitable and equipped for people to live in?"

"Sure, with a modest cleanup they are quite suitable to accommodate people. Why?"

Raine got nervous and began to feel like she was overstepping her position too soon, so she wavered from pursuing further. "Well, thank you for filling in the details, I have been curious about them since I saw them yesterday." She was willing to let the inspiration about what she had received earlier rest for the time being. The buildings were not going to leave so there was no need for her to be so impatient. Besides she felt uncomfortable to share right now.

While Raine gathered the dishes and moseyed around the kitchen making small talk about other things. She was confident the Lord would guide her when to approach Price further on the subject.

Price was not so easily sidetracked, he had learned to read his parents quite well and he could see this acquired talent was going to be helpful. He never considered that his ability to read people could become valuable in marriage as well. *Yes there is more to these questions about the adobes than Raine is letting on,* so he decided to stir the conversation to see if it went anywhere. "Sit back down with me a few more minutes and finish your coffee, there is plenty of time for household tasks."

Raine really was just avoiding the conversation for a while trying to get her mind off of the adobe topic. However, she chose a glass of water instead as she had too many cups of coffee already and joined him at the table.

Price continued stirring the conversation, "I am glad you asked about the adobes, it confirmed we are on the same track. Something was formulating in my mind concerning the ranch when I was out in the barn this morning. It occurred to me, we should discuss some goals, ones to put in motion for our future and for our children...you do want children, don't you?"

Raine timidly looked down at her water glass before allowing her eyes to meet his. She was feeling a bit sheepish over being asked, "Of course I want children. What type of things should be established for them?"

"Well actually...I believe it is our God reverent responsibility to set godly objectives concerning our future together and they will undoubtedly affect our children. I want to know what you feel about the ranch...Raine? Should we build the ranch like Uncle Cuate' thought or should we just continue to live off of what it provides? Like I told you my parents have done."

"Oh my, Price…I really think you need to be the one to make that decision." Although she felt honored he thought to ask her opinion

Price reached his hand across the table placing it on her forearm and gently caresses her skin. He looked into her eyes and spoke illuminating sincerity. "Yes, I could make the decision for us, but I truly desire to know how you feel about it. In fact Raine, I desire to understand how you feel about everything. I may be strange, but I believe it is important for a married couple to work together and come to an agreement on important issues. I got this idea from watching my parents who demonstrated daily this type of working relationship to me. Their marriage was solid and good. I want this solidarity for us." Price remembered how his parents went back and forth over different ideas until they were both content with the decision. *Yes, this is what I desire with Raine.*

Seeing how sincere he was about this, Raine obtained a modest confidence to share her thoughts. "Actually Price, I lean towards your parent's opinion. I certainly do not want you to be so overworked you become more obsessed with the success of the ranch and your children miss the opportunity of learning simple things from you." She hesitated for a moment to observe his facial expression in search for a positive reaction. He was hard to read. At one minute she felt he agreed, but then there was something he seemed to be preoccupied with, causing her to wonder. "Even though I lean in this direction, my mind is not set in stone, I am open for new ideas…how do you personally feel about it?"

Price leaned back in his chair and glanced around the room. In his mind's eye he could picture scenes from the past. "I want to be available to our children and I agree totally with your wisdom. When I think about my uncle, he was a good example of a hard driven achiever. If Aunt Arnett would have had children, I believe they would have felt like slaves in their dad's ambitious fervor. There were times working on the ranch alongside my uncle I felt that way. Yet, I am grateful for the protective wisdom of my parents, they would often liberate me from the labor claiming they needed a day to enjoy my company. I deeply appreciate them pulling out the 'parent plea' and rescuing me."

Price paused for a moment allowing more past memories to surface. "Yet at the same time, I confess during my younger years I wondered often what it would have been like to have other people around to share the load. Not to mention having people with new ideas concerning the ranch. Sometimes even the unidentified ranch-hands were mysterious heroes in my thinking. It is not easy growing up as the only child on a ranch living this far out of town...I didn't even get to go to a school to be around anyone my age. So I have mixed feelings about this and this is why it is good we talk it over."

Raine picked up on every sentiment portrayed on Price's face while he spoke about his young life on the ranch; trusting her with a special portion of his heart. She knew he had never shared this with anyone before, even his parents. This moment was tender and meaningful. She did not want to say anything to break the connection they were having. She poured another cup of coffee for Price and decided to have one herself, adding cream to hers and kept silent letting the words and deep emotions sink in.

Price realized the moment also, but from a seasoned man's perception. It was a relief to be able to tell someone about his fantasy, and how he wished his childhood had been a little different. He would have never told his parents for fear of hurting them. They needed to be far from others and he felt life with them was worth more than any heroes of a young boy's imagination. Price enjoyed the warm coffee and waited for Raine to speak first. He had been talking a lot; *being alone sure does give a man the gift to gab!*

The two sat quietly at the table drinking their coffee, it was not awkward sitting quiet, but refreshing. After a half cup coffee Raine wondered if she this was the time to share what she felt the Lord had given her while cooking. Oddly enough, it did seem like God opened the door on the subject. "Price, I have to confess, there was more about the adobes I did not mention earlier.

Price's perception was right, *now the mystery will unfold; I think I love this talent!* He looked up from his cup trying not to smile.

"Something occurred to me while cooking I could not shake it, so I have been praying about it quietly all morning. When you share about how you felt secluded and how you wanted friends nearby, hero's you called them. Well, that goes along with what I was thinking earlier. I thought about our children having the life you described, and then I thought about how you turned out so wonderful. Yet, I think being a schoolteacher I developed notions about when I would have children from observing my class. I figured they would establish young friendships in school and those friends would turn into lifelong companions. While I was processing these differences in my head something came to my attention, a solution you might find acceptable. Mind you, it is just an idea that came to me. It is however a way which could make it easier for our children. Maybe they would not need to seek imaginary heroes and at the same time we can maintain a simple lifestyle." Raine paused for a quick moment of silent prayer, because she did not want to say anything to give the impression she had it all figured out.

Not realizing Raine was silent because she was praying, Price thought she was having second thoughts about sharing and he was determined to not let her stop; his curiosity was thoroughly stimulated. "Don't stop now…you have my full attention. I admit having it both ways intrigues me."

Even though Price coaxed, she knew prayer would make the difference. So Raine continued to pray giving Price a faint smile then gently biting her lip. Meanwhile, she was contemplating with the Lord how to convey the idea.

Price was not tuning in to his talent of reading her so he still did not catch on that she was not giving up, but actually in silent prayer. Instead he was feeling anxious and thought a little push might be needed, "Raine, you are the helpmate God gave me. Do you remember what I said yesterday, when I told you God had you in the plans of this ranch from the beginning? I did not speak those words just to make you feel good, I was dead serious. This is a truth and there is no reason to ever holdback sharing your ideas with me."

Raine realized Price did not know she was praying and did not want him to feel dishonored any longer by withholding her words. She mustered the courage to explain, remembering the Lord's gentle instruction for her to keep respectful cautions and to not overstep her place. After taking a deep breath and exhaling, her words began to flow easily, "I am sorry for making you wait, I was praying."

Price felt a little foolish for pushing, but gave her his full attention.

"Yesterday when we were approaching the ranch I saw the ranch as a small community. The feeling was so intense I found myself looking for people. I looked for children playing in the yard when we got closer, but it was quiet and unlived. This morning I began conversing with the Lord about all of it, because of the intensity I experienced. My mind began unfolding at such a rapid pace I could hardly grasp everything. Hopefully there will not be much lost in the sharing of what was impressed upon me, as I am still trying to digest everything myself. Nevertheless, with the Lord's help I will try to convey it respectfully and unabridged as I can."

Price could see this was difficult for her, "Just Relax, there is no need for concern. I never have been a hard person to deal with," he grinned, "simply share from your heart what you remember and we'll trust God to take care of the rest."

Raine was still uneasy and began to doubt what she heard, *what if it were just a woman's foolishness.* She nervously poured more coffee to heat up their cups. She needed a moment in time to get out of the Lord's way so He could bring to mind what was most important to share. As she sat down at the table, the words began to bubble up, "Several wagon trains come through New Crossing every year, and often they try to cut some miles from their journey on the Santa Fe Trail, as did my family."

Price briefly interjected "I think it was the same for us."

"Because of these shortcuts or needs for supplies," Raine continued, "Stray wagons find their way into our town. Carrying people who are fatigued from the rugged unsafe travel they endured on their journey. Some of the travelers would have planted roots in New Crossing, as we did, but they were too low on funds to secure a place. Their circumstances put them in a desperate position to find a piece of land they could homestead or claim squatters rights one day. Some of them were open to stay if they could find work, but jobs are not plentiful. Ingrained in them to be proud people and not a custom to taking charity these poor souls just keep moving on hoping to connect again with the Santa Fe Trail farther up the trail. Eager to find suitable vacant land by continuing their journey westward; unfortunately leaving them temporarily vagabonds. All hoping to make it to their destination alive and we all know some never make it."

"There have been others who came from the North Country or California, unsuccessful at prospecting for gold. They too, attempting to take a short cut, traveled our way in a last ditch effort to make it back home to what was familiar. They were desperate for family encouragement."

"Every one of these people endured unimaginable hardships, for some it was lack of money which was supposed to give them a head start in a new land. For others it was devastation, giving their loved ones over to death along their plight. These roaming people found themselves separated from their relatives having nowhere to call home, becoming gypsy drifters or die in their attempts to survive. Many had children and a great many were extremely large families." Raine paused to wipe her tearful eyes and found it difficult regaining her speech, as she remembered the lost and hungry faces of the children.

Price felt compassion for Raine and the people she spoke about. *There is such grief in what she is saying,* "Raine forgive me, I can see this touches your heart deeply, as your telling of it moves my heart. I realize these conditions you have presented are incredibly wrenching."

"During our lives here on the ranch, we also have several wagons pass the ranch every year, yet with my parents being deaf, we were untrusting of strangers and protective. Aunt Arnett or Uncle Cuate' always directed them into New Crossing or to the Trading Post. After listening to your description of possible situations the Scriptures are resounding in my head from the Holy Bible, and convicting me as I speak. All the written instructions we are given to help those in need. Yet I am ashamed to say, I followed the same example of protecting my parents and sent people on their way as well. I realize how inexcusable this was."

By the time Price came to this point, his feelings of remorse for his actions were overwhelming and he got up to stretch his legs. He did not know what to do, but he needed to move or be humbled in the presence of his new wife, so he fed the dog some leftovers.

Raine realized the effect her stories had on Price and regretted bringing up the conditions of weary travelers. It was not her intentions to make her husband feel grieved over his actions on their first morning together. She empathized with his position, *how easily it would have looked like the right way, considering his parents condition. Lord what can I say to him to let him know I understand*? "Price, please sit back down. You did what you thought was best considering the circumstances. Try not to carry the burden of everyone on your shoulders. I am sorry I brought it up, I never meant to make you feel bad, I didn't know..." a tear escaped her eye, and she wiped it quickly away hoping no more would follow.

Price did not notice her tear when he sat down. The only thing in his sight was the cup in his hand; he took a sip pondering on the issue. *There will be time for me to repent and make this right with the Lord. Then this heavy conviction will ease, but the moment is not now. I will deal with it later.* His thoughts went to Raine, lifting his head to look at her, patiently sitting quiet and beautiful. He would never want her to feel guilty for sharing her heart. "Do not fret, I am alright…I admit, I will be better after my morning talk with the Lord." He forced a smiled, "however, I must confess I am a little confused. I do not get the connection between these weary travelers and our ranch. I do realize you must have a reason for mentioning them, yet frankly it baffles me, so please explain more."

Raine loved the tremendous strength she saw in this man of God and was comforted how he was able to handle his own mistakes wisely. Taking note of his remarkable character she continued, "It was about theses desperate travelers I was inspired this morning. If the Lord brings families our way now, would it be unthinkable to have them join us in the work on our ranch and allow them to make this place their home too? If the impoverished were to have any children, I could offer to teach them alongside our own. I know our ranch would no longer be a solitary oasis, but it could become an oasis of hope for displaced people and provide playmates for our children. They would develop into our neighbors and we could bring them to Jesus if they do not know Him, as you have with Caleb." She felt like she was rambling, feeling a twinge of excitement stirring within her. "Forgive me, I do not mean to sway your thoughts by my suggestions." She held back her enthusiasm for the desire to not take over his authority was strongly placed inside of her.

In Price's amazement he silently considered every angle of her suggestion, *it could work.* He recalled many lonely days as a boy roaming the ranch with his three make believe friends. *Poncho, my Mexican friend, Bear Claw, my Indian friend and Jacob was from back East,* he snickered at the memory for he had not thought about them in years. *Quite silly for a fifteen year old,* but he was lonely and they helped him survive.

Noticing Raine waiting patiently for his response, *is this idea Yours, Lord?* Immediately in his heart he felt he knew the answer and a surge of enthusiasm went thru him accompanied by an awesome peace, two emotions that rarely travel together unless God is doing something. "There is no need to be apologetic, Raine, you are a real God-sent to me and I love your passion about it. I actually think this is a magnificent idea. A splendid way for the use of our land, however, you do know if we gather too many people on the ranch we may need to expand our boundaries to accommodate them." He grinned.

"More land?" She spoke in a questioning manner. "Is adjoining land even available? Would it be difficult to attain?" She tossed out several questions as they came charging into her mind, then added, "Do you really feel this is a good idea?" Being concerned how Price would take such a suggestion of sharing his elite family ranch, especially from a wife of one day.

Price sensed her apprehension, *how could she possibly feel comfortable so soon, please help her understand I do not mind her ideas, but rather welcomed them?* Many times he requested a woman who would be actively involved with all aspects of his life and now without his parents making the decisions, he was pleased God had granted his request. *This must be a teacher's quality,* he thought before speaking to reassure her. "Yes Raine, I think it is a great idea. A perfect way to keep our children from the loneliness I felt growing up…I think the proposal is brilliant. I really never wanted to leave the ranch my family worked so hard to carve out of this barren land. I love it here! Now I want to share with you and our children all the great memories, it is our legacy. This could be the answer to my dilemma. I have been mulling over what to do about the loneliness my children would endure for some time. As for our property lines, it would not be hard to expand the borders of the land, once we came up with the money. There is plenty of available land surrounding us. Lucky for us no one desires to be out this far from town."

Reassured by his positive response, Raine excitedly offered, "You forget I still have a homestead for sale. When it sells we can take the money and apply it towards the land expansion."

"A very admirable plan, but are you sure you want to put your homestead money into the ranch?"

She cocked her head to the side and gave him an I-do-not-believe-you-asked-that look "You keep telling me it is OUR ranch, so why wouldn't I? It seems this also is a part of the Lord's plan."

He laughed and consented to her offer, "It is a faultless idea, something we can count on being there at the right time."

"Then it is settled, the money will be there when God deems so."

"I am sure it will. However, I do not think we should go out searching for stranded families. It would be easy enough to find many who have needs. I feel we should be wise about it, be patient and allow the Lord to bring them to us. If this is God's inspiration we can certainly wait for His selections of the right people. Ones we will be able to trust to be in our lives and to live among our children."

Just listening to Price's wisdom made it easy for Raine to drop her protective guard completely. She stood up, went around the table and threw her arms around his neck. "You are blessed with wisdom Mr. Barrett."

Backing away slightly, "I agree we will wait until the Lord directs them to our ranch."

Price scooted out his chair providing his lap for Raine and she welcomed it. She continued chattering while situated comfortably. "Although, I am pleased I want you to understand if you would have considered me just an impractical woman, I would have dropped the idea and not bothered you further." Raine Barrett meant just that and it would be difficult since she believed it was actually the Lord's idea, but she would not push her husband's authority. If he would not hear her the Lord would simply just have to talk to him in another way. After all if this was His plan, He would certainly establish His Will.

It impressed Price that she was willing to abandon the idea if it did not meet his approval. Yet he was also aware of his own obstinate trait and some things might require moving a mountain. "Never give up what you know deep in your heart has come from the Lord, just pray harder for me to get it."

Her thoughts exactly, Raine kissed his cheek, got up and went right to work on clearing the table.

Price opened the Holy Bible. He thought to read the Scriptures out loud as she toiled with the dishes. He looked down at the passage they were reading from last night and began reading the next portion, Chapter Four of 1st John. He read a few verses pausing at seven and eight, reading it over again. "Beloved let us love one another, for love is from God; and everyone that loveth is born of God, and knoweth God. He that loveth not knoweth not God: for God is love."

Price smiled and set the Holy Book to rest on the table. He glanced up at his new bride, "Raine, I do not think it is a coincidence we are reading the passage in 1st John on this particular morning. I feel God is letting us know we must provide a way to extend our love to those in need for His Name sake."

Price continued reading and when he was finished with the passage he informed Raine, "I think it is time for me to ride out to the Mesa. I should consult the Lord about the plans we discussed this morning." Price knew on his desert walk he could speak with the Lord more intimately. It was in the desert where Price could be certain of what the Lord was conveying to them and something as big as this would take a direct personal word from Father God before any plans were set in motion.

Raine laid down her towel, "I think that is a good idea," she walked over to give him a kiss. "That is where you told me you go to pray every morning, right?"

Price put his hat on and bent down to kiss her, "Yes you remember well. I won't be very long. I can see the trail and the ranch from there so you will be safe."

"I am not worried, for God will protect me when you are with Him." He nodded affirmatively and went out the door.

Raine watch him a few moments walking to the barn then she closed the door. She actually wanted the chance to become more familiar with her new home and would feel more comfortable unpacking her trunks in private, so the time alone was welcomed.

♥

Chapter 17

Price saddled up Girl, his favorite horse and headed up the trail to the Mesa with Trader running close behind. The dog showed no slack in his sprint, even with a full belly.

Girl seemed to enjoy a hearty run this morning. The wind blowing her mane almost straight seemed to energize her. Price gladly indulged his old friend in her gallop, only slowing down periodically for Trader to catch up. Price laughed robustly with pleasure as he watched the old dog keep a steady pace. Trader never ceased to amaze him with the endurance demonstrated for his age. While taking advantage of the moment, he slowed Girl down to a gentle trot while he viewed with appreciation the landscape. This allowed Trader a slower pace.

Looking over the terrain Price felt as if he was seeing it all for the first time. *Spectacular,* he thought, *what an impressive view. Father, did you put a fresh paint job on this land for me this morning. It has never looked more magnificent than it does now.* The weather also was pleasantly tolerable for July, feeling a northern breeze brush against his face. Price savored the time before picking up his pace, *not a cloud in the sky; Lord what a marvelous day You have made. There is none who can create like You!*

Trader did not relish the view as his master was doing and was beginning to grow impatient wanting to continue the run. He knew where they were going, it was the same place he traveled every morning with his master. Price noticed his dog's eagerness and obliged. Lifting the reins and giving resounding "YAH" for Girl to move faster towards the familiar destination.

Arriving near the Mesa's incline, Price had a perfect

view of the homestead and surrounding area. From this location he could see if anyone was coming down the trail for miles and could be back at the ranch before long anyone arrived. He discovered this location several years ago and he made him feel better about leaving his parents on the ranch alone, although he never told them. Now observantly Price would continue to look over the safety of the ranch for his wife and future family.

Girl and Trader knew the procedure; they would hang out in the shade of the plateau and wait for their master. Yet today the sun was already high in the sky, leaving only a thin jagged line of shade for them to rest in. Price noticed the location of the sun and felt the heat increasing. He wiped his brow knowing he had a good hour before the heat would overtake them. He generally arrived out at the mesa much earlier, but then again he never had a wife to detain him. Price realized he would have to make a conscious effort to master his schedule as a married man.

Raine was feeling more comfortable with her new surroundings; realizing this would be her home for the rest of her life. She glanced about the room embracing every unique detail. The exquisite design of the cook fireplace will amaze her for some time on how well planned and efficient it is. The windows were charming with a unique character all their own. She loved every part of this home and had not yet seen the whole house. Glancing from one door to the other she thought about looking in the rooms while Price was gone, but not wanting to spoil the tour she decided to wait. There was plenty of pleasure in this grand room alone to occupy her time.

The bread dough she prepared earlier had risen to

perfection, after putting the bread pan into one of the oven slots and sliding the stones back in front to keep the heat inside. She loved every part of this cook fireplace. Raine began working on a pot of soup salvaged from last night's leftovers and by adding a few additional items she found in the pantry; tonight's dinner was taking shape.

With dinner in the making she was free to start unpacking the trunks. Raine worked the trunk that held her clothing first. She placed them neatly in an empty drawer of the beautiful crafted drawer chest at the side of the bed. Underneath a layer of clothing were two quilts in which her mother and she worked on together, *I did not have the heart to let go of these.* Cradling them close to her heart only made the memory of her mother vivid. *I wish you could see me now mother, you would be so happy for me and I know you would adore Price.*

Since there was a beautiful quilt on the bed that Price's mama made for his wedding, she did not want to change it. So she relocated her quilts into a chest located at the end of the bed. She was glad to have these sentimental items to remember her mother by and one day she would share them with her daughters. Just like her mother shared items with her when she was young from Grandmother Carrie. Retrieving a hankie from her pocket she patted her eyes. She wished that her mother was still around to share this important time in her life. Wiping her tears, *this is no time to indulge in sentimental 'what-ifs'*, she scolded herself.

Returning to her trunk and retrieving several small items she safely tucked between the quilts and wondered where they would look best. Glancing around the room she noticed suitable places to include these little treasures coming from her family heritage. The delicate pieces being woven into the surroundings of the room was making it feel like home.

Reaching deep into the trunk to the very bottom, her fingers touched lightly upon the lace tablecloth which her Grandmother Carrie tatted. Tears formed in her eyes again, *my, my, I am a sentimental mess today, shame on me…on such a happy day too!*

Raine was tucking away her former life as she knew it with the memories finding shelter deep her heart. The truth dictated her reality; she would never walk those steps again. For many years Raine indulged in the memories of the past because they seemed to comfort her while waiting on God's promise. It was going to be strange to lay it all aside and actually live her life in the present, to look forward and not backwards for comfort.

Holding up the delicate tatted lace while mentally sizing the eight-seated table across the room, she doubted the cloth would be large enough to use. Approaching the table she flung it across the top and as she suspected, it was evident the lace would not even come close. *It looks tiny now*, she laughed, *it appeared much larger on the table back home.*

Feeling a little disappointed in not being able to use the lace tablecloth she proceeded to fold it back up. Then a creative idea came to mind about a possible use for it. While observing the light shining through the window the idea became more feasible. Walking over to the window case she held the lace next to it to measure the width and found it was plenty large enough. She could drape the lace on the wall over the bottled window just like she recalled her relatives back in Chicago had done. *To have on display a blessing from Grandmother Carrie,* the idea pleased her. *They had a name for it…* Trying to stir her recollection of when she was so young. *What did they call this? She searched her memory…a veil…valance…Oh yes…that's it! A valance over the window will look 'pretty'!*

Raine examined the window wall to see what she would need to put it up and spotted a large nail located on each side of the window a foot above the shutters. Raine wondered briefly what those imbedded nails in the stucco were previously used for, but only for a slight moment. She was glad they were mounted already because it saved her the trouble of having to ask Price about putting up some hooks. Standing still with her eyes closed for a brief moment imagining what it would look like, confirming in her mind that it would indeed be lovely. *It is going to need a little adjustment;* she considered looking at the piece of lace. *A little bit of stitching here…Yes, it will work out nicely and without the slightest interference of sliding the shutters closed. Those nails are long enough to allow a bit of lace to curve in front of the top of the window…splendid.* It was settled in her mind and she knew just how to make it all work.

Raine was excited to get started on the project, yet before beginning she needed to deal with the emptied trunk. She noticed a spot near the flour cabinet where the trunk would provide good storage, until she had another shelf built. Raine scooted the trunk over to the location and filled it with a few of her special cooking items from the other trunk. She was happy to locate her favorite teapot in the process, which she placed on the table.

The lace project consumed her mind and she was impatient to get started. Raine decided to leave the remainder of the half-unpacked trunk for a later time. It was enough she got to place some personal items around the room creating the atmosphere of her living here. She did hope the simple changes would not bother Price. She closed the lid on the second trunk and moved it near the window by the bench. She put her mother's choice table scarf over it and set her most favorite picture of her parents on top. Decoratively alongside it she placed the vase of wild flowers from the dining table. Backing away to view how everything fit together, she smiled feeling satisfied. Gathering up the lace tablecloth in one arm and her stitching satchel in the other, Raine found comfort in a rocker. She was all set to transform this beautiful tatted lace tablecloth into a curtain top, *a valance*, she reminded herself.

Raine was happy and light hearted; she sang boldly a powerful melody which would have inspired all the birds to join in…if she were outside. Her voice was soft and soothing (a gift of the Lord). She often sung special music on Sundays and during the holidays at the Missions Chapel. Raine loved to sing about the Lord Jesus and took advantage of this special time alone to worship Him as she worked gently on transforming her Grandmother Carrie's lace.

Conversations with Father God were essential to Price's life and he valued the morning necessity more than he loved food. He would often rise early and come out to the mesa while Mama was preparing breakfast. He wondered, *how much of my schedule will change with a wife.* Seeing the homestead in a distance he pondered over his new responsibility, *a wife*, then considered the possibility of children in the future. *I believe my time spent in counsel and prayer is even more important now since I am the one making the decisions…course Raine will share in this responsibility with me…we can't do it without Your counsel. I am going to need wisdom on scheduling my time Father.* His thoughts and concerns turned into a prayer for he knew God was always listening in.

If Price were to ever be transformed into the

compassionate leader his family deserved, he knew the Lord God had much work to do with his character. He only hoped he would be pliable. He mulled over the fact he was now the lead person in charge of making major decisions for the ranch. Although this was frightening, he was positive he could handle it if he kept his relationship with God in good standing.

Price provided the animals with a handful of water from his canteen then proceeded to walk and pray around the terrain. He began with rendering numerous thankful prayers to the Lord for blessings on his life and for the Lord God's faithfulness towards him with a wife. When Price finished thanking the Lord for all he could possibly think of he moved into a time of immense worship in song. Aunt Arnett taught him several hymns, which he sang from his heart with passion and boldness in this open chapel. It was during moments like this when Price was gracefully ushered into awesome laps of silent admiration and felt saturated in the Holy Fathers presence, this morning was no exception. During a worshipful aura Price submitted a simple song of his own making. The words embedded in his heart flowed out powerfully echoing off the mesa. As he continued pouring out his love for God in a song within his heart, the Lord approached him with a question: "What is on your mind today, my faithful?"

Being called faithful only humbled Price knowing his personal weaknesses quite well. Yet the Lord was always lavishing His love upon him, so much he had come to embrace his own personal humility. He accepted that even this feeling was undeserved.

In reflecting on the question Price thought of Raine. He expressed with thankfulness his great pleasure for the Fathers tender care in creating such a perfect woman for him. How could one even begin to deserve such favor? There was no natural way…it was pure grace.

After great a time of admiration which flowed between Father God and himself in his time of worship. Price felt it was an appropriate time to approach the Lord with the idea of sharing their land with displaced people. He began laying out the plan before God as he understood it.

As he was explaining he remembered his sin and promptly added, "Lord, the wife you gave me brought this plan to my attention. When she explained it to me, I was immediately filled with shame. I recognized my sin and I ask You Lord, please forgive me for being so insensitive. When lost and weary travelers passed through our ranch I was in the wrong frame of mind and I chose to protect my parents. I ignored their needs. Father, I am ashamed to admit I never once considered the needs of the weary travelers. My ignorance finds no justification and I know I am without excuse. You certainly know how often I have read instructive parables, especially the one about the Good Samaritan. How a priest and a Levite passed by the robbed and beaten man without even a care, but the Samaritan when he saw the man lying there in pain, he stopped and tended to him like a father. This is an example of how we should act upon similar situations with love and treat every man as our neighbor. The truth was always before my eyes, but I was blinded by my own self interests. Please forgive me for all those neighbors I have rejected. Forgive me for my lack of love for them and my lack of trust in Your protection. I am so ashamed for putting my mother and father before you." Tears of remorse began to trickle down his face as he confessed his inexcusable actions before the throne of God. Price Barrett was deeply grieved. He never intended to let Father God down. Yet his lack of genuine compassion for others in distress was truly uncalled-for considering the immense compassion the Lord showed towards his family for many years.

Price dropped to his knees in the desert sand and wept bitterly for what felt like hours. After a lull in time he experienced a calm flowing over him like gentle rain. It flowed from the top of his head to his feet and soaked him in a shower of peace. This awesome tranquility reassured him and tranquillized his spirit in captivating silence. Out of an atmosphere of serenity the Word of the Lord spoke a pure and simple fragrance of clemency, "You are forgiven. Remember it no more."

The shattered fragments of conviction lifted and left Price humbly changed forever. "Father I surrender to Your Will. I offer myself and I will open our home up for Your glory. If you desire for us to take in strangers I am willing and I welcome the privilege to be good to my neighbors. I know now that whatever I do to the least of men, I am doing to you. If You need a home Lord let me be the one to give it to You. I fully understand.

Now that You have cast out my fear with Your perfect love, I have confidence in Your selection of people. I know You will not bring anyone our way to bring us harm. Please Lord God, I ask that You give me the grace to treat each one with the measure of love I have for You."

In the silence of surrender Father God spoke with unyielding authority. "Price I need you to listen carefully. I have purposed in My heart to direct four families onto the ranch and with these four families you will establish a community of Believers for me in the desert. This is a beginning of a new life for you and Raine and for them. There will be some among them who have a need to know Me so I am counting on you to introduce us. When your children grow into men they will turn this community of Believers into a town to honor Me. A town is not what I require of your generation, however, I am asking you to give the community a name. This name will stand and endure as the name of the town in the years to come. When I see this name before Me I will remember this day and the roots that sprouted the town. Roots of love, obedience, surrender. This is what I am asking of you. This is MY Will for your ranch."

The powerful and authoritative sound of the Lord's voice made Price tremble. He was uncertain if he heard it audibly or if it were an echo in his head. Possibly he had fallen asleep and had a vision. In any case the impact absorbed everything around him and nothing stood, but the Voice of the Lord. He recognized in his state of awe a clear distinction of the Lord's Will. He stretched his hands out and upward to the heavens, openly receiving God's awesome direction. In the Lord's presence Price was able to comprehend the impeccable wisdom of His Father's plan. "Oh Lord my God, I am nothing and yet you have spoken to me, a mere man, lowly and undeserving of such a gracious visit. What grace You have bestowed upon a man of ordinary stature. I humbly accept your instruction. Thank You Lord for the immense clarity, I will do as you say...please help me not to fail you."

When Price become still and quiet the Lord whispered a further message, "Share what I have spoken with Raine and also inform her that she will have a visit from a young couple with a small child. They are coming to inquire about her family's homestead. Whatever the landholder has set to be a fair price, know that satisfaction will come with half the amount. The couple are Believers and will bring your home great joy and blessings in the days ahead."

Price agreed to deliver the message to Raine as the

Lord had spoken, yet he was uncertain how his new wife would respond. He prayed for Lord to prepare her heart.

Remaining motionless for several minutes, quiet in spirit, totally captivated in an atmosphere of tranquility Price wondered if the Lord might have more to say. He did not want to leave too soon in case Father God was not finished so he rested in the serenity, waiting. After the joy of silence began to fade he believed the Lord had said all He wanted to, but to be sure he inquired, "Is there anything else I need to know? Anything more You want to tell me?" The response was insightful, there was a quietness that penetrated everything, even a bird did not chirp. The air was unmoving, and he knew from past experiences this was a sign the Lord was finished. It was as if he was dismissed from the presence of royalty.

Price stood up and stretched, he moved vigorously back and forth, dancing while offering jovial praise. A breeze began to blow and the birds joined in worshiping. He glanced towards the ranch as he did periodically to be certain nothing unusual caught his eye. Discovering everything was satisfactory his attention drew to a unique desert plant the Lord created. Two little birds busily gleaning nectar from the blossoms, his mind encompassed the observation and immediately understood how these delicate blossoms were vital for the little birds allowing them to survive in desert terrain. *Creator God thought of everything!* The revelation brought forth more praises to his lips. He wanted to burst out in song again only this time he found it hard to concentrate on a specific lyric. With added surges of excitement infiltrating his mind he could not keep silent. He began humming praises for lack of words and spoke out a verbal praise of adoration periodically. This moment was pure ecstasy.

Price set his eyes upward and began speaking to

Father God as one would a trusted friend, "Lord, I remember the first time You spoke to me...it was on my twenty second birthday. I came here to the mesa to be alone that day. I was feeling forlorn and depressed about my life. After wandering and stomping about the area pouring my heart out to You in such a horrible display of selfish emotions...You spoke. I heard it clear as a bell, 'Happy Birthday Son'. I bet you laughed as I looked to where the voice was coming from. I thought the wind was speaking to me, and then You said it again. The very moment I realized it was You, I was instantly absorbed in Your love and I have never been the same since. Thank You for Your love, Your friendship and Your faithfulness to me all these years." Even though Price did not hear an audible reply to his rhetoric he knew in the deep calm valley of his heart the Lord heard him, and took pleasure in their friendship also. It was well with his soul, Price was at peace.

Price headed over to where Trader was resting quietly and Girl was grazing on a small bush. He was about to mount the horse and head back to the ranch when he spotted a bighorn sheep up the side of the mesa, not far from him. *What are you doing here with all the noise I have been making this morning?* He slowly took Old Henry from the holster located on the side of his saddle. Old Henry was a shotgun, a treasured gift from Uncle Cuate'. Price gently stroked Girl so she wouldn't spook, the good ol'gal had been in this place many times with him so she knew what to expect. Price took careful aim at the bighorn and fired a shot; it was a good hit, killing the sheep instantly.

"It's alright, Girl, you did good," he whispered softly while stroking her mane. The riffle shot woke Trader and without delay he began checking out the territory to see if Price needed him. "Stay boy," Price instructed the dog while he climbed up the ridge to dress the slain sheep. He first thanked the beast for providing food for his family and then thanked the Lord for His gift. When completed, he carried the sheep over his shoulders down the slope.

Once on level ground he took out his makeshift sled from the holstered spot. Caleb had taught him to always carry the sled folded for occasions like this. He proceeded to load the bighorn on the sled and strap him securely for transport.

Price was Feeling completely satisfied with all the Lord had ordained this morning and could hardly wait to get back to the ranch and share with Raine everything God had spoken. His thoughts pleasantly rested on his wife once again, a permanent smile invaded his face as he moseyed back to the ranch carefree and content. Life was good. He hoped Raine's time alone was as successful.

Price entered the front door of his home, excited to share with Raine about the wonderful thing the Lord had spoken. He expected to see his wife actively preparing a meal as the aroma indicated from the porch. Instead he found her sitting in a rocker covered in lace, "Hello Beautiful." The words fell off his lips spontaneously.

Raine stopped her needlework on grand-mother Carrie's tablecloth for a moment to glance over her shoulder to see Price. He was approaching with a tenacious grin, which he was struggling in vain to subdue. She was already blushing considerably from his greeting and naturally smiling at the very sight of him. "Hi, did you enjoy your talk with the Lord?" She did not stand to greet him, but went back to working on the lace.

"Matter of fact, had an excellent conversation and I think Trader enjoyed a good run." The dog could be heard noisily lapping water from his bowl in the cooking area. Price sat down in the rocking chair angled towards her, he was curious to see what she was working on. "What is that you are making?"

Raine proudly replied, "A curtain swathe...actually it is a piece of lace my grandmother tatted originally as a tablecloth, but it is not large enough to fit our table. As I was holding it and contemplating about what to do with the piece, I remembered how the homes back in Chicago had lace hung around the windows and I thought it might be a nice way to display her handiwork. I would like to put it over the top of the bottled window for a valance, if this ok with you?"

A valance? Price admired a portion of the lace with his hands exposing the unique pattern her talented grandmother achieved. "It really is an attractive piece of lace. I think it is a fine idea to show off her work," still unfamiliar with what a valance was exactly. He paused for a moment seeing an opportunity to introduce his reflection of the morning and added, "Especially since we will be having neighbors...so when I am home kissing my wife we will not need to close the shutters...."Price found his delivery clever and formed a sheepish grin.

"I am afraid to disappoint you, it is not actually meant to cover the window, but essentially hang decoratively over the top of it." Then she paused and considered his remark about neighbors, *the desire for privacy.* Slowly the corners of her lips began to curl up and she giggled out loud, "So you talked with God about the proposal, did you?" smiling confidently.

Price had to chuckle about her confidence, "Yes of

course, I did have a good conversation with Our Father about the idea and I am humbled to say I was also given wise counsel."

Raine was feeling a bit witty and responded with a jeering remark, "Did you expect unwise counsel from our Creator?"

Price was still getting to know her personality so her cleaver comment made him burst out laughing, and gave her a friendly poke. "Silly woman, of course not."

Raine felt at ease with him, taking a brief moment to relax she dropped the lace unto her lap, and quit stitching. She was dying to know the details, but Price stayed silent to prod her curiosity. It was working too. The hush was lasting far too long for the liking of Raine. When exhaling with a sense of impetuousness it all came rushing out, "Well...please do not stop there. Aren't you going to explain what Father God had to say concerning the idea?"

Price could not torture her emotions any longer and willingly complied with her request, however, he did find her adorable watching the suspense stimulate her inquisitive nature. "Alright, I have beleaguered you long enough by skirting the issue." He had to chuckle again watching her eyes widen with anticipation.

"I should have known God is in complete favor of everything. In fact, He made it clear to me that this was His proposal. In His wise and authoritative way He added a few instructions to guide us through the process." She listened attentively as Price shared. "The first thing He mentioned was hard for me to grasp, I was not thinking this venture would be quite as big as He elucidate. Yet from past conversations I have learned not to take what He says lightly, but as truth. He told me He would be guiding four families to share our 480 acres."

"Four families!" Raine spoke out surprised, "My...I

never considered that many, I figured two. Alright, four must be a sufficient amount of people to work together…He actually told you four?"

"Yes, He did, I also realized we will have to construct another adobe for the extra family as we only have three useable buildings."

Raine was hanging on every word, *four families*. Her enthusiasm to do what He was asking of them was lacking. She felt humbled considering what the Lord was beginning to perform with their meager lives. It was like being a missionary without having to go anywhere; the Lord would bring the people directly to them. Was she up to it? Could she please God in this endeavor? Could she still be a good wife to Price? Her mind was trying desperately to sort through all the emotions that hung on the fact of four families were coming here. *This is much bigger than I thought Lord.*

Price continued, "God is preparing us to build a small community, however, He made it clear that we are not required to assemble a town, the challenge of building a town is saved for our children. Since we are only asked to start a community there will not be any need to add more parcels of land right away, maybe later when the community is established."

"For our children…that's amazing! God gave us a timeline to know the projection of what our linage is destined to do. I guess setting up the foundation for a community is the first part of planning for our children. This is just what you wanted us to do this morning. If we do not build the community with strong values the town our children construct will be just like any other town and in the end, not give God glory."

Price considered the deep thought Raine put into her words and respected what she shared. "You are absolutely right, Raine. I did not have the chance to consider all of that, but it goes without saying that we must share the Lord's love with whoever we are near. So establishing love as the guideline and the worship of Jesus Christ with the people of a community would only benefit our children. It will certainly transpire over into the town they are predestined to establish. It is a fine calling of the Lord to be on the bottom of the ladder, when you can look up and see what the projected future will hold. However, if the ladder is unstable, whoever is on the top will fall."

"What a good analogy Price, you would have made a wonderful teacher." Then Raine corrected her statement, "I should say that you are designed to be a wonderful teacher of God's ways in the midst of the people He is bringing to us, and also to our children."

This time Price felt his face flush, he never thought of himself as a teacher. It was good to hear his wife say he would make a good one considering it was her vocation. Although he was flattered, he quickly thought to tell her another part of the plan, "The Lord God also said that you and I should decide on what to call the community. The name we select will stand as the name of the town in the future. If one comes to your mind let me know, we probably should make a list before we settle on one. It would be wise to have one established before anyone arrives."

Raine liked the idea. It would be fun to pick a name they both agreed on; she felt excitement start to bubble inside making her fears of such a big undertaking fade. "Alright, I will prayerfully ponder this idea, the selecting a name of a town of the future is an awesome privilege." She paused for a moment then offered, "Sounds like we will not need any money from selling the homestead for quite a while. Maybe that means the land will not sell for some time, which is okay since we are in no hurry for it."

Price was glad she brought up the Jordan property, because he almost forgot the directions he received at the mesa about it. "Actually…the Lord God gave me some instructions regarding the homestead. He specifically asked me to share them with you and I hope you will not be disappointed."

Disappointed, what would make me disappointed? I doubt anything could disappoint me today! Raine was attentive and sober waiting for Price to explain.

"I believe I heard Him correctly, but feel free to take this to Him yourself. He said you were only to ask half of the price of what the landholder says you can get for the homestead. There is a couple going to inquire about it and will want to buy it, they are Believers and have a young child. Now this being your family inheritance, I am leaving this decision up to you. Although, I am obliged to tell you, He did say if we do as He asked, we will find this couple a blessing to us." Price stopped for a moment concerned how this might sound to her, then added, "There is no pressure intended on you doing this Raine, please do whatever seems right to you, take it to the Lord and get confirmation. With something as important as this I do not want you to do it simply because I told you. I want you to know yourself what God is saying."

"Price, I am sure you did not hear wrong; you seem to have an incredible relationship with the Lord and it certainly hasn't taken a lifetime with you to figure this out. As for the home belonging to me, well, you certainly know from our talks I do not believe in dividing our money in such a way. Whatever I have or gain is already yours, I am your wife and everything has been combined from the moment we married. Now refreshing you on that fact, I do not need to take this to Him because I trust you and I know in my spirit it is truth. I am confident this is a holy request, important to Him and we should obey the Lord."

Price could not have imagined a better response, he felt so blessed God had given him Raine; *what an extraordinary woman.*

Raine had more to say, "Price Barrett, I am not in the least bit disappointed, God has blessed me far more than any amount of money could offer." She was grateful for marrying a God-fearing man, but realized her words were too empty to convey what she really wanted to tell him. Yet, she had to try. "I want to thank you Price for taking the proposal to Father God. It is comforting for me just to know you could not conceive of moving ahead on anything without consulting Him. The way you handle your relationship with God only makes me feel completely safe with your decisions for our life together. It excites me to know what God has begun here and I feel so unworthy of what He has in mind for us, but with you leading me..." A tear trickled down her cheek; she was profoundly moved at the revelation of all that was spoken.

Price moved closer, shifting onto his knees in front of her to offer comfort. Disregarding the lace on her lap Price gently cupped her face in his hands, holding it in position while he tenderly kissed her.

Raine felt completely loved.

As much as Price did not want to leave her side, yet there was still the bighorn that needed attention. Price stood and moved around behind her chair placing his hands gently upon her shoulders, he began to massage them. Raine began to relax and he knew she would be ok, no more tears. Leaning down kissing the top of her head then whispered softly in her ear. "Sorry Beautiful, I hate to shorten our time, but..." He moved in front of her to explain, "While I was at the mesa I spotted a bighorn sheep on the ridge as I was leaving, so I took time and shot it, now I need to go hang the carcass in the barn. The cooler night temperatures are better for butchering before the heat rises, so I will tend to it early in the morning. Tonight the carcass will drain out so I have to make sure it does not attract any predators."

Raine nodded she understood.

"While you work on your grandmother's curtain, ponder on a name for the community and we will talk about it later." Price started to move away, "If you need me just ring the large bell on the porch." He proceeded towards the door when the aroma caught his attention, pausing to look back, "Whatever you are cooking, it smells delicious…making me hungry."

Being so literally tied up in lace, Raine had not thought to offer, "Oh my, please forgive me for not being sensitive to your needs, I should have guessed you'd be hungry…it is soup I threw together from last night's leftovers. Would you like some now?"

"No, no, you stay seated…I am fine. The scent is enticing me…I think I will grab a piece of jerky to hold me over." Price went to the jerky jar and took a couple for himself and grabbed an extra one for Trader. Beckoning his faithful sidekick dog to join him, "Come on Boy." However, today Trader did not attempt to follow him; instead he was sprawled out on the woven rug without as much a glance in his master's direction. Price tried again and the dog still ignored him, "Alright you lazy mutt, stay with Raine today, but remember there is a job to maintain around here so I do not expect you to make this a habit!" Price expressed his amusement with a chuckle, "He only wants to hang out with you because he smells the enticing food also."

Speaking up for the dogs defense, "Well Price, what

do you expect, this rug is a lot closer to the kitchen than the barn is. Besides didn't you say he had an energetic run this morning?"

"He never let a little run stop him before." Trader lifted his eyebrows slightly, but did not budge. Price shook his head in amusement, "ok, I get to eat all three pieces," munching on a jerky strip while he left. Meanwhile Trader was contented laying on the woven rug and Raine continued her sewing, eager to have the curtain up in place before dinner.

Raine worked diligently on the piece of tatted lace, contemplating on what the Lord graciously revealed to her husband. While reflecting on his words she is able to foresee beyond the present time. The legacy they were creating for their children began to unfold in a startling way. In a vision…almost like a dream, only she was fully awake. It encompassed all the great blessings that were descending upon her children and their children. All originating from the inheritance God bestowed upon their father, Price Barrett. It was a clear picture before her eyes. One she would never forget. Raine held the picture in her heart and would revisit often with thanksgiving throughout the coming years.

Raine praised the Lord, she was grateful He enabled them to keep their vows and wait for the Sacred Promise of a spouse. Because she knew this was the beginning of the purpose her Lord had in His heart all along. With this understanding engulfing her every thought and staying at the forefront of her mind, she began to pray for her offspring's. *Lord I ask that my children do not dishonor You by rushing into a marriage that not of Your choosing. May they uphold Your standards, not only in their personal lives, but also by imparting godly examples to the town You have called them to build. I also desire to obey Your will Lord, guide my husband and I as we begin this journey together and help us to create a God fearing legacy for future generations, one with the enduring love you have had for us. Amen*

♥

Chapter 18

The harvest season was finally drawing to an end and Raine could hardly believe mid-October was already upon them. Through continuous toil and a lot of long hours, Raine had become quite accustomed to the art of preserving large quantities of produce. In the midst of backbreaking tasks she was still happier than she ever remembered. Price was a perfect husband and strange as it was to the both of them, so far they never found anything to squabble about. *God knew exactly who to join together so they would complement each other,* she decided. She finished canning the last jars of banno yucca, a wild type of sweet potato. While it was processing she gathered a few of the jars that were ready and took them to the pantry.

Placing the jars on the pantry shelf, reminded Raine there was already a sufficient amount of food in the pantry before harvesting this year. *Four shelves held enough food to carry us almost another year, and here we sit with such an abundance,* she tucked away loose strands of hair behind her ear and took a step back to view their obvious accomplishment. Eight more racks packed to the brim with canned jars. The baskets and barrels on the floor were all protruding with root vegetables, and three barrels of mariposa bulbs that Ruth helped her acquire, a root similar to a white potato. There was also a variety of herb bouquets hanging upside-down to dry.

She has a fleeting thought about her life and how different it would have been if her family would have stayed back East. O*ne must learn quickly how to survive in the West, always be prepared, whether you live in town, in a settlement or on a ranch like this.* It was common knowledge for the brave souls who ventured out West, to learn fast how unpredictable this way of life can be. It only takes one time when the planting, growing season, or harvesting could be hindered by an unexpected drought, or a bad storm wiping out crops. Not to forget plaques of pestilence. If you did not have extra supplies in the storehouse any one of these conditions could be devastating. All of your relatives were back East, and there is no one out here to fall back on for help. One must be prepared for anything.

Raine became overwhelmed by her own revelation, she understood a truth once taken for granted. The Lord blessed them with abundance and with good health to be strong enough to endure the long hours of toil needed to prepare this year's supply. She took a moment to baste in her heartwarming appreciation, for everything her Father God had done for them. He cared and was faithful continually.

Glancing again at the shelves, she knew they would be using the oldest jars from the shelves first and no one would be experiencing much of her canning abilities in the near future. With that thought, she smiled because she was a little unsure of her newly acquired ability. Raine returned upstairs to finish the last few items of produce.

A good thing Price was helpful to his mother over the years and learned the fundamentals of canning vegetation and small game, because he was able to pass this knowledge on to Raine. Once she became more confident in her abilities, Price focused his attention on snaring small game and hunting the larger ones, leaving her to the preserving department. He did manage to acquire a hefty number of wildlife, which they preserved together.

The summer was not the break time she was used to, one common for a teacher, but it was long hours of tiresome work. Even so, Raine found it fulfilling.

Price never lost sight of the calling God gave them about starting a community. When Raine felt worn-out He encouraged her to press on to prepared extra food, declaring, "God may bring another family this season." Needless to say, with the mission as a motivator, the dynamic team practiced great resilience in their work efforts.

While working Raine thought of Ruth, Caleb's wife, who has become a valuable friend in many ways. She looked above the water closet and noticed the spices and seasonings on the shelf because of Ruth. *Thank You Lord, what a good friend You have given me,* giggling at her own thought, *she taught this towns-woman how to forge off the land.* Raine now could recognize the yucca, ocotillo and the agave plant, among many others. She even knew where to locate lechuguilla, using the smaller plants root for soap.

Ruth, an expert at forging and preserving, educated Raine on the drying methods of wild herbs and desert vegetation. The two women found familiarity and respect for each other during the process; all barriers of culture came down in admiration.

There were large containers of various tea leafs; Ruth introduced each of them to her except for one. Price and Raine often took pleasure in a good cup of tea by the fireplace in the evening. Raine picked up the one container recalling how she obtained it, *chicory! I have to thank You again Lord for the large portion I acquired that day. It sure helps to extend our coffee supply and thank You for the travelers who must have lost the seeds along the trail...Bless them!* She found a meager amount on the shelf when she arrived, but never knew where to replenish the supply until she seen them growing along the trail to Cole's Trading Post. Raine recognized the plant right away.

Back East as a young girl she would pick the flowers for her mother. She was instructed to take the whole plant, roots and all, *"The whole plant is useable," Mother would say.* Locating it gave Raine pleasure to introduce Ruth to a plant she was not familiar with. It was good to contributed something, instead of just absorbing all of Ruth's knowledge. She set the chicory back in place and continued her work sterilizing the quart jars.

Giggling out loud, her mind wandered back to the time she managed to convince Price to teach her how to smoke a few batches of skinner fish. Breaking into a full laugh as her mind's eye saw vividly the wild look that came over his face when she had the nerve to ask him to allow her to make jerky out of his mule deer. He insisted it was his personal expertise. However, he compromised and said 'just one time'. She relished privately over the fact she had gotten her way.

Finishing the last quart of banno yucca she noticed there were enough screw-bean pods that were ripe enough for grinding into meal. She found, quite by accident, by mixing the mesquite meal and the screw-bean meal together it would make tasty griddle cakes. *These will have to wait for tomorrows chores,* she decided, knowing there were still several bushels of tomatoes to finish this afternoon.

Price explained how to make salsa, which Raine has grown to love; it was a Mexican recipe he learned from his uncle. *This last batch will conclude our preserving for the season.* While sterilizing the last jars Mama Barrett had, she concluded there was not enough to finish the salsa. So she went to the spare room, Price's old bedroom, and retrieved the new box of jars. Grateful for the trip to New Crossing she took with Price earlier this month, where she obtained the extra canning jars from Adam's General Store; *it was good to see Myra again.* ♥

At the beginning of the month the Barrett's had taken a day off from chores and preserving to go into town. Price needed to pick up a few things before the cold weather set in. For Raine it was a welcomed decision to journey back into New Crossing. She fared better at buggy-wagon traveling than she did back in July. Presuming the level of her endurance was because she was more physically fit due to working on the ranch, compared to her previous days as a schoolteacher. Not to mention the fluffy down pillow she had made for the journey.

The first stop the Barrett's made in New Crossing was the Land Settlement Office, Raine wanted to talk with her father's old friend. After Mr. Harrisburg got over the shock of her showing up in person to inquire about the homestead, he regretfully informed her he did not have any good news. It seems there was no one who expressed an interest in a homestead inside the town limits. There were a number of ranchers and farmers who were rapidly occupying the territory south of town and various clusters breaking away from wagon trains that have started small settlements east and west of town. He knew of three beginning just this past month. Although the words were not what Raine had hoped for, she was reminded of the Lord's instruction. Before parting company, Raine arranged with Mr. Harrisburg to have her notified on the ranch of any buyers. It was obvious how shocked he was about her marriage to Price and how close she lived to New Crossing. Raine had grace for his fumbling over words, which was very unlike Mr. Harrisburg. He was a man of eloquent speech and very businesslike. She left the Settlement Office embracing a few encouraging words, "it was only going to be a matter of time until someone would be interested." Since the Lord already revealed His plan about the couple planned for the homestead, she was in no hurry to sell until they showed up.

Raine asked Price to take her by the old homestead and they stretched their legs for a few minutes. Raine gave Price the grand tour. Then they settled on the front porch steps, as she reminisced about her youthful days. She was able to introduce Price to the Bartley twins and their younger sister, who happened to be passing by in her old buggy. She asked how the family was getting along and heard all the details. Those boys loved to talk, but not as much as their sister who seemed to lead the conversation, not wanting to leave anything out. As they were leaving Raine extended her greetings to be passed on to their parents. *It was good to see them,* she fondly thought.

Since it was approaching lunchtime, Price offered to take Raine to lunch at the hotel before going to Adam's General Store, but Raine declined the offer. She expressed how excited she was to see everyone and could not consider eating right now; Price understood. For that reason, he left Raine at the General Store to catch up with her friends and obtain a few supplies, while he went to various merchants in town to take care of a couple ranch needs.

Myra's chair was situated close to the window. It kept her entertained while George was busy working around the store. However, she never expected to set her eyes on Raine, who just pulled up with the fine Mr. Barrett from over by the Paints. "George!" she squealed. "It's Raine Jordan and you will never guess who she is with."

George turned from stacking the sweet-stick in the display bin just in time to observe Raine walking through the front entrance. Without hesitation he rendered his flabbergasted greetings, "Good grief Miss Jordon, what a pleasant surprise. Myra and I certainly did not expect to see you walk through our door this morning."

"It is wonderful to see you Raine," Myra promptly added getting Raine's attention to where she was at. Raine noticed the new addition to the store; a small parlor was added up front near the window, where Myra was sitting in a fancy chair.

It was good to see Myra, a big smile formed on Raine's lips while glancing back and forth, "It is so good to see you both. Look at you, my dear Myra! I see you are still blessed with child!" noticing her small protruding stomach. "You cannot perceive the numerous times I have wondered how you and the baby were getting along."

George Adams quickly retrieved his jacket from a rocking chair and insisted that Raine sit to visit with his wife, while he worked around the store. At the same time, he planned on keeping his ear open to the conversation.

"Yes, we are doing well," Myra proudly pausing to pat her protruding middle before continuing, "Thanks to Elizabeth, Doc Walker and my wonderful George for spoiling me. With all this attention I've been getting, I doubt I will remember how to do anything after the baby is born."

Taking the seat offered, Raine responded, "Myra, Myra, no need to fret a single day about it. Enjoy yourself now because soon you will not find a peaceful moment left in your day. I guarantee a child will keep you extremely busy..." Raine paused for a moment realizing Myra was not on bed rest, but out in the store. "I am surprised you are not still confined to your bed."

Myra was only happy to share the changes. "Well, it is like this, Doc Walker agreed relaxing close to George would be beneficial, provided we could work out a place in the store where I would be able to recline. I was getting so depressed at home while George was here worrying sick about me. Doc said if I were to continue feeling all this anxiety it would do harm to the baby. So as long as I am a good girl and keep my feet up in this fancy lounger, the doctor agreed that I could come into the store three times a week...Look at this piece!" Myra patted her hand on the exquisite piece of furniture trimmed in fancy carved wood and covered in red velvet; large and comfortable enough to keep your legs up. "George ordered it special from the Sears and Roebuck's catalog and the chair only arrived a week ago. It's called a Princess Lounger. Now don't I fit the description?" She smiled as she extended her hand as if in royalty.

Raine laughed at Myra's silliness, but the exquisite lounger was impressive, she had never seen a chair like this before; although she often read about such lovely things in books. "I am really happy for you, Princess Myra." giggling as she spoke.

As the laughing faded, Myra did not hesitate to express how concerned she had been. Wondering about what happened to Raine. Especially after Elizabeth's son, Daniel, informed them a week after he returned to New Crossing, "Miss Jordan did not accompany us to Albuquerque, he said. In the beginning months Elizabeth and I spoke often how you must be on your way to Chicago, we prayed for your safety. Then when Daniel tells us this news, we were shocked and did not know where you had disappeared. We questioned Max several times and he would only make a crude remark about you having a secret lover, but we all figured it was just a Max story...we knew you better. Elizabeth watched for you around town, but felt it peculiar no one ever seen you. Except one time, Preacher Matthew made a small comment about how you probably got married, and then he would not elaborate, which only made us more frustrated. Since George seen you leave that morning with Max, but Daniel never saw you; he said his father picked him up on the way out of town. It was all very mysterious and we had no answers. Max was the last person to see you and he was vague about it. Our worst fears was that you were dead someplace."

Raine listened intently to Myra, feeling responsible for the worry she caused her friend, who was fragile with child. At the same time, she silently praised God for His marvelous rescue, as the incident became fresh in her mind. She vowed to never reveal anything to Myra about her brother Max. The miracle of her marriage to Price certainly would sway the direction of the conversation about what had taken place that morning in the covered wagon.

"Myra, as you see, I am not dead, but I am dreadfully sorry to have caused you any worry, especially in your condition. I must confess everything took me by surprise myself and things happened so quickly I did not have time to let anyone know."

Myra interrupted her speaking to interject, "Do not concern yourself about me, I and baby are doing fine...I am so relieved to know you are all right."

"Actually, I am also very thankful to see you, little mama, completely healthy and still carrying your precious baby," Raine affirmed.

The look on Myra's face displayed she was patiently waiting for the full explanation. Raine did not make her wait long and proceeded, "Preacher Matthew was telling you the truth. I'll admit I'm a bit surprised he felt he needed to be so evasive and quiet concerning my marriage."

"You are married!" Myra gasped laying her fingers in

front of her mouth. The woman looked like she seen a ghost, and was completely astounded to find out Raine was definitely wedded. She barely got the word out of her mouth when there was a large noise, getting both of the women's attention. George Adams dropped a few canisters and was promptly scurrying to retrieve them from the floor. He was glad he was able to hide his face in the midst of his embarrassing misfortune, as not to be noticed eavesdropping.

Raine's smile carried an arrogant smirk; she was not unaware that the population of New Crossing never believed her claim about God's Promise of a special man for her. Nonetheless, it was becoming evident to Myra, George and the rest of the town's folk, the Lord indeed planned a 'Blessed Promise' awaiting spinster Raine Jordan. She felt a pronounced satisfaction of the Lord's faithfulness and was eager to tell Myra the whole story.

"Yes, it is true, I am married. Remember the man who came into the General Store back in the spring, the one I inquired of Mr. Adams…that same man was coming into town to ask me to marry him the morning I was leaving for Albuquerque. When he saw me in the covered wagon with Max heading out of town he was confused for a moment, as the Lord told him we were chosen to be together. So he turned his buggy around and caught up with us and convinced Max to stop at the edge of town, near Elizabeth's home. He boldly, with such confidence approached our covered wagon and simply informed me I was going the wrong way." Raine's face flushed a little and she giggled at the memory of that moment before gathering her thoughts to continue. "I felt a drawing attraction to him from the time our eyes met outside the store back in April. I found my words telling him that he was absolutely right and I got off the wagon. It was like I was in a hypnotic daze. I could not stop myself from getting off with him because for some strange reason it just felt right."

Myra was listening attentively, her mouth hanging slightly open in wonder. While George forgot he was trying to be inconspicuous set his work aside to come in closer to give full attention to Raine's explanation.

Raine decided to finish her account of that day and keep the precious details to herself. "Price and I talked for a while sitting on the side of the road in his buggy-wagon. He was pretty direct and confident about why he journeyed into New Crossing that morning. I admit I was the one who was in a bit of a stupor, even after all my sharing about Mr. Right and God's Promise. Yet as he spoke, I began to realize Price also had been given the instruction to wait for God's perfect choice. He told me I was the one God promised him. He knew from the moment he saw me at the General Store. After he explained, he asked me to marry him and without hesitation I said yes. Preacher Matthew married us that morning. Once we were wed, I journeyed back with Price Barrett to his ranch as Mrs. Barrett...didn't Gus tell you anything? He was there and gave us Gretchen's ring," she held out her hand to show the ring. "Sorry Myra, it never crossed my mind to inform anyone. I was in such a daze, what I had believed and waited so long for just occurred."

There was a sacred awe that permeated the air and no one spoke for several minutes. Myra made the first attempt to respond, while George was totally lost for words marveling over the whole story. "Gus never said a word...did he, George?" George still speechless stammered, "n.n.no...no, nothing"

Mira continued, "I am amazed with your story Raine. Hearing about it makes my faith soar to greater heights just knowing the Lord God is so faithful. You have told us all along God had a man saved especially for you. I wish I could tell you that I stood with you and believed you. However, I was one of the skeptic's, I'm embarrassed to admit it and it was my thoughts that were unwise, not you. Forgive me, my dear friend, God is greater than my meager understandings; just look at my blessing from God," she fondly laid her hand caressingly on her stomach. "This child growing inside me is going to be alright, and I have felt all along God has heard my prayers…a true miracle for my weak condition. Your life and faith confirms my hope. Now I can speak it boldly as you did all those years."

George still silent, feeling overwhelmed with what his wife just spoke, turned his face and wiped an escaping tear. He had been waiting so long for a child, and now in his later years God was going to bless him. He felt his faith ascend to a new level and knew in this very moment he would not be missing a Sunday meeting from this day forward. George went back to his work a new man, and let the women continue their visit, while he privately talked to God himself.

Before Raine could speak another word, Myra continued, "I am delighted for you Raine. I am so glad you listened to what the Lord was telling you, even when the town's folk did not support you in your 'Promise' from God. It is like I am seeing you for the first time, you look so radiant and happy. It is clear…being married satisfies you. If my George is a good judge of character, then I believe Mr. Barrett is a fine man."

Raine was touched deeply by Myra's maturing faith. How she expressed that she knew God would allow her to carry this special baby full term. She was humbled her witness of God's faithfulness could confirm such an important part in Myra faith. "Thank You Myra, I hold no hardness against you or anyone in town. Who could have really known outside of me, and it was a long wait...but doesn't that only strengthen our faith? It was good lessons in growing for me to have to wait. Price Barrett is a wonderful man and I cannot imagine life being any better. I am so grateful I am not in Albuquerque or Chicago, besides our ranch is only a day's travel from here. This means, I can visit you from time to time and I'll be able to see the newborn. Remember, we are friends, you will be in my prayers always, as you have been each day since I left."

The conversation was drawing to a close when Price entered the store. George Adams promptly greeted him with a handshake, congratulating him. Price responded with a welcomed friendliness and then exchanged affectionate glances with Raine. Price and George chatted friendly for a few minutes then Price let George assist him in several purchasing needs. Price also collected all the mail for Raine and himself. He knew the Postal Rider would not be arriving on the ranch for a couple of days. He also filled out the forms to change Raine's mailing address so her mail would come directly to the ranch in the future.

Raine was enjoying her visit, nevertheless the long trip back to the ranch meant they should be heading home, it was getting late.

She remembered there were fresh tomatoes and lettuce to put on the bread she baked yesterday for tonight's dinner. "Sure hate to leave, but we have quite the ride back. " Raine stood and moved over to where Myra was reclining on the Princess Lounger. "This has been really a nice visit Myra." Feeling a draft, she picked up an afghan lying on a nearby chair and tossed it neatly over Myra's legs. Reaching down with a hug she whispered softly, "We are friends by a divine plan, Princess...I believe God's blessings is definitely on your baby."

Myra realized she had wasted many good years of not having Raine for a friend when she lived close by, but even though they were further apart in distance now she would never take this friendship lightly. It was good knowing she would be seeing her again. "Thank You, it means a lot to me just knowing you are praying for us."

Raine moseyed through the store collecting a few items while Price was busy conversing with George at the counter. She selected a few necessities to finish the food preserving and some coffee.

While Price loaded supplies in the wagon, Raine invited George and Myra to come for a visit after the child was old enough to travel. "The ranch is called Barrett's Promise. Once you cross the river there is still a couple of hours travel, but when you come to a fork in the road you'll see the ranch sign on the trail that bears to the left. Our ranch is located at the end of the trail." Price came back just in time to confirm the invite. The Barrett's left the General Store looking forward to another day with the Adams in the months to come.

"Wait until I see Gus! They sure look happy…don't they George?" spoke Myra while watching Price help Raine into the buggy-wagon from the window.

George agreed with a nod "aha." At the same time, he was lost in his own thoughts about Myra and his child. He had spent too many days worrying, but now his faith was soaring. He felt this profound peace to trust God completely. "Do you think Doc Walker will allow you to attend church on Sundays if I drive the buggy slow?"

"A splendid idea George, we will have to ask. I have been good for several months…if I have to, I could sacrifice some of my time in the store to attend a meeting." Myra noticed the beginning of miracles unfolding and she felt a deeper closeness to George for mentioning it.

Before leaving town, Price and Raine went to the Hayden Hotel, owned and operated by Myra's parents. As they were waiting for their food to be served, they expressed to one another how delighted it felt to have the opportunity to witness about what the Lord has done in their lives, declaring God's good faithfulness for individuals who chose to follow Him. Raine had no doubt that her meeting with Myra and George was a divine plan of God.

When their food arrived, Price led a prayer. He asked God to bless the food and all the people they had the privilege to have spoken with this day.

Recalling the experience fondly, Raine finished the jars of salsa. She proceeded to clean her work area while the jars were cooling on the table. Raine still felt warm and giddy over her affection for Price. She never once felt marrying him was a wrong choice, but rather she was amazed how fast her love had grown. From that first magical glance permeating her whole existence... *how blessed I am. It will be three months exactly tomorrow when I became Mrs. Price Barrett,* but to Raine it was as if she spent her lifetime knowing him. Pondering lovingly over her husband she carried the last of the quarts of banno yucca down to the pantry, placing them carefully on the shelf.

Closing the pantry door, Raine looked around the room to see what was left to do; the meal was prepared and the home tidy. Taking off her apron, she went over to the mirror, took out her braid and ran a brush through her hair. She arranged it to hang down her back. She was trying to do this more frequently because Price liked it down. Raine wanted to look extra special tonight, knowing Price always noticed when she took the time to primp and she had grown to appreciate his compliments.

Raine went out on the porch to rest in the cool of the day, feeling content and happy. Singing praises under the veranda, Raine waiting for her husband to return home from his day of hunting with Caleb.

♥

Chapter 19

In the late afternoon breeze Raine relaxed on the veranda. She had come to appreciate the tranquility of her desert ranch. Oh how she had grown to love it here, just like Price said she would. Resting in Father Barrett's beautifully crafted rocker, gently tottering her feet to the sound of the rasping windmill. The view from the veranda was breathtaking and the landscape continues to impress her daily. The scene was always changing, no two days were duplicated.

This evening Raine felt fortunate to be observing the sunset casting a rainbow of harvest shades on the horizon. *My...what a magnificence bouquet of color.* She began expressing silently what her eyes were witnessing. *Deep shades of purple mixed with gray and hints of orange splashing streaks. Like the brush of a painter's hand, passionately in love with color...Very artistic, very beautiful! Then why shouldn't it be, my Lord God is certainly is a wonderful painter. He display's splendor in everything He creates.* She sat mystified, watching the great expanse of a desert sunset layering most of the sky.

Raine turned her face to the wind and let her hair blow in the breeze, it felt fantastic, so freeing being unpinned. She continued to bask in her moment as she waited for Price to return. She was optimistic his hunting day was successful, *Price is an efficient provider.*

As Raine rocked, her thinking went in several directions entwining and she enjoyed each one. Life was good; her outlook was completely void of anything to make her feel dismal. She still marveled over how everything fell into place for the Barrett family to purchase this land. Although she never met Price's family, she felt grateful for the foundation they laid.

Certainly her children were going to reap the benefits their grandparent achieved. Neither Price's relatives, nor his parents had any foreknowledge of the vision the Lord revealed to them recently, but there is not a doubt Who was behind their every move.

Realizing that her thoughts were all over the place, and encompassing many areas, she profoundly understood how limited her thoughts compared to His infinite ways.

Holding in place wayward stands of hair, she turned to see the surging waters of the river displaying the winds strength. It was a view just this side of the barn where she was able to watch the river from the veranda. *The river is racing rapidly,* she noted, *it's a blessing to not have to choose between the two views, and this river view is just as gratifying as the desert sky.* She could even see reflecting in the waters colors of the sunset dancing off the current. *The river also changes without rhyme or reason, just as impetuous as the desert, everything here changes daily, leaving magnificent sights for the eyes to behold.* She silenced her thoughts momentarily to appreciate the splendor.

Over the past months, Raine had chosen the river as her quiet place to meet with God; taking solitary walks along the riverbank. She found the movement of stirring waters peaceful, comforting her and escorting her tenderly close to her Creator, which has deepened their relationship.

Her thoughts went back to Myra. Since her visit to New Crossing they had begun corresponding by letters. The ranch was located along the mail route to the Trading Post and Wiggins the Postal Rider stops by twice a week. Normally in the West you were lucky to get a delivery. Pick up was made at the General store and it depended on how close your property was to town on often you checked for mail. *Sweet Lord, You thought of everything.* Raine felt blessed even more tonight while she was enjoying this marvelous spot on her veranda.

Barrett's Promise, she heard the words ring in her head. *How appropriate this name suits our ranch, our upcoming community and future town, I am glad Price thought of the name.* She shook her head in amazement, *it fits so well…we are merely embarking on the very beginning of Your Plan,* she conveyed to God in silent words. *What a privilege.*

The brilliance of the sunset was beginning to fade and Raine realized she had been sitting a long time. She was starting to feel a little nervous, Price was not home yet. Worried, she walked the length of the veranda a couple of times with hopes of getting a glimpse of her husband coming up the trail, but there was no sign of him.

She sat back down in the rocker trying to put her mind on better things, trying not to worry. *I wondered how much time God intends before I am blessed with carrying a child, a son who will one day transform the settlement into a town.* She thought she would certainly be in the motherly way by now, looking down at her flat stomach. Her heart began yearn for a baby, placing a hand on her stomach wishfully. At the same time, she had mixed feelings and did not know if she was ready to sacrifice the wonderful moments alone with Price. *Am I ready to give it all up for a child?* This though stirred her emotions; certainly God would not bring a baby before she was ready. *Maybe not yet Lord,* she prayed.

Glancing up from her lap, Raine noticed the dust blowing on the trail and a wagon rapidly approaching the ranch. She did not recognize the wagon or the team of horses. Raine hurried into the house to get her revolver. Putting the gun into her skirt pocket she returned promptly to the veranda. She obtained her former position, rocking, appearing casual and unconcerned as the wagon moved into the courtyard.

Raine sat cautiously with hand in pocket on mother's revolver. A sturdy team of gray horses advanced gracefully towards the house. Raine noticed a man and woman on the front bench. Her apprehension began to ease some as they appeared harmless.

Moments after, she became aware of the wagon being a two-seater and a young child about the age of five was enticed by the chickens scratching and pecking the sand. Nevertheless, Raine thought it was strange for the family to be so far from town at dusk, obviously they were not on a trip westward in a wagon of this type.

When the wagon drew to a standstill the man quickly scrambled out, speaking immediately, "Mrs. Barrett?" He took off his hat and held it politely in front of him. "My name is Skylar Thompson," then with a hand gesture pointing to the attractive young woman and the blond haired boy in the wagon, he added, "This is my wife Rhoda and my son William."

Raine was surprised the man knew her name, yet she held her poise and offered only a quiet nod until she knew his intentions. At the same time she silently questioned the Lord about them, *Father, have You led them here? Are they 'a family in destitute' guided to Barrett's Promise?* Although, the Thompson's looked more like a family out on a pleasure ride to a picnic or grandma's house.

Noticing a bewildered expression on Mrs. Barrett's face, Skylar Thompson realized he should reveal promptly why they were here. "Mr. Harrisburg sent us to talk with you."

The mention of a well-known family friend quickly lightened Raine's demeanor, "Oh, I see, have you come concerning the homestead in New Crossing?" She stood up to move closer, but not leaving the security of the veranda, she positioned herself near one of the pillars. A twinge of anticipation rose up in her as she recalled the Lord's insight.

Skylar could hardly restrain his excitement, "Yes, oh yes indeed, Mrs. Barrett, we have come about the homestead…" pausing momentarily to look at his wife. "My wife and I have been to your family's home several times walking around the yard. We took the liberty to sit on the front porch steps and observe the neighbors. One time we viewed the inside with Mr. Harrisburg. We are feeling a special attachment to the home and can see raising our children there. Mam, we are very interested in purchasing the homestead. Mr. Harrisburg relayed a fair price and it is suitable to us… we were hoping by coming here to talk with you in person that it would make the transaction go faster. It would be good if we could move into the home and get settled soon as possible."

Since Raine had not said anything just quietly listened, he continued. "Rhoda, my wife, is a teacher and accepted the teaching position at the New Crossings Schoolhouse. We were told you held that position until last spring. It seems like the town school board had not found a replacement to open the school this year until Rhoda showed an interest. Now with harvest ending, the children's classes are ready to start…soon as we are settled." Skylar approached the veranda, eager to settle the deal. "Would Mr. Barrett happen to be available so we could discuss the details with both of you?"

Skylar had Raine's attention, although she glanced in the direction of Mrs. Thompson recalling her own first trip to the ranch and her mind wandered. *Possibly this woman and child are weary from the journey.* "Mr. Barrett will be home shortly and we can discuss the matter in full detail then. You are welcome to come inside and rest while we wait on him," she offered.

"I appreciate your hospitality, but it is not our intention to impose Mrs. Barrett. We'll be comfortable enough in the wagon until he returns. If you do not mind, maybe we could walk around and stretch our legs a bit," Skylar replied with sincerity. He thought it was not fitting to burden the landowners of a homestead he wished to purchase.

Raine did not quite know how to respond and took a few seconds to collect her thoughts. *Lord, I am listening; yes, these folks are new to the West and obviously not familiar with our customs. I know they probably feel uncomfortable with my sporadic hospitality to mere strangers. Ok Lord, just help me with the words.*

After talking with the Lord, Raine felt confident to take charge of the situation. "Don't be silly Mr. Thompson. You and your family are not an imposition. You are in the West now and folks out here are either friendly to a fault or cold as ice. Come on inside, I have a hardy pot of soup on and there is plenty for all of us."

Raine pointed in direction of sundown, "If you did not realize the time, the sun is already setting and it is a long ride back to New Crossing in the dark, on an unfamiliar trail. Besides, people tell me that crossing the river at night is often treacherous. With this in mind, I suggest you relax…we have all night to deal with business."

After her assertiveness Raine noticed a forlorn look on Skylar Thompson's face. If she was reading him correctly he was still hesitant and uncertain about her offer. She felt compassion for him.

Raine continued, "Your family is welcome to enjoy the comforts of Barrett's Promise tonight. I assure you we have suitable accommodations for sleeping." She could tell the idea was too new and had not settled into a reality for the Thompson's. She turned up her persistence a few notches to energize his thinking. "Might as well get comfortable with the idea Mr. Thompson, because you will not be traveling back tonight with a young son and wife." She hoped her firmness mixed well with her western hospitality.

Skylar was put in his place and was lost for words; he did not know how to take Mrs. Barrett's firm approach. He never considered the drive home at the onset of their journey. While the parents seemed puzzled, young William spoke bluntly his opinion, "Oh yes! Can we stay Mama." His eyes sparkling looking towards the chickens, which Raine realized she had not yet secured for the night. His mother Rhoda, feeling timid about the offer looked to her husband for guidance.

Raine's former experiences with children made it easy to recognize the lad's interest in the hen house. She moved from under the veranda, "If you will excuse me for a minute, I have to lock up the chickens for the night." She did not wait for Skylar Thompson's affirming answer. Instead she promenaded past him, stopping to extend her hand out to young William. "Ask your ma and pa if you could come help me? I could use an extra set of eyes to watch the chickens, while I get them all inside."

Young William's eyes darted impatiently from his father to his mother waiting an answer. He prodded his mother, "Can I go help Mama, can I, can I?" Rhoda's heart was quick to melt watching her son's hopeful anticipation, his yearning to be around the chickens unrestrained and it was difficult to deny him. "Yes, I suppose it will be alright William, but you listen to Mrs. Barrett." She looked over to Skylar and he nodded in agreement.

"Thank you Mama, I will...I will be real good Mama" and William gave his mother a hug, smiled at his pa, then he reached for Raine's hand.

Raine took a firm hold of the young lad's hand assisting him off the wagon, while speaking to Rhoda and Skylar Thompson. "Feel free to rest on the porch until we return and you can discuss how you feel about spending the night with strangers." She smiled hoping they would realize she did understand their hesitations. "We have a private bedroom inside the main house equipped with fireplace. Yet if you prefer complete privacy to feel more comfortable, we have one of the adobe homes," she pointed across the courtyard directing their eyes to the bunkhouses, prepared for guest. "You are welcome to use it for your stay. Either one is fine, it's your choice."

Raine proceeded to walk with William towards the chicken coop, sometimes she would skip in step with him and he giggled. She could not hide her amusement and giggled too. She was delighted in having a little guest accompany her. It has been months since she had the privilege to be around children and she missed the fun filled interaction she had with them.

When they reached the coop, Raine asked William if it was ok to call him Willie. "Call me Willie, my grandma use to call me Willie before she went to be with Jesus; I like it."

Raine appreciated the uncomplicated honesty of children. She felt sad he lost a grandmother, but chose not to pry, "Ok...than, Willie it is."

The boy's face radiated, expressing his joy.

♥

Rhoda Thompson eased herself out of the wagon without the normal cordial assistance of her husband, who apparently was uncomfortable with the whole situation. It did not help Skylar's ego any to have Mrs. Barrett define it so clearly. Skylar stood motionless with his head downcast feeling extremely foolish for not planning more efficiently. Rhoda walked up beside of him, touching his arm and speaking empathetically, "Let's sit down Skylar."

She had admired the beautiful enticing rockers from the wagon, but instead guided her husband to the porch bench, so she could be close to him. Rhoda understood Skylar well and his perplexity about what course to take concerning Mrs. Barrett's offer. "Skylar, there is no need to fret over what we should have done. Since we are already here maybe we should spend the night and return in the morning. Mrs. Barrett appears to be a reasonable woman, and it is obvious she loves children, so William will not be a problem."

"Rhoda, I certainly wasn't thinking when I brought you so far from town. I should have left you and William at the hotel...I should have come alone. I simply was not using my head, not considering the dangers...I was thinking with my heart...I love having you and William with me."

Skylar looked up from his lap and spontaneously his hand caressed the outline of Rhoda's face, smoothing her hair gently around her delicate features. "The thought of taking my precious family across a raging river in the dark is unthinkable...Mrs. Barrett is right; it would be too dangerous...I do not know what I would do if anything happened to either of you. We have come a long way to have this opportunity...I will not take the risk of losing you over my stubborn pride," dropping his hand to his lap, feeling melancholy.

Rhoda comforted him with a hug and he responded to her tenderness. She held Skylar close for a few moments before she scooted back to face him, "Look at me," she said. He lifted his eyes, "You are such a good man Skylar Thompson. Coming out West was a wonderful exciting idea and coming here to see Mrs. Barrett about the Jordan homestead was also a good idea…it will all work out, you will see. We are going to have a wonderful life together in New Crossing… it is a great place to raise our family. So Darling, you have nothing to regret, besides, I would not have let you leave without me this noon. I was in need of an adventure and William was so bored around the hotel. He was driving me daffy! If I had to come up with another game, I do not think I would have been a sane woman when you returned."

Skylar gave a half smile. He loved this woman and appreciated her encouragement, yet he did not want to ever forget this lesson, ever! He made a firm decision to not let a careless act like this happen again. They were not taking a simple joy ride around a city block any more like they did back East. He definitely would be more cautions with future adventures.

"There are many settlements around New Crossing Darling, and I must consider safety measures in my travel activities from here on. I will not be reckless with your lives anymore, Rhoda." She gave a nod that she understood.

He was amazed how the West was so different. "Before coming out West, have you ever imagined the vastness of this terrain? When I was in Boston I never considered there was this much barren land…until we set out on this journey. This short venture today has opened my eyes to the realization of what the West is really all about. It's not just an endless trail of scattered little towns like I presumed. Some people have chosen to live in very remote places where their closest neighbor may be a day's ride…in some places probably longer. Rhoda, I believe there is a lot I need to discover about timing if I am to be helpful to the people in neighboring settlements. It is a bigger undertaking than I considered and frankly I am not sure I am up to it." The whole reality overwhelmed him. "However I promise you this, I will to do my best to adjust my old ways to adapt to this life. This is our home now!"

"Skylar, I think we all must learn new ways to adjust in this place. You are right; it is very different from what we were accustomed to back in Boston. Be that as it may, I think you are the right man for this job and so does Doc. Walker. We will get use to these new ways and soon we won't remember it being any different."

Rhoda glanced around the ranch, "I actually love the area with its vast vacant land…I find it peaceful and unhurried. As for New Crossing, it is certainly a perfect place for us. The people we have met are so resilient and accommodating, even out here, Mrs. Barrett seems to be delighted to have us stay. She even has offered to feed us on a moment's notice…this would have never happened back in Boston."

"The woman believes I am a reckless man, lacking any sense to care for a family."

Rhoda laughed, "Oh Sky, I am sure she has figured out we are new to these parts. After all, we came here with the intention of buying her homestead."

Skylar laughed outright, it was his first uninhibited relaxed expression of joy since they arrived, "You do make logical sense, but I will have to catch on to western life quickly. I do not want to come across as a complete obtuse to all of my patience's."

The peaceful scenic landscape from the veranda

embraced her, and Rhoda was beginning to relish the idea of staying the night. The hush of twilight lingered and with the gently breeze luring her, Rhoda hugged serenity. Glancing briefly at Skylar and leaving him to him to his mulling, she did not share her tranquil thoughts. Rhoda was confident of her husband's resilience, knowing the time was right for her to be quiet and allowed Skylar his thinking space. *He will sort it all out...he always does. Sky will come to his own conclusions; I am so glad God gave me a brilliant, caring man.*

In the silence, Skylar was also pondering, *what a great wife I have in my corner, one who always makes sense of me.* The two sat quietly on the bench for several minutes.

Skylar broke the silence, "I would have come here to get acquainted with the Barrett's anyhow. They are one of the neighboring settlements who will probably need doctor on occasion...we just did it a little soon than I planned." He was beginning to feel better about the situation.

Rhoda was glad to see Sky's countenance lifting, "Yes, this trip might have been good for many reasons unknown to us, and God will use this moment for something far greater than our buying a home."

"You are probably right again. I need to trust the good Lord more in my many blunders. I know He gets a good chuckle from watching me!" Skylar snickered. He was feeling more relaxed and began to notice the scenic view which had his wife mesmerized, "It really is beautiful here."

While the Thompson's were coming to terms with their situation, Raine escorted Willie inside the hen house. She pondered a few ideas concerning this family's unexpected visit. *The Thompson's must really be interested in the family homestead; after all they were quite impulsive, not to mention careless, traveling out here so late in the day.* In her formulating an opinion, God instantly reminded her of the many impulsive careless things she's also done in this life. She instantly regretted her thoughts and told Him she was sorry. A gentle whisper followed her repentance, "This is My doing Raine, enjoy the company." Humbled again, she turned her attention to the boy.

Young Willie quickly focused his interest on some baby chicks. He became quite enamored with them, coming up with names for each one. Raine enjoyed having Willie around. He was satisfying the homesickness she had been feeling for the children in her class. She caught herself pondering often this week about them and wondering how much they've grown over the summer. Now watching Willie, each child's smiling face came to her, picturing them vividly in her mind's eye. She remembered how the first day back in class unfolded and how each of the children would share their stories of harvest time. The town children would tell different things that kept them busy over the summer. Oh how she enjoyed reconnecting every autumn. A bit of sadness overcame her realizing this was the time of year when she would normally be preparing to open the school house. Funny she never thought she would miss teaching this much. Skylar Thompson's words resounded, realizing this pleasure would now be Mrs. Thompson's.

Making every effort to tuck these thoughts away, she shifted her attention to the lad. "Would you like to help me collect the eggs tomorrow morning?" she asked him.

Willie concentration being absorbed with the chicks, found it hard to answer. Raine repeated the question again. This time the words penetrated his hearing, "If Pa lets us stay…I would very much like to collect eggs, Mrs. Barrett." While Raine changed the water and filled the feed troughs, Willie was gently petting the chicks yellow fluffy down.

When the chores were completed, Raine offered her opinion, "I think your dad is a very smart man and once he realizes the lateness in the day I expect that you will be staying. Nevertheless, collecting eggs will require you being up early. We will need to retrieve them before breakfast to feed everyone…do you sleep late?"

He giggled at the thought of her asking, "Mrs. Barrett, I turned six last week!" as if she should have known, for no boy of six sleeps late. "I get to go to school this year with Mama."

Raine squatted down to be closer and picked up one of the chicks, petting its fluffy down, "Oh, I should have known, silly me. Guess that would make a big difference to your sleeping late.

He quickly responded, "That's ok. I am short for my age."

"Really I thought you were seven." He smiled

"Willie, it's time to go back to the house now and let these chicks get to sleep with their mama. Besides the older ones will need to be up early so they can provide us with plenty of eggs." She gently set down the little chick she was holding and stood to wait for him.

"Ok." Willie positioned the baby chick carefully down beside the flock. He already decided on a name for this particular little fur-ball, calling it Puff. It was his favorite he confessed. Then he went out hanging onto Raine's shirt as she had instructed. She paused outside the coop securing the door tightly to keep out any predators and wondered if he would be able to find Puff in the morning, as they all look alike, laughing silently.

Raine and Willie were approaching the porch, where Skylar and Rhoda were sitting, when Price arrived. He was dragging a sled behind him, carrying a longhorn and a mule deer tied to it. Before Price could say anything, Raine informed, "These are the Thompson's." She waved her hand motioning to the couple sitting on the porch, "Rhoda and Skylar." Ruffling the blond hair on the young boy standing beside her, she added, "and this big boy here is Willie."

Willie smiled from ear to ear and waved his small hand to greet the giant man upon the horse. At the same time he was quick to get close to his parents, embracing the comfort of their protection. For he was sure the big man killed those animals with his bare hands.

Raine continued telling Price the details surrounding their unexpected guest's, "The Thompson's will be staying at Barrett's Promise tonight and have agreed to join us for supper." She looked at Mr. Thompson, making sure she did not offend him with her confidence and he quickly gave a favorable nod of acceptance along with a slight boyish grin.

Price removed his hat. He certainly did not want the visitors to think him rude natured, even if he was a little famished. Then in a mannerly way he let them know they were most welcome. "It is my pleasure to meet everyone, Skylar, Rhoda, young Will." He gave a personal nod to each. "I am looking forward to sharing a meal and the company. It is a luxury we rarely get in these parts. However, if you will excuse me for about an hour, I have to hang these carcasses in the barn."

Skylar spoke promptly, "If you would allow me to accompany you Mr. Barrett, maybe I could be of some help. I am not skilled in such matters, however, I learn quickly...if you do not object to guiding me thru some things."

Price looked pleased at the offer and replied, "There's not much to hanging a carcass, Skylar. You'll catch on pretty fast. I would welcome your help and even more some talk." Price fashioned his hat back on his head, "By the way, the formalities can be left on the porch, call me Price." Circling his horse and sled around, he looked back over his shoulder to Skylar. "Bring your wagon to the barn for the night, we can water and feed the horses…they must be tired from the trip out here. I am assuming you journeyed out from New Crossing."

"We did! A trip I am eager to make more often in the future." Skylar looked to Rhoda and she confirmed with a glance that the arrangements were pleasing with her. He climbed in the wagon, looked intentionally at Raine and nodded, "Thank you for your offer Mrs. Barrett."

As Raine watched the men making their way to the barn she took a brief moment to appreciate the breeze in the post evening air, *it feels strange to entertain guests. This visit from the Thompson's is quite different than the visits with Caleb and Ruth. When they come over, it involves some labor worked on together and if time permits, a short relaxing moment for tea or coffee afterwards.* She turned to Rhoda and Willie, walking around them so she could open the door hospitably, "Come inside, I am glad you decided to stay."

Young William was more than eager to respond, "Me too Mrs. Barrett." While Rhoda gave a gentle response, "Thank you for opening your home to us."

Opening the door, Raine replied, "Don't give it a second thought, it is going to be fun to have company."

Rhoda pitched right in helping Raine with the final preparations for supper. It was not long before the women discovered that they get along extremely well.

Both being fond of teaching, gave them a great deal in common. They enjoyed sharing classroom stories; from back East to the rugged West, realizing children were not much different. Miraculously, a deep bond between them was rapidly taking shape. It was almost as if they were natural sisters who had not seen each other for some time. Oddly enough they had similar mannerisms and felt the same about a variety of topics, just as sisters growing up together would.

Raine had to articulate this similarity, "If I would have had a sister I am sure she would have been a lot like you. We are so much alike, it is incredible."

Rhoda was glad Raine expressed her thoughts, because she was experiencing the same feelings, "I never met anyone I have connected with this quickly before and I did not have a sister growing up either. I have two brothers who are much older; it was almost like being an only child. By the time I was eleven they were both out of the house. We are going to be great friends…I really like you Raine."

Raine smiled, picking up a warming basket for the biscuits, "Thank you, I like you too Rhoda." As she filled the basket she wondered what was taking the men so long, *I thought they would be in by now.*

Raine watched her new friend setting dishes on the table and she decided to set aside her jealousy. She felt foolish now being so envious of Rhoda, *taking over my teacher's position,* as if she held an exclusive entitlement to the job. Instead she sincerely wanted to support Rhoda, by giving her exclusive insights on the students.

Raine began filling Rhoda in on the special needs of different children in her class. She even managed to share her method of exams and grade passing procedures that was different than the board wanted. She explained it was to prevent children from experiencing ridicule from their peers. Defending her stand based the principles that every student had their own individual speed in which they learned. Rhoda was impressed with Raine's insight and decided she would carry out the same method in the tradition set by Miss Jordon.

Then the topic came up about her most difficult student, Billy Sprats, just in case he should return this year. They both agreed, it was time for Mr. Sprats to take his son as an apprentice on his farm and keep Billy at his side, but after discussing the issue they both had the gut feeling, it was highly unlikely.

Willie was a boy with great resources within himself. Once he seen Trader, he was on a mission. All during the time his mother helped with the meal, he was happy to entertain the dog on the floor. As for Trader, let's say he was overly delighted having a child in the house to take care of. Amazingly the dog showed no signs of scuttling around the desert all day. In fact he had an abundance of energy, more than Raine had seen in him. He was never this energetic in all the months she had been on the ranch, a child around simply brought out the puppy in him.

As they waited on the men, Raine and Rhoda continued to converse over many topics. Raine explained what life in New Crossing was like and how different it was from what she remembered as a young girl in the bustling city of Chicago. Rhoda found the information helpful in adjusting to her new life on the western frontier.

Raine on the other hand, was intrigued to know all about Boston and the ways of life back East nowadays. About things she had only read about in periodicals and she especially wondered about the motorized buggy.

The conversation of the two women came to an end

when they heard Price and Skylar approaching the house, as the men were laughing and talking loudly. "They apparently are getting along," Raine giggled and Rhoda agreed.

♥

Chapter 20

As they gathered around the table for supper Price drew everyone together for prayer, "Shall we bow our heads?" Without hesitation the Thompson's folded their hands while Price extended his hand to Raine, as it has become their family custom. "My gracious Father God, Thank You for our new friends, our time together and for their safe journey. May our lives give honor to Your name, we appreciate our daily portion, which You have generously provided; bless the food, In Jesus Name, Amen."

Skylar was not in the least bit bashful about eating, being brought up in a family of twelve, he dug right in like a starving man. After the first couple of mouthfuls he rendered compliments to the cook. "The soup is great Mrs. Barrett, so delicious, and the bread…I have never tasted a grain of this type before."

"Thank you, the flour is a mixture of desert grains and maize; it was new to me also. When I came to the ranch I had a lot of adjusting to do. I cooked different things back in town. I learned about desert foods from my husband and his friends." She paused for a spoonful of soup, "Please call me Raine. There is no need to be so formal in our humble home…besides, we will no longer be strangers after we share a meal together, Mr. Thompson."

Skylar almost choked on his soup from a slight snicker and set his spoon inside the bowl. "Alright RAINE (he stretched out the syllables). It is a common professional respect back East to use the last name, I realize that is not this way in the West. So I really need to curb that habit. However, after you encouraging me to change with such a great speech, did you notice that you still called ME Mr. Thompson? I give you permission to call me by my first name too, Skylar." He was smiling along with Rhoda and Price, for they caught the formal address also when Raine spoke it.

Rhoda already felt less formal with the Barrett's. Also finding the soup full of flavor she added, "Thank you so much for sharing your meal with us. I must agree with Sky, everything is delicious."

Young William paid little attention to the adults. He ate studiously while managing to sneak a few tidbits from his piece of bread to slide under the table for Trader. He thought no one was watching, however, Raine noticed, and kept it to herself.

Price added to the conversation, "Knowing my Raine, there is absolutely nothing you could have done to get off this ranch without a hot meal that would have worked, especially after traveling so far. Nonetheless, I agree with you, she is a remarkable cook." His eyes shifted in Raine's direction and gave an affirming wink. "Did I mention she is an incredible wife," and with that affirmation he took a bite from the piece of bread he was sporadically waving while he was speaking.

Raine felt her cheeks flush. Was she ever going to get use to this man's outward compliments? *I wish he would not be so flattering in mixed company…he leaves little room for imagination about our romance.* She felt self-conscious, although truthfully she would not have him any other way. Raine quietly ate her soup, listening to the conversation at the table, but her silent thoughts were on her husband. *I wonder if my husband's affection will end someday,* she did not like that idea. *In my observation of marriages in town, innocently those bubbling romantic people are now taking each other for granted and have forgotten the precious love which brought them together in the first place.* This thought made her sad. *Maybe we will be different.*

Remembering it was not the love of each other that brought them together, but rather their love for God. *Myra & George seem to have rekindled the flames since the pregnancy.* Raine wondered what kind of marriage and Skylar and Rhoda had; *they seemed attentive to each other.* She hoped it was a good marriage; she really liked them. Raine let her thoughts rest, and focused on the topic being discussed.

The men were rambling on about life in the desert. Skylar was very interested and being new to the West hung on every word Price spoke. The women listened with interest. Periodically Raine would add something. With Price being a skilled desert rancher of thirty years, his experience created a fantastic educator about this way of life. Raine considered the details that cultivated Price's knowledge. *Price was fortunate to have his Uncle Cuate' and Caleb in his life, no doubt their knowledge added to his success. Being friends with Caleb is a great advantage, for generations his native culture knew how to survive the barrens. Uncle Cuate' skills of adobes and farming desert land in Mexico, was the right blend to make life adaptable for people not naturally raised Indian.* Price Barrett was destined to have this life, and everyone in his life played a cultivating part in it. God did not leave one detail out.

Everyone finished eating enough soup and bread to be well satisfied. While placing the bowl of wild berries on the table for dessert, Raine asked Skylar about his vocation. She knew Rhoda's, but they never got around to discuss what Skylar did for a living.

Price could see a friendship developing between Raine and Rhoda probably because of their passion for teaching and quietly hoped there would be children on the ranch soon. He could tell Raine missed this part of her life. Returning his focus to the question Raine asked and thinking, *she is going to be so delighted with Skylar's answer*. Meanwhile he offered a dish of berries to William and served himself some.

After three bowls of soup Skylar was stuffed. Leaning back in the chair he gently rubbed his belly. He was about to speak before the question was asked, so impulsively he continue on with his own thoughts first. "Before I answer your question, I have to mention how very blessed men we are," he glanced over at Price then back to Raine. "You and Rhoda are both exquisite cooks. Once we are settled in our own place you have an open invitation at our table...Seriously, any time either of you are in town, please stop by the Thompson Diner for a meal." With this remark he saw an appreciative look on his wife's face, affirming she was in complete agreement.

"I have to tell you, when we set out to come here today, I had no thoughts other than business ones," he chuckled. "How foolish of me! I have gained more on this trip than I ever anticipated. We have found friends in the West at last, and looking how comfortable Rhoda & Raine have gotten in such a quick time, I am guessing we are going to be close as family." Everyone around the table felt the same God-given connection that Skylar expressed. "You spoke the truth Raine, after a meal together we are no longer stranger, we have grown into family." Raine could only smile, her & Price needed family.

"After leaving our natural families," Skylar continued, "this is truly an unexpected blessing. I never realized until now how many of the Scriptures could actually apply to us in a personal way. The one that comes to mind is where Christ spoke, 'no one will leave family behind that he will not gain more family.' I think we are an example of this truth."

Price knew the passage Skylar was referring to. He did not add the part about leaving 'for the gospel', because for all he knew God could have called them to the West. He noticed many times Skylar and Rhoda mentioned God, *Thank You Lord for sending them.* He was glad the Lord had revealed to Skylar how the Scriptures are living and active in our lives. It was a good reminder to him too.

For the first time since they arrived in the area Doc Skylar was not feeling like a stranger or an outcast in 'The West'. *Through my own thoughtlessness of not planning sufficiently, God revealed true family to me.* Skylar was on a roll and the words just continued to flow out his mouth. "My wife encourages me often with this saying, 'God will use everything, including our blunders to bring about His purpose'. I can't tell you how often I needed to hear that on our journey from Boston to New Crossing. Many times when my faith was faltering and I felt guilty for taking my family from our protected surroundings, she would remind me."

"The journey was merciless, even in all the trials, with her encouragement I was compelled to continue the course in spite of my fears. Today, with my leaving New Crossing so unprepared, I realize just how absolutely right her saying is and how faithful God is."

Surprising himself of his openness, feeling grateful, he looked at Rhoda and said "Thank you Darling." Rhoda gave a faint smile and wiped a tear from her eye.

"It must have been hard on you to have to keep me positive."

She simply responded, "You were not that bad Sky."

"You are too kind My Dear."

Remembering the question Raine asked. "Forgive me, for not answering your question right away. I am not sure what got into me, my babbling on does not happen often."

The Barrett's thought it was good for Skylar to

express what he was feeling. They also were experiencing an unexplainable family attachment to the Thompson's and were confident it was a God intervention because of how quickly it had transpired.

While Price continued eating berries, Raine spoke up, "We appreciate what you shared Skylar, no apology needed. We feel the same about you and Rhoda." Price nodded in agreement with his mouthful. "We understand how difficult the journey West can be, Price and I made the trek as teenagers, but we will never forget the emotions attached to that trip with our own families…I did not mean to pry about your job. I was just being inquisitively nosy," she added.

"I never once considered it a meddlesome question, and I would like to answer. I am a doctor by profession and a Christian by heart."

The Barrett's smiled in approval and Rhoda was delighted Skylar explained it the way he did.

"I had a small practice in Boston for eight years, when one day I read in the newspaper about the great need for doctors in the West; I was instantly inspired. I began talking it over with God and the more I prayed, the more intrigued I became to answer His call to the western territories. God was beckoning me. Rhoda became equally excited to go west; she also believed it was a call on our lives. Her vocation as a teacher only added to her excitement. Knowing she would have a place to serve in this new uncultivated territory, because where people gather there would be children… and sick people."

Skylar continued to share how New Crossing became their destiny. "yes as I have said, the journey was long and rough yet we were being drawn like a magnetic to some unknown place. We really had no idea where we were going to end up, we just trusted the Holy Ghost to lead us, like they did in Biblical times. We were getting exhausted and extremely weary from traveling, when our wagon train paused outside of New Crossing to make some needed wagon repairs before continuing over the mountains. While waiting for repairs to be done on several wagons, I used the time to visit the local doctor. I was hoping he might know of a place on the route we were traveling that could possibly use a physician. I thought having a little insight would be to our advantage."

Skylar gave a mild chuckle, "At first Doc Walker acted shocked at my question, then promptly showed tremendous excitement to see me. Unbeknown to anyone, Doc was in need of another doctor's help but had not yet sought out any. He was planning to get around to posting his need on the board in the general store and send a telegram to a newspaper back East advertising for one, but time had not allowed for this. So when I showed up, all he could do was rub his bald head, shake it a few times, and looked up to the heavens dumfounded as if to say...You knew!"

"God was orchestrating, and it was the break we both were looking for."

"Doc and I had a great afternoon discussing all the possibilities together, but I still needed to talk with Rhoda about it."

"When I returned to the wagon I asked Rhoda what she thought about staying in this town. It did not surprise me when she told me, during her prayer time she had the strongest feeling that we were to stay here. Once again God had us in agreement and confirmed His Will to us. So the following day I gratefully accepted the position with Doc. Walker."

Raine loved the whole remarkable story. "I just love to hear how the Lord leads His children. He is such a faithful Father," speaking out with excitement. "I must confess I am delighted He led you to our area, but is New Crossing actually becoming big enough for two doctors?" she inquired.

"Well, it depends on how you look at it...Doc is in his late-seventy's. He believes he should be more relaxed and unhurried, and the only reason he has not slowed down before now was his deep concern for the community. On top of his age factor, when you take into consideration all the settlements springing up around New Crossing, it has doubled his practice. With these nearby communities forming, there is great need for a doctor who will visit them once or twice a month. Not to mention the ranches and farms on the outskirts of New Crossing who would benefit from house visits too. There are several homesteads as far out as your ranch surrounding the town. Although it does appear most of the newer ones are springing up in the south area, fanning east and west.

Think about it, just one trip to your ranch, if you had a crisis come up, would take a doctor away for the whole day. Leaving the town without a physician; heaven forbid there are two emergencies."

"So in answer to your question of supporting two doctors, I would say yes, definitely! In fact Doc and I are hoping to publicize the need for another physician. We feel it will support three easily and maybe even four. I am certain God will bring someone when the time is right, just like he brought me."

"For now, Doc is going to handle the town's people and any crisis that come up there. I will be taking care of the surrounding areas. This way there will always be a medical doctor available in town."

Listening attentively to Skylar explaining the area needs and realizing what a large undertaking this would be, Price decided to interject his thoughts. "I never noticed how populated the area is becoming. You have painted a vivid picture in my head to this fact…my word…pretty soon we will be like the cities back east."

"Not likely Price, least not for a long, long time. You would not believe how crowded Boston is today. Especially with the new invention of the automobile; the streets are becoming a dangerous place to walk. On this side of Kansas, there are still many miles of vacant land without any settlers at all. The growth seems to be developing around established settlements. People are gravitating to areas where they will not be totally alone."

Price ignored the topic about the automobile, saving it for another time and kept focused, "It sounds like you will be on the move a lot Skylar, are you prepared to be away from your family this much? "

This is something that has concerned Skylar also, giving it a great deal of thought and prayer. He welcomed the opportunity to share his thoughts with another man, "Rhoda and I have discussed every angle in full detail many times and since the Lord brought us here. He opened the doors for both our jobs; we trust He will supply the grace enabling us to handle whatever this entails for a season. We know this is not forever; even now there are things in the works to make it easier."

This sparked some curious listeners, they had no idea things could be moving any faster for the Thompsons. They asked to know more.

"Doc and I are in process of setting up a small medical station at a mid-way location in the south. If this works out, I will only have to be traveling to the south two days a week, unless an emergency. The medical station will be close enough to service five of the growing settlements. We are hoping to find a person who would live at the station full time, a person to handle minor cuts and things of that nature."

The Barrett's were intrigued by the plans. Price continued, "I think this sounds like a great plan Skylar, I am glad to hear you are careful to not lose sight of securing time for your family because William will need his dad close by as he grows into manhood. I will be praying for God to inspire another doctor to move out West to lighten the load for both you and Doc Walker." Price cautiously shook his head showing his concern. "Still sounds like a tremendous undertaking to me, but I see you are a god-fearing man and I believe God is in this venture. With that, I guess everything is going to work out just fine…forgive me if I sounded negative and if I have overstepped my bounds any."

"Of course…Price…No problem at all. I share your concern for my time with Rhoda and William, and by you asking me only confirm what I said earlier, God has blessed us with family." Skylar set his hand on William's shoulder and excused him from the table to enjoy the dog, "Yet someone has to do this Price. Rhoda and I understood the time involved and the sacrifices when we agreed to stay in New Crossing."

"I would never attempt to manipulate what a man feels God has called him to do, Skylar. All I can do is ask him to be sure God has called him to do it, because without Him in the process we all know things will certainly go sour."

"Thank you Price, I appreciate your Christian friendship. I will always take what you say to heart and to prayer because I know the purpose of your speaking it is for my good…did I mention Millie?"

"No, I do not recall hearing the name." Price replied. Raine also shook her head no.

"Well, Millie is a nurse, who recently moved into town. The woman is the sole supporter of her family and is presently helping out at the feed store. Millie's husband Hank had an accident two years ago which left him with a wrenched leg, and he uses a walking stick to get around. They have three children. One child…a little girl who is slow minded, the older daughter helps care for her. Millie's son is fifteen and is a brawny lad who does not appear to be lame in work ethics and abilities. I think this is the perfect family to keep the medical station open. She acted interested when I spoke to her about it. One thing is for sure, if Nurse Millie takes our offer at the Midway Medical Station, it will help me tremendously. I'll be aware of who is sick in the settlements and what their needs are without investing the time to visit each home."

Price was impressed with the thought Skylar and Doc Walker put into this idea, and that the Lord already sent a nurse to town who could be interested in the offer. "Do you have a place already picked out for this medical station?"

"Actually, there is an abandoned ranch located in a perfect location to maintenance all the settlements and the owners moved back East last week. Doc. Walker has been talking to Mr. Harrisburg about buying it for this purpose. I rode out there with Doc to look at the homestead and it was more than we hoped for. It would make a great medical station. Golly, it is a big place; the family had 14 children. There are eight rooms to this home, a large main room and seven bedrooms. On one side of the main room is a unique wing which has a central room with three rooms off of it. This will serve as doctor's station, with the three adjoining rooms. The other side has three rooms off the main one which serves as a living area with cooking; perfect for Millie's family. The home would be a real benefit to her as they are living at the hotel right now."

"I tell you, Price, it is like God designed this ranch with our medical station in mind. With the three extra rooms on the medical side, it could serve like hospital rooms for the ones who need extra care. Millie could care for them while they are recovering. Sorry for getting so excited...it just amazes me that when we need it...it becomes available and the way it was built is so perfect...if God wills it so, it will be."

"This is fantastic Skylar!" Price was excited "It looks like God is already moving. The place does sound like God designed it perfectly for the medical station. He knew the future of the large family would one day leave it at the right time. He is very much in the business of planning and creating long before we need it...I am excited for you! I will be keeping this in my prayers...Do you have any plan for people who live on ranches away from settlements and town, like we do?"

Raine had been quiet listening attentively and also wanted to know this answer.

"Yes, yes, I am planning on visiting them once a month; unless I get word there is a serious need. Wiggins the Postal Rider goes out to the Trading Post twice a week. He will relay to me any medical information, if you have any needs. He also has routes passing by a couple of other settlements and homesteads and desires to be of service. I already spoke with him about it."

Rhoda, who had been quiet, taking in every word of the conversation, decided to express a few of her personal thoughts on the topic. "I am not worried about the time it will take Sky to get the medical station running. I believe it's going to work out fine. This season, I will be busy checking papers after school hours and doing thing's to prepare for the following days lessons...Raine, you know how a teachers life can be. In the summertime, William and I plan to travel with

Skylar to the medical station and to neighboring ranches."

Raine knew Rhoda was right, "Yes, I remember well, teaching is not a profession you leave after the day is over, it is one that comes home with you…just like a doctor or for that matter a rancher and farmer."

Price was beginning to understand this was just another way of life. Men were called to walk different journeys according to what the Creator designed them to handle. However, he felt extremely glad he and Raine had the privileged to be home every night together. This is a blessing he would not take for granted in the future.

Raine was glad to know Skylar would be making scheduled visits to their ranch. It would be good to have a doctor available and coming out to their ranch when children start arriving. To be certain she heard correctly, "Are you saying, you will routinely come to each ranch?"

"Yes, I am planning to schedule regular visits. If an urgent situation comes up and I have to alter my schedule I will send word with Wiggins so you will know when I will be able to make the trip."

Price chuckled, "Skylar do not let my sweet wife put you on the spot, and we are both in good health. Since we do not have children yet, we are just grateful you will be available to us…my family never had a doctor available for all the years I have lived here."

Raine recognized the awesome benefit this would be for them, and persisted, "When you do come out, please schedule a time when you can bring Rhoda and young William with you…plan on staying the night."

"Are you trying to make sure we will come to visit again?" Skylar asked.

"You bet she is," added Price smiling.

"I happen to think it is a wonderful idea, to come out

to visit on a scheduled routine trip, don't you agree Skylar?" Rhoda willfully interjected. "You will have to carefully schedule the Barrett's."

Knowing his wife was all for this idea, he said lightheartedly, "It is an excellent idea and I promise that I will put forth a good effort to have it work out this way…as much as possible. Furthermore, I myself would not mind some of Raine Barrett's delicious soup from time to time. Not to mention, your home is very relaxing and being on your ranch will only benefit us, it is such a serenity atmosphere."

"Skylar, you certainly will need a place to ease up from your busy schedule, so consider our ranch available for you and Rhoda anytime for some rest and relaxation." Price warmly added.

It felt good for Skylar to share all his plans with his new found family, but he knew it was time to get on to business of buying the homestead. "Even though being here continues to be a priceless experience, unless we can come to an agreement on the Jordan homestead all our travel plans will go on hold. We do need a home in New Crossing so we can start moving forward. Besides, William is outgrowing the hotel lifestyle rapidly!" Skylar chuckled knowing the truth of his statement, "no pressure intended." He looked over at his boy being very well entertained by the dog. "Seriously, the Jordan family homestead is simply a perfect place for us and we are willing to offer you exactly what Mr. Harrisburg said you were asking."

Raine looked over at Price, recalling the discussion

they had concerning the amount. It was clear, the Lord instructed them to ask a different amount for the homestead than what Mr. Harrisburg considered fair; one a great deal lower. Since Mr. Harrisburg was a family friend and was selling the home as a favor, he was not expecting to make any profit off of the Jordan homestead. Thus putting no strain on him to what price they decided on.

Price did not hesitate to speak, "Skylar and Rhoda, we have a different amount in mind than Mr. Harrisburg has conveyed to you..."

Skylar quickly responded before Price could finish, "We are willing to work with whatever you want, if what you need is higher than we can come up with right away, maybe we could make an agreement to pay you directly some annual installments or barter some medical services along with the payments."

Price stopped him, "Wait Skylar, your offer is very gracious, however you have misunderstood…"

Skylar cut Price off again, "You did not make an arrangement with someone else already, have you?" Rhoda looked worried, but held her breath.

"No…no that's not it at all, Raine and I want less than the quote Mr. Harrisburg told you, not more."

Silence filled the air.

Price continued, "We prayed concerning this a while back and decided to take the Good Lords advice on the matter. We only want one half of what Mr. Harrisburg had claimed its worth." Price clarified and Raine nodded in complete agreement.

"Did I hear you correctly…you are asking half of what Mr. Harrisburg relayed to us?" Skylar asked in shock.

Rhoda sat dumbfounded, not knowing what to think, she glanced over at William who was lavishing his attention on the dog; *could this be really happening, my son is going to finally have his own home. It's been so long...he has been so good about it.*

Price and Raine Barrett harmonized their response, "yes."

"That is correct" Price added.

Skylar scooted his seat away from the table, shaking his head, completely flabbergasted. "I truly do not know what to say." It was obvious the lower amount blind sighted him. Never expecting this just made it hard for him to fathom why the Barrett's were giving them such an unbelievable deal. He never met anyone in all his thirty-eight years who apparently did not want to get the most out of their product...never the least! *These people were not in the least bit greedy. They must be the most generous people in the West,* he thought. *In the world!*

Rhoda finally got her voice, "I do not believe I have ever seen my dear husband completely speechless."

"Not often," Skylar mumbled in agreement, as he got up from the seat and strolled erratically around the room trying to comprehend this idea.

Price got his attention by bringing up the actual transaction, "We will sign any papers you brought with you and the home is yours. Show us what you have Skylar, so we can put this behind us and get back to socializing." Making light of the moment, "You forget we do not get company very often."

Raine sat quietly letting her husband take over the rest of the business transactions. She was very proud; he always knew the right thing to do. She was also delighted to know she would be able to visit her family home on occasions. She could not have asked for any better folks than the Thompson to move into the home her father built.

After the papers were signed and deal completed,

Skylar wanted this to be a fair deal for both sides so he verbalized a promise to the Barrett's. "I will not charge anything for my professional services or for any medicine to your family or whoever lives on this ranch, be it a ranch hand or relative. If they are on this ranch they are family and there will never be an exchange of money or goods for services rendered. This will stand as a legal part of this transaction for however long we both live as neighbors and I would like you to write it in the paper work as a part of our deal."

Price replied, "We do not expect special treatment Skylar," and refused to put it in ink.

"Alright, I will not push you into writing this in the agreement. Nevertheless Price & Raine Barrett, I am serious, I will not charge you or the people of this ranch a penny. Besides if I heard correctly, you will be providing a meal and a place to sleep on my visits and often for my whole family; that has to count for something." He was not giving in, determined to work out a method to repay them for their kindness and generosity.

Seeing they were not going to win this conversation, Price and Raine agreed in good humor. "It will be whatever you decide Skylar. Just enjoy the home; it gives me tremendous peace knowing your family will be living there." Raine meant every word.

"You are not the only ones who get nudges from the Lord, you know." Skylar added.

Raine remembered what the Lord had said about the blessing these people will be to them in the coming days. She wondered if the agreement really meant the four additional families, but did not bring it up at this point.

After getting to know the Barrett's, the Thompsons changed their mind about staying in the adobe and decided to spend the night in the main house. It was unthinkable to leave, when they were enjoying the company so much. The room where Price's uncle and aunt stayed was very accommodating, large with a sitting area and close enough to lay William down to sleep, allowing the four of them to continue visiting.

The two couples sat around the fire, sharing stories about their personal lives, talking way into the wee hours of the morning. When they became exhausted they had no choice, but to retire.

♥

Once the Barrett's were alone, Raine thanked Price for helping out with the sale papers, "Price Barrett you perpetually find a way to surprise me daily of your wisdom...How do you know about such legal dealings?"

Price was flattered, his arms found his wife's waist and drew her close to him, and her long hair brushed the top of his grasp. Looking directly into her eyes he smiled, yet he felt humble and replied, "I don't know anything about it, but I trust God does...there is nothing beyond our ability when we stay close to the Lord. He is all knowing and so eager to instruct on every detail, be it hunting pronghorn, canning banno yucca beans or assisting with some legal papers. It is all the same to Him, He loves to assist the same way a father enjoys helping his child."

"Someday, I hope I can feel as confident as you do with God whispering in your ear all the time. As for me...I don't hear his instructions very often, mostly silence." She looked up into his ebony eyes and melted as if she seen them for the first time, she adored him and cherished the God who created him. "I am glad I heard Him on the waiting for you part."

Price's heart filled with compassion, from her remark, "I am glad you did too! Raine honey, we all have unique gifts from God. I noticed one of yours is to see future events. That is amazing! Also you are very gifted with compassion and love for others. You display it in hospitality and have been motivating in this gift all night. Honestly, I don't have one of those gifts in me. I guess this is why God has put them in you, so I would not be without them." Even though everything he spoke was truth, he could still feel the longing in her to have a more intimate relationship with the Lord and he admired her passion.

"But Price you have..."

He cut her off by laying his finger on her lips silencing her, "We are not supposed to compare ourselves with another, but rejoice in what the Lord has given us." She knew he was right for she read it once in the Holy Scriptures.

Price brushed a strand of hair from her face, admiring her beauty inside and out. He explored her face silently, trying to read her expressions to see if she understood all it meant to be joined as one. To know her gifts were for his benefit as well as his were for hers.

Paying attention to her eyes always caused him stirring, it was a deep well to her soul, and he felt himself fall entirely into them...into her. He kissed her before she could articulate another word. "I have been waiting all night to find those lips next to mine," he whispered softly.

Raine forgot every thought she had previously and instantly was transformed into this spellbound woman, *he always does this to me, but no, no, not tonight,* she resisted letting herself go. Raine loved being close to her husband, yet she had no choice but to shake off this desire of what transpires from a single kiss. Tonight she would be wearing bedclothes appropriate to having guests in the house.

It was as if Price could read her thoughts, reluctantly he let go of her, but only after one more kiss.

Feeling weak-kneed as their wedding day, Raine proceeded to make the bed ready for slumber. She turned down the covers and crawled in while Price finished adjusting the fire to burn throughout the hours of sleeping.

Confident the house would be warm tonight; Price already lit a fire in the fireplace in the guest room for the Thompsons when Skylar laid William down. He left a bucket of fuel in the room so Skylar could tend to it throughout the night, if needed.

Walking to the other side of the bed, he slid out of his overalls, and crawled into bed next to his wife.

In the darkness, she lay motionless in her husband's embrace; Raine could not help but wonder about what miracles the Lord was orchestrating for them...the Thompson's were very nice people. She snuggled closer into Price's arms feeling safe and drifted off to sleep.

Price said silent prayers for the Thompson family, for Skylar's new job venture and for Rhoda's. He prayed for William, and for their relationships with each other and with God. Then he remembered Raine's temptation to want to be like him. He prayed for her to find contentment in the personal unique relationship she already had with Father God, knowing all things come to those who love the Lord. A gentle peace overcame Price and he felt his prayer was immediately delivered to the lap of God. As the peace surged with waves of love, he fell asleep.

♥

✝ During the quiet hours of the night when all in the Barrett house was sound asleep, resting peacefully, the Spirit of God visited them unnoticed. He delighted in their faithfulness and obedience. He placed His blessing upon each of them and on their mission endeavors. His heart overflowed with everlasting love for his children. These five gave Him great joy.

Concept inspired by
Psalm 5:12, 3:5,
John 14:15-23

♥

Chapter 21

As the morning light penetrated the glass bottle window, a fragment of lace drooped slightly over the top of the casement, casting a shadow print on the wall. Price lay motionless barely awake observing the shadow art, then noticing the piece of lace; *it was a peculiar idea when Raine suggested hanging it there, but I have to admit, I like the appearance of it*. Once the thought was fully formed, he felt foolish for thinking it, so much he almost laughed out loud. *What is this woman doing to me; I lay here considering the frivolity of window dressings?* His silly thought stirred him wide awake and he adjusted his eyes to the daylight. Raine was still sleeping soundly in his embrace. He tenderly stroked a strand of her hair that lay across his arm, moving it aside he kissed the back of her neck and whispered softly, "Another day to love you Mrs. Barrett."

Raine responded with a full body stretch, turning to face him she uttered a groggy, "Morning."

He shifted his arm to prop his head up to look directly into her face. He loved looking at her in the morning, she was just as beautiful after a night's sleep as she was in mid-day & evening. He attempted to find those green hazel eyes he has grown to admire. Only this morning, it appears they are having trouble holding themselves open. Trying to stir her awake, he spoke, "Every day I wake up with you lying in my arms I am reminded of how grateful I am that you were saved for me." He kisses her forehead.

"That's nice," stretching again making a slight attempt to wake up, "I feel the same way." However, this morning Raine was feeling exceptionally tired. "You are so alert this morning, how long have you been awake?" She proceeded to stretch once more, twisting her shoulders in a circular motion.

"Here, let me help you," reaching around her body to rub her back between the shoulder blades in an upward motion towards her neck, a generous attempt to get the blood circulating. He massaged it for several minutes and asked, "Does this help?"

Gratefully responding, "Yes, it is working; you always know just the right thing to do."

She appreciated his tender thoughtful ways and could lay there relishing his touch for hours. She nuzzled closely knowing what exactly would wake her, in fact she wondered if it were ok to initiate her affections. In the midst of a soft comfortable cozy feeling, her memory jarred her fully awake...*we have guests; the Thompson's were sleeping in the next room!* "Oh my, the Thompson's, I need to get up and make breakfast, we have guests." She gasped as she spoke in low tones, fully realizing the situation.

Feeling quite enamored with the moment Price whispered, "They are not awake, Beautiful, the sun is barely up." The back message was no longer trying to wake her. He was tenderly caressing her back and snuggling close.

With alacrity, she whispered back convincingly, "But they will be, with the sun up and in an unfamiliar place...no one sleeps sound in a strange place."

Price reluctantly rolled on his back, tucking his hands behind his head. He had to find some humor in this, a full pearly white smile found its way to the surface. Realizing, his sweet delicate wife felt a little shy about their guest finding her in bed...with her husband nonetheless. Price cordially obliged her, "You win, let's have a cup of coffee on the porch. The morning air is going to be a bit nippy so we'll need to bring a quilt to wrap around us. Even if you think the Thompson's are stirring, I will try to be light on my feet in case they are still sleeping. We were all up late last night."

Raine whispered, "Coffee...great idea," she could use a cup this morning with her feeling tired. More so, she was relieved to be getting out of bed, she did not want Thompson's to come out and find them all cozy. Giving Price a quick kiss, she was swift to her feet and dressed hurriedly. Price rolled out on the other side, slipping himself into overalls and pulling up the suspender straps. In no time he was ready.

To subdue the early morning chill, Price took care of fireplace, with more fuel to raise the heat. Meanwhile, Raine started her own fire in the cook-fireplace on the other side of the room. She put on a pot of coffee and set a few things out to cook after Skylar and Rhoda were awake. Not wanting to break her promise to Willie, she would wait to collect eggs when he woke up.

Price waited patiently for Raine before going out on the veranda. Yet she could not stop thinking of what was needed for her to prepare breakfast, and continued a few more minutes setting up. A few time saving steps to make her cooking go faster when all were awake. She quickly stirred a batter for hotcakes, set it aside and retrieved a jar of some homemade precooked venison sausage from the pantry; an easy addition on a hot griddle. She felt it was a good start.

The coffee was not quite done, however not wanting Price to have to wait any longer, she poured a couple of cups anyway and by adding a little more water to the pot, she let the rest brew slowly. Price had found something to do while waiting, he got fresh water and a few scraps from last night's dinner for Trader.

When finished with dog chores, Price picked up the quilt and a shawl for Raine. Placing it around her shoulders and with his best persuasive mannerisms, he escorted her to the door as she carefully steadied the cups in her hand from spilling.

When Price opened the door for her, she paused for a second and spoke softly, "What an incredible view." The sky was arrayed magnificently with a golden haze that faded out parts of the mesa...*breathtaking.* Price gently nudged her out the door where they lingered a few moments more before settling down on the bench. She handed Price his cup and took hold of her side of the quilt. Both taking their portion of the quilt and wrapping it snug around them, while burrowing close together for heat, because as suspected a morning chill was in the air.

Price took a couple of sips of coffee and was ready to talk, "Looks like it is going to be a fair-weather day...what are your plans today?"

"As a matter of fact I did have something in mind. Right before the Thompson's pulled in our lane yesterday, I was sitting here admiring the landscape and I notice the adobe I have neglected to clean up. With the food preserving I have not found the time to tackle it. After Skylar and Rhoda head back to New Crossing, I just might start in on the second adobe; I should make it presentable for our future neighbors. You never know when God will bring them." Raine spoke feeling encouraged about the plan.

"You certainly did a fantastic job with the first adobe. I doubt anyone will ever guess it was originally designed to be a bunkhouse. Now it looks like a house to live in. I think Pa and Mama would be glad we are finally finding use for those two buildings."

"Thanks to your fathers carpentry work, we have two extra double beds to use. Perfect for each adobe to have one in them...bunks may be ok for children, but not the parents." She felt her face flush mentioning it, but Price never noticed. To him, it seemed a perfectly normal assessment. "Those few things I brought with me and some of your aunt's belongings have added a little a touch of welcome, I think."

"I agree, when I saw what you had done on the inside I felt so welcomed I wanted to lie down on the bed and stay there with you all day," snickering, Price followed through with a gentle squeeze on her knee. *He did notice,* Raine could only smile, he loved to make her turn red, but she turned her head so he could not see it.

After the amusement of the moment settled, Raine thoughtfully added, "When I was working on the first adobe; I remembered what you told me about your parents holding on to the dream that one day you and Sharla would live in these buildings. Then after Sharla passed away, I imagine they still felt they wanted you to be close when you married, because in your father's workshop there are many treasures he created for setting up a home."

"You may be right, Pa made both of those double beds before we lost Sharla Jane. After that, he was pretty quiet about it. I figured he just occupied his time making things he enjoyed. Pa could have assumed Aunt Arnett and Uncle Cuate' would move out of the main house."

Raine laughed silently to herself, she could imagine the close living of his aunt and uncle, and his parents feeling the way she felt this morning. "Maybe your father was hopeful one day he would live alone in the big house with just you and your ma, maybe he was the one who needed the privacy."

"Hmm...maybe so...I noticed Pa would tend to get a bit frustrated off and on. It was often difficult for the three of us to find time to interact alone. There was generally someone else around. After Aunt Arnett died he may have wondered when I was going to find a bride too and move out so he could be alone with Mama. After all I was in my forty's," smiling at the thought of his parents enduring love for each other. "They just needed to wait a little longer."

Raine noticed a hint of melancholy on Prices face, but said nothing, just listened.

After a few silent moments of reflection Price continued, "I know my Pa, he would have never expressed any discontent. I was his only son and he also appreciated what my uncle and aunt sacrificed of their own lives by moving us here. From what I heard of Pa's life back in the city, it was very difficult, even humiliating to the point of outright persecution. On several occasions my father was beat up by a group of bullies, just because he was deft and would not speak to them. It was just an ignorant excuse ill-bred men would use to show off in front of their friends. Yes, my father was very appreciative of moving out here; living on this desert ranch was a meaningful and fulfilling life for both him and my mother, thanks to my uncle and aunt. This was a place they could be themselves."

"Sounds like his life in the city was terrible, I cannot imagine people being so cruel. Then again, I guess I have seen this kind of meanness in bullies, even in New Crossing, but it is so wrong."

The moment gave way to silence, both pondering on the reality of how depraved certain individuals could be.

Raine broke the silence first, "Your family had the right idea to keep children close by. It does need consideration these days with so many families moving out West, away from relatives and their heritage. I think we are most fortunate God has given us the insight of knowing our children will live close, because they are a part of His plan for this land. Not every parent receives this kind of privileged information." Raine was referring to her offspring being the ones to construct a town around the new community that was to be established on the ranch. "Barrett's Promise is a good name for a town."

"Now that's what I was talking about last night, all gifts are unique and God has blessed you with a gift of foresight! Until you mentioned this, I never considered the possibility as clearly as you just put it. You are absolutely right though; we are blessed and privileged to be given this advance information. Humbles me though…makes me feel like Abraham & Sarah." Price noticed the two adobes across the circular dirt clearing, "With your cleaver fixing, those adobes will be comfortable homesteads for a family to start out in."

"Did your father ever plan on selling any of his carpentry? His workmanship is exquisite. There are several tables with a variety of chairs hung up on the walls inside his shop. I admire them every time I go in to look for something."

"I know Pa could have sold them in New Crossing or at the Trading Post and maybe he was planning to do just that before Uncle Cuate' went back East. It would have been my uncle's job to do business with the merchants. After he left, I suppose Pa simply took pleasure in making them. Who knows what he was thinking, but it kept him busy and close to the house, where Pa liked to be. I took care of the ranch and the only thing he really took part in was feeding the small animals. I think it was his protectiveness of my mother. It was something he began to do early on in their relationship in the city. Those early days shaped how he watched over her." Price paused for a moment to sip on his coffee while his recollections of past times shuffled through his mind. "My Pa certainly did take pleasure in making rocking chairs. I have given several away, one to

Cole at the Trading Post and I gave one to Tracker Joe for his help with Trader. Pa even had me take two rockers over to Caleb and Ruth's pueblo, which they and their family have enjoyed. It even inspired them to construct several raised sitting stools for themselves; Caleb was pretty proud of his girls for making them. Pa started constructing a double rocker, but never finished it. Maybe I will complete the project someday for us to use."

Raine felt it was good for Price to talk about his father, his parents had only been gone several months and remembering these things made them feel closer. Not to mention, she loved hearing stories about them, so she listened attentively as she sipped her coffee. It was easy to identify with the high esteem Price felt for his parents. Raine adored her departed parent every bit as much. There is a sense of stability in families who are close. With their good heritage and God's blessing by having them wait on His Promise, she expected her & Price would also have a close stable family. She was appreciative God was so thoughtful in His planning of her marriage to Price. Focusing her attention on the comment about the double rocker she said, "So you have talent in carpentry also. I should have suspected as much." With a coxing smile she suggested, "A double rocker would be perfect on mornings like this." She snuggled in to stay warm and Price responded by holding her close.

Raine had a way about her that made Price want to do everything to please her, a well-kept secret he vowed never to disclose. As if she could not tell. "Is that a hint Mrs. Barrett?"

"Maybe," She said coyly.

"Alright I will do it for you. There should be time to finish it over the winter," he offered. With the adobe buildings still in view, "I am surprised you did not find any critters harboring in there when you scrubbed it down."

Raine pulled up the quilt close around her neck. "To my surprise, I did not see any droppings or nests that indicated infestations. However, it is good the Thompson's did not choose to stay there last night because I never checked the chimney in the cook fireplace. I would feel much better if you would be there when I do." She wiggled closer looking for more heat, at the same time feeling squeamish at the thought of finding a homestead of some critter.

"Ok, I am ready for a critter hunt...sounds like fun, especially if we find any," he chuckled. "Let me know when you are ready to explore and I will be there!" Teasingly he added, "Bring your broom."

"I hope we don't!" she had to laugh about how he liked to pick on her.

After sitting there quietly for a while simply enjoying being with Price, she asked, "What are your plans for the day?"

"I have some work to do with the game I brought in last night, stripping the pelt off to tan it. The hides will make good coats for the winter. I will be passing some of my work onto you later...more meat for you to preserve."

"Your game...oh yes...it completely slipped my mind with company. I was just thinking yesterday I was done preserving for the season; silly me, I was not thinking about the meat part. I believe I can handle preparing the meat alone now, you have taught me well. While you are doing the pelt I will take care of the canning part alone. I have thoroughly enjoyed working by your side preserving foods, but now we can get the job done quicker. Thank you for your patience in teaching me."

"I know you can, in fact you could have done it a month ago, you learn quickly. I just wanted to spend time with you and this was a convenient way." He had to admit it, he did not want her to get the impression he felt she was not capable.

"Thank you, I have enjoyed our time working together. I do have one request, if you don't mind, maybe we can smoke some of the meat, but this time not for only jerky. We certainly have made plenty of that." Raine set down the empty cup.

"No more jerky!" Price exclaimed, pretending to be shocked, all the while maintaining a grin he found hard to hide. "Certainly you must know, jerky is my upmost pick-me-up food. You just wait Mrs. Barrett and you will observe just how quick the jerky can disappear in this house."

A little surprised at his response she replied, "I know you love it and jerky is great on fatigued days…but we have forty jars of it!"

"Only forty jars? Well, to be perfectly honest let's not forget the fifteen jars of smoked sausage snacks we put up. If I limited myself to one jar a week, it will only last a year. Provided you do not take a hankering for any of it. I already share with Caleb and Trader...Are you beginning to grasp just how meager forty jars really are?" Price chuckled then quickly mustered up the best semi-serious expression he could, "You hate the taste of jerky, correct?"

"Your point is well taken Mr. Barrett, I do not hate it and it is clear to see a man would wilt away without jerky. So one can never have too much of it in the house," shaking her head and smiling in an I-give-up way. "However, just this once I would like to preserve some smoked flavored meat for a few cooking ideas I have floating in my head…if there is enough."

He felt strangely satisfied in an amusing way. "Of course there will be enough, besides I promised Caleb a few more hunting trips before the cold weather set in. So Beautiful, we can smoke this batch for your wild creative recipes and we will make more jerky later." After a short pause Price added, "When I get them skinned, I will bring in half for you to preserve, and before nightfall I will hang the other half of it in the smokehouse."

"Thank you."

Raine enjoyed Price's wit and humor, leaning her head onto his broad chest, enclosed in his strong arms, *there is no place as good as this,* she thought. The calmness of the desert in the earliness of the morning left the ranch emerging like an attractive oasis, the mystical golden haze only adding to its personal charm. *God must have put His most precious imprint of favor and beauty on our ranch.* Price and Raine Barrett silently sat content in each other's embrace enjoying a serene landscape.

Sunrise relaxing on the veranda was a pleasure the Barrett's had not indulge in for a while, the demands of harvest time won their attention, and often waking up with an agenda for the day. However this morning's break from daily routines was gentling on their soul. Price and Raine were discovering, the more they trusted each other in conversation, the deeper their bond of friendship seem to grow. It was a great wonder how they ever made it all these years without a companion, because neither ran out of anything to say. Their quiet moments would always be followed by a lengthy exchange.

This morning was no different; they sat comfortably

in silence, simply enjoying being there together. The golden mist lifted leaving the natural beauty of the desert to gracefully emerge.

Price contemplated all morning about sharing a surprise he secretly placed in the house for Raine to find, apparently she never noticed it. The suspense of her not mentioning it was driving him crazy, so he decided to inquire, "Have you been able to read any of the books you brought with you?"

"Truly I have thought several times about picking one up to read, then I think I have read them all, some several times over. I am waiting for one to beckon me again and one will…at the right time. Would you like me to read one to you sometime…I really miss reading to the children?"

"I don't think I like being compared to your students," he chuckled.

"Sorry, I did not mean…"

Price stopped her, "It just sounded funny," then added, "Actually I think that might be a great idea. There is a book that caught my eye."

"There is….which one?" She spoke with a tinge of excitement.

"I guess it is time for a small confession. I set a brown clothbound book on the shelf amongst your collection...I assume you did not see it. I had hoped you would have found it by now, but rumor has it that your husband has kept you far too busy these past few weeks."

Surprised, she exclaimed, "Oh my, No! I did not notice a new book on the shelf. Since we married my books have become secondary to my time with you."

Price was flattered. He felt important knowing this beautiful teacher would put him above her books.

A book perhaps I never read. Raine became impatient and felt impulsive. She wanted to go get the book, but refrained. "What is the name of the book and when did you buy it?"

"I came across this little book on our trip to New Crossing a few weeks ago," he said, feeling quite smug and proud of his actions.

"It has been on the shelf that long! Are you teasing me? I cannot believe you never offered one solitary hint about it before this." It amazed her he could keep a secret for this long.

Raine could hardly keep herself seated, she attempted to tame down the excitement she was feeling. However she did not fool Price. He could see it written all over her face and wondered just how long it would take before she stampedes into the house to get it.

Raine was antsy and could not concentrate on anything, but that book. She was just on the brink of going into the house to locate the book when Willie appeared at the door. She stood to greet him, pausing to kiss Price's cheek and whispered, "Thank you." The she turned to William, "Good morning Willie. Are you ready to collect some eggs?"

Young William stepped out on the porch looking pale, his hair tousled, rubbing his eyes with his fists and visibly shivering. "Its cold out here!"

Raine laid aside the idea of the book to tend to a young shaking boy. "Then get your cold bones over here." She sat back down and held the quilt open, "Climb in here with us and you will warm up fast." William obliged, climbing in on her lap and she closed up the quilt, fashioning it around them. Her warm hands began rubbing his upper arms. "Does this help?"

It was difficult for Raine not to display pleasure in the lad; he was as cute as a button. The blue eyed boy with hair light as wool just like his mother's. Willie's delightful character also fascinated her, *his parents certainly have taught this lil'guy how to charm adults, because he has mastered the skill.* "Quite the chatterbox, you are this morning." He spoke non-stop once under the quilt. To this statement he just smiled and continued talking about everything under the sun.

Price paid close attention how Raine interact with the young boy. Never seeing her with children, he found her natural abilities fascinating.

"Oh no!" Raine screeched, jumping up as she spoke, nearly flooring the boy, "I forgot about the coffee pot, I left it brewing slowly...it is going to be so strong and possibly muddy!" Her excitement over the book had now changed to desperation. She quickly handed Willie over to Price's lap and sealed the quilt to keep them warm. Abruptly gathering the two cup from the porch floor, "I will bring you back another cup when I get everything under control, but I may need to add some goat's milk and honey in this batch."

Price hardly got a word out before she vanished into the house. He thought about the coffee with goat's milk and honey, a *change is often a good thing,* he reckoned, *but goat's milk and honey...in coffee?*

Raine purposed herself to be quiet, not wanting to disturb the Thompson's as she entered the house. The coffee had brewed for almost an hour and the outcome was not going to change by her hastiness. When she passed by the guestroom she could not help noticing Skylar and Rhoda sleeping soundly; Skylar was snoring massively loud. *How could Rhoda even sleep through that noise*? She wondered while cautiously closing the door Willie left open.

Then Raine went directly to check the coffee...it was as she feared. Very dark and smelling strong, however she was amaze that it did not appear to be muddy. After adding a little warm water to it, she poured two cups and sipped hers carefully. The flavor was powerful even with the water added…yet tolerable. Nevertheless, viewing the goat's milk and honey, she decided to spruce it up. After a quick taste and feeling confident it was suitable to serve, she fixed a half cup of warm milk and honey for Willie, so he would not feel left out. She added a little more hot water to the pot and set it in a spot with lower heat. She decided not to fret about the taste and offered a quick prayer for the flavor to be perfect when Skylar and Rhoda woke up, then left it in the Lords hands.

Raine was on her way to the door when she remembered…she sat the three cups on the table and walked over to the shelf. Price had built her a fine wall shelf to hold her collection of books. Raine's eyes beheld the new book immediately, *there it sits, plain as day, a clothbound book, more brownish-orange than brown, but she knew this was the one*. Picking it up, she read the title, *With Christ by Andrew Murray*. She held it in one hand while rubbing the cover endearingly with the other. Raine Barrett was truly a lover of books. She softly let her fingers flip through the pages to get an idea of the contents. The inside page read, "*With Christ in the School of Prayer: Thoughts on our Training for the Ministry of Intercession.*"

The next thing Raine noticed was the `chapters' were listed as `lessons'. She was familiar with lesson books being a teacher, but she had never read one like this. The enticement of reading this book had already captivated her. The topic and selections brought clarity why her husband liked it. *I cannot wait to read this to him,* she thought, knowing how much their relationship was held together and designed by God. This book reading would only add to their bonding.

Raine reluctantly set the book back on the shelf until

they could read it together. She picked up another shawl to put around Willie and returned to the porch with the three drinks.

Raine handed Price his coffee and sat the other two down, so she could fasten the shawl around Willie's shoulders. After the shawl was tucked around him setting his arms free, she gave him the cup of warm sweet milk. Willie was happy to receive it; his stomach was beginning to growl, as he confessed. Willie scooted to place himself between Price and Raine, so he could hold his cup with both hands. Raine secured the quilt on their laps and was grateful it had warmed up a little.

Price felt a little apprehensive over having his coffee a new way. Not willing to show any hesitation he took a sip. Surprisingly it was tasty and nothing like he had imagined. "Good flavor…it would have never crossed my mind to add milk and honey to my coffee, but I may switch to drinking it this way, after the coffee sat all day. If cream & honey can take away a burnt strong taste, I am sure it will transform old coffee too."

Raine gave a sigh of relief; being worried he would not fancy the taste. "Oh yes it does. My mama liked to drink her coffee this way, and I have used this to perk up day old coffee. I actually fancy the black coffee best, but it sure does well for a strong-bodied cup…I am relieved you find it satisfactory."

Listening to the conversation, young Will asked if he could have a taste and Price accommodated him with a sip. However, he was not greatly impressed, which showed on his comical expression. Price and Raine secretly smile at each other, holding back their laughter.

Raine was enjoying the company and watching the changing view of the landscape. "I noticed the book when I was inside…a wonderful choice and I cannot wait to begin reading it with you…thank you."

"You're welcome, I was hoping you would find it interesting. I was intrigued by it and was hoping it will expand my understanding of the Holy Scriptures. Since it was about the Bible and the Holy Bible is the only book I have ever read. I am sure the author found the Scriptures fruitful, after all he wrote a book about it."

"It does look like a book to teach us more about Scriptures and prayer. I too am eager to find out what we are going to learn. When I glanced through the pages I noticed the sections were broken into lessons. It declares the author, Murray, is a preacher."

"Really, I did not notice that," Price was thankful she found the book intriguing. "I was hoping with teaching being your profession that you would appreciate this book. I have to admit, I never heard any preaching I remember, except from Uncle Cuate' & Aunt Arnett, therefore this will be a good book for me too."

"Price, I am glad you found it, I dearly love the book...you were thoughtful to buy it. I think we will get good idea of Andrew Murray's preaching from his written pages," she responded.

Raine shifted her attention to Willie who was politely quiet throughout their conversation. In a soft tone she spoke to him, "When I am finished drinking my coffee, we will go see if any chickens are early morning layers and check on Puff to make sure he had a good night's sleep." The blue-eyed boy shook his head affirmatively and voiced an eager sweet, "a-ha."

Price and Raine gave a fleeting look to each other, then both spontaneously looked at William, welcoming this scene to be replayed one day with their own children.

As Raine enjoyed the last drops of her coffee, she reflected on her life with Price and wondered if she were ready to have children. Presently she enjoyed being alone with Price. She could see children would definitely change the dynamics of their relationship and alter many things she loved about being Mrs. Price Barrett. One thing for sure, she would have to come to a place of knowing a child would complete their relationship, and not quench it. Which she at this time she was not fully convinced it would do that. *Since children are really in the hands of the Lord, He's going to have to nurture this confidence in me, before the time for children.* For now she would not be too concerned with the idea and simply allow God to choose the appropriate time for them to be parents.

As for today, *I am simply going to enjoy our young guest and when the moment is over, hand him back to his parents. Then after they leave, I am joyfully going to continue to focus all my attention on my dashing husband.*

Raine gaze over at Price, admiring how handsome he looked with his sparkling hair absorbing the sunlight and falling attractively across his face. She studied him while he conversed with Willie about his boyhood likes. It delighted her to watch him interacted with the boy and realized he would make a wonderful father one day. It would be wrong for her to not want this for him...but not now.

♥

Chapter 22

Doc Skylar kept his promise. Twice he made it back to the Barrett's Promise Ranch with his family before the year was out. The first time he was on an official routine doctor's call and the second was merely a pleasant visit where he and his family spent four restful nights. However, today the doctor was alone on a scheduled professional visit.

The old timers around town had him spooked; they were predicting the weather was just perfect for some hazardous snow. Skylar feared risking an unsafe trip for his family if the old men were accurate. Nonetheless, with Thanksgiving approaching, dutiful Doc Skylar needed to make sure his friends were healthy before a harsh winter could make routine visits difficult. On the ride out he recalled the time Price sternly informed him how some years were quite difficult for wagon travel and crossing at the river treacherous. Nonetheless, Wiggin's did not have the option; his job delivering mail demanded he ride this way twice a week no matter the weather conditions and he promised to keep Doc informed of any needs.

After Doc Skylar was satisfied that his friends Price and Raine were in good health, he was eager to return to New Crossing before a storm blew in, staying only a couple hours. Just long enough to eat a bowl of stew Raine had on the stove and enjoy a warm cup of coffee before the cold trip back.

As the old timers predicted, a storm was beginning to stir; coming in from the northwest. Raine felt sure Skylar would be home before it got too bad. He had a couple of hours start before any signs in the sky appeared. She was comforted to know he was heading southeast and would escape any harsh winds during his travel, not being use to the change of seasons in these parts. Nonetheless she covered his trip with prayer.

Lately when Raine prayed, she noticed herself praying with more fervency, in the Spirit, as she learned from her weekly reading in the With Christ book. It had proved to be good study for both of them. Price and she would ponder on the message together and when alone with God they would contemplate privately over the lesson again. It was not uncommon for Raine to read the same pages several times over throughout the week, because both her and Price had a deep desire to absorb every concept before moving on. She realized today was a good time to put the prayer lessons into practice, as she observed the dark clouds approaching in the distance!

Raine began securing the outer shutters, latching them firmly in place. The wind was picking up and a cold chill penetrated her clothing. She shooed the chickens inside the coop, hens were cooperative, but that old rooster was giving her a difficult time. Finally she was able to coax him into shelter by threatening him with a stick. Afterwards fastening the latch bar, making it impossible for the wind to jar it open.

The advancing black sky was quickly turning the afternoon into night. In the distance she could see the violent lightening flashing. Raine promptly ran out to the barn and was glad to see these animals, unlike the rooster, instinctively knew to come in. She secured each door and fastened the latches to keep them from opening in the wind. Once satisfied the horses and goats were safe, Raine closed the outer barn door even though Price had not returned yet. Lifting her head to thank God, she noticed the windmill was spinning faster than she had ever observed before. So she rendered a quick prayer for it to withstand the strong winds.

Price had left for Cole's Trading Post to obtain a few supplies shortly after Skylar left. Raine tried not to be concerned; *he should be on his way back soon, unless he ran into someone to chew the fat with inside the post where he could not see how quickly the storm brewing*. Looking in the direction of Cole's, *that sky looks pretty dark and violent.* When she did not see him coming up the lane, she had only one option, PRAY! Raine flowed spontaneously into relentless ardent prayer. It was like she was in two places at the same time, one action taking place in her spirit, while the other was completing the needed chores in the physical. It amazed her that she could successfully do both without any distraction from the other. Only recently she heard about this being possible, a person could be in the Spirit simultaneously while maintaining their fleshly duties. Today she believed it undeniably because she was experiencing it firsthand.

As Raine started back to the house the high pitch squeals of the whistling wind echoed throughout the ranch. She was shocked how quickly this storm was approaching and how aggressive it had become over the last half hour. The velocity of the wind being strong and forceful hindered her from being able to walk upright. She moved towards the house hunched over and struggling with every step to stay on course. It felt like she could easily be tossed about like tumbleweed. The air had become even colder and she feared the storm could bring a blizzard like Skylar told them, although it seemed much too early in the year for this. Even so, she did remember a few abnormal years when there was snow before Thanksgiving.

Rain continued to move against the harsh squalls which abrasively showered her with sand. Squinting and pausing only for a moment guarding her eyes from the sand with her hand. She managed to look down the lane once more hoping to see Price riding in. He was not there. Instead she noticed a covered wagon heading up the lane being hammered by the blustery weather. *Whoever it is, they will need shelter.*

Raine arrived at the main house exhausted and out of breath. Under the veranda was meager shelter. The house modestly blocked some of the sand sprays as she waited for the wagon to get closer.

She stood looking over the cul-de-sac, a word she only knew of in English books describing a circle end of a road without any way out, but the way you arrived. This is what Raine named the area in front of her home. It was a wide space that all the building sat off of.

Raine could not believe her eyes, she had seen dust devils before, but this was an uncontrollable imperfect one. The sand showed the wind twirling in a sporadic fashion without rhyme or reason. This storm was the worst she had ever witness and she feared how bad it would get once it was totally upon them. *Oh Price please come home!* The cry in her was becoming worrisome, although she tried to hide it through prayers.

Raine held onto the stucco column and watched the covered wagon arrive. As it stopped, a frantic man of color spontaneously jumped out of the wagon, covering his face from the blowing sand. He moved closer so she could hear him over the screeching wind. He spoke hastily, "My name is Elisha Blake. Mam, my wife is six months with child and I am asking permission to seek shelter on your ranch from the storm. Please Mam. I'd be obliged if you'd permit me to park our wagon close to a building to protect it from these gusting winds," He pleaded, as he held his hat from blowing off while also protecting his face.

Raine answered as loud as she could, "Nonsense, you and your wife will take shelter in the house. Bring her inside, then go secure your wagon on this side of the barn and take your horses inside, there is an extra stall." She was still holding onto the post to secure herself.

Believing he was infringing upon her hospitality the man spoke again. "Mam, we would be more than grateful to settle with the wagon beside the protection of the barn."

Raine was quick to retort, "Sir, I will not have it! Quickly bring your wife in the house before this storm is wickedly upon us." *Hurry up. We have no time to dabble over male pride,* she continued in thought feeling frustrated with his hesitation.

The man conceded. He went to the back of the wagon and assisted his wife down. The woman looked to be of Indian decent and huge with child. Raine immediately felt compassion, *Oh my, she must be over six months from the size of her.* "Come quickly," she motioned with her hands while holding the door forcefully in place with her whole body, as the wind was making it difficult. Raine encourage the man again to go secure his wagon. While talking to him, she took another look beyond the wagon, hoping to see Price. Still shouting over the wind, "Quickly secure your wagon and get the horses in the barn, then come inside...your wife will be safe in here." Raine took a firm hold of the woman's arm as the man let go of her.

After helping the woman inside and shutting the door a welcome peace engulfed the room, muffling the noises of the storm. Raine guided the mother-to-be to a soft rocking chair, "This should be a comfortable spot for you to sit out the storm. It is far better than battling the wind gusts inside your wagon." Raine could not help noticing the marking of a spider on her left upper cheek bone and wondered about her tribe and customs.

Raine promptly built a fire to take out the chill settling

in the home. She attempted to camouflage her uneasiness of the storm and her concern for Price, by being lighthearted and friendly. She tossed a lap quilt over the woman's legs and sat down in a rocker near her.

Being women, it did not take much for the two women to begin conversing. Raine started the conversation by asking questions about what brought the couple this way. The meek mannered Indian woman did not hold back her explanation. She told Raine they've been wandering from one place to another for over a year, looking for a place to settle down and raise a family. However, due to her being an Osage Indian and her husband, a free-black-man, they were not pleasantly received anywhere; even her own tribe shunned her. She was betrothed to marry another prominent brave within the tribe, but ran off marrying Elisha Blake in the white man's way. This did not settle well with her father.

After hearing the details about a variety of ways brutal people in towns and settlements treated them, Raine understood why Mr. Blake was apprehensive about coming inside. The whole report of these injustices made Raine indignant over the cruelty demonstrated. "My, my, what distressing situations you both have endured. It truly grieves me that you have been treated so maliciously. Rest your mind, for you certainly have nothing to fear here. You and your husband are very welcome in our home. As a matter of fact, I am sincerely grateful we will be sitting out this storm together." Unspoken, Raine was still in turmoil. She could not get Price off her mind and prayed simultaneously in the Spirit for his safety.

The Osage woman told Raine the full story to see her reaction. If she was going to be rejected by this woman it was better to know now. However Raine's reaction left her in disbelief, *did settler express welcome? Does she speak truth? Many have taught me.* The blatant and devious rejections of so many people made her hesitant, *I not trust her so fast.* Yet she wanted to believe.

After a few moments of silence she decided to trust her with her name, since they will be sharing the storm time together. At the same time she would hold on to her uncertainty and observe this woman. She would not allow herself to be blind-sighted again. "My name is Cholena," she said politely, "Thank you for kindness. We sit out storm here…home warm. We go when danger passes."

"I am pleased to meet you Cholena," Raine never heard the Osage name before, "Your name is very pretty, my name is Raine and my husband is called Price Barrett."

Cholena nodded to the introduction, "my name means bird in your tongue, I know what your name means," and she smiled softly.

"We have a friend who calls me Rainwater, I like that."

Cholena did not respond but thought to herself, *if I were around you long, I call you Rainwater too.*

Raine continued, "My husband and I live on this ranch alone, so you will be safe here and be protected from the weather. However, it is not uncommon for a storm to last most of the night in these parts. If this one does not let up before nightfall, you are welcome to lodge with us. We have a suitable guest room." Raine added a question amidst her ongoing silent prayer for Price, *"Lord, is this one of the four displaced families? Are they the first to be a part of the Barrett's Promise Community?"* Raine did not receive an immediate answer, but either way she was glad for the company. It was a good opportunity to show two people God's acceptance and love. Not to mention, she was becoming more fearful for her husband whereabouts and did not want to be alone.

"Very kind, Raine, we leave when weather good."

Cholena no sooner got the words out of her mouth when the door burst open. Elisha hastily entered and the wind just as hasty and fierce incoming with him. Elisha secured the door, as the aggressiveness of the wind pounded violently in protest against it. Being a man of smaller statue, he demonstrated he was more than capable to handle himself.

Raine took a mental note, *smaller than Price, maybe George Adams size, only more muscular, not in the least bit frail.* Elisha dusted off his hat and eased inside closer to the fire to warm up. "I got the horses settled down and I put them in the empty stall you suggested, thank you, they should be safe there, although the two geldings in the other stalls were expressing displeasure for the company."

"They aren't use to newcomers," Raine gave a half smile; "I hope you fed them something and gave them water." Raine tried to be hospitable while hiding her disappointment that her husband had not accompanied him in the door.

"I did, I had a bucket of wheat hay and oats in the wagon. I did not impose on your supplies," he offered. Elisha squatted down beside Cholena's chair to inquire on her condition. Being a protective husband and almost-father he did not hesitate to demonstrated his concern for her.

"It would not have been an imposition, Mr. Blake. We do not mind if you used our feed to care for your horses, we have plenty."

While Raine prepared tea, she was overcome with a fear that went into the bone. She was certain Price would have been home by now, even in this weather. *Lord*

Please take care of Price wherever he is. Keep him safe and thank you for sending these people here to keep me company. She wiped a tear away and then turned to her guest to serve the tea.

♥

✞ Father God kept a watchful eye on the situation as it unfolded on the Barrett's Promise Ranch, nothing escapes His sight and no storm had the power to block His view, for nothing is hidden from Him. He observed in silence, not disclosing the full purpose to His children. The hospitality Raine gave strangers in the midst of her turmoil was examined with love.

Inspired concept:
Psalm 34:15, 139:16, Luke 12:2,
Matthew 25:35&40, Hebrews 13:1&2

♥

The violent storm howled and stammered all evening, prevailing lightning with long terrifying rolls of thunder. Wind gusts battered the shutters. All made for a very unsettling evening. The storm alone was unnerving, but Raine endured more in her mind.

She fought desperately not to linger her thoughts on her worst nightmare. The concurrent prayers she had been experiencing earlier had ceased when her fears increased. She wanted to continue offering these endless prayers, yet it was difficult to muster up sufficient words, other than a simple silent cry, *Lord, please, please, please help Price*. Struggling spiritually to keep the faith, Raine sadly endured a kaleidoscope of emotions which only exhausted her thoughts. *I'm in my home with two people I hardly know, my beloved Price is out there somewhere in this horrible storm, maybe struggling for his life and worse yet…no, no I won't say it...I will not believe it.* Tears filled the cavities of her eyes. When she blinked to focus on her father's pocket chronometer, the trickles of tears gave way to an avalanche, swiftly flooding her face; it was already past midnight.

Raine was relieved not to be alone tonight. The endless squall of wind and bullet size hail gave ample support to convince the Blake's to stay the night.

When it was obvious Raine's husband had not returned home, Elisha offered to go search for Price. Although with his unfamiliarity of the inconsistent terrain made Raine apprehensive. She was certain both would be lost and her conscience could not allow it. The possibility of something tragic happening to Elisha, that could leave Cholena an expectant mother alone was more than Raine could handle. 'Price will be fine. He is familiar with the area. He's lived on this ranch for many years. I am sure he knows what to do in storm,' she told them before they reluctantly retired.

The Blake's did not want to leave her alone, but Raine insisted. She needed to be alone so she did not have to act brave. Nevertheless she was grateful they were close should she need them.

Raine slid open the shutter, forgetting the outer shutters were in place blocking her view. She bravely opened the front door a little, holding it tightly. *The wind is still fiercely wicked.* She stood watching the sky brighten from the lightening, showing no signs of letting up any time soon. She stayed there for a moment enduring the wind, hoping to envision her husband in the cul-de-sac when the next blast of light gave her temporary sight. The thunder which made hair curling clamor throughout the evening, was beginning to carry a numbing sound to Raine's ears. She was no longer startled by the exuberant echoes.

Sadly she closed the door and moved back in front of the fire, seeing their bed nearby only made it worse. Raine missed the way Price comfort her making her feel secure before going to sleep. Now she felt vulnerable. There was no way she could even consider going to bed without Price safely home.

Sitting in the rocker, she adjusted the Holy Bible open on her lap. Raine desired the comfort of the Words of the Lord. However, she was unable to grasp anything. Her eyes blurred and made them run together. What she could read she found hard to comprehend. It did give a flicker of hope simply by having the Scriptures open and near her. She still had the mind to reason inside how it would be a lack of faith to give up so easily, so she fought back the tendency of screaming out her anguish.

Raine glanced at her father's timepiece again, *how did it get to be 2 a.m.?* She sighed deeply and her heart was breaking from fear, *I wish you were here with me, Father…I am so scared.*

She recalled a time in her youth when her family were traveling westward with the wagon train. They had stopped for the night and Raine could not get to sleep. Outside the camp she could hear wolves howling. Being a frightened child she was certain they would be attacked that very night while sleeping. She clung to her Father for dear life. She remembers how he made light of it, reassuring her by saying, 'Darlin' we are all too skinny for any wolves to desire, maybe if they would have caught up with us in Kansas we would have provided a healthy meal. We are not worth it now. Beside once they hear Mrs. Keller snoring they will hightail it the other way.' 'Clay!' her mother spoke out. Raine forgot all about being afraid because every time it got quiet she would hear Mrs. Keller in the next wagon and she would chuckle. As for the wolves, they simply went away. "Just like daddy said," she mumbled.

The memory made Raine feel like her Father was still besides her telling his funny stories. This briefly eased her mind. In this lull of memories, Raine's eyes lids became heavy and she drifted into a deep sleep. The woman's petite form went flaccid in the rocking chair, covered with Mama's quilt and the Good Book lying open on her lap.

The brutal vengeance of the night subsided. The wind could not even whisper and stillness hovered over the ranch. Every life form was idle. Except for an exhausted dog slowly approaching the main house.

Raine was awaken by a sudden noise battering against the door. At first, she considered the wind, but it happened again and in between the sound was an uncanny silence. It was not the sounds she had grown accustomed to all night...not the violent raging storm which sent chills through your body at every crack of multiple thunders and lightening! This was an eerie calm with an occasional bump into the door.

Startled fully awake, Raine arose abruptly leaving the quilt and Bible drop onto the floor. She moved anxiously to the door. Unlatching it nervously, she desperately hoped to see Price on the other side. Yet when she opened it, a visible emptiness pierced her heart once again and she looked over a calm lifeless ranch.

Relieved the cruel storm had ceased, but there was still no sign of Price. However, when she hung her head despairingly, there at her feet laid Price's old dog, unresponsive and battered. "Trader!" she cried out and gathered him carefully in her arms. Although the dog was heavy, she did not hesitate to get him inside. She carried him with precision and velocity, setting him by the fire on the Indian woven rug. Although alive he made no attempt to move.

Raine went to retrieve a water basin, cloth and towel to clean his wounds. Proceeding first to dry the ice patches off of him so she could better assessed his condition. After his coat was pliable again she looked for abrasions and checked his bones. Thankful every joint moved freely, no swelling and only a few abrasions were visible. The poor old dog was in pretty good shape considering what he had been through. Trader was merely exhausted from enduring the rugged storm.

It was obvious Trader was weakened after the unpleasant ordeal, nonetheless Raine was hopeful when he still had an appetite. He ate all the food Raine set out for him and was drinking water. Before long the dog returned to his fit self. He was refreshed enough to even wag his tail.

Observing the dog regain his stamina, Raine considered her options. Her first thought was an impending compulsion to find her husband; she needed to know he was alright. Looking at the timepiece, *5:15 a.m., I wish I had not fallen asleep, Oh Lord, where is Price? Why is he not here with Trader?* She questioned momentarily, *Is he with You, Lord?* Her lip quivered, hoping he was not. *Please Lord, do not let my time with Price be over…I have only had five months, I was planning a lifetime…no…no…I am not willing to let him go…Lord. Please do not take him from me.*

As Trader rested in front of the warm fire, Raine paced the floor contemplating what to do. She opened the inside and outer shutters on the bottled window allowing the dim light to enter the room. *Trader has been home over an hour, what should I do?* This pondering was foolish, for Raine knew precisely what she needed to do. *I have to go…I must search for him,* she determined. *But where…oh my, where would I look...Trader must know*! Looking down at the dog warming in front of the fire, Raine felt sad she could not let him rest a minute longer. It was time to do something and he was her only hope of finding Price…*in case he needs me.*

Raine gathered a quilt, bandaging rags, a jug of water, and jerky. Then she bundled up in the warn pelt wrap Price made for her. Raine had allowed Trader to rest while she gathered supplies, but now it was time for him to move. Trader roused slowly getting his strength back to his limbs and in no time he was ready. It was as if he understood clearly his mission and where they were going.

Raine had no idea how treacherous the ground was until she stepped off the veranda onto the icy slush, catching her balance quickly. *I figured the never-ending hail last night would cause bad conditions, but this is worse than I thought.* She was cautious of her footing, being vigilant with each step she took while carrying an armful of supplies to the barn. Trader was doing better with his four paws. He seemed to have mastered the slippery ground.

The wagon was not the best option for these icy conditions. Nonetheless, it was a perfect choice for a rescue. If Price were injured, she would not be able to get him home without it. Raine harnessed the geldings to the wagon, making sure every strap was secure and maneuvered them out of the barn. Calling out, "Trader, where is Price?" Repeating herself several times as the old dog instinctively led the way.

She stopped several times, calling Trader back into the wagon to warm his paws, while moving slowly in the direction of the Trading Post. Trader would not take it easy for long, he recovered swiftly each time, jumping out of the wagon and taking the lead. The dog was completely in charge. He seemed to know the precise route, while Raine followed close behind with the wagon. She was amazed at the courage Trader displayed. She had never been more thankful than now that Price had such a smart faithful dog for his sidekick.

Raine welcomed the sun sweltering on the horizon and was hopeful its warmth would melt the compacting ice. The wagon wheels were coated thick and she feared they could break. Even with the unpleasant thought, she could not help noticing the breathtaking landscape. It was as if everything were cut out of glass. Nevertheless regaining focus she declared vocally, "It still needs to go!"

Raine was almost to Cole's Trading Post when she spotted Price's horse in a clearing off the trail. Raine brought the wagon to a halt and climbing down coaxing the mare closer. Girl willingly ambled towards the wagon and met Raine halfway. Taking hold of the old mare's reins she led her to the wagon. Holding the horse still and calming her with tender stroking, she examined Girl's condition. When she was satisfied there was no visible injuries, she affixed the reins to the wagon.

After the horse was tied securely, she examined the saddlebags and found the items Price purchased from Cole's. This meant Price was leaving the Trading Post not arriving. This was insightful to know where to begin her search.

"Trader!" she shouted firmly, "Where is Price!" With encouragement, the dog moved promptly. He led her to a place where the ground was rugged. Raine continued to follow the dog with the wagon uncertain how far she would be able to go. Slowly holding the reins steady, with Girl tied to the back, Raine moved the wagon further than she knew was safe. Yet the wagon endured the harsh ground. Raine halted the movement, it was evident she was closely approaching a cliff. Feeling slightly defeated she groaned, "What next!"

Overtaken with worry, Raine could hardly think. Price was nowhere to be seen. She got out of the wagon and began to follow Trader on foot. Although finding it difficult to walk with her feet slipping frequently in the bitter slush. Even so, Raine continued vigilantly without stopping. She had to keep up with Trader because the dog seemed to know exactly where he was going. She was already exhausted, but watching his determination gave her hope she would find Price. Although with the dangerous rocky decline of the land Raine was fearful of what condition he would be in when she found him.

Raine tried to visually search out the area, noticing everything. Every bush, rock, shade on the ground, but nothing was moving. Not paying attention to where she was placing her feet, she slipped, unable to keep herself from tumbling until she hit at the bottom of the crest. She was fine and slowly regained her stance. Evaluating her predicament she wondered if she would be able to make it back up the ridge to high ground, especially with this sludge of ice everywhere. Her mind started running wild with assumptions, *maybe this is what happened to Price, and he could not get back up the slope in the ice storm.* Her eyes searched the landscape hoping for any sign of him, yet saw nothing…not even Trader! Yet Raine could not give up; *he has to be here someplace*, so with whispered prayers, she pressed on alone carefully.

Raine searched for hours in the hazardous terrain at the bottom of the ridge. She wandered along vast clearings and searched several brush areas without any signs of Price. She checked every possible place he could have taken shelter. She was out of ideas of where to look when Trader showed up. She tried several other places each farther away from the cliff she had tumbled down. Yet the dog did not follow her. Trader seemed to lose his momentum and stayed at one location.

She began to notice that where Trader refused to leave the ground was empty of slush. She walked back and checked the area again. *Strange…no icy covering by this small ditch, indicating an animal or someone had been here during the storm.* Raine was certain it was Price. However he was no longer here, *he must have moved to a safer spot*. Since the land did not show any tracks; she had to rely on her instincts to figure out which direction he could have gone. Raine tried to coax Trader to help her, but he was fixated on the spot and would not leave it.

Wearing the heavy pelt wrap only added to her exhaustion. She wished she left it in the wagon. *It did protect me when I fell!* There was no choice Raine had to endure the weight moved on.

Raine continued to search the lower ground the best

she could, determine not to give up. Yet there was no place left to look. It was time to consider other options. *This endless search is not getting anywhere, I am so frustrated Lord...maybe Price made it up to the Post, or someone else found him and took him there.* Raine decided to go to Cole's Trading Post and see if anyone knew anything, *maybe he is still there.*

Raine went back to the spot Trader was resting, feeling compassion on him she stroked his head. "You are a good dog...I am worried too...let's go find Price, he is not here...Trader, let's go find Price," she repeated it as she began to leave and was able to convince the dog to come with her.

Some of the slush melted during the hours Raine was searching. This made the hike up the rough ridge somewhat easier than expected, but not without minor incidents. Her footing slid from time to time, accruing some abrasions on her legs. It was of little concern to her. She was steadfast on finding Price. Trader had his own route up the cliff, one he probably found his first time up when he came to get help.

At the top of the ridge Trader joined her at the wagon. Raine found maneuvering of the wagon back to the main trail a bit tricky. Coming out to the ridge was much easier because the slush actually made the ground smoother for the wagon and horses to travel. Now she found herself in a rock-strewn field. These rocks were not small by any means, most were the size of melons, only rougher. Raine had to physically lead the horses over the bulging rocks slow and carefully. The horses were not her only concern she needed to take precautions to not break a wheel. With persistence and patience she was able to get the wagon and horses back on the main trial safely. At which time she got into in the wagon and proceeded to Cole's Trading Post.

After talking to the men at the Trading Post, Raine regretfully gave up the search; no one had any information about Price. She wanted to cry and fear continued to plague her, yet Raine refused to give up hope. She was hanging onto optimism by a thread. Hoping someone had rescued Price and he was healing well in a trapper's cabin. *Then again, maybe Price is home now.* Feeling frightened mixed with hopeful ideas of this turning out ok, she climbed back into the wagon.

The weather was visibly warmer, yet Raine was still chilled. The sun was up in the eastern sky and from the location, it was nearing lunchtime. Raine took off the pelt coat and tossed it over her legs. Her shoulders felt better, they could not endure the heaviness a minute more. She rode back to the ranch with Trader resting on the floorboard under her feet, covered also by the coat.

Once in comfort of the barn Raine took extra time caring for the geldings. They needed a little pampering after being out in such horrible conditions. She gave Girl a little more attention and wished animals could speak, so Girl and Trader could tell her what happened. A part of her was anxious to run into the house and find Price, but on the other hand, she did not want to be disappointed by his absence. Raine made sure the horses were all brushed, fed and watered. While she was out there she took care of the goats as well. On the way to the house she stopped to care for the chickens and got a pale of fuel for the fireplace.

Raine approached the door and hesitated…opening it slowly. As feared, the home was still missing her beloved husband. She looked into the faces of Elisha and Cholena and could not speak. Slumping into a straight-chair at the table, she buried her face into her hands and began to weep. Raine was weak, exhausted and frustrated. Her time searching had not changed a thing.

Combined with the lack of sleep, every facet within her exploded into an emotional breakdown. At the table, she cried and wailed; inflicting her body with vicious tremors. She could care less about the Blake's being there, it never entered Raine's mind to subdue the outburst any longer. Her pain was too deep.

Elisha took the pail from where Raine had left it and proceeded to refuel the fire, while Cholena looked around the house to find some coffee or tea to make for Raine. She wipe a tear from her eye sympathizing with the pain Raine must be feeling. Both of the Blake's were saddened by the situation, but uncertain of what to do.

Raine continued crying and did not even look up, when Cholena brought her a cup of tea. She offered it to Raine hoping it would somehow help, but Raine refused.

Tormented in her anguish she lifted her head, dazed and looked over at Elisha working on the fire. Remembering the Blake's did not have a home, she managed to ask him to stay on the ranch for a few days until her husband returned. When Elisha agreed, she went to her bed, burying her face in the pillow she cried herself to sleep.

♥

Chapter 23

When Caleb came by to check on his friends he was not surprised about the calamity. He already had suspicions of something not being right at the Barrett's. He and Ruth prayed several times together throughout the storm for them. Elisha explained to Caleb what he knew about the situation and Rainwater was able to pull herself together momentarily to share a few things about where she had been searching. Caleb left telling them the search is not over until Price is found.

Caleb proceeded to search for his friend along the trails, streams, and brush area Rainwater described. He looked under every crevice and stump in the area and decided to expand his hunt outside the circle of reference, without success. Three suns have risen and set since Price Barrett disappeared and the storm in its viciousness had erased all evidence of his trail. No signs of man or animal were seen in the vicinity where Girl was located. Nothing was found at the spot where Trader seem to identify with and even the faithful dog, now at Caleb's side, could not pick up his master's scent. Apparently the storm was efficient in its cleansed with hail, then rain and now days later covered by blowing sand. Nevertheless, Caleb was determined to continue looking for Price until God says 'enough'. With his Indian upbringing knew he had an advantage and Caleb will do what he knows best, TRACK! He could not surrender to fear, which Rainwater's agony beckons his painful soul to do, he had to keep trying. *It is good Ruth stays with woman while I hunt friend.*

Darkness had Raine clutched tightly in its grasp claiming that her worst fear developed into reality. As daylight pierced her poorly lit room, she increasingly became more enraged with God than she was the previous night. Words of despair and anger echoed in her mind regularly, *why did You not answer my prayers… how could You do this to me? You had me wait for forty-two years to be a bride…to have him, then only give me his pleasure for five months; You are a cruel God!* Raine tossed the feather pillow over her head to block out the fourth day's sunrise and wept again. Her tears had not dried out in the normal fashion, but an abundant supply drizzled out puffy sockets. Even when Raine did not weep, her eyes kept up the practice.

The Blake's conscience could not leave Raine Barrett alone in her condition, so they continued to stay trying to be of help. They believed some strange fate brought them to the Barrett's ranch at this time and they would stay with the grieving wife until she was on her feet again. 'How long' was a question they often asked themselves? Even though Raine made no attempt to know them personally, they still felt committed. It was all they could after she was so willing to help them. So they continue to be there and watch her slowly drown, in the midst of overwhelming trauma.

Caleb stopped by the ranch several times during the day in the midst his endlessly searching for Price. Ruth never left Raine's side during the daylight hours, tending to her needs. She brought a special blend of calming tea and burned relaxing herbs inside the house. She administered regular applications of an Indian potion to the abrasions on Raine's legs.

While at the ranch, Ruth observed Cholena's service fixing meals and cleaning the home and Elisha caring for animals and needs of the ranch. After spending time with the Blake's and observing their character, how willing they were to help Raine during this troubled time, was a comfort to Ruth. She openly placed a lot of confidence in Cholena's care. With her being an Osage Indian she was already familiar with herbs and teas to prepare in the evenings after she left. There was only one concern, but it was temporal. The Blake's were not Believers...*All in Creator's time, our Master has plan.* She knew in her heart if they were to stay on the ranch long enough around Raine, they would soon find their faith.

Before Ruth left each evening she made it a point to have her friend join her in a time of prayer. Raine would reluctantly comply, so Ruth would go away. For the time being, it seemed Raine preferred to indulge privately in her own misery. This unspoken compliance was no secret to Ruth, yet they did pray.

Cholena consistently tried to persuade Raine to eat something, but it was of little avail. "Raine Barrett, four suns you not eat enough to keep bird alive, please come to table...eat today," Cholena coaxed. Only this time she did not give up easily, and became insistent that Raine eat something. Ruth joined in the effort, also being persistent.

After great deal of persuasion from both of the women, Raine finally gave in. At a snail's pace she came to the table to eat some of Cholena's Osage stew. Raine toyed methodically with the spoon, finding it hard to put anything into her mouth. She lacked enthusiasm and appetite to eat. It was not that she was ungrateful and lacked appreciation for Cholena's help. Nor was she totally oblivious of the time Cholena invested in cooking; she simply did not have a hunger for anything, in fact she thought she was doing well drinking that strange tea.

Once getting Raine to the table, Elisha, Cholena, and Ruth sat down to join her for dinner, when Trader became ecstatic, barking and scratching at the doors.

Raine glanced up slightly from her bowl, not giving it

a great deal attention. She figured the dog had become attached to Caleb after all the time they spent together searching and he was just making a fuss because Caleb was back. She could not bring herself to respond in any manner, good or bad.

The front door swung open and the dog ran out, and Caleb spoke loudly for Elisha to come help him. Raine paid little interest as Elisha left the table. The only reason she was at the table at all was to appease Cholena and Ruth. She certainly did not wish to greet optimistic Caleb tonight. The best thing she could do was to force a few bites down and retreat quickly to her bed. Maybe then Caleb would not bother her for a meager comment and just go home.

Raine glanced towards the door when it opened. Caleb stepped in first, behind him a stretcher in which he and Elisha were carrying. On the stretcher laid Price Barrett. Raine refused to get up, she caught a glimpse of him and knew who it was, but lowered her head. She was afraid to look fearing he was dead. *All wondering is over;* she despaired giving a side glance towards the women, who were beginning to stand. Raine remained seated, not wanting to acknowledge it.

"Beautiful," she heard his whisper.

Caleb took care of Price's injury using the traditions taught him by his grandfather, while Cholena and Ruth assisted him. Cholena filled the house with fragrant smoke as she sung a peaceful melody. Caleb placed herbal poultice wraps on Price's arm and leg. Each time he lifted the bandage up to the Lord and a melodic blessing was proclaimed before placing it on Price. Ruth gave Price a strong cup of herbal tea which did not smell very tasty. He was too weak to refuse.

Raine watched closely as they worked their healing customs on Price. She stood near to him with her hand on his shoulder. She just had to touch him while she quietly spoke her own prayers in the midst of her dazed condition. The words, *"You are home and not dead"* replayed many times in her head while she prayed. She ran her fingers like a comb through her hair, *I must look a mess, my eyes swollen,* but there was no way she would leave his side to get presentable.

Raine watched Caleb work diligently to help Price. She had no words to express the gratitude she felt for Caleb's persistence to find his friend and her beloved. She would always be beholden to him.

Caleb was finished dressing his friends wounds, he knew the leg may need more attention later, but felt sleep would be good medicine for Price now.

Price was too weak to convey what happened to him. So after the healing traditions were completed, Caleb told Price's account for him. "Rainwater, I will tell you story. Girl scared…lightning strike three times fast in front on trial…make horse go off path. Strike one more time, horse rear up, Price fall. Slide down rock cliff. Leg broke and hurt arm." Raine remembered the area from her search and could visualize everything in the order as Caleb spoke.

He continued to explain, "Price, no have horse. Told Trader go home for help. He there long time…no shelter from bad storm. Price strong man, with Great Father's help, he find safe place. Price crawl on ground many hours…he try to come to ranch. The weather bad…earth bad…like crawling in field of blood where braves die, night long…storm long. Left leg, right arm no work…his journey not easy. Great Father stay with him. Stop in bushes for fast shelter. When he rest…he get strong.

Brave man move again, find crevice in earth. Mighty winds cannot get him, soil warm when he dig...safe spot he stay there. He pray rest of storm. When storm go, Price move to place he can sleep safe...small cave by river. He in cave when I find him".

"Rainwater, we go now, come back first light...man will sleep...you will be alright. Not worry, Price Barrett get better, he strong man of God. Great Father is good. He led me to place Price sleep in cave. Price stay with you, Great Father wants him to live."

Raine thanked Caleb for being diligent in searching, her eyes were still full of tears, which motivated Caleb to step out of his inbred customs and offered Raine a gentle hug to reassure her everything was now going to be alright. This act of kindness touched Raine deeply. With this single action, Caleb had become her brother. Ruth did not hug Raine, but rubbed her back briefly, showing she too was glad this nightmare was over.

Before leaving, Ruth and Caleb talked over a few healing remedies with Cholena and Elisha, in case a need would come up during the night. Raine did not get involved in their conversation, her attention stayed on her husband.

Elisha went out to secure the animals for the night, while Cholena cleared the dinner dishes. Neither one said anything to Raine. However both of them noticed a remarkable peace in the home. Cholena wondered if this peace she felt, was something familiar to the Barrett's before the nasty storm, nonetheless, it felt wonderful. She watched Raine tend lovingly to Price, brushing his hair out of his face. Then she took off his boot from his right leg with care trying not to disturb his injured leg. Raine covered him with a quilt and made him comfortable. Cholena knew Mr. Barrett would not be easily disturbed, as the medicine Ruth gave him would keep in a deep sleep for most of the night. There was no point to explain this to Raine.

Cholena was glad to see Raine take the brush to her own hair and work the tangles out. Raine had beautiful long dark hair, any Indian maiden would love to have and it was every bit as dark as Ruth and hers. Cholena brought a basin of warm water with a cloth over to Raine. She sat the basin on a chest at the foot of the bed. Raine notice and was truly grateful, but she did not speak, only smiled. She wet the cloth and washed her face. The warm water felt good, like she was washing the bad days away. It was so refreshing she leaned over and gently wiped Price's face also, but he made no response.

Price Barrett slept soundly in his own bed for the first time in four nights. Raine was afraid to lie on the bed beside him, so she scooted the rocker close and covered her shoulders with a small quilt. She really did not need to lie down, as she already spent several days in bed. Raine just needed to be near him.

Elisha came in and with Cholena went into their room, leaving Raine to be alone with her husband. Raine was grateful the Blake's were sensitive to her. She already knew what remarkable people they were and was pleased that they were here.

She felt relieved, Price was sleeping peacefully, after all he had been through. Raine's gratitude turned to the Lord for His keeping a protective watchful eye on Price's life. While she pondered on His faithfulness, the words of Caleb resounded, *'Price Barrett get better. He strong man of God. Great Father is good. He take me to place Price sleep in cave. Price stay with you, Great Father wants him to live.'*

Yet the consoling words echoing inside her only brought conviction. The realization of what she had done became overwhelming, and her own relationship with Father God was damaged. She had not trusted

Him. In fact she had been bitterly angry with Him. Raine knew she needed to repent and offer sincere remorse for her inexcusable behavior, but even though she was grieved over her sinfulness she felt unworthy of His forgiveness. He was faithful, she was not. Shame taunted her and she cried again, but this time it was not out of fear or anger. It was because of her personal unfaithful actions which exposed a wicked heart. For the fourth night in a row Raine Barrett fell asleep exhausted by her own tears.

♥

Elisha and Cholena were happy Mr. Barrett returned home alive. They were running out of ideas on how to help Raine. Their main concern was how long it would take for her to get back on her feet so they could move out before winter set in. She needed to be in good health to handle the needs of the ranch and they could not just leave. Now this was no longer a problem, with Price Barrett's return. He would be back on his feet in no time and Raine would now be motivated to take care of the ranch chores until he could do them. It appears their time here has come to an end. There was no longer any need for them and it was not their way to impose on anyone. A goal now could be set for a time to depart.

Now alone in the guest bedroom, while Elisha was preparing the nights fire, he asked his wife, "Will you be all right to continue further down the trail in the wagon?" Elisha's voice carried a deep concern for her condition.

Cholena already in bed, trying to find a comfortable way to position her body, replied, "Husband, please no worry, many babies come in world every new sun…child and I will be fine."

"Even if you will be ok physically, how are you going to handle leaving here? Has this ranch begun to feel like home to you in these few days? You look comfortable here, but we must not forget the only reason for us staying this long was to assist a hurting woman in her time of need, now this time is over…we must find our own place to settle."

"Yes husband, I happy here…helping Raine Barrett, no hard…I know not my home. We find perfect place…raise children. Family is home, not piece of land." Just then the baby kicked stirring her attention elsewhere. "Come feel Elisha," she laid her hand on her stomach.

Elisha placed another shovel of fuel on the fire before looking back at his wife. Her expression portrayed a pleasure he never witnessed before. Cholena's hand was moving across her abdomen as she urged him again to come closer. Laying the shovel down, he did as she requested and went to her side.

Cholena took his hand and laid it upon her stomach, holding it firmly in place, she instructed, "Wait." At first he felt nothing different, then the babe gave a walloping kick, jarring Elisha's hand off of his wife. He laughed and asked her, "Did that hurt you?"

"No hurt…Your child is strong…has strength of bear, only brave punch hard," Cholena suggested as she began to reason the child inside of her was a male.

"I don't know…if my mind recalls correctly, I know a brave Indian girl who defied her whole tribe for the love of a simple man; that to me is an act of absolute strength." Elisha moved his hand, placing it along side of her face and bent down and kissed her lips. "I am such a lucky man and our child is lucky to have you for a mother," he whispered, gave another tender kiss and then went back to tend the fire.

"We should decide when to tell the Barrett's of our plans to leave. I only want to stay as long as we are needed, but at the same time Cholena...we need to find permanent shelter before it gets any colder. We have already lost a few days of travel and before the baby arrives it would be good to have our own home."

"Yes, papoose needs home…" she hesitated, "we need to stay…Mr. Barrett not well…not worry Barrett's with ranch work and cooking…Raine weak, not leave now." Cholena was suggesting the Barrett's needed to be in better shape before leaving.

"I know we need to be sensitive, yet the baby will not wait for us. The day of arrival is already set and the child will need a home. The weather will not wait either." He felt responsible to do right by his family first.

"Yes Husband," Cholena understood, if his mind was made up she would not challenge it. "When Barrett's are better, we tell them. Raine very kind in bad storm…has good heart."

With the fire stabilized, Elisha crawled under the covers by Cholena. "I know we owe Mrs. Barrett our life. I cannot imagine how we would have fared that storm. I do care about their predicament, but I will not stay past a week. That is seven suns," he smiled. "You and child are important to me. The Barrett's have Caleb and Ruth to help them." He snuggled in and kissed her cheek before spontaneously drifting fast to sleep.

Cholena felt it was a fair request and she would leave on the seventh sun. She lay awake for several hours with too many uncertainties running through her mind. One in particular, was about the white-mans-God which Caleb and Ruth also embrace. The God who saved Mr. Barrett was strong and brave. One to be respected. In Cholena curiosity she decided to approach this white-mans-God in the way her tribe would speak to the ancestors, in her native tongue. "Great God of Mr. Barrett, Caleb, Ruth and of Raine, I do not know You…but I know with wise bravery You kept Mr. Barrett safe and showed Caleb the cave he was in. I hope you not mind me talking to you. A God so strong can do anything. I ask for Your help to find our home…raise child inside of me…place where people not look at him as bad child. My Elisha, good man…he needs Your calm, Your bravery to find home." She spoke softly as to not wake Elisha. She hoped this God would understand her Osage words. "This is all I have to say." Somehow in the stillness, she sensed this white-mans-God heard her and understood. Cholena went to sleep peacefully.

♥

Chapter 24

Doc Skylar received a message from Wiggins concerning what was taking place at Barrett's Promise and how Raine went through a grueling ordeal searching for Price. As Wiggins conveyed the whole drastic story he added, 'her legs have suffered some major abrasions'.

Upon hearing this news the Thompson's spent a long time in prayer. They were grieved to the heart about Price's disappearance. They just could not imagine life in the West without the Barrett's support. Skylar was convinced he should make the trip to Barrett's Promise in person. "Rhoda, it is not uncommon for a simple abrasion, if left untreated, to turn into gangrene. I have to go out there to check on Raine. They are like family to us, with Price being as close as any brother."

Rhoda understood, she was just as concerned about both of the Barrett's. Family must be there for each other in bad times as well as good. So with his wife's blessing, Skylar left at 3 am promising to be careful.

To his amazement the ride was not bad. One could hardly see any evidence of the storm on the trail four days later. By leaving when he did it put him into Barrett's Promise the very next morning after Price was rescued. Although his friend was looking quite battered, he was relieved to see him home and alive.

Raine was in better shape than Price so Doc began his checkup with her. When finished examining the abrasions on her legs, he had only compliments for Ruth and the medicine she used that brought about good healing results. "With the knowledge you have of herbs and tinctures, Raine will not suffer any lasting injuries, thanks to you." He spoke directly to Ruth.

Now it was time to take a good inventory of Price's condition. Doc Skylar examined Price with extreme carefulness. Doc knew the man was in severe pain, even if Price was careful to hide it from his wife and friends.

It was obvious the right arm suffered a massive strain, constricting the muscle. The swelling had decreased over the night again with the help of his friend's medicinal knowledge. He complimented Ruth and Caleb generously. "I am so glad the Barrett's have you two as neighbors." Nonetheless, it will take time for the arm to work properly again. Although with rehabilitation treatments to manipulate the muscle, Doc was encouraged Price would gain all his strength back in that arm.

It was Price's left leg Skylar was most concerned about. It was swollen beyond a normal swelling and his toes were beginning to turn blue, indicating the circulation was being hindered. After a careful assessment, Doc was glad to only find one fracture, as he feared multiple breaks. He needed to establish where the circulation problem was located. But first Doc needed to tend to several deep gashes, some requiring stitches. So he proceeded to take care of the outer surface knowing the next step would be difficult.

The break was unusually high, close to the knee and the way it lodged was putting pressure behind the knee, apparently semi-clamping off an artery. He hoped it did not puncture it.

In spite of the seriousness of the break, Skylar could see the hand of the Lord definitely on Price, for there were no signs of infection or gangrene. All quite uncommon after five days, especially with a brake that is hindering poor circulation. Not to overlook the deep gashes incurred. The chance of an infection setting in was not uncommon.

However along with the good news, the bone still required attention. It would have to be pulled out of the place it rested without injuring the artery. Skylar prayed silently, *Lord please do not let the artery be damaged when I move the bone, if it is, put your finger on it, so he does not bleed out.*

Doc Skylar suggested the women leave the house while he set the bone in place. He knew there could be complications in the procedure, not to mention how painful it will be to Price and he did not want to frighten them.

Skylar observed the women walking in the open area, on their way to the barn. He turned back to Price and began to explain the procedure along with the complications involved. After this he asked, "Do you need anything for pain, maybe you have some whiskey or moonshine around the house. People seem to have a private stock in the West."

Price declined the offer; as he did not succumb to any strong drink, nor did her have a private stock.

Doc presented, "I have some ether in my medical bag. It will put you in a deep sleep so you will not experience the magnitude of the pain."

Price declined this solution also, "I can handle it Doc, just do what you have to do."

Doc Skylar wished Price would have chosen the antistatic. However, he was not surprise, knowing the headstrong character of Price Barrett.

After Doc applied a tourniquet to the thigh he implored Elisha and Caleb to assist him by holding Price completely still so he could carefully manipulated the bone back in place. With Price's large frame the procedure would have been difficult to maneuver without their help.

Skylar began prayerfully pulling the bone out from

where it was lodged. Sweat beads were formed on Skylar's forehead as he manipulated the bone in place. He would never get use to inflicting pain on a patient, even for their own good. After inspecting the artery behind the knee, and slowly loosening the tourniquet, he was relieved. There was no massive bleeding and the artery appeared to be undamaged. He took out a handkerchief and wiped the sweat from his brow.

Through the whole procedure Price proved himself to be a brave sort, not letting out a single moan or screech. Although it was obvious from the tension on his face he felt the pain. "You are certainly a man of valor, my friend. I have never in my profession seen a man go through a procedure of this nature without making some sort of grunt, even under whisky or an antistatic."

Before coming into the house Doc had gathered two wagon spokes from the barn to use as a splint, not knowing the seriousness of Raine's leg and he wanted to be prepared. Skylar had Elisha sterilize them for him and set them near the fire to dry.

He wondered if the Lord had nudged him to pick them up because he would now need these splints to secure the bone in Price's leg. He took a small break to stretch his legs. He searched the house to see if there was anything else he could use. He remembered in the back room the construction for the stairs was not finished. There he located two pieces of bowing wood. *These two pieces of wood now have a new purpose, it will aid in protecting the splints from moving, like a brace. Yes this will be just perfect.*

Doc came back and set the bowing wood to the side. He put the splints on Price's leg and finished the bandaging. The bowing boards was five inches longer than Price's leg which Doc knew would aggravate Price enough to detour him from putting weight directly on his leg. He secured these boards in place. Faceting them with straps so it could easily be removed during wash times. *Perfect.*

After Doc Skylar finished, he helped himself to the cup of tea Cholena set aside for him in the warming slot on the stove. Doc sipped his tea and rested in the rocker by Price's bedside.

Once he was sure his patient was recovering nicely from the strenuous procedure just inflicted on him, Doc did not hesitate to give strict instructions. "You must stay completely off this leg. Even though it is bandaged, it is not able to take any weight. I will return in six weeks to examine the leg. If it has healed rapidly, I will release you to gradually do more and start transferring yourself. However, if the healing process shows to be slower, you are looking at an extra month or even longer. The outer bandages are to be changed daily and the leg washed. You will have to accept Raine's help to accomplish it, yet remember to not remove the bowing brace for any reason except washing and the splints never remove. If you notice any red streaks or discoloration, send word to me right away. This is nothing to ignore or put off."

"Alright Doc, whatever you say. What about sitting up in a chair to eat or do I have to stay in this bed continually?" As Price inquired his stomach growled and both heard it. A throbbing appetite was beginning to surface and he felt like an empty cave was inside of him.

Doc smiled, remembering how Price literally made an art of eating. He leaned back in the chair and gave it some thought as he sipped his tea while Price waited for an answer.

He recalled something they used back East that might work, if modified. "If you are insistent to get out of bed, I have an idea. However, I will need your solemn word you will not leave this house for any reason short of a fire." He gave Price a serious look to let him know he was not joking and then waited for Price to answer before speaking further.

Price felt trapped, he really had no choice and with a gruff sigh relinquished any further hesitation, "Doc…It looks like I am at your mercy…you have my word."

Doc Skylar began to explain his idea, "With a little help from these two men, I believe we can construct a chair with wheels to assist you in moving around the house. We will have to assemble an attachment that will hold your leg in front of you. With your break being so close to the knee, we cannot chance bending it."

"Skylar, if you can construct such a contraption, I will be exceptionally grateful for any independent movement you could give me. I promise I will not push my recovery. I know you are the expert and I will not do anything to mess up the healing progress. I certainly do not want to be in this position a year from now. I am no different than most men and I want to get back to working on my land as soon as I can. Yet I am also smart enough to obey wise instructions, especially when it comes from a friend whom I trust."

Doc was grateful Price Barrett was a sensible man, but wondered if he really knew what he would be facing for the next couple of months. "Price, I would like you to consider what you can do with your time while you are confined. Having a plan will make the time go by easier."

"Actually Sky, I have one," presenting a smirk on his face, "I am going to get to know Raine even better," with this he laughed. "All kidding aside, God and I had a few talks while I was in the cave. I think I will do some extensive reading in the Scriptures. I am not sure why He is calling me to immerse myself in His Word, never the less, I feel I may need to know them as well as I know my own. The days ahead are full of uncertainties regarding the plan He has given us about the Community. I am getting the impression that I need to be ready for this undertaking far more than I am.

Price paused for a moment then added, I do not need know all the detail today, only to obey what He gives me. My meager perspective can honestly use a bit of clarity on some issues. Come to think of it, there is a great deal I need to grasp. After those days in the cave alone with Him I am compelled to know more of how He looks at things." He humbly spoke in a lower tone, "I owe Him a lot Skylar."

Skylar admired the courage and devotion to God Price Barrett demonstrated. He always looks at the positive side of every situation. "After looking at your condition my friend and hearing what you went through, I can definitely vouch the Lord Hands are on you. I'm a believer in providence. God saved you for a purpose. I trust you have the right idea on how to spend your days."

Skylar paused when the realization hit him, God indeed had something in mind for Price Barrett. The impact of this comprehension on Skylar was almost as strong of feeling as it was the day he knew God called him to be a doctor out West.

With this thought Skylar returned to the doctoring part, "I want to encourage you to take any herbs for pain and healing that Caleb, Ruth or Cholena suggest for you. It made a big difference in Raine's leg.

"That tea is horrible!" Price exclaimed, then looked over at Caleb, "sorry".

Caleb did not mind, "Truth!" he voiced gracefully.

Skylar ignored the complaint, "I was sure I would find her with serious complications, but quite the opposite...I have now complete confidence in their medicine. Not to mention the swelling going down in your arm as well. Guess the medical schools do not have the exclusive on healing medicines."

"Well Doc, I guess we all can learn something. I have always been receptive to Caleb's medicine, even when it tastes nasty." He chuckled. "So accepting their cures will not be too hard for me...Now tell me more about this chair with wheels. What are you going to need to construct it?"

"Boy you are eager to get back your independence, even though you have not been in this bed twenty-four hours...patience my friend, patience." He paused, "ok, I will give you credit for the time spent in the cave, but still it has only been five days," he grinned.

"Five days seems like a month, Skylar!"

"Alright, I will give you that. Do you have any chairs your father started to make, but did not complete? If so, we may be able to convert one of them into a chair with wheels."

At this point the women returned. Ruth was not among them, as she had returned to her pueblo. Now Raine and Cholena were curious for information tossing out many questions simultaneously about the procedure and if Price was going to be alright.

Price interrupted the women, "Ladies, ladies, I am fine. I will inform you both of all the gruesome details later, but first Beautiful, would you mind taking the men to my father's workshop and pick out an unfinished chair for them. They are going to convert it with some wheels? I am going to have a little independence around the house. Isn't that right Doc?"

Skylar responded "That is our goal."

Although Raine was a little puzzled, she moved on the task her husband asked of her and led the men out the door. *Wheels?*

Once inside the workshop, Raine considered a specific chair she had her eye on and wished many times it was finished. The craftsmanship on it was uniquely sculptured, but for some reason his father did not make any legs to match its quality. Pointing to it hanging on the wall, she asked "Doc is that one suitable?"

Seeing the chair, Skylar knew it was a perfect choice. "Caleb can you get the chair down for us... Elisha, have you seen any wheels around the barn that aren't the size of a wagon?" As Caleb was getting the chair off the hooks, Elisha was off to the barn in search of suitable wheels.

Before leaving the woodshop, Raine observed the beginning conversion of the wheeled chair masterpiece; the beautiful armed chair was indeed a perfect choice. It was as if God inspired Price's father to make just this part and set it aside for this occasion. The arms were curved and solid, no spikes, just solid curved wood like you would see on a deacon's bench. The back was also curved and on it was carved a unique tree, which looked a lot like a juniper, *Beautiful work.* Raine admired the piece many times and now she was happy that it was going to be used. She remembered Aunt Margaret mentioned Uncle Bentley being in a wheelchair, but she had never seen one.

Cholena stayed at the house, she did not ask Mr. Barrett any questions without Raine, but kept busy starting the evening meal. In the meantime Price took the liberty to rest quietly, closing his eyes to regain strength. After a while, Price realized Cholena had begun to work on food preparations and they were still alone, he took the moment to speak to her. "Thank you Cholena, for helping Raine...I am totally indebted to you and Elisha for looking after her. If there is any way I can repay you for such kindness, let me know and as soon as I am back on my feet I will see to it that I meet your request."

Cholena heard a sincere gratefulness in Mr. Barrett's voice, yet in her perspective he had the situation backwards. "No, no Mr. Barrett, storm bring us together…Mrs. Barrett, good to us…said 'you stay in house…not safe in wagon,' she give safe place to sleep…we not leave her…she afraid for you, very sad."

"That sounds like Raine. She could not turn a duck out in bad weather. Yet when the storm passed you could have left, but you stayed. Not only did you stay, you and Elisha kept the ranch running while looking after my wife. I am grateful. Thank you." Price closed his eyes again and Cholena felt he needed no response.

When Raine returned to the house, she could not hold back her inquisitive nature. Sitting down in the rocker by the bed she began asking Price clear precise questions. She wanted to know Skylar's professional opinion and on how serious the break was and how long it would take for Price to recover. Raine was concerned, even frightened, she could not lose him again, he had to get better. Meanwhile Cholena listened attentively while cooking. She also wanted to know, but for personal reasons. Elisha only gave her a week before they would be leaving and this weighed heavy on her heart. If the Barrett's were fine and ready to work their ranch, she would feel better about it.

Price was confident he would have a full recovery and wanted to ease Raine's mind. He was ready to share every detail, yet he thought best to omit the horrific pain which accompanied setting the bone.

Once Raine listened carefully to all the details and seen the confidence Price had regarding his recovery, her worries began to eased up. However, there was still the issue of redness and discoloration Doc warned about. The next couple of months were going to be challenging. She did not mind caring for Price, she was just grateful to have him home. She knew they could conquer anything if they were together. After Price finished, she relaxed and set aside the fear of losing him which had entangled her. Raine simply inquired, "Is there anything I can do for you, to make things easier."

Price gave a thoughtful reply, "Just be here for me, Raine, I am deeply in love with you. The time I had in the cave thinking about you just made me appreciate you even more. I am so glad you are my wife. God did a wonderful job of picking you out for me, you are much more than I deserve." He reached over and took her hand and knew she felt as deeply for him. "I do not need you to do anything specific, we are going to get through this. You know it will probably not be the only time we will have to go through a less than perfect season in our married lives." He smiled at the realization of that comment, "Yet every time we go through a crisis, we will not be alone. We have a faithful God who walks closely with us. When each trial is past, we are going to come out of it better than we went into it. That is part of His wondrous love for us."

Price notice Cholena working preparing dinner, so he lowered his voice to not make her feel uncomfortable, "We must thank the Lord for the Blake's, because in His mercy, He put us together to help each other."

Raine added, "They have had far worse situations, our trial of uncertainty is only for a few nights, but theirs has lasted much longer." Both glanced over at Cholena, who continued preparing the evening meal. She was trying hard not to show she was listening, wiping discreetly a tear from her eye as she turned.

Even though Raine never said a word about how the past few days were extremely difficult, her pain was not easily hidden. The eyes have a way of being transparent. "Beautiful, you were very close to me every minute in the cave, I cherished every memory. They inspired me to hang on. Father God reminded me of His promises to us and about our children. He would not have told us His purpose for our lives if He were going to end our relationship so soon. So you see, Darling, it was only a matter of time before I would be rescued. I knew Caleb would come...Now I don't want to mislead you, there were times I was very weak and I felt like giving up. Then a memory would come like a vision and I would gain strength. One memory was of a time when you read to me out of the Andrew Murray book. Your voice was a healing balm and I heard the words spoken by you. They were clear and resounding. This vision or whatever it was, administered hope."

Raine had not taken her eyes off Price. She hung on his every word. However, when he mentioned reading Andrew Murray, she felt uncontrollable shame and looked away. She wondered how she could ever be able to tell him about the days when she had not trusted God, calling Him cruel God and in her anger claiming she would not follow Him anymore. *All the while Father God was faithful. What would Price think of his wife now? He snuggled close to the Savior and I pushed Him away,* she fretted, unable to regain eye contact.

Price noticed the quick change in Raine's demeanor, and thought she might be reliving the nightmare, but before he could inquire about what was wrong, three men were wheeling a chair through the front door laughing.

It did not take much for Price to see why his friends were experiencing the hardy laughter. This weird looking chair was the strangest thing he ever set eyes on. His mother use to have a cart to move heavy things around the ranch and he was certain they robbed the wheels from that cart. Only Mama would use a goat to pull it around the yard and now he was going to use the same wheels to roll himself around the house. Price had to chuckle, noticing the look on all of their faces. Everyone was staring at this contraption and all voicing their curiosity. Was it safe for a grown man to be in? How can he maneuver it alone? Price heard their questions and also wondered the same.

This thing had two big wheels and two small ones. Knowing a little about how things were constructed he presumed the small ones was for balance. He looked at where the left leg was supposed to rest, a ledge that conveniently went up and down. It was being braced underneath at two levels and he actually considered, *this contraption just might work as long as I have enough room to move about with my leg sticking out.*

At this point Elisha jumped in the chair and tried it out and everyone got a good laugh. Elisha being a small sized man looked like a child in the chair. After he got out, Caleb got in and that got another laugh. Caleb looked like a king in his stately appearance needing his subjects to push him around. Price wondered how he would look, but realize he would not look as silly as those two. Although the alternative was not a choice for him; no matter how silly he looked.

When the fun was over, Skylar took charge of the introduction and wheeled the chair beside the bed. "Ok Price, this is it, since I will not be here to help you into this chair every day, Raine and Elisha will have to assist you." He motioned for the two of them to come close so he could show them what to do.

Price was easily ruffled by Skylar's suggestion, "I am certainly capable of moving into the chair by myself," he said with defiance.

"Oh no, you are not, Price Barrett. I will not have you straining that arm because of your pride. You work regularly on those treatments I showed you to do. When your strength is good enough to pick up an iron skillet and hold it out in front of you for fifteen seconds, then you may try to get in the chair yourself. Only with someone close by, just in case you are still unable to hold your weight with your arms and remember no weight on the leg." Skylar was firm and unmovable in his deliverance.

Price unenthusiastically received the reprimand given by his friend the doctor and even though he hated to admit it, he knew he deserved the rebuke, *but why did he have to use that PRIDE word? Now I will be up half of the night sorting out my motives with the Lord.* Price looked up at Skylar, conceding he would surrender his stubborn will and agree to the help.

Skylar demonstrated to Elisha and Raine how properly to assist Price into the chair with wheels. He stressed the point of being careful, not to allow the knee to be bent in the slightest and how to help without putting any strain on his right arm. After a couple of practice attempts, Doc was satisfied on how smooth the transfer went and gave his blessing.

Price felt some exhaustion from the transfer practices, but now sitting upright he liked how it made him feel more like his old self despite his lack of energy.

Skylar did not plan to spend the night on the ranch as he often did. Today it was imperative he return to New Crossing. Feeling confident of his friend's stability made leaving easier. Before starting his journey back Doc Skylar repeated the instructions once more. Then he prayed with the Barrett's for a complete healing and left them in God's hands, promising to return in six weeks. Nevertheless, if any complications should occur they were to send word and he'd come out to the ranch immediately.

Caleb was out helping Elisha hitch up the horses to Skylar's wagon for travel. After Skylar left, he came inside hoping to secure a few quiet moments with Price. Meanwhile Raine feeling more like herself was helping Cholena preparing the night's supper.

"Come sit with me by the fire Caleb, I have not had the proper time to convey my gratitude for your persistence in searching for me." Caleb took a seat and Price continued, "I actually wondered if I was hid away from everyone…in my own grave. Every time I felt like giving up, God would shake me awake and remind me of promises He gave Raine and I that had not come about yet to give me hope. When you shook me yesterday I actually thought it was the Lord again. What a good sight for sore eyes you were, because when you showed up I was at the point of doubting I would leave that cave. I tell you truthfully, under great stress your mind plays tricks on you, and the devil lies to you, even when you know the promises. One minute I would be full of faith and then next in despair."

Caleb responded understandingly, "I know this truth from time on mountain when bitten by snake. Until Shinning-Light found me, I too struggled with devil's lies. God is always there in battle; sometimes in shadows, sometimes in clearing, always watching!"

Caleb and Price enjoyed a lengthy conversation about Father God faithfulness and encouraged one another. Trader was stretched out on the Indian woven rug, in the middle of his two favorite men, just like old times the three of them together doing what they enjoyed.

When Elisha came in, Caleb knew it was time to leave. He extended his hand to Price and said he would be back tomorrow. He walked over to Elisha, with deep respect gave his hand of friendship. No words needed to be spoken, but Elisha knew it pleased Caleb they took care of Rainwater and the ranch while Price was lost from them. That moment was sealed, knowing they would be friends forever. Elisha hoped he would find a man with the integrity of Caleb up the trail, where he and Cholena would settle. It had been a long time since he felt this acceptance. Unfortunate, there was not an abandoned homestead close by. Or he might be tempted to stay in the area.

As Price watched both men extend friendliness to one another, he silently thanked the Lord for people He graciously put into his life. He pondered a moment before closing his eyes, Caleb was right about the Father's faithfulness, He is always watching.

♥

Chapter 25

Price was pondering over the idea of getting to know Elisha better. It had been two days now since the big excitement of the wheel chair and Elisha had only spoken of small things or things pertaining to ranch chores. Tonight as he & Elisha sat in the rockers catching up from the day, he thought it might be a good opportunity to talk on a more personal level while the women were busy cooking. "I am curious Elisha, what brought you to the desert on such a stormy afternoon? We do not get travelers every day so I am interested in what brought you to our area."

With this question, Elisha was intimidated. He stood up and moved closer to the fireplace, asking Price if he would like him to start a fire for the evening.

Price thought it was a warmer day and a little early as the sun had not set yet, but if Elisha was cold he would not prevent him from starting one. So he agreed.

While Elisha proceeded to make a fire he pondered the question Price asked him, uncertain what he felt comfortable to divulge. He realized his silence and inability to answer promptly probably made him look suspicious. Yet in actuality, Elisha felt shame mixed with anger concerning his reasons for being in the barrens on the day of the storm. *How do you tell someone a bogus man ran you out of town, because of the color of your skin? A white man in the middle of a desert would have no idea how to respond to this truth.* Elisha found no words to express the situation. At the same time, he considered the question was not unreasonable. *The mere fact of being in his home and what the man went through... certainly gives him the right to an honest answer; especially in a home we both occupy presently.*

The fire was taking off and Elisha knew he would have to say something. He turned to go back to his seat and shot a look to his wife across the room.

Raine caught it plain as day. It said without words, 'can I trust him?' She felt compassion for Elisha, recalling the conversation with Cholena the night they arrived. How people severely persecuted them, for simply being a free-black-man and Osage Indian…this still disturbed Raine to know people were cruel to such kind folks as Elisha & Cholena. She pretended she did not notice, but wondered how Elisha would respond to her husband's question.

It was obvious Elisha was holding back and Price Barrett respected the rights of another man's privacy. However while he waited patiently to see if Elisha would answer, Price was involved in his own clandestine questioning with God and amazingly getting prompt answers. This gave him the confidence to pursue further. "I didn't mean to pry, Elisha. I respect your right to be private, but it might be easier if you understood why I was asking."

This got Elisha's attention.

"Elisha, my family lived on this land for thirty years and I plan to die here, leaving it as a legacy to our children. However the work is hard and long." He smirked at how that must have sounded. "More so now with my leg and arm out of action, but if you are in need of work and not running from the law…maybe we can persuade you to stay on the ranch longer than what an unpredictable storm dealt us."

From across the room Raine understood very quickly what was happening, God had whispered to her husband again. She waited for Elisha's reaction, presuming the Blake's could be one of the families God was bringing to build a community. The possibility excited her, glancing at Cholena working beside her. Raine kept busy with chopping vegetables, although anxiously waiting to hear Elisha's response. Then memory of her secret betrayal crept into her thoughts and took away her joy. *How can I act as one who welcomes God's plan with my unfaithfulness?*

Cholena and Elisha exchanged another glance without anyone noticing; they both were stunned by the offer Price presented. Considering they had decided to go and were waiting for an appropriate time to break the news to the Barrett's. Now with this offer Elisha had a fresh scenario to consider and wondered what Cholena thought of it.

Cholena remembered her talk with white-mans-God and wondered if He was really answering her request this quickly.

Elisha got up again, pacing in silence, while running his hand repeatedly through his hair on the top of his head. He looked at his wife standing in front of the cook fireplace, her delicate condition carrying his firstborn child. The need to settle somewhere before the baby is born was his foremost thoughts for days. This offer confused him, and his previous experiences made him cautious. He had lost all hope of finding a place where they would be accepted. He was convinced on the idea of locating a place far away from anyone; a place off by its self with just Cholena and the child. This new concept was difficult for Elisha to process, after having his mind set in another direction. Then again, he had to admit he never once felt degraded here. In fact the past few days he forgot momentarily there was ever an issue. Yet, he never once gave a thought of staying on the ranch. *It was never consideration, let alone asked to do so.*

After tossing all the contradictions around in his head, Elisha felt it was time he break the silence and say something. He sat down and looked Price square in the eye. "Mr. Barrett, first off I am not running from the law, but I am a bit confused. I do not understand why you have presented this offer to us. Certainly you have others in mind, people you are more accustomed to, ones who help you in times of need…people more like yourselves."

Price heard the last statement Elisha said, 'people, more like yourselves', but chose to ignore it for the time being and tried to explain what he was asking in a better way. "Actually Elisha, this is not about helping us because of my present situation. I am asking if you would like to stay and work beside us on the ranch. I understand you think my condition calls for drastic measures and I am making a wild offer because of it, yet this is not the case. Raine and I considered long before the night of the storm to have people live and work with us on the ranch. In fact we named our ranch Barrett's Promise to accommodate these plans".

After a considerable amount of prayer, we've come to believe Father God was going to bring to our ranch specific people who needed a place to settle; people who would be without a permanent dwelling location. He would guide the right ones here...Correct me if I have presumed wrong. It seems obvious to me you need a place to settle, especially with Cholena being with child. Unless you have work somewhere we do not know about, you wouldn't have a lot to lose by accepting my offer, if only temporary."

Elisha was trying to comprehend the idea of staying on the ranch with a permanent job. *Why does this bother me, it does not sound bad, but there has to be a catch somewhere.*

"I know you may not understand this, but sitting here in this crazy-wonderful chair-with-wheels," Price slapped the wheels, "God whispered, 'invite Elisha to stay and offer him work'. So that is what I am doing. I hope I have clear up any misconception you may have had about this being temporary, due to my present circumstance. Because plain and simple I am offering you a permanent position on this ranch, a home for you and Cholena as long as you want."

Elisha still had reservations, *why does this man appear so confident and this God whispering stuff... fanatical.* "Mr. Barrett, I cannot comprehend what in the world you are telling me. Saying God whispers to you...He is bringing people to your ranch and I am one of these people...offer me a job? I am sorry, save the religious stuff for someone who cares. You want me to actually believe some weird God far off in the heavens has informed you about us..." he laughed. "This whole idea is foreign to me, bordering on spooky. How could you possibly presume this God of yours was controlling my steps to bring me to this ranch? Mr. Barrett, I have to tell you, this gets more bizarre as it unfolds inside my mind...I cannot even begin to grasp the concept of my life being controlled by some far off mystical being." Even while Elisha was rattling on, he knew silently how completely bewildered he was about how he had come to this place in the first place. However, he certainly did not want to buy Price's explanation...and yet *could it really be a divine providence? I have to be losing my mind to even consider this!*

Cholena listening to the conversation was very impressed with what Price told her husband; however she knew better than to share this with Elisha. *White-mans-God, help Elisha accept, if You want us to stay,* she whispered in her native tongue.

Raine also kept working, silently praying, *Lord, I know You have all of this in your hands, Your will be done.*

Well, guess it is obvious; Mr. Elisha Blake is not a

believer...yet! "I realize this is a new idea to you, Elisha and as you just shared you do not understand the workings of God, but try placing that aside for the time being. You have to admit your present circumstances are demanding a secure place to live. Laying out this fact, I don't need to convince you this is a good idea. Our offer stands. However, if you chose to stay and later you do not find this place to be what you are looking for, you are not obligated to stay any longer than you want to be here. Be that tomorrow, after the baby is born, or two - three years from now."

Even though Elisha still felt uneasy about Price's alleged-connection with a so-called-Almighty, *he is right about one thing, I do have an important need to consider.* He began calculating the advantages of accepting Mr. Barrett's offer over the disadvantages. He reasoned, *guess it does not matter how we came to be here at this specific time, coincidence or providence, nevertheless, I do need stability for Cholena and my unborn child.* He was also aware of Cholena's subtle glances and Elisha could tell she did not want him to be too hasty in turning this down. After all, *isn't this exactly what I promised her.* 'One day they would find a good community to raise children'. *This is not a large group of people, in fact only a two, but they seemed to accept us, maybe...* "What can I say, Mr. Barrett, your assumptions are absolutely correct. We are as you say, in dire need of a home. This forces my hand to consider your offer even before speaking with Cholena. Since my wife will deliver early February, it would be good to not worry about be stranded somewhere along the trail." He was humbled, but he had to risk it for His wife and child.

Price was glad to hear he was considering, and stayed quiet.

"I am a hard worker Mr. Barrett and if we decide to

stay, I will do anything needed. If there is something I do not know how to do, I confess honestly…not bragging…I do learn quickly. I took care of your livestock while you were away. If you could go out there, I am sure you would find your animals and barn in excellent condition. I do not think my work will disappoint you."

Price replied, "I am sure your work is excellent Elisha. You and Cholena took good care of my wife. I need not inspect the barn to see the caliber of man you are.

Elisha wondered what made this man different, comparing him to those he encountered in his recent past. The brunt of previous towns and settlements were still fresh in his mind, the constant hostility and crude remarks. In all the places they tried to make their home, not one single person befriended them. Instead they heard repeatedly how much *they did not want 'the-likes-of-us' living anywhere near them.* "I am driven to ask you a simple question before I can accept your offer and I need for you to be honest with me. I have tough skin and will not be offended," (which was not totally true). "Mr. Barrett take a good look at me, look at my wife…is there anything you see that would bother you about us staying on your ranch, being your neighbors, maybe not now, but in the future?"

Price had never been asked such a thing in his whole life; it took him off guard. It troubled him why the man felt Cholena or he would be offensive. With careful discernment he knew it was important to answer Elisha quickly. "Well let me see, it is obvious by looking, Cholena is an Indian woman about to have a baby…we like children and my friends are Indians. As for you, well you're not very tall with dark skin, why should this be a problem? My Uncle Cuate' was short and had family who were darker than you. Elisha, I certainly would not suggest you to stay at Barrett's Promise if there was anything I felt would bother us." Elisha Blake's question was a great insight to an area which needed great healing and Price Barrett knew he was just the man to fill that order.

"You do not find my skin color offensive or the fact that my wife is an Osage Indian a problem?"

Price wondered why Elisha pushed the question again. *I thought I answered, is Elisha feeling bad about how God made him? This must be a learned insecurity, a rejection from his past.* In a flabbergasted tone, "What could possibly be the problem with that? Why would your ethnic linage be a reason to not offer you a place to live and work on my ranch? You have a need of a home; I have a place for you to live. This arrangement would benefit us both and again I am not referring to just while I am recovering, but also afterwards when we work together to build up the land...You are not hunted by some angry slave owner, are you?"

"No sir, I am a free-man," Elisha snapped abruptly with immense pride and confidence.

"That's good, but if you weren't a free-man, we would just have to settle up with the owner to acquire your freedom; after all the Lord led you here."

Elisha intentionally ignored the implication to God again because he was absolutely stunned, knowing he heard acceptance in Mr. Barrett's voice. "Now that takes all, Mr. Barrett, you really surprise me. Are you telling me that you would actually go through all the trouble to buy a slaves freedom and for a complete stranger? That beats all, I do not understand."

"Our Father God is incapable of making any mistakes, Mr. Blake. If He brought anyone here in need of help, for any injustice, we would do all we could to assist them. I personally do not believe in slavery, yet living in the desert, I have not witnessed it. However, it makes me angry to think people could treat other human beings harshly and force them to work against their will…while the owners get the benefits." Price stopped there, if he continued his course of talking he could say some unkind things himself and it is best to flee from a sinful thought than to embrace it. Remembering The Israelites in Scriptures, being owned by Pharaoh and how appalling they were treated, when he read about it, he made the opinion; slave-owners were not nice people.

"Elisha, I know we are not personally acquainted with each other, but if you choose to stay on the ranch, we may have a lifetime of being neighbors to develop a respect and a friendship. In a short time you will discover Raine and I believe in God-fearing-rightness and you can count on us to back up God's standards, which never indulges in cruelty."

I can see I will have to get use to this God jargon if I am going to be around this man much. "I appreciate your opinion Mr. Barrett. I must admit you are the strangest man I have ever encountered, but nonetheless likeable. Rest assured, you will not have to buy freedom for me. I already have it, but I have to admit it is an honorable act to know you would try."

Price felt he and Elisha went about as far in this conversation as they could. It would be good to have the women's view on the topic. How would they feel about sharing the work load with each other? Price pivoted his chair so he could look over at the women, "How close are we to supper?"

"It will be a while, we just got all the pots filled and they are cooking now, Are you hungry…I could get you something to hold you over?" Raine offered

"No, I am fine. If you can leave your cooking, I was just wondering if you and Cholena would come over and join us. I would like the four of us to talk over a proposal I just made to Elisha." He added cleverly, "I know you both have been quiet so I am pretty sure you know what we have been talking about."

The women looked at each other coyly and smiled. They were caught even when they were trying to not show they were listening.

Price continued, "Understand this is only a temporary arrangement to see if Elisha finds us easy to live by." He let out a chuckle while spinning his chair around to position him to face Elisha.

Speaking to Elisha, "Actually, I guess I should explain our vision for the ranch, so you can best assess the offer. Even if you stay for only a short span of time I think it would be good for you to understand the full scale of what we are planning. I would not want it to be a surprise to you later if you decide to stay."

When Raine and Cholena joined the men, they brought a tray of coffee with them. The men were appreciative and without hesitation welcomed the hot drink. All the while, Raine was serving her heart was leaping for joy, God's design of Barrett's Promise Community was beginning in spite of her betrayal. She tried to set the thoughts of guilt aside for now so she could join in without showing her own inadequacy. After everyone was served, she joined the cluster, taking a seat next to her husband's moveable chair. Cholena and Elisha sat together across from them.

While everyone relaxed sipping on their hot coffee, Raine realized setting her guilt aside would not be easy. In reality, how could she possible get all enthusiastic about the 'community' when she had her betrayal hanging over her head like a cloud of darkness? Father God proved faithful in everything from bringing Price home, to bringing the Blake's here, even when she proved to be cold-hearted towards Him. She had no comprehension of how great His mercy was before this trial, but Father God was starting His community just as He declared to them. Shame engulfed her. *I will not be able to be a good witness to Cholena and Elisha until my own heart has surrendered…*As she sat quietly drinking her coffee and listening to the other converse she made a firm decision to talk this over with Price later tonight. She knew it was essential for her to repent and have her relationship restored. Yet for now she would have to approach this meeting proposal with a confidence she did not have, *then again…my confidence is in God, not myself,* she was reminded, *I guess, if He could use a donkey, He can use me tonight.*

While she was lost in her own thoughts, Price shared with Elisha a few simple plans he had for the land, expanding the garden, adding another community pantry, more privies and buying more cattle.

When the conversation took a lull Raine spoke up. "I hope you both have been comfortable in the guestroom these past days," Raine said with genuine kindness. "I'm glad the room has a fireplace, it is pretty chilly this November. Price's family really thought of everything when they built this ranch."

Price smiled nodding his head and gave an affirmative, "They did."

Raine continued, "If you decide to stay, I would like both of you to walk across the cul-de-sac with me tomorrow and check out your new home…I hope you will find it just as suitable. If not, feel free to make any adjustments necessary for your family, the home will be yours as long as you stay. This way you can start unpacking your wagon...once you have some of your own familiar things around you it will begin to feel comfortable." Five months ago when Raine came to the Barrett Ranch she needed to see some of her things out before she felt like it was her home. She assumed it was the same way for Cholena.

Cholena, who was quiet, listening to the men talk, could not stay silent after Raine's offer. "What you say? You give home to us? Mrs. Barrett, you good woman...big heart...no give home, we stay in wagon. Elisha no stay past spring...I hear right, Elisha?" She looked to her husband for confirmation.

Elisha affirmed his wife's statement, "Certainly, we can move out of your home in the morning. For us to stay in the wagon will be sufficient. With it being on the ranch and it is definitely a more stable location than we have seen in months. Being parked next to the barn provides good shelter from the wind. If in the spring we should decide to stay on, I am capable of building our home in a spot suitable with you. There is no reason for us to be any bother."

"NO!" Raine cut him short; she would not let anyone reside in a wagon longer than absolutely necessary, especially not with winter months ahead of them. "No...You are not inconveniencing us to stay in our home. I just thought it would make you feel more a part of this place if you had your own home. If you want to stay with us there is no hurry to move out. Just know that one of the adobes could be your home while you are here, if you choose it. Even if it is just for the winter, right Price?"

Price quickly agreed and added, "We have already a prepared two adobe homes for people to live in and Raine has made them quite suitable for anyone to start making it their home. If in the spring you decide you would like to have one and raise your family there, you can add whatever additions suitable to your growing family; there is plenty of room for expansion. However, if you stay on and have it in your heart to build your own home, we can work with that idea also. Besides Lord did tell us we were going to have four families to assist in building a community and we would need to build two homes anyways. If you stay, it might as well be your place we build to suit you."

The Blake's were shocked silent, *a community…four families coming?*

Cholena still feeling confused inquired again, "Sorry…Mrs. Barrett…I no understand you…more come…live in camp?"

Raine softly smiled, giving Price a silly look, realizing all of this must sound extremely strange to the Blake's and hard to grasp. *We have had several months getting use to the idea.* "You must forgive our excitement, although we did not know you, we have been waiting for your arrival since last July and we tend to forget, you were not aware of what our vision is before today.

Price closed his eyes; it had been a long day. But he was feeling too excited to doze, *there would be time to sleep tonight.*

"If you give me a little time I am sure I can bring some clarity to your confusion," Raine suggested.

The Blake's confirmed they were ready to hear more.

"We are expanding our ranch to become a place of refuge for people who do not have a permanent place to settle. The idea is, if four families work together, we can make Barrett's Promise Community a sufficient place to meet all of our needs. You happen to be the first to arrive…now being first has some benefits and will give you some advantages. To begin with, you will be established here before anyone else arrives and the community will grow around you as a founder. Your ideas and opinions are going to be very important to us in our planning. The Barrett's and Blake's will be working side by side to put the community framework in place and what we set in motion together will become the structure that will stand. Even if you are only here for a short time, your ideas will live on as a part of our established community and you will be remembered fondly for ages to come. We appreciate your help for however long you feel you can stay.

Raine felt she explained most of it sufficiently, but she still sensed some apprehension. With Price being worn-out he was content to let his wife handle the explanation, "Ok, from the look on your faces, I can see this is still confusing to you. It is a lot to grasp all at once, but maybe if I can share how we got to this point, it will answer some of your questions."

Elisha looked at his wife then back to the Barrett's, "It is a little confusing, and I am wondering what we have stumbled into? First I am offered a job, and then it is a partnership in building a community which will contain four families. Am I right?"

"Yes," Raine answered, while Price grinned and shook his head affirmatively thinking, *they understand better than they think.*

"Yes, yes, please do continue Mrs. Barrett. I am sure this has to get clearer, because I am certain it cannot be any more confusing." Elisha wanted an understandable picture of what exactly he would be agreeing to. Much of it sounded too good to be true, with fragments sounding like a fantasy.

Raine desperately wanted to help them understand, even if they did not have vision for what they were doing. Starting from the very beginning she explained the whole story and the Blake's were attentive listeners.

Cholena even wiped a tear from her eye at the thought of many without a home like they were. Elisha now understood what a great necessity the Barrett's were providing. He may not have comprehended why they were so compassionate, but he sensed their genuineness and realized they may be good people to live around.

Price got his second wind and interjected, "We did not think we needed to go search for people. We asked the Lord to bring ones with impeccable character to us, like He did when He brought you here on the winds of a storm. I cannot tell you when He will bring others, it may be tomorrow or it may be years from now. If it's the latter, we will wait until His selections are ready. If you are agreeing to accept our offer, it looks like it will be just our two families who will have the privilege of being neighbors until God says different. I figure we can work together to secure a better life better for our young. We do not have children yet, but we are hopeful the Lord will grant us several. Just married five months now."

Elisha sat calmly without responding, although on the inside he felt like tossing his hat and shouting a loud boisterous 'yippee!' At the same time the practical part of him felt like he was living a fairytale, but if not a fairytale it was a great vision to be a part of.

The Blake's were surprised to hear the Barrett's were only married five months, both thought the couple had been together for years. Elisha wanted to get alone with his wife to talk this over privately, yet Cholena spoke first. "You give good welcome, like dream…must no Elisha's heart, we talk."

Elisha realized Cholena depended on hearing his side of things and knew he wanted to hear what she thought. This is new to him, *I guess all these months of my asking her ideas has shown how I value them.* He was glad she spoke up and he added his words of appreciation for the kindness that was shown to them.

Raine had another encouragement, "If you decide to stay on permanently or simply for the winter, I can assist with the newborn once the child is here. You need not worry about childbirth either when your time comes for the baby to be born. Ruth would be happy to bring the baby into the world in a manner you are familiar with."

When Cholena met Ruth and Caleb, it warmed her heart knowing the Barrett's were friends with them and certainly the idea followed. Any people, who opened their hearts to other Indians, could open their lives to her as well. After meeting them, the Blake's began to let down their guard a little and relax in the Barrett home, but not fully until this night. "This is good, thank you" Cholena responded.

Since there was nothing more to be said and everyone was hungry, Raine moved to finish the meal. Cholena stood up to follow, "I help."

"Not this time. You been overworked for days while I was indulging in self-pity," Raine replied. "This would be a good time for you and Elisha to go for a walk and talk privately. It is always good to get together with the husband to make everything clear."

Cholena looked at Elisha, who agreed it was a good idea. They excused themselves with the understanding they would be back for supper. The Blake's walk out to the barn, but when passing the two adobes they took special notice.

Before Price rested his eyes, he compelled Raine to come close. He took her small delicate hand and held it between his. "Beautiful, you did a wonderful job explaining to the Blake's. I apologized for being too tired to help you."

Raine did not let him feel indebted, "You are the one who got the conversation going with your insight from

God. I only filled in the blanks. She leaned over and gave him a kiss and with a fluttering heart Raine resumed working on supper while Price rested.

Elisha and Cholena returned faster than was expected, it did not take long for them to come to an agreement. After comparing mental notes, both thought it a worthy venture to stay here and have the baby and a good opportunity if all worked out. Nevertheless, there were a couple of questions Elijah needed answered, if he felt comfortable with the issues he would agree to stay, if not, he would decline the offer. Even though Elisha implied he would consider it before talking to Cholena, everyone understood if Cholena had reservations, no one expected Elisha to make her stay.

Once back at the house, Cholena immediately offer to help with meal preparation, but Raine insisted, "Just rest at the table and converse with me, while I finish. There really is not much left to do...you already completed your share earlier and you should take it easy, you work too hard. Besides, I am dying with curiosity to know what the two of you have decided and I do not want your thoughts on food." Raine giggled.

Cholena smiled, reluctantly sitting down at the table allowing Raine to finish alone. "No need rest...women made to have child," she sipped on her coffee.

Raine laughed, "You are right, Cholena, but you are a hard working woman. I appreciate all you have done for me." Raine lowered her voice, "Now what about the decision?"

Cholena smiled, cupping the outline of her ear and spoke simply, "you hear."

Raine smiled and listened as Cholena suggested. The recent tragedy and unique circumstances gave the two women a level of respect for each other.

As for Elisha and Price the previous awkward conditions that once prevailed subsided as they relaxed in the company of each other. They spoke over a few things that were unclear to Elisha and Price was able to present the picture with a man's view, which was exactly what Elisha needed, to have the vision unfold all the way for him.

Raine listened and when she felt the decision was made, she announced supper was ready. Elisha simply said "Mr. Barrett, we accept," shaking hands as partners in developing the framework of the Barrett's Promise Community.

♥

Chapter 26

Supper was ready, complimented with special touches from both woman and the two couples were ready to sit down at the table. They first allowed Price to maneuver his chair into place. He needed to sit where his stretched out leg would not interfere with the table guests. Then everyone took a seat and Price spoke the blessings which Elisha tolerated.

The meal was pleasant. They conversed as they ate enjoying the time together. Taking time to get really acquainted was long overdue. After all they have been through together a unique friendship was in the making. The recent tragedy seemed to intensify the closeness, even before knowing each other well.

When everyone was satisfied, the women began to clean up the table, and the men retreated to the sitting area. Elisha contemplated the earlier question and felt it was time to answer Price. He had intentionally kept his past private, but if he were going to be around these people, he knew he would have to take the risk and open up at some time. *Might as well do it now...would make living around them easier without me sidestepping all the time.*

Elisha shared about his upbringing in Toledo, Ohio. Which instantly invoked Price's attention, considering his own family roots were in Ohio. Elisha rambled on, explaining the full story. How he set out to pan for gold in California, but after the welcoming he received from the Osage tribe he decided to stay in their village and learn from them. He spent a year with the Osage before unexpectedly falling in love with Cholena, the Chief's daughter. Since she feared their attraction to each other would bring trouble for her father, they kept it a secret.

"It all changed when Cholena, the Chief's only child, refused to marry a prominent brave chosen to be the next leader preceding her father. Cholena went to her father and confessed our secret six month relationship. She explained to him that she could not marry the brave because she was already in love with me...to say the least, it was not well received. In her culture this was a big disgraced to her family and to her ancestors. Chief Ahanu needed his daughter to marry the next chief so the honor would remain with their lineage. If she refused, the honor would be taken from them when her father dies. It would have been different had Chief Ahanu had a son."

Price admitted his friendship with Caleb made him somewhat familiar with some tribal customs. Realizing there were differences among tribes, but acknowledged the basic traditions appeared to be similar.

Elisha continued, "Chief Ahanu became furious at hearing the news, and he threatened to kill me. However once he spoke it publicly he had to no choice. Although it deeply troubled him to do this, it sealed our fate. The Chief wanted to retract his own words, but did not know how to alter the traditions of his ancestors in order to accept his daughter's request. Moreover, being the Chief, he needed to back up what he said."

Elisha continued to explain how the Chief would not have been in such turmoil, had he not previously embraced Elisha as his son. This betrayal was another tug on Chief Ahanu already torn heart. After bringing Elisha into his household, treating him as his own blood and then have Elisha disgraced him. Price could see how this grieved Elisha.

While Cholena's father was apologizing to the ancestors in a secluded tent and talking with them on how to handle this situation, Elisha and Cholena decided to seal their commitment to each other in fear of being forced apart. They went to the nearby town and took wedding vows in a mission's chapel.

When Chief Ahanu heard this, he was hurtfully enraged, telling them both to leave the village and never return, they were dead to him! "Thus in his heart killing both Cholena and myself."

Cholena sat down next to Elisha, "My father call me Cholena Ahusaka...means bird wings. After I marry Elisha, father said 'he cursed own daughter by giving this name'...he very sad, much weight in heart."

Cholena found simple words mixed with hand gestures to express how she worries for her father, but has no regrets in her decision to marry Elisha. "If Father see daughter this sun," she laid her hand upon her stomach, "he see Cholena Ahusaka fly high with happiness."

Elisha lovingly rested his hand on her arm, then continued telling the story, "At first, I figured taking Cholena back to my hometown would be the best for us. I was under the impression my family would certainly love someone I chose for my wife. Unfortunately my own family and relatives did not welcome her. Several of the neighbors were too pious to show friendship to an 'Indian squaw' as they called her; taunting us with thrashing ugly words every time we were out walking together. The mass rejection of my own town was devastating to Cholena. She was dead to her family and now mine did not accept her. In her cultural upbringing, it was extremely demoralizing to be without a tribe, no family or roots to bring up children."

Both Price and Raine were deeply moved with compassion for the couple as the story of their lives unfolded, it was becoming clear why God chose them to live in Barrett's Promise. Their need was extreme.

Elisha took hold of Cholena's hand. *The thought of you laying down your life and everything you have known for me is an action I will never take for granted.* "When it became obvious we could not make our home in Ohio, I set out on a quest to provide a home for my gentle Cholena. Some town or settlement would certainly accept us and we would make our neighbors family...to grow old together and raise children. Little did I know how difficult that would be and how unfruitful our pursuit has turned out?" Elisha paused for a moment then with a tone of sincerity he added, "at least until now." Giving the Barrett's the benefit of doubt.

Price's heart grieved with them, sympathetic of the struggles they endured simply because they fell in love. He rendered a silent thankful prayer to the Lord God that He ended their quest by guiding them here.

Now that Elisha was sharing his heart for the first time with other people, he could not stop. The high walls were no longer there to hold back his feelings. More personal history unfolded, their time in Toledo only lasted two months. Then Chicago, Kansas City, St. Louis, then many smaller towns, wherever they went townspeople and settlers all displayed the same contempt for either his skin color, or hers, or both. People's negative responses kept driving them further west, hoping to locate a place for them to settle without ingrained prejudice. There were several settlements between Kansas and Albuquerque, where Elisha found meager work, but eventually their presence was not welcomed, either from the people themselves or their acquaintances. "Outside of Albuquerque we came upon an abandoned homestead. After finding the owner's relatives back in the town, we were able reach an agreement with them and we would sublet the land for half the crop. Things were looking up, for two months

Cholena and I labored hard on the land. We even sold some of our belongings to get started. However it did not take long for word to get around in town about us living on the homestead. In the middle of the third month, while we were relaxing in our home after supper disruptive men rode out from town and a few began circling the house, shouting insults while others were riding through our planted crops. I wanted to go shoot every one of them, but Cholena would not let me leave the house. She was frightened, so I obliged her and did not go out. I was only one man compared to the mob and I probably could not have done much, but get myself killed."

Hearing the frustration in Elisha's voice, being a man Price could identify. A quick glance at Raine, he wondered what he would have done in that situation, having your heart torn between the love of your life and your manly integrity.

Once again the Blake's met with the same discrimination, forcing them to leave the property. "I still cannot understand why that happened," Elisha said, scratching his head, "We were over ten miles from their town. No one even seen us for the most part, unless I came in for supplies. Which wasn't often."

"After that night, the crops were destroyed and we were unable to keep our end of the agreement. I tried speaking with the landholders, but the couple was aged and scared, they did not want any trouble. Unfortunately they lacked the courage to stand up to the townspeople. So regretfully we packed up and continued our plight."

Talking about it only made Elisha aware of the anger he felt, mixed with a lack of understanding over the insane actions demonstrated. "Even when passing through New Crossing, we met with the same insidious reaction. A burly man came into the hotel restaurant while we were eating. He belligerently demanded us out of the establishment and out of his town. We tried to peacefully finish our meal, but not a single person came to our defense, so we left…with Cholena's condition I could not chance her getting hurt."

When Raine heard what took place in New Crossing she knew instinctively the burly rude man mentioned was Max Harper. The hotel restaurant was his family's enterprise and no one would ever question his actions there, in fact most were afraid to cross him elsewhere. Max was in a league all his own, completely disreputable. Raine still was uncomfortable about the deception he pulled to get her alone in that covered wagon. *I am so grateful Price came by when he did…thank you Lord.* She looked at Price remembering him now as her rescuer.

If Price had known it was the same man who trapped Raine, it would have stirred up some unsettled feelings. He had not encountered the man he saw in the wagon on either of his trips into New Crossing. Listening to Elisha's explanation disturbed him enough to know the nearest town was not exempt from such evils.

Elisha felt a sense of satisfaction to finally be able to speak with another man, with his family ties cut and the abolishment of Cholena's tribe, there was never a man to confine in during their struggles. Now that he opened the door and let Price into his world, he felt an awkward safety. "Before that violent storm brewed, I had made a decision to stop searching for a family-friendly-settlement," speaking mockingly, "instead I had a new quest to find an uninhabited place where Cholena and I could dwell alone; I was desperate. You cannot imagine how shocked I was when Mrs. Barrett showed kindness, yet I did not trust her. I was uncertain if it were a trick of some sort...In fact, I decided not to trust anyone, even after we were here. Then you go make a generous offer to me, which really confused my mind because I had come to believe no one would ever accept us. I convinced myself the only reason we were allowed to stay here this long was because your wife had a need. I am still having some difficulty adjusting to new thoughts of our living here."

Price was listening, but his body felt weak and if it would not be for Elisha pouring out his soul, he would have excused himself to rest awhile. Perceiving a greater need was taking place, Price continued to listen as attentively as he could. At the same time he conversed with the Lord about this situation. Not to mention, Price was able to see the parallel of Elisha's struggles to his own family's plight. In fact, discrimination was the very reason they looked for a place so far out of town to settle themselves.

Price wanted to encourage Elisha, he was praying God would give him the right words, so when Elisha became quiet he took his opportunity. "Elisha Blake, I assure you as long as you and Cholena live on this ranch you can expect to be safe from prejudice behavior. We will never tolerate this sickness in Barrett's Promise."

"I'm going to suggest we make our first Law in Barrett's Promise, to ban this infectious behavior. If anyone demonstrates any form of prejudice, we will have a meeting and they will be in danger of being asked to leave our community. This issue tare's right at my heart. My family moved here because of discrimination. They were deaf and could not speak. They were often ridiculed back east in the town they lived in by a group of ignorant men. In their honor, with your help, we will stop this disease before it leaks out on their land...See Elisha just you coming here, God has brought this to our attention. I never thought of it, but now we will be on guard."

Elisha was surprised to find out Price's parents were motivated to established this piece of land out of their own private mistreatment. Even if it was unfathomable to even consider the enforcement such a Law. *It should not even need addressing... and what is the significance to my coming here have to do with anything...it is that God thing again,* he concluded.

The whole topic stirred Price to the core, he felt strongly about not tolerating this behavior on Barrett land. "I will make a sign, but we can post these moral laws on the barn for now. Later we can put a sign out by our entrance so everyone who journey's onto our land will know what we stand for and what we simply will not tolerate. I refuse to put up with this type of injustice from anyone, visitor or neighbor."

Elisha was quick to informed Price Barrett of the repercussions he could endure to have such a bold statement posted, since he recently experienced the world first hand. "You cannot possibly begin to perceive how a position like that could affect your family, or this community you are planning. There is a great deal of unwarranted hatred out there Price, people do not live by the same rules. You could be signing up for tremendous trouble."

"This does not scare me or surprise me. I know how deeply men are overcome by evil. I trust Father God who will uphold superior standards by His power. He is able to protect our land from the likes of evil men. Besides, that would not be a law that stands alone. It will be posted with our first Laws for this land. Like 'Honor with all reverence, God the Father, God the Son Jesus Christ and God the Holy Ghost'. It was His Commandment first and it will be our duty to abide in it."

Elisha felt he could go along with this proclamation as it was after all Price's land to do what he felt best. He just felt Price was asking for trouble with the other one.

Price was fidgeting in his chair, feeling quite uncomfortable, but his mind was soaring with ideas overriding the discomfort. "Actually this prejudice law goes with the second commandment Jesus gave us, which would be the second law posted, 'Love Your Neighbor as Yourself'. We can simply add after that, 'No Prejudice Tolerated.' What do you think?"

"What do I think?" Elisha scratched his head, "Golly Price, you sure do speak like you know this God personally. Frankly, I am not so certain about Him, but I am quite pleased to have met up with you. I like your ideas just fine."

"Well, Elisha, someday I would like to introduce you to Him. I am certain after you meet Him, you will find Him to your liking also," Price said with confidence.

The room became silent as each pondered over specifics of the conversation. They relaxed and enjoyed the flames dancing colorfully in the fireplace. It was very clear to Price why the Lord chose this couple. The Blake's had gone through a terrible time trying to find a home and needed a break in their struggles. By choosing them a foundational stone was added to the building of the community. One Price had not considered. At the same time, they needed to know the Savior. *Yes, Elisha Blake and Cholena, have first-hand knowledge of man's implausible evils, I am persuaded to demonstrate the difference.* He knew Father God would adequately prove Himself desirable. God's choice of people for the community pleased Price very much, if he had any doubts about this undertaking; they all left with the meeting of Elisha and Cholena Blake. *Why would I even doubt it, You planned Raine for me!*

Elisha gazed into the fire, lost in his own thoughts. He wondered about this God who Price revered like a favorite relative. Elisha's mind drifted back to a specific time in his childhood. He could remember the period as if it were yesterday. He and his friend Johnny Harris were walking back from Noah's house. After Johnny went inside at his house young Elisha continued walking home. On the corner was a church with music and happy singing echoing out into the street. Being a curious sort, he went to peek in the doors and came face to face with a man who had a big smile on his face. The man invited him to come in and sit down. *I went back a lot of times after that, for about a year, they were a loud bunch of people, but always happy…I loved those songs.* Elisha tried to think of the melody to one of them but couldn't. *In a day it all ended. Pappy found out about me attending a service and forbid me to ever go there again.* Pappy Blake did his best to convince his son 'church was for foolish superstitious people'. Elisha never visited the church again, because he certainly did not want anyone to consider him foolish. From that time on he took the long way home so he would not pass the church for fear the singing would lure him in. *Yet now this grown man, Price Barrett…quite different in many ways from the people in that church. Yet there is something that connects them,* but Elisha did not know what it was. He wondered now if his Pappy was wrong and where this venture in building this community with the Barrett's would lead him.

When Cholena and Raine finished the dishes, they took a cup of tea at the table. The men seemed occupied in the sitting area getting more acquainted.

Raine was surprised with the artistic quality Cholena possessed. She drew a simple sketch of her father, Chief Ahanu, on paper. The appearance of it seemed life-like. "Cholena, you have a beautiful talent. I am lucky if I can write legibly," Raine complimented.

Cholena was modest and felt it was her heritage which gave her the ability to recreate things onto animal hide, pottery and paper.

Raine viewed the dusty tools from Price's mother over in thc corner asked Cholena if she spun wool or made patch quilts. "I spin cotton, animal hair, plants…yes…quilt hands on blanket."

Raine showed Cholena the coverlet for the bed. "My mother and I made this quilt together. Price's mother quilt also."

"My village make many hand quilts. I make blankets with string…buffalo…horses…many things on blanket. I make bowl with clay dirt. You have clay dirt?"

"I do not think so," looking at Price for some input, but he had drifted off to sleep, so he was not of any help. "I make shawls, neck scarf, work gloves, hats, slippers and afghan's from string." Raine added.

"You teach me…I teach you blankets...this is good...yes?" Cholena said with pleasure.

"Yes it is good, we will learn from each other, I also make baby blankets." Raine smiled, "we are going to be great friends."

Cholena nodded with pleasure, her thoughts drifted to the powerful white-man's God who had answered her request. She would consider Him more in the days to come. *He prove Himself to me, I will be respectful.*

Raine wanted to stay excited about her new friends and the entire plan which the Lord was unfolding, but her guilt continued to come back and plagued her. *How could I burden a tired man tonight*? Looking at her husband sleeping upright in his wheeled chair. *It has been a trying day for him.* Even though she predetermined to take the first opportunity to talk with him about her failure. She would be flexible if the moment did not present itself.

Raine encouraged Cholena to go sit by her husband while she did some menial tasks around the home, stoke the fires and set things up for the morning. It would soon be time to get Price settled in for the night with Elisha's help.

♥

Raine finished the nightly chores and made evening tea for everyone. She brought it into the sitting area with some biscuit's and honey. Price woke up from his cat-nap, refreshed and alert, and talking up a storm. Elisha and Cholena were finally relaxed and comfortable in the company of the Barrett's. They were sharing ideas and adjusting positively to the proposal, even catching the vision of Barrett's Promise.

During coffee and biscuits, all four were interjecting suggestions for establishing a community, yet each looked to Price for his final say. While they all had an equal say as Price often reminded them, everyone knew he was the one to govern meetings and the community. Not because he was the owner of the land as much as it was his character. He showed a solid gentle way of leading which made people take notice and follow. While each realized the qualities they possessed were not intended for leadership.

Raine experienced moments of short-lived temper outburst over injustices, not to mention her betrayal. Cholena, her timid insecurities and Elisha's limited forgiveness of past acquaintances which often left him bitter and distrustful.

For Raine to look to Price for leadership was explainable, she was his wife and privately understood he would take every suggestion before the Lord before acting on it. For Elisha it was also a simple equation, Price owned the ranch, so it was natural he would have the ultimate say and for Cholena, she simply recognized the making of a chief.

The evening come to an end and Elisha assisted Raine on helping Price into bed. Then he and Cholena excused themselves, they too were exhausted. Raine was also tired, but prepared the night-fire in the sitting room before turning in for the night. Once in bed, her head barely touched the down pillow before overtaken in slumber.

Price however; after cat-napping earlier, now lay restlessly awake, with his leg uncomfortable in a splint. Yet this discomfort and pain was minor compared to his personal attitude problem that surfaced when Doc Skylar was here. He generally did not let things go this long without dealing with it, but he had been tired and he thought the tea Ruth prescribed for him knocked him out. For some reason he did not get it tonight and his eyes were wide awake in the darkness. *My pride, why did I give in to it? What motivated me to let evil surface like that?*

This greatly disturbed him and knew had to take care of it. He silence his thoughts and listened to the Holy Spirit. He wanted to identify the evil intention of his heart. *Father, forgive me for not dealing with this sooner, my two days adjusting to the splint or even feeling tired is a poor excuse. Lord, forgive me for wanting to look strong in front of my wife and friends. I am embarrassed to have them dote over me. Please help me accept my fate and this circumstance. I know it is for my good and at the end of this season I am sure I will embrace the changes made in me, even if I do not understand them now.* Price mulled regretfully over his sin until he heard the gentle whisper of the Lord, *"Forgiven, Remember it no more"*

Since Price was wide awake; he took the time to pray over burdens heavily on his heart. While he was praying for the Blake's, Raine, and God's protection over the ranch, in the midst of his plea, a strange sensation overtook him. He sensed in the Spirit, that the devil was indeed angered over the Lord's abundant blessings on the ranch and its inhabitance. This sharp pierce to his heart was an insight he would not take lightly. He realized now how important it was to pray daily for the protection of each person God brings to reside in Barrett's Promise. Another thing he understood was God's cultivating in him intercessory prayer, the way it was mentioned in the book, With Christ. *I accept this responsibility Father.*

Price thought of Ruth and Caleb, and felt confident these were perfect people to help the Blake's accept this as their homeland. His friends could certainly identify with the struggles the Blake's endured, because Caleb and Ruth were also rejected by their tribe. Caleb decided to establish a pueblo for his own family away from the tribe who rejected their Christian beliefs. The separation of family for a love principle is felt by both. *Please establish the relationship between these two families, Lord.*

After several hours of praying, his restlessness ceased and the discomfort of his leg was not noticed. He relaxed, in peace. It occurred to him, this would be how God would meet with him for the next few months. It was obvious he would not be riding out to the mesa in the mornings. Although he would not be able to bellow out a hymn or a song from his heart for fear of waking the house. Yet in the quietness of his mind he could sing to his heart's content, loud enough for the Lord to be pleased. He was satisfied with this new way. He loved spending time with Father God, while everyone sleeps.

Price's eyes were getting heavy and soon he would be joining his wife in restoring sleep. Snuggling close to Raine, the best he could, feeling relaxed and tranquil. He sensed everything was according to God's plan, and fitting together like a puzzle. Each piece a part of something not only useful, but beautiful. With this contentment, Price drifted into a restful slumber.

♥

✝ God kept a watchful eye on Barrett's Promise. Blessings of health and restoration were released the moment Doc Skylar prayed.

Price endured his trial admirably, and it pleased God to see his committed heart steadfast and unwavering.

The Lord recalled the Sunday morning when eleven year old Elisha Blake walked the isle of surrender. A glorious moment. Back then his young heart was tender desiring forgiveness and closeness. With Price in his life, his heart will wake up to believe again and the intimacy he once desired will be his reward.

Cholena, my sweet daughter, I have many blessings for you.

God took a moment to feel a daughter's anguish. He was privately acquainted with Raine's heart and was confident she would find her way back and be restored. This experience will not destroy her, He declared.

Yes, everything was on schedule. The Lord God gave His angels charge over Barrett's Promise to protect His children and create a platform on which the Glory of God will be magnified.

Inspired Concept: James 5:15, 1:2-4; John 3:16, 17; Psalm 1:1; 17:3-8; 34:7-9; Jude 24, 25

♥

Chapter 27

The next day Raine presented the two adobes to the Blake's. Cholena and Elijah took their time and viewed both places carefully. One was equipped to handle a large family. It had several bunks in the main room. The table was large enough to seat eight to ten people and the sitting area adaptable for the same. This adobe was built with a separate bedroom on the back side of the cook fireplace, which provided another fireplace like the one at the main house. The Blake's commented, "It is a beautiful home, very well set up."

The second one was smaller. It had less sleeping arrangements. There was a bunk built-in against the wall and five feet from it a free standing larger bed. On the far side of the bed was a wall the length of the bed. On the back side of the wall were shelves for dishes and books. Next to this was a small dinner table with six chairs. The back wall held the cook fire place which also heated the whole adobe. There was ample living space in the sitting area. It was simple, yet cozy. In the area were two chairs with cushions, a rocker and a small bench that sat under the bottled windows. This adobe also had a small room in the back, but it was not big enough to use as a bedroom. More like an above ground pantry with lots of shelves. Although this adobe was visibly smaller it had plenty of room to move around. Raine liked that the small wall shelf gave each area an independent feel about it. She had a real knack for making an area into a home and this showed in the two adobes she had cleaned. They were homes instead of the bunk houses they were created to be.

The Blake's thoughtfully chose the smaller adobe, the one closest to the barn. It was a sensible choice given that there were only the two of them until the newborn arrives. As it sits, this adobe would adequately house two children, maybe three.

Raine suspected if Elisha stayed passed spring he would want to build their permanent home, but for now she could see both of them looked pleasingly satisfied.

Cholena walked around the home looking at everything. *It was better than Raine conveyed the night before…it is our home, for now anyways.* Elisha vocally acknowledged that it was a very comfortable place and humbly admitted it was a better choice than life in a wagon. Nevertheless without any words spoken, Raine was correct in her assumptions, because inside of Elisha Blake was an undeniable passion to build a family home, *maybe I will build in the spring, if this works out,* he reflected. Even though many uncertainties still lingered about where they would be in the spring. He would not steal the joy he observed on Cholena's face this morning, *she loves this place.*

After Raine left, Elisha and Cholena allowed themselves a moment of lighthearted indulgence, bursting out in laughter and both flopping on the bed, looking up at the ceiling. "The mere fact we have left the wagon lifestyle, makes adjusting to this adobe quite doable, especially for the winter. We'll see what spring brings, but even a break is nice," Elisha suggested. Cholena smiled in agreement, feeling very contented.

Elisha started a fire in the cook fireplace; it did not take long to adequately warm the home. The two walked around the room getting familiar with every corner, seeing Cholena's eyes sparkle, confirmed to Elisha this was a good decision.

Raine had left a selection of teas as a welcome courtesy, so Cholena found a pot and brewed some for them to enjoy. While sipping on the warm tea, Elisha suggested, "Cholena, settle us into our new home in the Osage traditions," which basically meant she would burn selected herbs and sing songs blessing their new dwelling.

"I will." She smiled, recalling he had witnessed her blessing the last ranch. Only this time Cholena planned to include a request for the white-man's God to protect them and to come visit them frequently.

Once Elisha finished his tea, he went to retrieve their belongings from the wagon, and making certain to bring the herbal basket in the first load.

On Raine's walk back to the main house, she stopped by the coop to feed the chickens and gathered a few eggs. Left alone to her thoughts only troubled her, uncertain how to break the news to Price about her betrayal. Tending to the henhouse was actually a way of procrastinating, for she had already collected a few eggs this morning. She wanted some time alone to sort things out in her head because she was uncomfortable about having this confession conversation with Price.

Raine entered the house carrying a batch of eggs in her apron, and proceeding straightaway to the egg bowl sitting on the wash cupboard without making any eye contact with her husband. As she unloaded ten eggs from her apron she wondered if they would need more laying hens for the upcoming community. Which meant a larger hen-house and allowing some hens to sit this spring, to hatch more chicks. *The chicks Willie enjoyed are now ready to lay eggs...that will help with the Blake's, but I think we should prepare for more.*

Price was in his chair with wheels near the fireplace reading his Bible. He glanced up when Raine entered and noticed her wearing the same forlorn look he observed on her face the past few days. Price lowered the Bible to his lap and watched Raine for several minutes toiling with eggs then moving ambitiously around the area without even acknowledging his being in the room, which was very unusual. Price did not roll his chair closer to make her notice him, but continued watching from a distance, wondering what was wrong. Had he done something to cause this? *Lord what have I done?* Price could not handle seeing his wife look this troubled and being evasive. After a short prayer he knew it was time to find out what was causing this troublesome demeanor.

"Raine, come over and sit with me for a minute," he spoke patting the chair next to him. "I'd like to know which adobe the Blake's chose. I am sorry I was not able to go show it to them with you…this bum leg!" Price slapped his leg pathetically, displaying his anxious thoughts.

Raine hardly noticed Price's anxiousness concerning his leg. She was determined to not sit and proceeded to inform him about the Blake's choice, commenting how she believed they felt the home was more than satisfactory. While explaining she only glanced briefly in his direction. All the while continuing to make her actions busy fixing lunch in an attempt to keep her secret a little longer by not divulging anything in conversation. Raine Barrett was running from God and now also from Price. Recognizing this obvious fact, she became more disappointed in herself for not bringing the issue out in the open before now.

Price caught on quickly to her avoidance technique and boldly addressed it. "Why are you keeping yourself busy so that you hardly notice I am here? You have barely slowed down since you woke up this morning. Are you purposely trying to avoid me? What have I done to make your love turn from me? Have I done something to hurt you?"

Price's voice was heavy and demanding answers. Raine had never heard him speak so decisively direct before and when he asked about her taking her love away…it was more than she could bear. She never intended for Price to feel she was rejecting him, not loving him, especially now after he already endured so much. It was just the opposite. It was her deep love for him and not wanting him to know how ugly she had become in such a short time, this was the reason for her avoidance. Compared to Price's enduring faith, her betrayal was a miserable contrast, leaving her more shameful than ever. It hurt her that her actions had inflicted pain on Price. Reluctantly she knew it was time to get the whole torturous idea off her heart.

Turning to him with tears running down her face, "I'm sorry, I am not avoiding you Price for lack of love. I do love you and you have done nothing wrong." Her voice trembling as the tearful emotions could not be contained, "forgive me I..."

Just then Elisha Blake hastily entered the front door blurting out, "Price we have a problem. The windmill has suffered great damage from the storm and it is not delivering any water into the well."

Raine quickly turned her tearful face away from Elisha's sight and proceeded to work on lunch, while Price directed his attention to the crisis at hand. "Explain what you have found Elisha," again feeling extremely helpless.

Elisha bent over, his hands on his knees catching his breath, then straightened his body up and began to inform Price the complete situation. "I did not notice the water level dropping this past week since the storm subsided, but today it is clearly visible. I checked the windmill and two of the arms have been damaged. They are not catching the wind. I think I can climb up and fix it alone. However, it would go a lot faster and actually be safer if I had some help. I know you cannot do it. I just thought maybe you knew another rancher we can get to help us. If not, I am capable of fixing the problem alone, but it may take longer. I figured you needed to know right away so you would be aware to conserve some water for a while…I could go get water from the river and you can boil it Raine, if your supply is low." Looking over at Raine who gave him her attention, he continued without noticing anything was wrong, "I am going to have to do that for Cholena before I get started anyways."

"I appreciate the offer Elisha, but I have plenty and if I need more I can go to the river myself and get it. Don't trouble yourself, just take care of Cholena's supply and concentrate on fixing the windmill." Her words were sincere, as she laid aside her personal troubles.

Elisha heard what she said, but planned on including water for the main house in the morning anyways when he refilled the supply for Cholena.

"Sorry Elisha, because of our location, I do not know another rancher living out this way." Price searched the Lord quietly for an answer. "I do have one idea," Price interjected. "Ride out to Caleb's pueblo and recruit one of his son's to come help. He has three strapping strong braves, Shinning-light is the oldest, then Faith-Walker and Good-Follower. I am certain one will come and offer good assistance. Caleb has raised those boys very well."

To hear of Caleb's three sons was encouraging. Elijah quickly replied, "I will need some directions. I have no knowledge where the pueblo sits or what direction I need to go to get there."

Price began to lay out clear and precise directions for Elisha, drawing a map on a piece of parchment. Meanwhile Raine grabbed her shawl and went near the barn to access the damages herself. This way she could confirm the findings to Price, being his eyes by proxy. She could see the two distorted arms of the windmill from the veranda, but getting closer she noticed the missing board slats and one of those arms were only half there. She passed Elisha as she headed back. He was going in the adobe to inform Cholena that he was leaving the ranch to recruit some helpers from Caleb's family.

Raine placed her covering on the hook and proceeded to tell Price. "It is as Elisha described, but he did not mention about one of arms being gone completely."

Price was at the door observing the damage from his distant view, but the wind direction had the blades turned so he could not see much. He was glad Raine thought to go look for him, knowing two sets of eyes on a problem was a good evaluation. Price thanked God openly for bringing the Blake's here at this time, he could not have handled this situation alone. Price centered his attention back on Raine, "The windmill will be fixed, but I think we need to refocus on us. What were you about to tell me before we were interrupted?"

Raine did not hesitate this time; she promptly took a seat by Price and placed her hand in his for security. "I have something to tell you that I am dreadfully ashamed of."

Raine began pouring her heart out to Price. Explaining how fearful she became at the thought of losing him. "It was too soon to lose you, after waiting so long for you to come into my life." She continued, divulging her moments of anger and did not withhold the blatant statements she had spoken to Father God.

Price could not help feeling somewhat flattered to know how deep her love for him had grown. At the same time, he felt terrible her relationship with the Lord suffered by not trusting Him, knowing this is a greater loss than losing a husband.

She confessed openly, "The part that bothers me most is I shouted at Him saying, He was a cruel God and I did not want to serve Him anymore. I feel terrible about it now." When she revealed this part she let go of Price's hand and lowered her head, because she could no longer bear to look at him. Focusing on the floor, she mumbled a tone scarcely above a whisper, "How can God forgive me for saying such terrible things?" The tears came rapidly and she began to sob. She was too ashamed and did not raise her head, but covered her face with her hands.

Oh this stupid chair! Price thought trying to get his body close enough to comfort his wife by embracing her in his arms, but he was unable. Taking the only approach available to him, "Raine," he spoke gently above a whisper. While at the same time affectionately rubbing her back as she slumped over on her own lap. "I want to hold you and take your pain. You cannot imagine how much it grieves me to not be able to do that. This chair prevents me. How can I comfort you?" She remained unspoken, weeping. "My anguish for you is great, nonetheless, I have to consider my restriction is not by accident at this crucial time. Our Father God does not make mistakes and He is very detailed. Many things in life we are required to endure alone. Maybe this is your private plight. If there was any time for this to be different I wish it were now, because my heart is breaking along with yours." He caressed her back and leaned over enough to be able to kiss the back of her head. Laying his head gently on top of hers, "Beautiful, have you spoken with the Lord about this? If you have not taken time to sit with God and express your regrets, than you must do it. Stay with Him until you receive His peace. He will not reject you. Do not avoid Him." He paused momentarily waiting for a response, then asked again, "Have you talked with Him since you realized you were wrong?"

She shook her head 'no'.

"Oh Darling, I recommend you comply with your heart right now and do not put it off any longer. I should leave you alone for a while. I can take my Bible into the guestroom and read for a while, because this is something I cannot fix for you. I will be praying continually while you pursue Him to have your relationship mended…trust the Lord, He loves you."

Raine did not lift her head and kept her hands over her face. She knew Price was right and weakly replied, "I will do as you have asked…I have put it off too long already."

"Trust Him Raine, Our God is not a tyrant. He is a loving Father, and always faithful." Price gave another gentle rub to her back before removing his hand and clumsily motivated his chair into the other room.

"Raine heard Price fumbling to get the door to close. When she heard it shut, she lifted her head and looked around the room. She was alone, yet not really. There was a deep intense feeling of the Lord's presence, as if He was waiting for her to speak. Wiping her tears on her apron, "Father, I am so sorry." The tears fell again, "I should have known with the promises you already gave me about our children and the community, it was not your intention to bring us harm. Rather You would keep your promise. You would take care of Price. I was being selfish and bratty, worst yet, I was not keeping You first. I put my wants and Price's life above You. Please forgive me. I did not mean those words I said out of my selfish fear." She wept mournfully, desiring a quick reply, but nothing came, only more silence.

Raine's heart felt empty, as if it were missing the very element that brings the beat. It was like a hole so deep inside she feared it would swallow her and she would be lost within this nothingness forever. Raine's mind was terrorized. A deep apprehension was moving over her, as she feared being lost from the Lord forever, "I called you cruel. You are not. You are kind, loving, and I am the one who is cruel. In my anger I said I did not want to follow You. I was self-centered. I was mad because everything was not going my way. Forgive me...Lord, please in Your mercy, forgive me. I do not know how to live without You." Still the bitter emptiness surrounded her and desperation multiplied, "Lord...I do love Price, but I give him back to You. I do not want to put him before You ever again and if being married will turn my heart away from You...than Lord remove me from it, by any means you see fit." She then added weakly, but still fully submissive, "even death".

There was a melancholy silence in this surrender. She meant it. Life without the Lord was harder than life without Price.

After what seemed like a long time of silence, Raine began to sense a trivial breakthrough. Nevertheless it was not anything big enough to identify as releasing her from the immense grief. Although it occurred to her, God was letting her know His ear was attentive to her cries. "Father, have mercy on me a sinner, full of sin...I have been an unfaithful and ungrateful servant. I do not deserve your forgiveness. Yet I have read in the Holy Scriptures, 'Your mercies are new each morning' and Father, I need some fresh mercy today. Your Word also says You are longsuffering and not willing that anyone should parish...if I have understood that correctly, it means even me. It is not Your desire for me to parish, but rather I come to repentance…I am here Lord. I would like to be able to say from now on, I will be always full of faith and trust You, but I fear I am weaker than this. I cannot promise you vain words. All I can say is here I am. If You are willing to change this wickedness in me and grant me Your forgiveness, than I am willing for You to fix whatever unrighteous is in me, no matter the cost. I surrender all to You." Raine poured her heart out, weeping and still feeling doomed. She was at the point of giving up and considering her loss when she heard. *"Forgiven, speak of it no more."*

"Truly Lord, Are You accepting my repentance?" and again she heard, *"I accept all true repentance; I was waiting for you not to be consumed by your own pain, you wanted the pain to stop more than you desired Me. Now speak of it no more, I do not want to be reminded of your sin, you are clean."*

Raine knew the words of the Lord spoke truth. She was even selfish in her repentance. *How can He put up with me, is there any hope?* She thought. Then she remembered a passage *'the Lord is the Perfector of our faith.'* In her relief she spoke openly, "There is hope…thank You Lord. Make me worthy of your grace, and perfect my faith." Peace sheltered Raine like a thousand veils in the wind, and she was restored, not unexcused for her betrayal, but forgiven. *I am clean.*

Tap, tap, tap…the sound of Raine's hand knocking on the guest room door before entering.

Price looked up from his Bible to see a glow restored to his wife's beautiful face and without words, he knew her meeting with God was successful. His mercy covering her was evident. *Thank You Lord.*

Raine knelt beside Price, laid her head on his lap and he embraced her. She lifted her head to look at him, and with tear stained hazel eyes, she spoke softly. "Forgive me Price, for risking everything we have built our foundation upon…I will not make it a habit. With God's help, of course. I love you deeply and I am so glad you are alive, but I must confess, I love Father God more."

"As it should be," Price leaned forward and kissed the top of her head. He understood everything was settled, his wife was going to be all right. "I love you, Beautiful."

♥

Yesterday's ride to Caleb's pueblo was a success, not only were the three boys available, Caleb was happy to help also. All four arrived on the ranch at first light, waking Elisha and checking out the damages. After the men constructed a plan on how to tackle the problem, they went right to work.

When Price heard the pounding, he asked Raine to look out to see if Elisha and the others were working on windmill. She confirmed it, seeing Caleb and his son's horses tied to the rail in front of Elisha's adobe.

Raine took advantage of the unaided morning to clean Price's leg before assisting him into the chair by herself. A task the Lord was gracious to let go smoothly. However Price was not as model of a patient as she would have liked, nevertheless she was quickly becoming familiar with the male ego.

While Raine busied herself cooking breakfast, Price wanted to observe the work going on. He rolled his chair to door, but when he finally got it opened, a blast of cold air rushed inside the house making his wife shiver. Price was too restless to feel the drop in temperature, but noticing it was a problem for Raine, he closed the door. He was antsy…slightly edgy about not being able to get out there and join in the labor. Having to rely on others to do his work just did not feel right. He vented out loud, "Things have sure changed…Pa and Mama gone. I'm married to a beautiful wife and now it appears I cannot even work to take care of her." It was not because he did not trust the men involved, he knew they were capable of accomplishing the task flawlessly, *here I sit drinking coffee while my friend's labor on our damaged windmill,* he mulled over in his head.

Raine heard the grumble and silently prayed. In all these months she never saw Price ruffled by anything, but being confined to the house really had him bothered. The best thing she could do was give him as much space as he needed to work this out, and continue to pray. It amazed her on how quickly her prayer life returned to normal. Even though she was working on breakfast she was praying fervently in the Spirit again.

Price picked up his Holy Bible from the table and wheeled himself into the guestroom, "I will be taking some private time with Father God. Maybe He can help me make some sense out of this." Informing Raine as he closed the door.

Raine held breakfast until Price was ready. The biscuits were finished cooking and in the warmer. Some fried mush was being kept warm in another opening in the fireplace. *I love this cook fireplace!* Setting the eggs aside as they would not take long to prepare when Price come out. Meanwhile she paced the floor praying silently for her husband.

It was about an hour later when Price came out looking like he had received a scolding. Although his demeanor did not display any of signs of previous agitation, he was unusually quiet. Raine was grateful, reckoning he found some peace. She went right to work preparing the breakfast eggs, setting out the mush and biscuits.

It felt a little awkward eating her meal in silence, as it was apparent Price was not ready to talk. After breakfast was finished she cleared the dishes, poured a second cup of coffee and sat down quietly to drink it. She continued silently praying for her husband, who appeared to be unaffected by her presence.

Price lingered at the table with his coffee in hand, trying to muster up the courage to share with Raine the conclusion of his conversation with Father God. "Thank you." he said, holding up his cup before taking a drink.

"You're welcome. I was hoping I would not need to add goat's milk and honey this morning." She smiled trying to make light of the moment.

"Sorry I was so long."

"That's ok...as long as you are alright."

"I am fine, a little humbled, but fine."

"Do you want to talk about it?"

"Actually, I have been sitting here wondering how I could tell you that your husband is a prideful man."

"Really, I think he is a good man."

"You are too kind, Beautiful...God gave us the desire to share our land with others in making a community and look at me, I cannot even let go of a simple windmill. If I feel possessive of this windmill, how can I begin to let go of the rest of our land and allow others to unite in the responsibility of it?"

Raine was silent, what could she say? Her heart hurt for Price, but she had no words of comfort.

Price continued, "The Lord was quick to remind me of this fact. He let me know in no uncertain terms my being in this chair confined to the house was exactly what I needed to get a right perspective of the ranch. God does not make mistakes! This is why Elisha came when he did. Elisha is the first one I have to convince this land belongs to him too. It is no longer my family's sole possession and frankly I do not know how to do that. Will you help me...if I get overly possessive and controlling, showing ownership? Do not hesitate to let me know. I do not want to disappoint God anymore. This was the first time I actually raised my voice to Him and I am so dreadfully ashamed of it. He owns our land now Raine. We willingly gave it to Him, and we are just equal settlers on our Father's land."

Raine's compassion for Price was immense, however she still didn't know how to answer him. Especially now, seeing they both had disappointed their Father. She stood up and moved around the table to his side. Bending over his back, she threw her arms around him. "I will do whatever I can. I understand how very hard this must be for you Price, but we will learn to trust God while He teaches us both how to let go. You are so close to Him. I know His strength in you will triumph over these feelings of ownership. You will learn to let go...what greater honor can you give your parents than to present their land to the Lord for His use?"

"You always say the right things. I love you so much Beautiful."

The manual labor on the windmill lasted three days, nevertheless with great diligence the men were able to fix the damaged paddles and the water level began to rise abundantly in the well. Caleb and his sons took daily lunch breaks in the Barrett's home to spend time with Price. Elisha joined them, as Cholena was determined to help Raine prepare meals for everyone.

During this time, Price took pleasure in Caleb's daily friendship. They carefully deliberated on certain Biblical principles, especially ones on not holding on to anything too tightly or selfishly. Price considered these conversations over lunch quite beneficial. 'Surrender to God what is already His' became Price's theme, and he would remind himself every time he felt the twinge of ownership. Caleb never really struggled with any possessions. He believed God gave the land to everyone to use, but never to possess. So his insights were meaningful to Price, helping him to grow in understanding.

When evening came the Barrett's had adequate private time for fellowship, where they would read the Good Book together and review Andrew Murray's book. Then every evening Elisha returned to help situate Price in bed. Although Price was getting fairly good at moving the splint around. With his strength was returning to his good leg he needed less help to do the simple things and was feeling more independent.

Since the time of correction and refreshing in the Lord Raine and Price's relationship grew even closer to each other and to Father God. Once again they were enjoying unstrained rapport with each other. Talks about the Scriptures and the lessons in prayer flowed freely. Life for them was a new form of normal. Everyone seemed to be managing with Price's limitations.

Price was faithful every day to do the treatments Doc prescribed to strengthen his arm. Earlier tonight he tested his skill. He attempted to pick up a cast iron skillet and was instantly humbled, he barely got it off the table. To top off his humiliation, he had to observe frail petite Raine pick it up and put it away without even a sign of awkwardness. Lying on his bed tonight, he pondered, *"Lord I continue to be humbled, return my strength to me so..."* interrupted by *"Patience is a virtue, My son."* Sigh...

♥

✞ God smiled. It was good to see Raine & Price back in fellowship. He sent strength of body, mind and soul to Price. Surrendering his ranch was indeed harder than moving a lame arm.

Inspired Concept:
Isaiah 40:28-31

♥

Chapter 28

It was unfortunate for Price that Doc Skylar was unable to come back to his ranch in the month timetable as previously planned. Those two extra weeks were not easy for Price. He was thankful for the never-stopping Wiggins to able to bridge the gap between doctor and patient. Nonetheless, no matter how certain Price felt he was ready the Lord disagreed, and spoke decisively to him, "*Doc. Skylar would come at the right time.*" Price came to realize this was God's providence and understood He detained Skylar. So Price continued listening to the doctor's orders and waited for the time Skylar would be free to come before adding any weight to his leg. Truth was, if Doc had come earlier, Price would have needed to endure another full month before Doc would be able to return a second time.

The only solace he had in waiting was the accomplishment of the iron skillet challenge and he was now able to transferring himself. With this achievement his arm was gaining strength daily.

When Skylar arrived two weeks later than scheduled, everything had healed perfectly. After examining the leg and a whisper from the Lord, he had the confidence to release Price from the splint and wheelchair. The leg was notably weaker and Price would need exercise to build up his muscle. However, a walking stick would add sufficient support until his strength returned. As for Raine's abrasions, they were no longer a concern, completely healed. Doc Skylar could return to New Crossing with a good report to Rhoda, without any more fretting for his friends.

After visiting Elisha and Cholena, having a pleasant lunch, and healthy chat with Price, telling him about the new med-center station where Millie's family now lives, he was ready to head back. Right after praying together. No one was sure when Doc would be able to come back with winter setting in.

♥

The winter of 1912-1913 proved to be most trying for Doc Skylar; the western wilderness was a far cry from city life and his travels to the settlements were often perilous with blowing windstorms, yet he was determined to adjust to this new way of life. He had not visited the Barrett ranch since early January, when he checked on Price.

It pleased Doc when he had heard about the Blake's decision to stay on the ranch for the winter. Recalling the Barrett's idea of building a community, made this arrangement with the Blake's even more interesting to observe. However, Cholena being with child did concern him. He was too far away to deliver the baby in a moment's notice. After examining her last January, he felt she was healthy and strong enough to deliver naturally. With Ruth close by and experienced in bringing infants into the world, there should be no reason for him to make a treacherous trip back before spring. Just the same he gave some simple instructions to make her delivery go easier and promised he would check on the child soon as the weather permits. Cholena and Elisha were content with this arrangement, besides there was always Wiggins if he were needed sooner.

Price recalled Skylar's past visit to the ranch and felt his timing was always impeccable. His coming the morning after being found in the cave, to the exact time needed for his leg to heal. It continued to amaze him how 'God worked all things for the good of those who love Him' and he knew Skylar was listening.

Price had begun making his regular visits out to the mesa. Even the cold blowing winds did not stop him. Although he was wise enough to know some mornings would be hard on Girl, his mare and Trader. On these days he retreated to the guestroom for solitude, like he did this morning.

Refilling his coffee cup, Price noticed Raine absorbed in reading her Bible. Not wanting to disturb her, he put on a jacket and went out on the porch. As Price sat down in the rocker, *it still feels brisk this morning. The rampant dust seems to have settled down...the growing daylight will quickly make the day tolerable.* Looking over the quiet ranch, Price began to evaluate the winter events as he enjoyed his coffee. *Often on winter days the workload is unbearable; this year certainly has met that criterion.* Price began to review what had taken place; *Elisha, Caleb and his sons started out last November...after the storm, repairing the damage to the windmill.* He looked over at the windmill turning, visible in the morning dusk. *They did a great job...Next was the unexpected job of repairing wagon wheels; all four suffered serious damage after Raine's adventurous search in the icy slush on rocks. Elisha eagerly rebuilt four of them, then replaced the worn-out ones before I was able to leave the house. Once I was released to walk again, my first job was to build several more wheels to have on hand. It was good to have Elisha work with me on these.* This brought a smile to Price, it really was about all he could do in the beginning with his uncooperative leg. Shaking his head recalling how weak he was. *I was pathetic.*

Glancing in the direction of the fuel shed then on the lean-to shelter he & Elisha set up. It was where the constructed privies were being stored. Considering another unexpected job that had required attention. The winter's strong winds blew over the privy, destroying it. *Together we immediately build five of them, replaced the one and four are ready to install in the spring. If that wasn't enough to do in the past month, now we have another unforeseen situation.*

It was Late February. *The blistering cold nights caused the gears in the windmill to lock up*! This slowed down the water to a light trickle in the well. *I have never known it to freeze up in all my years on the ranch, but then again this is unusual weather.* He wrapped his coat tight to his neck and continued to enjoy the fresh morning air, even while mulling over the winter's chore list.

Price was grateful to have Elisha's help. He was certain without his new friend to sustain the ranch this winter, it would have been impossible for him to maintain it alone. *God always comes through at the right time, giving us what we need and this year we needed Elisha Blake.* "Thank You Father for Elisha", the words barely flowed out of his mouth when he looked up to see Elisha stepping out on his porch ready for another day, *what a blessing!*

It was a tiresome day struggling to free up the gears on the windmill. After constant determination the parts finally began moving freely. Relieved, the men headed to Price's house for a bite to eat.

Cholena and Raine had planned a special dinner to show appreciation for their two hardworking men. They were looking forward to an evening of relaxation and socializing. However when the men arrived, they noticed the table was not set for a meal as expected. Instead they found the women in the sitting area, where Raine was reassuring Cholena, telling her, "Everything was going to be fine". She had gone into labor.

Price sprang into action and headed for the barn to

saddle up Girl to ride out to Caleb's pueblo. He had to get Ruth, this was his designated job. Meanwhile Raine and Elisha assisted Cholena back over to her home where preparations were already made for the delivery.

Raine waited impatiently with Cholena and Elisha, hoping that Ruth would arrive soon. She was a bit jumpy being unsure of what to do if Ruth did not come in time. Raine had never been around anyone who was having a baby. In fact, without doubt, she certainly was not the person to help Cholena with birthing.

Her head was spinning with thoughts, *Golly gee I never even seen an animal give birth*; she felt helpless. Although Raine had the general idea, mostly from books she'd read. Yet at this precise moment, *Book knowledge is not very comforting on my skills as a midwife.* She felt more nervous than Cholena, as they waited for Ruth to arrive. Although Elisha had her beat.

Raine did her best to hide her fears and comfort Cholena, dabbing her forehead with a damp cloth as she lay on the bed. "Ruth will be here soon, dear friend."

It was Cholena who made the decision for Elisha to go over to Raine's house to wait for their son's arrival. He acted twice as nervous as Raine felt. Displaying a very restless behavior and making Cholena worry more about him than concentrating on delivery. She was putting more effort in keeping him calm, way more than she needed to be doing at this time.

Elisha knew she was right so he left, but with reservations. He would be pacing no matter where he was at and he could see he was not helpful to Cholena.

After he was gone Cholena felt she could begin to concentrate on bringing her young one into the world as lovingly as she could. She gently caressed her belly and in between her pains she hummed a melody. A calming gesture for her, the unborn, and Raine.

When Raine peeked out the door to check if Ruth was coming she noticed Elisha still pacing back and forth on her veranda across the way. *Lord, help him not to worry.*

It was not long after when Price stopped at the Blake's on his way back to the house. "Caleb and Ruth are right behind me", he informed. "She wanted to gather some herbs to bring."

Raine felt distraught, but tried not to show it, "I do hope she gets here soon...Oh...there is a pot of soup on the fire. Please put it on a warming shelf and help your selves to some. I hope it is ok. I never got the bread out either, it might be burnt...I'm sorry"

"Do not let it worry you. I can take care of everything. Where is Elisha?"

"Cholena sent him over to the house because he was extremely restless and making her nervous. A few minutes ago he was pacing the porch, he must have went inside."

Price hugged Raine and turned to say something comforting to Cholena before leaving, but Cholena let out a loud cry. "I better go." He was swift to leave and went out the door. It happen to be just as Ruth and Caleb were approaching. Price took Caleb with him to locate the panic stricken papa and Ruth went inside.

Raine was never more relieved to see Ruth's beautiful face. She embraced her with a hug. This was not a common gesture for Ruth who was not the hugging type, but Raine could not hold back her relief in seeing her. Then she spontaneously moved aside so Ruth could tend to Cholena, who let out another excruciating cry. Indicating a contraction.

Raine had kept the hot water pots boiling gently for sterilizing in the fireplace so everything would be ready. Now with Ruth here, the home became a warm safe environment. Cholena was genuinely relieved to see her.

Ruth went right to work and examined Cholena. She looked around the room for what she would need when the time drew near, moving somethings to locations closer to the bed.

Raine was still quite nervous, she picked up a stack of clean towels and gave them to Ruth, thinking Ruth would be using them straightaway.

Noticing the panic in her friend, Ruth calmly said, "Raine, you need to settle down, it is just a baby and everything is happening just as it should."

"Yes Raine, please...sit...rest...oooh...." Another contraction, "pray, you pray good," Cholena managed to say between her groans of pain.

Ruth interjected, "Brew herbs in pot, first make tea then sit."

"Ok, ladies, I get the point, I will brew some tea and sit and be quietly praying. However if you need an extra hand for anything, feel free to tell me what to do...I follow orders well."

Cholena and Ruth both expressed she would indeed be needed to assist later. Ruth stressed the point, "You must calm yourself down, or you are not going to be of good service when time comes."

As much as Raine tried to relax, every scream Cholena let out, only increased her apprehension. Once the tea was ready she poured a cup for Cholena as Ruth instructed, and one for herself as Ruth insisted, Ruth did not want any.

Raine sipped the tea, it was flavorful and she was beginning to feel calmer drinking it. She browsed around the room, keeping herself occupied and somewhat detached. Cholena had turned the vacant adobe into a very comfortable home. The tapestry Cholena was working on sat in the corner. Raine examined it carefully and was impressed with Cholena's talent in this art. She remembered the sketch she had drawn of her father, Chief Ahanu. This tapestry was fast becoming a real beautiful piece to hang on the wall. It was a picture of her tribal family, recognizing the Chief. The sketch of him sitting with family on the cloth was excellent and life like in its quality. Raine surmised it would be used in sharing her heritage with her children. *I love it, she is so talented!*

Raine was surprised to see a Holy Bible on the shelf. It looked old, but unused. She took it down from the ledge, dusted it off and opened to the first page. The hand written inscription was: To: Elisha Blake on Dec. 24, 1890, *Elisha owns a Bible*? She was astounded, *he has never expressed any reference of being familiar of the Faith.*

Raine took the Bible back to her seat to read. She opened the pages to Psalm's in hopes to receive some comfort from her trepidation. While reading, she occasionally glanced up to observe Ruth and Cholena. She felt such admiration for these women. Each worked their role perfectly and they did it exceedingly better without Raine. She wondered what was in the tea that made her calm down so easily.

The birth was not as quick as Raine hoped for. Only once was Raine asked to do anything. To keep herself busy, she looked after several pots of water and kept the home fires toasty. That was the extent of her toil during the night. The rest of the night Raine maintained an appearance of half-awake, half-asleep, propped up in the corner rocker. On the times Raine was awake, she would read aloud the Scriptures and felt a calming rest on all of them, making her feel useful.

The light began to peek through the bottle windows, yet there was still no baby. Raine felt empathy for Cholena, who was noticeably exhausted. However, Ruth was amazing. She stayed steadfast at Cholena's side all night, fully energetic. It was a good thing she was still lively, as Cholena began to labor more severely with the light of day.

"It's time," Ruth called to Raine, "Come here, sit behind Cholena and allow her to lean on you, while you steady her in a sitting position." After Raine was positioned correctly at the back of her laboring friend, Ruth began confidently coaching Cholena in the final phase of delivering her child. "Gently push," then "push hard...gentle. Hard...again...that's it...three more sets and you will have this child."

With Raine securing Cholena's back as instructed, Cholena did exactly as Ruth coached her to do, allowing the sweet miracle to happen. Ruth graciously received the new life entering the world. "It's a beautiful brave," Ruth informed as she set the infant on Cholena's stomach for her observation. Next Ruth cut the umbilical cord and packed the area with white sterile cloth. She promptly took the infant up by his feet, smacked his bottom and the cry of a newborn baby resounded throughout the home. Ruth bathe him tenderly cleaning the mucus from his body and face.

Raine could not believe how fast the actual delivery and clean up was. Only a matter of minutes. She felt safe knowing Ruth would be the one to deliver her child when she begins a family. She could hardly take her eyes off the new babe, while helping Cholena reposition herself in the bed. She took a wet cloth and wiped Cholena's face, refreshing her. Then adjusted her hair behind her ears and situated the pillows so Cholena head would be slightly lifted.

All the while Raine was making her friend comfortable, Cholena's eyes never left her baby boy. Watching Ruth as she bathed him and wrapping a soft piece of yellow flannel around her son. When Ruth finished she handed the beautiful babe to his mother.

The women stood in awe admiring the newborn. There is something that transcends the hearts of all who witness the miracle of birth. Raine's heart melted finding a pure golden ember burning inside of her which revealed a clandestine truth. Having a child would only complete her relationship with Price. Understanding this certainty, in this moment she found herself longing for a baby. Raine admired Cholena's little one and noticed his miniature resemblance to his father, Elisha. As she observed Cholena holding her fine-looking son, she understood what a privilege she was given in this moment. To be a witness to the most beautiful miracle, God's creation of birth.

Cholena's gentle sweet voice broke through Raine's encompassing thoughts to ask, "Please get father…he be worried."

Ruth added, "I will clean bedding when you leave, everything should be done when he comes. Do not rush."

Raine happily agreed and swiftly put on her wrap. She then bent over to kiss Cholena's forehead and whispered, "I am so happy for you…he's beautiful." She squeezed Ruth's hand and smiled as she passed by her to go retrieve Elisha. What a privilege she was given, not only to witness the birth, but also to ease Elisha's mind from worry and announce the arrival of his son.

♥

When Raine opened the door to her home, she witnessed three men sleeping. Elisha slept upright at the table with his head resting upon folded arms. While Caleb slept with his chin tucked onto his chest in a rocking chair and Price lay sprawled out across the bed from corner to corner. Even Trader was sleeping soundly on the woven rug. When she closed the door in a normal fashion no one woke to the sound of it, *they must have been up late.* She spoke out the news, "It's a boy," but no one budged.

Raine walked up behind Elisha laying her hand gently upon his shoulder, she spoke softly over him hoping to stir him awake. "Your son has been born Elisha."

Elisha abruptly jumped, startled by her voice and touch. Once he noticed it was Raine, he instantaneously asked, "Has the baby arrived yet?"

Being happy to inform him, Raine replied proudly, "Yes, you have a healthy beautiful boy, Elisha."

A smile covered his mouth and he stammered, "A boy…a son." His countenance shined like a man who accomplished something important and at the same time there was an element of humbleness, entwined with joy. Raine did not miss a thing in her observation.

After a few moments feeling dazed, Elisha anxiously remembered the boy has a mother. "How is my wife, Cholena…my wife…how…how is my wife?" He anxiously questioned.

"Cholena is beautiful as ever and doing fine. She is a little drained, it was a long night, but she is now laying comfortably tending to your son and waiting to share this joy with you."

Jubilant Elisha quickly stood to his feet, pushed his hands into his hair. A gesture to make his appearance look proper. Then added, "You mean Cholena is awake and I can go home to be with them now?"

Giving a gentle chuckle, she encouragingly patted his back, and replied, "Of course Papa, oh I forgot…should I say Pappy?" Raine heard him refer to his father in those terms of endearment before, so she figured this would be his title also.

"The delivery time is over and now the celebration of life begins. I know you must have felt festive when Cholena found out she was with child. Well Elisha, my friend, this time you have family to share in the rejoicing of your son's birth."

Elisha picked up his coat. He turned back to look at Raine. "We were so happy. I stopped the wagon right in the middle of grassland between Santa Fe and Albuquerque. We danced. I swung Cholena around in my arms…I tell ya, she never looked more beautiful than she did that day." Then he paused, remembering the responsibility that followed and shared. "It took me two days before I began to realize the magnitude of our need. We had to find a place for us to settle. Thought we found it once…but now…I am so grateful to you and Price for inviting us to live on the ranch to become a part of this growing community. It really means so much to us. We have already decided to stay after the spring." Elisha slid his arms into his fur coat, while buttoning it he finished his thought. "We actually feel like we belong somewhere. The peace we have knowing our son will be loved and treated with respect is so very important to us…we are so glad to be a part of Barrett's Promise! Thank you for inviting us to stay on."

It delighted Raine to hear the Blake's had made a decision to stay, as she had come to love them both. "Elisha; we could not have done any different. You only have God to thank for bringing us together, because it was all His idea. Price and I are so glad you are here, we've grown to love you as family. Not to mention the great help you both have been to us…what an encouragement you are Elisha Blake!"

Elisha walked over to the door, cracked it opened

then turned back again. "Raine, I did thank Him…God. Just last night and a part of me is thanking Him now." On that note, Elisha left closing the door behind him. Swiftly hurrying home to welcome his son into the world and kiss his lovely wife, *Praise you Lord God, Thank You.*

The words Elisha spoke affectionately about God penetrated the very core of Raine's heart, bringing tears to her eyes. Instantaneously she began to praise the Lord for Elisha. Rejoicing that he turned to God in his need for comfort. She wondered if Price and Caleb knew this, if they had a part in his awakening last night. He had lived among them for over three months now and not once gave any indication of accepting Price's explanation on Salvation. Although she heard several conversations her husband and he had about the topic. *A newborn child can certainly make a big difference in how people perceive things.* It comforted her, *Elisha would be raising his son to love the Lord and this family is now Christian.* She had already heard about the conversion Cholena received a month ago. Cholena shared her delight in Jesus with Raine while washing the dishes one afternoon.

Raine was in high spirits now. She put on a fresh pot of coffee, and cleaned up the soup bowls the men had left on the table. This was a beautiful day!

Elisha entered the home cautiously not wanting to let any cold air into the home. Quietly took off his heavy fur covered coat and was hanging it on the hook when Ruth approached him, speaking in a soft whisper. "She tired…labor long time…she wait to see you…eyes heavy, she fall asleep."

Gathering her wrap, Ruth informed Elisha she was going over to the Barrett's to get some sleep herself and would be back later to check on them. "If any problem, wake me…I think no problem…everything good. Brave papoose healthy…Cholena strong woman."

After Elisha expressed deep gratitude for Ruth's service, he put his hand on the door latch to open it for her. Ruth reached out and laid her hand on top of his to keep him from opening it, "Our family pray for Cholena and papoose many moons, old woman pray with young in pueblo, Shinning-Light pray, all pray every rising sun." In her way, she was letting Elisha know to be directing his gratitude to the God of creation who hears prayers and grants life. Ruth's hand left his with the end of her comment.

Elisha caught on to her implication and right before he opened the door replied, "God answers prayers, thank your family for praying."

The quiet spirited Ruth was satisfied with his comment and left, knowing the Lord would magnify himself to Elisha as He did to her.

Elisha was now alone with his wife and child. He walked over to the bed and stood there quietly observing his beautiful Cholena sleeping. She looked so peaceful holding his son in her arms. He wanted to talk to her, but knew it was better if she slept. The boy was a bit of heaven to his eyes.

While standing a long side of the bed caught up in this overwhelmed feeling of gratitude and love for both of them, he felt a slight draft on the back of his neck. Promptly he went to tend the fire, realizing the home must stay extra warm for the baby.

As Elisha was stirring the fire and adding more fuel, Cholena awoke. In a weak tired voice she said, "We have a brave papoose, Elisha Blake…a son."

Hearing her voice, Elisha turned around exposing a huge grin on his face. He felt such admiration for her.

Walking towards her, he asked, "How are you feeling pretty Mama. I was so worried about you when I did not hear anything all night."

"Yes…you would be. I feel you with me in labor. Your love help me…white-man's God and you give me strength." She did not care what he thought about her mentioning God, because she knew God was here during the birth.

"I am extremely proud of you, I too am very thankful to God for making everything possible. I know you and my son were in His hands last night. I could do nothing. I felt so helpless. I desired to be with you and make the harsh pain stop. To my dismay it was not possible. I had nowhere else to turn. After a conversation with Price and Caleb, I decided to turn the situation over to God. Look how faithful He is to me even in my stubbornness. He took good care of both of you. I felt His peace cover me. I gave Him my life, with a promise to share His love with my child and with you." Elisha took hold of her free delicate hand, the one not embracing his son and placing it inside of his.

Cholena, heart warmed with satisfaction hearing his testimony. He did not know she had accepted Jesus herself a month ago. Now tonight she felt even more blessed. Not only did she realize God was no longer a white-man's God, but her God too. He gave them a beautiful healthy son and He gave her husband faith. "Elisha, I am happy. I meet Jesus…three suns in month called January…I am learning calendar," she smiled. "I want to tell you…afraid…your story when child stop me."

"My Pappy was wrong Cholena. He was very wrong and I only sought to make him proud of me. That is why I left the little church and those happy people. I suppose, I always knew deep in my heart there was a possibility

Pappy might be mistaken. Maybe this is why I held onto the Holy Bible. It was a ChristMas gift from the people in that church. I found it in a box of keepsakes when we were in Ohio. I figured if Pappy was wrong about our marriage and our love. I needed to know if he was wrong about this too." Elisha kneeled down beside the bed and could not control his emotions, he began weeping. With his voice cracking he told Cholena how last night he confessed remorse for his sins and his stubbornness to the Lord God. The same way he did as a child at the altar of the little Toledo Community Church.

He was grateful how God's saving peace returned. Wiping his eyes, he looked at his wife holding his son and knew he was looking through the eyes of a new man. With sincere thankfulness, "I am glad the Lord brought us to Barrett's Promise, this is our home now."

Cholena smiled and nodded in agreement. She looked at her son, as her hand affectionately caress the tender head of her newborn child.

Elisha noticing her affection, "I was looking at our son while you were sleeping and he looks like a healthy lad. He actually resembles you."

Shocked at his remark she retorted, "No…no Elisha, he has face of his Pappy." She felt justified in a pleasurable way to rebuke him with this compliment.

"You think so?" he smiled.

"Yes, Husband, wait see…his little eyes open…truth will be there." Cholena look intently at her husband kneeling upright at her bedside. He appeared to be somewhat afraid to get too close to her or the child. She implored him, "Come close, sit on bed near me."

He wanted so much to take her up on that suggestion, but he restrained himself. "I do not want to hurt you or our son. I'll get a chair and bring it close to you."

"No, not sleep in chair, you rest in bed with us. In village father with mother…night papoose born…you no hurt us."

He still was hesitant, "Cholena, are you sure it will be all right?"

She pulled the blankets back for him to climb in, but Elisha did not oblige her. He insisted on pulling them back up before retrieving a quilt and hen lay down on top of the coverlet. Once settled comfortably, he pulled the outer quilt over him. "For tonight, I think this will be safer."

"As you wish," she consented. It was only right to have him close to her tonight, even on top of the blankets. Cholena adjusted herself and turned to face him, setting the sleeping child in between them.

Elisha lay on his side propped up on one elbow looking closely at his son. He took his finger to rub the baby's hand, but the boy instinctively closed his finger's around his father's. Elisha smiled, "He is very small, but has a strong grip."

"He grow…be great man like his Pappy," she spoke confidently and proud.

"But now he is incredibly small and fragile." Elisha did not add how he thought she also looked exceptionally frail to him tonight. "Cholena, I think we have a good life to offer our son now…living at Barrett's Promise. Do you feel comfortable here? I hope you do, because I told Raine we would be staying on past spring."

This information made Cholena very happy. She was hoping they could make their home here and not leave in the spring. "Oh yes, I like it very well…I like Barrett's. Good people…like family."

"I feel the same way, in fact Raine said the same thing to me tonight. She said we were like family to her. We are going to have a good life in this place and our son will not feel hate living on this ranch. It is good to protect him from the evil we witnessed before we come here."

"Elisha, when keep son safe, we no teach him to be acquainted with hate in heart...did I use word right?" Elisha nodded yes, surprised at how quickly she was learning English from Raine. Cholena continued, "he will no feel hate to people who show hate, he no hate anyone." At this word, the little baby boy stirred and stretched his body, cupping his fists and tossing it over his head.

Elisha delighted in watching his little fist stretch out. "I do not know Sugar, you used the word right, but I am not sure if that is going to be possible. Maybe this little man is up for a good fight, look at that fist," he chuckled.

Cholena replied reluctantly, "He will be, if he like his Pappy." Her eyes were having difficulty staying open. "I tired now...I sleep...soon hungry son wakes."

"Of course, rest now my beautiful wife." He moved her black hair away from her face, cupping her jaw line fondly with his hand for a second. Taking another look at his boy, he wanted to touch him again. Elisha ran his finger gently on his son's cheek, but the little guy was not easily disturbed from his peaceful sleep. "You had a big tiring night yourself son, what a brave thing you have done coming into this world." He was whispering quietly so he would not wake him or Cholena who drifted into slumber.

Elisha lay on his back, being extra careful not to hurt the child who lay next to him. While he mutely spoke to God about his plans for the child and imploring the Lord to protect his son from hate. He realized they had not named the boy and wondered why Cholena never mentioned one. He had a name in his heart for the child and hoped she would like it, Joseph Ahanu Blake, to honor both of their fathers.

Elisha was motionless, but dreadfully awake inside his active mind. He thought about how the Lord revealed Himself in his hour of distress. Elisha felt appreciative for Father God's mercy. Reminded of the Holy Bible laying upon the shelf, he was instantly filled with love towards the people who had given it to him. Moreover, he welcomed reading the pages openly, now that he and his wife were both going to follow Jesus. In just one day he already felt a softening taking place inside of his heart and wondered how much this newborn faith would change him after a year. The word 'newborn' struck him, yes my son and I were born on the same day. *Thank You Lord, for Cholena, my son and for the love You are showing me by taking me back.*

♥

God smiled

♥

Chapter 29

Several hours passed since Raine had fallen asleep on top of the coverlet beside Price, her shawl lightly spread over their shoulders. Blinking several times, her eyes began to focus on Ruth and Caleb. They were stretched out on a quilt tossed on the floor in front of the fire. She wondered why they did not use the bed in the guest room. Although she could see that Trader was contented to share his spot, snuggling up to Caleb's back. Raine could feel the heat generating from the fireplace and was grateful for warmth embracing the room.

Lying there barely awake, still feeling exhausted from the night before, Raine wondered how late in the day it was. She noticed daylight was still entering the room. *Guess it does not matter, besides everyone else is still embraced slumber.* As she lay there looking at the ceiling, she reflected on the special moments preceding her sleep. Elisha, Cholena and their new baby boy, she felt sincere in her joy for them. On the other hand, she began to question why God had not allowed her to be with child yet. She was silent and contemplative, *we've been married for seven months going on eight. Maybe I should not have asked God to let children wait the first morning Willie was here. It was a selfish idea…not wanting to share my life with Price to include a child. Oh Lord, perhaps could you forgive me for my inconsiderate and selfish traits. I understand now a child is an expression of love, not a hindrance to it. Lord, if you would allow it, I would love to have Price's child. Or was it my denial of You the reason I am not conceiving…You knew my heart was unfaithful and I was undeserving of such a blessing. Oh Merciful Father, as you have forgiven me, please don't let my sins keep me from having a child.* She felt a tear run down her cheek, realizing she lost faith and trust in Him again...so soon, *You did say that our children would build the town, that means children are in Your plan for us. Please forgive my foolishness and my disobedience for bringing it up, after You said not to mention it anymore.* She knew His forgiveness is greater than her inconsistent wavering heart.

Raine's faith was reassured. She was secure in God's forgiveness and snuggled in to her beloved Price, wondering if she would have to confess this to him also. *How would he feel about my selfish nature? He already forgiven me of my lack of faith and trust, now this...betcha he did not bargain for such a woman as I have become.* This troubled her and she yearned to drift off to sleep to escape her own thoughts, yet she lay wide awake.

Price stretched, stirring himself awake and was delighted to find Raine nestled close. It was not long before he noticed she was awake. He cuddled her closer and she welcomed his tenderness, "Beautiful, it is nice to have you beside me. How is Cholena?"

"She is doing just fine. Elisha and Cholena have an adorable son."

Price moved a strand of hair from her face. "Elisha must be thrilled to have a boy, although he said he would be glad for a healthy child either way."

Raine wondered if she should tell him. She looked over at her guest still asleep on the floor and decided now would be as good a time as any. She did not want to make a habit of holding back anything again. "Price have you wondered why I have not become pregnant yet?"

Price had anticipated this question, he understood this would be a soft spot for his wife in light of the new baby. "I have thought about it, but I also figured Father knows the best time for us to begin a family, and there will be children. It is in His promise to us."

"Raine blurted it out, "I think it's my fault we had to wait. I was unfaithful and God knew my heart. I also asked him not to give us children too soon, so we could enjoy being together as a couple…I was selfish with you." Raine could not shed a tear this time, she was merely too drained to be emotional. However she felt grieved about doing this.

Price moved his arm and leaned on his elbow to secure his head as he studied Raine's face. He found it hard to believe she actually requested to not have children. This news surprised him, yet he found it difficult in his heart to toy with getting upset. Price only had compassionate words for his wife, "Raine, my beautiful wife, babies are a gift from God and He alone determines the time of birth. No child was born by accident, or by will of any man. It is His divine plan to bring forth life for a purpose. You cannot sway the plans and purposes of God by your humanness. He is the Creator." *Did I just say that? Lord You have a way with words. This is also mercy to my soul. Thank you for being the Creator and for giving me words for Raine. Which also completely heals my heart about this news as well.*

Raine was captivated by the wisdom her husband spoke, she could not argue the point, or dabble a second longer in any despair. He was a man of God and these profound words released the guilt she was chaining herself to. A smile came to her lips and peace flowed over her countenance, "Thank You Price Barrett. I needed to be reminded of that." *How could I possibly think I could stand in God's way, another folly I have placed on myself?*

Price's hand brushed her face, "I think I needed those words too…we will have children Raine, when God is ready for His plans to be fulfilled. For now, we can be contented with our life as He designed for today. We are beginning Barrett's Promise Community and we have friends, the Blake's, Thompson's, Caleb and Ruth; God is good to us Raine Barrett."

She regained vision in what the Lord was doing in her life with this wonderful man, "Yes He is, Price Barrett…I love you…second to God."

"I love you second to God too." He sealed that sincere affirmation with a tender kiss.

"I love you both!"

Coming:

Barrett's Promise Community

Can a healthy community actually develop with strong ethnic and denominational differences? Will the Blake's really stay? How will the Barrett's handle these new challenges?

Join us and find out in ***Barrett Promise Community*** to see who the Lord brings to live along side of the Barrett's to take their unique position on the 480 acre ranch, transforming the ranch into a desert community.

Any comments welcomed at
MaryAutumnGrace @ Outlook.com
Or my facebook page
Mary Autumn Grace

About the Author

Mary Autumn Grace grew up in the suburbs outside of Detroit, MI. USA. She is mother of six children and grandmother of ten. With her husband Jim, she fostered thirty-two children and still maintains a close relationship with several of their extended children. Mary presently resides with her husband in Northern Michigan, where she occupies her time teaching a Ladies Bible Study and writing. It is her personal relationship with Jesus Christ that motivates each endeavor of life and provides the inspiration shared within the book.

About my friends who set time aside to help me in editing this book.

Barbara J. Layow, spent her adolescent years in Redford Township MI. where she and Mary became lifelong friends. Barbara resides in Northwestern Michigan with her husband Mike. She is the owner of Camp Hosanna Ministries, a horse ranch instructing children on the fundamentals of horses while incorporating God's way of living in her teachings. The Layow's have one son, and many adopted by heart children and grandchildren. Barbara is a devoted Christian and a good friend.

Without the commitment Barbara gave me, this book would not be in print. Thank you.

♥

Lisa Revall lives in the same town as Mary. She is a retired teacher and works part time to fill her days. Married to Kelly and the mother of four. She loves the Lord and volunteers at her church.

I am grateful for the time she set aside out of her busy day to help me and for the encouragement she gave to finish the goal of the final editing this book. Thank you.

♥

THE BEGINNING

Made in the USA
Middletown, DE
24 April 2021

38245452R00235